DATE DUE

BL

PRINTED IN U.S.A.

D1264521

ISBN: 978-0-578-76734-5

BLIND SIDED

ERICA HILARY

When you choose a partner, you've chosen a story.
Often, you've been recruited for a play you never auditioned for.

−E PEREL

Destitute didn't seem all that bad now; it had just been trumped. By *dead.*

A muted squeal followed by the thrump of a cork being wrenched from a bottle.

"The *how* is your job. I don't care to know details. I simply want to know when it's done. It's awfully hard to bear such a tragic accident," he said sadly.

A glass was placed firmly on the granite. Liquid was poured generously.

"The gentleman is automatically accorded everyone's empathy—you see? The widower that soldiers on. And when he finds love again, whoever it's with, everyone will be on his side. He deserves it, after all."

The cracked plaster of the walls in the tiny closet squeezed in more tightly; my cell was airless and claustrophobic. Anxiety was no longer inanimate. It clawed at me. From the inside out. An alien straining to escape the constraints of my body.

Six years earlier

CHAPTER 1

COLD OPEN

Crack. An emphatic smack on the bumper jolted my silver car forward in the otherwise quiet parking lot, jerking me sharply against the snug seat belt. *Damn it. Not today.*

Massaging the back of my neck, I winced, shaken more by the memories it stirred than by any physical injury. The jarring crunch of metal on metal always transported me back to my parents' tragic fate. My heart twisted in my chest.

Breathe. Like my sensei said: *Deep breathing allows for clarity of mind and emotion.* In and out, in and out; my pulse steadied. Sighing, I flipped my sunglasses to the top of my head and pushed sun-streaked blonde hair from my face. I peered in the rearview mirror.

The shiny black SUV that hit me loomed large over my tiny BMW. Naturally. It couldn't be a fair fight, could it? That behemoth versus my just-off-the-lot Matchbox car. A glint in my side mirror, movement—the other car's door opened, but no one emerged yet. Wiping away my prickly expression, I threw open my own door and stepped out to see what dope couldn't navigate a routine parking lot.

I heard him from inside his car before I saw him. *Oh.*

"Sorry, that's totally on me. A bit knackered today."

A charming English lilt. Didn't hear that every day in Washington, DC.

Grasping the car doorframe over his head with one hand, he swung his long legs out. Dropped from the Range Rover to the concrete in one fluid motion. Athletic, compact. Cool move for a guy in jeans, maybe, or board shorts—entirely unexpected from a guy in dress clothes.

And I was captivated by his … everything. *Holy hellooo.*

Exasperated with himself, he coolly tugged a business card from his breast pocket without looking up. "Just have someone ring this number here. It's my assistant, Emma."

Have *someone* ring this number? Well, there was our first teeny issue; I didn't have a "someone." My someone was just me. Did everyone else in the world have a someone?

To this guy, this episode was simply a nuisance to be delegated.

"She'll look after you," he said, thrusting the card in my direction, only the tips of his index and third fingers holding the edge. When I failed to reach back, he looked up brusquely.

All at once, his agitated demeanor softened, and the detached facade evaporated. *Yikes.* Tanned. Tall. To me, anyway—I was barely five foot six, so he had to be six feet. Square, slightly too-strong jaw, meticulously tousled auburn hair. A touch of silver at the temples. *Forty? Midforties?*

His once-polite smile morphed into a zero-to-sixty grin. The hand with the card dropped back to his side. Cocking his head and turning up the wattage, he crinkled his eyes disarmingly.

Sorry, you're wasting your wattage on the wrong girl.

My friends teased me: I'd been impervious to men since my divorce. Cornered into ending a dysfunctional marriage yet blamed for its demise. Alex had cast himself as the victim. Even to our daughter. "Mommy wants the divorce. I don't." *Men.*

Immune to all men the past few years, I automatically delivered them the "Reilly Heisman." As in the make-*no*-mistake you're-staying-at-arm's-length vibe.

Parking Lot Guy was apparently exempt, his curiosity undeterred; his smoky hazel eyes flickered up and down. Dropping from my eyes to my mouth and lingering. On my lips.

I … I was speechless. Ironic, since being extemporaneously charming was my most marketable attribute in broadcasting. I slightly opened my mouth, once, twice. *Oh, come on!* Social Interaction 101—you speak, I speak, you speak. And yet his eyes remained on my lips. My eyes on his eyes, the lush sooty lashes. And I … closed my mouth again.

Words, I know words.

"My sincere apologies," he said ingenuously. One dimple appeared, a single freckle embedded deeply within. He slid the card back into his pocket. "Not to worry, I'll see to it personally that this is taken care of." The french cuff of his pale-blue shirt peeked out from his suit sleeve. Classic Tiffany silver knot cufflinks gleamed. Dignified, pulled together, ready for his close-up. And then there was me.

I hadn't exactly dressed for a meet-cute parking lot moment—in fact, I'd *un*dressed. After my "Life of Reilly" segment, I'd peeled off the body-conscious teal number, swapping it out for Sweaty Betty workout gear. *Ugh.* At least they were new, not the everyday utilitarian ones. Still, though, I was wearing spandex. And this guy was french-cuffed perfection.

"I'm Rick. Rick Lynch. And *you* would be Reilly," he said, hands spread apart and raised up as though pleased he'd correctly answered the game-winning question.

Oh, so he knew me. Or the TV me, anyway (a carefree, looser version of the real me, the one with no backstory and no baggage). A point for that, I supposed. *Still not happening, bud.*

"Nice to meet you, Rick. Considering," I managed, adopting a wry smile.

Almost apologetically, he followed up. "I'm with Butler." Smile gone. Of course he was.

Butler Industries. *Figures.* I couldn't get a break.

It had just been announced, to some consternation, that a private equity firm had purchased our station. We'd been through this before. They didn't care about us—they consolidated; they trimmed. Translation: they downsized; they fired. Any change in my life right now would be a disaster. I was looking down the barrel of a tenuous transition as it was.

Gripping my hand firmly, he was one of *those*—he clasped his other hand over mine immediately. The doubly-nice-to-meet-you shake, the one I was never sure was authentic. An electricity passed between us, an actual shock. I froze.

With a start, he said, "Your hand is ice cold, and it's got to be eighty degrees out!"

My gaze followed his, the sight of our hands intertwined oddly mesmerizing. The acute tingle was unexpected. And undeniable. Snatching my hand back, I tucked it in my pocket, curled it into a ball.

Eyes still fixed on me, he was soaking it in, this crackle of energy. Incredibly, words still eluded me—nuanced, interesting ones, at any rate. *Speak.* I grabbed at the first words floating by.

"Cold hands, warm heart," I said, the trite phrase slipping out before I could stop it. *Cringe.* Having no words at all had been infinitely better. *Zero game.* Less than zero.

I sensed our satellite trucks weaving around us, overburdened with equipment for remote broadcasts, engines revving with the effort. Muffled chatter as anchors and producers passed by. But here I stood with this virtual stranger, in this alternate universe. So far from our dingy studio lot, yet engulfed in the long, triangular shadow cast by our prominent broadcast tower.

The guy was handsome, no doubt about it. Not the bland, pretty-boy handsome of our TV anchors; he had more edge, a masculine energy, a hint of a unibrow that somehow ... *big damn deal.*

He ran one hand through his shiny tangle of hair. "Most unfortunate. Come, let's pop around to Giselle's. I'll handle this. *You*"—he pointed—"are not to be put out. I'm sure your life is hectic enough without me bollocksing it up." Not waiting on my reply, he headed to his car. "Pull her back in. We'll put this episode behind us."

Pull her back in. Kind of presumptuous, actually. A man a little too accustomed to people respecting his directives.

My annoyance flared. I was irate at his take-charge manner. Already late to kickboxing, I wasn't about to fall into line for some guy telling me how it was going to be.

I don't think so, Clooney. Calling after him, I said sharply, "I can't. I'm late as it is."

Turning, his eyebrows raised, he asked, "You've an alternative idea?"

"We could just handle it old-school, like other people."

He tilted his head, the concept seeming foreign.

"Exchange information. License, registration … let insurance deal with it."

Sheepishly, he stroked the nape of his neck. "I'd … I'd rather not put this through my insurance, if it's all the same to you. I'm good for it. I'm not a complete screwup."

"No doubt." I made a point of eyeing his pricey car. "I'm sure you're not a total screwup, but your driving record? Most definitely a little sketchy."

"None of those incidents were my fault." He laughed. "If you'll join me for a coffee, we'll ring the BMW in Bethesda, and I'll get it sorted. Honestly, you would go a long way to making *me* feel much better about this mess." His palm was pressed to his chest.

It was tempting in a way; no, that was a lie. Really, *he* was tempting. Disconcerting, given he was so damn abrasive. All lanky … and confident … and dimples … and *I'm sorry, you were saying?* His mouth was still moving. I hadn't heard a word. "Sorry?"

"Good to go then?" he asked, poised at his car in his springy, athletic way.

Still fuming that my logical suggestion had been summarily dismissed, I was unable to conjure another reasonable objection. I finally just bobbed my head in agreement.

"Excellent." He leaned against his car and watched me maneuver into a spot. *This isn't a spectator sport.* I hadn't had parking anxiety like this since driver's ed. Over a guy who couldn't even come clean with his own insurance company. He had it, that veiled look men perfected: as though you weren't measuring up, as though you were inept at simple things.

No. This I could do; I did it every day. I knew where to break for the turn … wait … *now.* Gliding to a stop before the barrier, I was startled by his double tap on my window.

He grinned disarmingly as I powered the window down and motioned to the two spots I'd parked diagonally across. "So I gather you think those white lines there are just a vague suggestion, do you?"

Deflated, I saw I'd meandered badly into the next spot. Fail.

A crimson flush warmed my neck and moved up to my cheeks. Blushing. *I can't even.* Gripping the slim leather wheel, I reversed and pulled in again. Properly. Tossing my small backpack on, I stepped out and channeled my on-air composure.

"You know, I don't think I'd be quite as judgy as you if I'd just rear-ended someone in a parking lot," I said, dropping my sunglasses back on.

With a delighted glint, he said only, "Cheeky."

The beveled glass door at Giselle's swung open, and he motioned me in before him—I glanced sideways through my glasses at his reflection. His eyes had dropped. He was checking out my behind appreciatively. I smiled to myself. *Cheeky.* In all the right places, it seemed.

A striking flame-haired hostess greeted us with blank indifference. She tapped on a table up front, the inside of her toned arm tattooed with vertical Chinese symbols. Spying a table he preferred, Rick swept past her to a booth with a window overlooking the National Cathedral's outdoor amphitheater of curved stone and manicured grass walkways.

"This looks perfect. Thanks much," he said, all but winking at the hostess and sliding into the quilted leather banquette. Her eyes drifted up. Annoyed at first, she was quickly smitten with his naughty-boy grin. Her resting bitch face evaporated. She smiled back brightly and removed the RESERVED card from the table to accommodate him. He had a way, no doubt about that.

"Well. A man who gets what he wants. Does anyone ever say no to you?"

"Ah, lesson number one, Reilly: if you simply don't leave space for a no, there's no *no*." He draped the black linen napkin across his thighs.

No no ... *maybe for you*. With that confidence, he'd climb the Butler ladder quickly.

As the waitress filled our water glasses from a terra-cotta pitcher, she held up a rustic farmhouse slate with chalked words across it. Classic French music floated in the air: "La Vie en Rose."

"Special today, if you're interested. We're trying out a new version of our caffe mocha."

The intense fragrance of recently ground coffee beans wafted from the adjacent table, the supersize cup heaped with froth and a drizzle of syrup. "Mmm. I'll try that, thank you."

"I'll join you. Deux caffe mocha, merci." A satisfying roll of the *r* in *merci*, I mused.

"Merci," I echoed, rolling my *r* in response. "Raising the question: How many languages can you say *thank you* in?"

"Thank you?" he repeated. "Several. But with a real grasp on the language: four. French, Spanish, Italian. English, of course." He ticked them off on his long fingers. "My Latin is more than adequate, but I find the dead languages so rarely come in handy these days," he added with self-deprecating humor.

Exactly, if I had a dime for every time ...

Charming, sophisticated, larger than life. Everything I didn't need. Everything I gravitated toward. What was it that he'd said? No *no*.

Chin on his hand, he propped his elbow on the weathered wood table with interest. "Enough about me. Tell me about yourself. If you're so inclined, of course."

Me? What did he want to know? What was there to say? He knew where I worked so ...

"Well," I began, "I got my first TV job in Boston. I produced the movie critic segments; I landed his job when Bo eventually left and nudged it a little more into the pop culture arena ..."

Smile lines creased his upper cheeks, one nearly intersecting with that dimple. "Well, this isn't an interview, for Heaven's sake; you *have* the job. It's *you* I'm curious about, not your CV."

My what? Right, curriculum vitae. My résumé. Got it.

"I've seen some 'Life of Reilly' pieces, so the career bit I get. You seem to have created quite a nice niche," he said admiringly. "But ... outside of that?"

Our mochas appeared quietly.

"Well, lately ..." I faltered, aware suddenly that my recent personal life had been less colorful than my career. "I've been a little busy outside of that. Raising a teenager. Between the gig and the girl, I've been woefully all work, no play. But with Sloan off to college soon, I ... get my life back," I said, selling the excitement of that with a beaming smile. The one that hid the truth.

His double take was authentic. His eyes widened. "You have an almost-grad? You must've made a deal with the devil to have cheated time like that. No offense intended."

As if I'd tire of hearing that kind of compliment. "*Please.* Most of my on-air colleagues are actual *embryos*, so thank God I've cheated time to some small extent."

Faux relief. He drew his fingers down his neck. "Whew. It would truly be a dodgy introduction to tap your car in the car park *and* offend you—all in one go."

"*Tap* my car?" I shot back. "We'll see if BMW classifies it as a tap." A tap. *Really?*

"I suppose you're right; we'll see about that right now." Placing a call to his assistant, he arranged for her to give BMW his information and to tell them to expect my car in the next few days. "Emma," he said drolly, his eyes on me, "have I told you lately that I couldn't manage without you?"

While he updated her, a round-faced woman with a chestnut shoulder-length bob held in place by a slim headband paused by us. "I know ..." Then the recognition. "*Oh*. You're Reilly Anderson, right? I ... watch you. We always have you on in the fitness center at Equinox."

My turn to amp it up now for a loyal viewer. ABG, our mantra: always be gracious. Slipping into work mode, I smiled. "Well, hi. I totally appreciate that. What's your name?"

"Oh, sorry. It's Britany. I ... didn't mean to bother you. I shouldn't have ..."

"Britany. And you're not—it's sweet of you to say hello. I was noticing your skirt, by the way. Super cute." The cheery, oversize daisy print suited her and her sunny disposition.

"Thanks for saying so. My daughter informed me this morning that flowers are out."

"*No*. Well, I have a tragic problem then. I'm kind of partial to a floral," I confided.

"Ha. It's weird, but I feel like I know you. Like you're one of my friends. I'm sure you get that a lot. Anyway, nice to see you—in person." Britany gave a little wave and headed out.

Rick chided his assistant with affection, "It's nice out. Get out for lunch today. All hell won't break loose because you actually take an hour to yourself." Ending the call, he turned back as I wrapped my hands around the ceramic bowl of mocha and took a long sip.

"Sorry to miss you entertaining your adoring public. Must get old," he teased.

"Not really. Except when I'm spotted after crying my eyes out at a movie. Or with the dreaded seventeen items in the twelve-item-only checkout, hoping to squeak through with no one noticing. Just my luck. Say hi, smile bright, go with it. Without people liking me, I wouldn't have a job."

"Spot on, give them what they want. And that's *you*." He picked up the tiny oval spoon. "Curious, that. People care about you; they want to be your friend. *You* are your brand." His eyes clouded as he stirred. "With me, it's about the bottom line. My return on investment—my success at *that* is my brand. Full stop. Who I *am*: irrelevant; no one cares." Inhaling the fragrance of the mocha, he sipped. His tongue flicked at the bit of froth left on the rim.

Poignant, really; I inferred a certain loneliness. A man on an island. Intrigued, I leaned in to speak.

Smoothly, having forgotten to impart crucial information apparently, he pivoted: "Ah! All sorted about your car. You'd please me if you'd take it to the dealer; I can be relatively sure they won't bodge it."

They won't what? Oh, got it. "Bodge, a Britishism," I said, smiling.

He grinned playfully. "Hey, when called for, I can do American with the best of them." Adding in a dead-on Midwestern accent, "This is the *real* me, ma'am. Just a cowboy at heart."

I giggled; the silly impression was damn cute. Rick abruptly glanced at his sleek watch and grimaced. "Good Lord, I've been so caught up, I'm about to miss a meeting at half past."

He pulled bills from his money clip and rose in one swift motion. "Sorry to dash. Let me know how it goes with the car." With a double tap on the table, he sped off at a near jog. He hustled past the hostess, touched her inked forearm lightly, and slyly slipped a bill into her hand. A thank-you for the table, I guessed. She squeezed his arm. And he was gone.

Disoriented, I scanned the café and eyed his half-full mug. I followed him onto the street. The transformative music faded the instant the door closed, replaced by a glaring summer sun. The two-tiered red DC tour bus ground to a stop, a plume of exhaust rising from the rear. *WTF.*

The ping-ponging between annoying and intriguing, it left me dizzy.

At the lot, I assessed the damage to my car—the fender was bent noticeably in a few spots. Not bad, considering his massive SUV. Galling, though, given it was avoidable to any human paying even moderate attention to anyone beside themselves. *Come on.*

Stepping closer, I saw a paper—no, a business card—tucked in a wrinkle of the bumper. On the back in neat, block writing: *My info would help. No excuses now, no no! Rick*

Below, his cell number. And a smiley face. A smiley? Fascinating.

Flipping the textured ivory card over, I caught my breath sharply. *No. Effing. Way.*

CHAPTER 2

B-ROLL

His card read, RICHARD W. LYNCH, CHIEF EXECUTIVE OFFICER, BUTLER INDUSTRIES.

Holy shit. This guy isn't with Butler Industries. He is Butler Industries. My head was spinning. I had just had coffee with one of the big boys of Butler.

Dropping onto the ancient linen Shabby Chic couch with the swirly cabbage roses, I curled like a cat into the far corner, where the sun gathered on June afternoons. Details played back. The fluid way he'd vaulted from his car. Guiding me through the door at Giselle's, his hand on my back. It still tingled. His reflection in the glass as he checked me out. Typically, I was offended by a man scoping me out. To my dismay, though, a tinge of excitement had tempered my annoyance. *Stop, you don't even know him.*

But there was something oddly familiar about Rick; the dynamic between us was a dance I knew. *Oh my God.* Was it that the CEO was a bit like Alex? Charming, successful (Alex owned a PR agency), larger than life. "Pull her back in." Rick's unilateral decision that my car was to go to the dealer. God, that was so Alex. Was he controlling, asserting his will over me, or was he simply trying to make the situation right after his embarrassing car mishap?

The front door slammed shut. It reverberated through the house. That girl: a bull in a china shop. Kicking her stinky tennis shoes into the corner, Sloan called out in a near panic.

"Mom! Mom? What's going on? Are you okay?"

Jumping from the couch, I popped my head into the kitchen. She was tense, her tanned, lightly freckled face paler than usual.

"What's the matter, sweetheart? Why wouldn't I be okay?"

She off-loaded her tired Sidwell Friends bag to the floor with a thud and tossed her thick blonde ponytail. "Because I saw your car, that's why. Doesn't look good. And you just got that car."

"*That,*" I said. "Tell me about it. A guy slammed into me at work. Some people are completely unconscious, but nothing to worry about."

She exhaled in relief.

She was on me in one spindly move, her arms around my neck. "Damn. Well, sorry, Mom. You're okay, though. That's the important thing." Still in rumpled tennis whites, she stuck her head in the refrigerator and stared—waiting for food to jump out at her, it seemed.

Dramatically, she said, "Need. Rations. Now. Warning. Last you'll see of me—it's all required reading and packing. Pre-orientation next week and I still have tons to do."

Any hopes for a quiet night with my girl were dashed. Victim to pre-college prep. I'd thought we'd Netflix a few episodes of her favorite show, *Gilmore Girls* (in her mind, she and I were the original Lorelais), and munch on cheddar SkinnyPop. But no.

Reheating the pesto pasta, I added clipped, fragrant basil from the window garden. Sliced a plump yellow tomato and swirled on aged syrupy balsamic. Off she went, balancing the plate precariously on top of a few books and an iPad. *Don't say it, Mom.*

Half-packed trunks and you-assemble-it empty boxes littered the hall. There was no denying it now. In nine short weeks Sloan was off. I'd be dropping her at college and returning to a Sloanless home. How did people do it? Hell, I'd been a mess leaving her at pre-K. She'd skipped off happily; I'd peered through hand-print-smeared windows just to get a glimpse. What was life now?

My source of affection, my spirit animal (her words). She'd become my significant other.

I tried to resist, but I couldn't. I slipped my laptop from the couch and moved into my little office, sliding the pocket door closed. *Idle curiosity, nothing wrong with that.* Guiltily, I pulled up Google. First result, the Butler home page. Raised in Surrey, England, Rick had attended the London School of Economics and joined Butler in England ten years ago. They'd brought him here two years ago. A thumbnail picture of a man who looked like him, albeit a stiff, sterile version of the guy I'd met. My own headshot on our station site was equally as generic, though—another in a sea of smiling, telegenic, interchangeable blonds.

It was thin after that, the Rick recon. Smiling at charity events, parties, different women in tow. A brooding brunette— Hermione. A hungry-looking Asian beauty, Aiko, who clung on to him like a life raft. Swirling my fingers on the touch screen, I made the image bigger. He was younger, the thick head of hair a darker auburn. The new lightness at the temples suited him, softened his strong features. Clearly no Mrs. Lynch. Was it wrong to wonder why he was single? After all, I was, and I didn't possess some fatal flaw. At least I didn't think so. *Let it go, Elsa. Do something useful.*

I pumped the soapy foam from the red grapefruit-scented bottle and washed my hands in the kitchen sink. The packing list on the counter stared at me. It never seemed to get shorter.

After four trips up and down the narrow metal basement steps, I dragged up a portable air mattress (the kids bunked communally at orientation). Thumping awkwardly, it heaved over every step. I was almost to the top. The sharp rap on the front knocker was accompanied by the door opening, then slamming shut.

"*Yo!* Is this where my party people at?" Always made an entrance, Billie. She'd been my bestie since college. Sloan and her daughter, Amy, were a year apart. Amy looked up to Sloan, and she counted on her for the invaluable help a "big sister" could provide navigating her teens.

I dumped the unwieldy bag at my feet and yanked the unattractive yellow scrunchie from my hair before Billie could mercilessly mock it. "As luck would have it, the hotties just left," I said.

Her husky laugh filled the room, and she kicked off her suede clogs. Eyeing her, I shook my head in amazement; she wore tight, distressed bell-bottom jeans no normal woman could get away with. Had to love her.

I scrawled *Orientation — Oak House #3* in Sharpie on two sides of the box and pushed it away, shoving it with my foot until it hit the wall. Billie thrust out one angular hip and screwed up her nose at the smelly marker.

"Jesus, girl, clock out already. Way past wine o'clock." Leaning into the wine cooler, she pulled out a sauvignon blanc. I grabbed glasses, the supersize ones, and poured generously. The golden liquid almost reached the rim. Billie wandered to the landing, stretched her toned body along the rail, and shouted up, "Amy! Rollin' out in ten minutes. Not fifteen, ten—got it?"

Sloan's door opened to muffled giggles. Amy was singing along to Ed Sheeran's "Happier." But she broke off mid-lyric and her voice wafted down, "Mother. How could I not get it? You're *yelling*. Ten, not fifteen. Got it."

Amused, I put our glasses on the dark, distressed coffee table and adjusted the mason jar of honeysuckle. "Wow. I had no idea your daughter was upstairs. Mother of the Year over here."

"Very stealthy, Miss Amy," Billie said. "She's here, she's there— can't take your eyes off that one." Pulling a cozy throw from the couch, she snuggled into it and flopped back onto the sofa with a swoosh. *Ahhh.*

Resting was tempting; I sank onto the oversize leather club chair, propping my bare feet on the ottoman. "At last. Cheers," I toasted, holding my glass up. We both took a long sip.

"Damn. It's really happening. Kid's spreading her wings." Billie eyed the piles.

I misted up. I couldn't help it. "My mom used to say, 'Why do kids have to grow up and get their own lives? Why are they allowed to leave us?' God, I used to roll my eyes *hard*—but I get it now. That sure wasn't in any parenting contract I signed."

Billie answered with a raspy giggle. "I'm bad. Some days I look forward to Amy getting on with it. She's sixteen, and I feel like I've been raisin' her for thirty freakin' years. At least Brian stuck around, helped. Not like …"

Jerking her thumb-ringed thumb toward the towers of boxes and rolls of Bubble Wrap, Billie asked, "Is he gonna show? Will we be honored with an Alex sighting?"

"He texted Sloan that he'd meet us in Boston. But the day before yesterday, he reneged. Said he has a big client and that he'll try to visit in the fall. Once she's settled."

She muttered under her breath, "Jesus. How'd the kid take it? That's just …"

"She looked sad but not surprised. She just sort of accepts it now, his coming and going at will. If he's around—great—if he's not, well … he's not."

Billie scowled. "Well. You don't need his help. Still effin' weird to me he's never around. Even for her. It's like that's how he punishes you."

We'd dissected the dynamic often. "I guess he'll always be bitter, since the divorce was 'my decision,'" I said, with air quotes. "Which I now understand, after all the therapy—*one* person may say the words *it's over* first, but it's not like it was that person's decision. It … just … wasn't working."

"Ha! It worked perfect for him. He liked it the way it was. *You* pulled the plug."

"Perfect," I echoed. "You saw how controlling he'd gotten. I could hardly fend for myself when it ended." I sighed, recalling how close I'd come to having to file for bankruptcy. I'd been so adrift I hadn't managed simple bill payments. Alex had handled all that.

I'd tried to hide it from Sloan: how untethered I was after my parents' deaths, the divorce. I'd *failed*, epically, failed to keep a family together for her. The bottom had fallen out of our world. Any sense of security had vanished. And I'd been to blame. The agony of guilt had ground me to a pulp.

I'd taken a leave of absence citing personal reasons—they were personal all right. I could barely get Sloan to the bus before crawling back into bed. Images, sounds, the smell of food bore actual weight. They'd pinned me down and held me captive. At one point, I didn't shower for four days. Four days.

Billie tried to swallow a devilish laugh.

"Now what?" I asked.

"Controlling! Ya think? Just because Alex bought you *boobs* for your thirtieth birthday, for Christ's sake. Boobs you had never, ever said you wanted."

I mustered a smile-grimace. "Classic take-charge Alex; he decided I could be curvier. If he would've just stopped at the typical guy stuff—the dishwasher must be arranged exactly this way, recyclables go out at exactly this time, the cars are my sole domain. That stuff I *miss*."

"Hell yeah." Wickedly, she assessed my breasts. "But they're still the best set I've ever seen. Cheers to those girls right there." We laughed and raised our glasses to that. To them.

Before we'd finished our wine, Amy materialized in her waiflike, ethereal way, all auburn waves and enormous Keane eyes. She admonished her mother, tapping her phone with a delicate finger. "Ten, not fifteen, Mother."

Billie shrugged off her throw and said slyly, "Yah, yah, boss." Nudging my slate lazy Susan aside, she rummaged deep in her tasseled bag on the counter. "Hey. Amy's babysitting tomorrow afternoon; wanna meet me at Soosh at five? You could do takeaway for Sloan," she coaxed.

Ticktock. Soon there wouldn't be takeaway California rolls tacked onto our order. *Stop.*

"Sounds perfect. I need to escape this."

Before closing the door, Amy called upstairs, "Sloan. Call me tomorrow about the Segway night tour. Sounds way cool."

Segways. Electric two-wheeled scooters. *In the dark.* What could go wrong? I stood at the door watching Billie and Amy meander back to their car, their walks nearly identical.

I passed Sloan's half-opened door and peeked in. She was nearly obscured by a towering mass of clothes. She sat cross-legged, and only her knees protruded around the pile.

"Please, *please*, for the love of God, tell me that is a 'stays at home' pile."

She leaned out from behind and giggled, pushing her hair out of her eyes. "Well, I'm happy to *tell* you that, if it makes you feel better, but ..."

I pulled out graphic tees, each seemingly with a band on it. I folded them efficiently. Sloan squealed and clasped her hands over her eyes in anguish, peering through her fingers.

"Mom! No! I just folded all those."

Critiquing the haphazard heap skeptically, I asked, "These?" I dangled a loosely rolled example from one finger. "I love you more than life itself, but folding is so not your thing. How about I do these and you pull out sneakers and flip-flops?"

She moved to the closet and proceeded to toss sneakers and sandals into a tan plastic crate. Watching pair after pair thud in, I finally caved with an inevitable mom question: "You need all those? Must be six or seven pairs of sneakers there."

Sloan sighed. "For tennis." She pointed. "For running. These are for ... being super cute."

Sporty Spice. She and Alex shared that. She played on Sidwell teams, and that helped fill the Alex void. We found other outlets that we enjoyed together. We rented kayaks at Fletcher's Boathouse and paddled to Roosevelt Island. Watched the lithe rowers traversing the river, the strokes so smooth, so strong. She'd come to Pilates with me occasionally. We paddleboarded on vacations. She'd forced me to parasail. She'd kick my butt on the tennis court every so often.

After twenty minutes, she threw herself across Nanny's patchwork quilt atop her bed. All arms and legs in her black leggings and *Abbey Road* tee. Still coltish at seventeen. Yawning contentedly, she tucked her favorite fuzzy, mohair pillow under her. My cue.

"'Night, sweetie. A bubble bath beckons. Don't stay up too late." I was crazy to give a man even a passing thought after what we'd survived. Not now.

I tiptoed past her door in the morning and peered in as if she were still a child. With masses of blonde hair strewn across the pillow, she slept soundly. Ticktock, Mom.

I headed for the studio. It was always quiet in upper Northwest at this hour, just me and the Dunkin' truck. A few cars here and there, most heading down to the Hill for an early start.

I checked the show sheet. *Meh.* Celebrity gossip, not a segment the hosts vied for now. No interviewee or anchor to bounce things off. Nothing to eat, drink, wear (no kitchen prep, no fashion). What I called a static segment. It just *was.* But with the camera solely on me, it ramped up the need to look good. Rifling through options, I pulled a brick-colored jersey dress and held it against my face in the mirror. That was it—it lent a rosy glow even pre-makeup.

The segment was fine, if not inspired. Everybody did a version of scoop—less important all the time since anyone interested checked online sites. It was filler. I kept it moving, sold the stories, and I was relieved when the floor director gave me the wrap sign.

Falling in beside me, our meteorologist prattled on. "Going to the meeting?" Sunny could be nails-on-a-chalkboard annoying, but she was tough not to like. Couldn't quite figure out how she did it; she was like a lovely glass of wine—sometimes the tannins made your teeth ache.

"Meeting? I didn't know about a meeting. What happened to once a month … ?"

"All-staff email just came out. Butler's here. Maybe they'll cut to the chase—let us know if it's 'off with our heads' day." My mind hummed, on the representatives as much as the result.

With supreme indifference, I asked, "Who's coming from Butler—did they say?"

She sputtered. "Like it matters. Same old boring guys. Saying the same old boring stuff."

Filing into the soulless, airless conference room, I sensed the mood among the staff was decidedly glum. Not much eye contact was made as we found seats. We knew the drill. We'd been sold twice before and steeled ourselves for the worst. There could be sweeping changes, possibly to be announced today. The rustling and murmuring stopped.

Our general manager, Gus, stepped up to the lectern. Less frumpled than usual, his black curls tamed somewhat, he said, "As you know, Butler Industries acquired our station. We're pleased to be part of such a distinguished company. They'd like to say a few words." He motioned some men up. Men who had silently entered and stood stiffly in the back of the drab room. The "suits," on-air talent called them. Generally considered stuffy and dull. And perhaps about to tell you that you're terminated.

Spotting those broad shoulders and his easy gait, I knew it was Rick before he even turned. My heart did that foolish twinging thing again. Maybe it was attraction; maybe it was abject fear. Losing my job right now would be devastating. My pulse raced. I clenched my hands under the table, but I maintained a nonchalant expression.

Rick smoothed his striped tie and surveyed the room, seeming to scan for someone. In near synchrony, pairs of knees shifted toward him. The air crackled with trepidation.

Ascending the steps, he stood assuredly at the lectern. His palms rested on top, long fingers lightly around the edges. No notes. "First things first. For those of you I've yet to meet, I'm Rick Lynch. My door's always open. Having been through these situations, I wanted to get in front of you as quickly as possible. Butler acquired this station due to its performance and potential for growth on the current investment horizon. Due to that, we plan no changes. We do not intend to interfere with your management team, which has led this entire group, each of *you*, to great success." He clasped his hands and raised them up. "I salute you. The media arena is not my milieu. In fact, this is our first toe in the water in broadcasting, but having done due diligence for this transaction—I can only say *Brava* for the fine work you produce day after day. Our goal in partnering with you is to help you capitalize on your successes," he said with a step back. His arms outstretched, he exuded respect for our team.

A smattering of applause. Gus started it, the news anchors joined in. Our sports anchors whistled and stomped. Relieved, I rose as the groundswell of the standing ovation took hold. A peculiar sense of pride overtook me for a man I barely knew; he had won over a resistant room.

The door creaked open. An older, robust gentleman stepped in—ruddy face, tidy silver hair. Rick called out, "Better late than never, Franklin Butler, everyone. Executive chairman of Butler Industries." Escorting him to the lectern, Rick stood deferentially to his side. Our eyes met, Rick never shifting his gaze. I couldn't look away. I couldn't breathe ... Mr. Butler said only, "Richard handled this masterfully, I'm sure. I simply wanted to be here to applaud your efforts. United Airlines, however, made it tough on me. At any rate, on with your day, we won't keep you." Clearly going table to table, he happened to start with ours. I stood and put out my hand, which he grasped tightly. Before I could introduce myself, he said, "Reilly, I like your work. Personable, authentic, you're the real deal."

"Thank you, Mr. Butler. And I'm sorry about your delay. They may promise you the friendly skies, just not the timely skies, but that's only in the fine print." A hearty laugh.

"Touché, my dear. I'll be seeing more of you." He squeezed my arm and pressed on.

Seated next to me, Sunny (her real name, she always insisted, not that I'd ever asked) poked me. "Smoke show," she whispered and cocked her head wickedly toward Rick. His eyes were still trained in our direction, each of us believing we were the subject of his scrutiny.

People started the exodus out with lighter moods. Melting away with the early leavers, a weight was off my shoulders too. Behind me, his unmistakable voice rang out.

"Pretty tricky, miss. Is that the Irish exit you just pulled there? The one where you vanish without so much as a hello," he elaborated, jogging to catch up with me.

"Seemed you were a little busy allaying everyone's fears, inspiring continued greatness."

"I hope so. Well! It seems our fearless leader has a crush," he teased me. "Mr. Butler doesn't light up like that around *anyone*. You are a unicorn." He'd been charmed by me. *Score*.

We passed a tired, barely used reception room. "Come sit? I wanted to talk to you." Sitting in the beige, flecked chair, he threw one leg over the other and rested a hand on his thigh.

"Much better meeting like this, now isn't it? I didn't hit it out of the park the first go."

"Not tough to beat the tap in the parking lot. You set a pretty low bar." I smiled.

"Ah, so I rang back the auto body just to be sure there would be no issues, and you're meant to ask for David when you take your car in. He's the manager."

"David. I'll do that." Presumably, he was speaking to each of us. Standard operating procedure. I sat expectantly, watching colleagues walking the halls and peeking in. I squirmed.

"Such poor form," he added. "I never actually apologized."

Car talk? Still? "It could happen to anyone. I mean, it obviously happens to *you* more often than most—since you're on a first-name basis with your insurance company and all," I said with a saucy smirk.

"You just love having something on me, now don't you?"

Taking a perverse pleasure in it, I had to agree. The man definitely got under my skin.

"And just to clarify, I wasn't talking about the car … debacle." He grasped for a term I wouldn't tease him for. "I was actually referring to leaving you at Giselle's on your own."

"Oh please. So you're not punctual, you're a bad driver, and you terrify my colleagues."

His eyes sparkled. "At least I've made a memorable first impression. You must appreciate that. Aren't you the one that passed out her first day on air."

I cringed at the long-buried recollection.

"Hey! That was in Boston … years ago! How did you … ?" The Cheshire cat smile. "You googled me …" A flash of indignation or guilt; I mean, it was one thing for *me* to google …

"Now, I did *not* google you, miss. The story is classic. You know that. You passed out cold. And carried on to finish the piece. Kudos for that."

Flustered, I muttered, "I didn't pass out. I … fainted. It's different. My blood sugar was low."

Funny he gave kudos for that. Alex had been convinced it was a stunt to garner attention. Aghast when people stopped me in the street to ask how I was, he'd melted away as though he didn't even know me.

"Truly didn't mean to make you self-conscious. The other one that follows you. The day that big actor asked you on a date. With cameras rolling. Hugh Grant, was it?"

I grimaced. "Close. Charlie Sheen. Tiger blood Charlie," I elaborated, since it had been amid his scandal days.

"Charlie Sheen. Was he the one with the angels ... or the harem ... or ..."

"That one. And he *didn't* ask me out; he *asked* me to have his baby! Hard to come back from with two minutes left to fill." In mock horror, he ran a hand through his hair.

"Good Lord. The things you deal with. Men must come on to you every day of your life."

My cheeks burned. *The Misadventures of Reilly*. He twinkled, toeing the line with that well-constructed flirt. I squinted back; the summer sun had shifted, blinding me temporarily.

"All in a day's work, you just field it," I said weakly. "So. These meet and greets ..."

He raised an amused eyebrow. "Back to your impression I only talk business? This isn't a meet 'n' greet." His frame blocked the sun as he leaned in. His expression was guileless and genuine, there was a sweetness. "As it happens, I wanted to speak with you about something not work related. Something I hope you'll consider."

Tongue-tied again, I was at a loss. A silky voice interrupted before I could respond. Sunny. After a wardrobe change, she was in tight black jeans and a chili-red sweater that bared a bit of midriff. Smoke show indeed. "Mr. Lynch, I have a question for you. I'll only take a sec."

My Sunny escape route; sliding past her quickly, I squeezed her elbow. This time *I* was the one who took off without a word.

CHAPTER 3

SIDEBAR

Exhilarated by the "no pending changes," I challenged myself with a higher-level kickboxing class. Hard-core. Zero socializing. It was a women's class in tony, leafy upper Northwest—but despite the fancy workout gear, these ladies weren't messing around. They worked the speed bag and jumped rope before class even started. Happy to have made it out alive, I headed around the corner to meet Billie at Soosh. That lilting voice still in my head—"Something I hope you'll consider." What was that all about?

Just disappearing through the door, you couldn't miss all five foot eleven of Billie. We'd met modeling in Boston during college. Funny and tough, she called it like she saw it. And I'd liked her right away. Covers, runways, Billie had done it all. I was just a fit model, there to fit clothing to a sample-size body. But you couldn't begrudge Billie a thing. She was true blue with a big heart she hid under a tough veneer. She now worked tirelessly with veterans, assisting their reentry.

"B!" I called out over the usual clatter of the place. The din of happy hour mingling, the tinny snaps of half-priced Sapporo cans popping open.

"Ordered you merlot!" Jumping up, she swooped me into her trademark bear hug.

I eased onto a stool and shook my head. "I'm still in shock that Amy's babysitting now."

"Hard to believe when she can hardly look after herself." Text-book beleaguered mom.

"Oh, she looks after herself just fine. She's still alive, isn't she?"

"Way alive. Kid's got a raging case of the sixteens."

We giggled. She tossed her wavy black hair over her shoulder with a sigh, her octagonal silver hoops swaying from side to side. "That girl actually forgot she had a concert. And she had a solo. Barely made it."

Amy had been into music forever, singing with an a cappella choir now. Shy in person (until you knew her), she had a dynamic stage presence. With twenty girls performing, Amy was the one you watched. Her soulful eyes were captivating.

"At least you have her with you for another year. Wish I did."

Billie rubbed my back. "You'll be good, Reilly. And Sloan's gonna kill it."

The bartender put our glasses down. I ordered Sloan's California rolls so they'd be ready when we wrapped up. Billie turned, she was coming in hot. "You know what really sucks?"

"Give me a category at least." I drew my teeth along the bright-green edamame pod.

"Hell, I'll give you a bunch of categories. Here's the …"

At that moment, a text lit my phone up. I pulled it closer.

Sunny DaMonte: How can a guy with that much zhoosh miss the obvious bread crumbs I was dropping. Sunny has lost her mojo. Where oh where can it be? She added a crying-laughing emoji.

I tapped back: The horror. Tomorrow's another day, Scarlett. With a heart emoji.

"Sunny, totally on the prowl … ," I said to Billie as my phone vibrated and shimmied on the bar. A call, not a text. Better check, I decided. I picked it up to look at the screen.

I turned the phone over instantly. Put it facedown on the bar and let it go straight to voice mail. RICK LYNCH, the caller ID had said. I took a long, long sip.

"So what is it that really sucks today?" I circled back to her original question.

Intrigued, Billie spun my stool around. "Hey. I saw that. Who's Rick what's-his-name?"

My cheeks burned when Billie busted me. I grimaced and pushed the phone away.

"I don't ... really know. I have no idea what he could possibly ..."

"Well, damn, girl, never seen you blush. What the hell is up?"

"Oh, please, that's just the merlot. Nothing is up. As usual."

Letting my eyes drift to the sushi chef to my left, I watched him intently. He deftly brushed wasabi on the seaweed and scooped in the rice and raw fish.

She drummed on the bar victoriously, wickedly reveling in my discomfort. "Bullshit! This is non-merlot-related blushing. I *knew* somethin' was up with you. I *knew* it."

"Fine. I had coffee with a guy. I ... I don't know ..."

Her ice-blue eyes lit up.

Before I could stop her, she'd reached out and flipped my phone back to see if there was a notification. There was. She tapped her tapered, glossy red fingernail on it.

"One new voice mail."

Why? Endorphins evaporated; agitation returned. I stalled. Reached for more edamame.

Billie squealed. "Right on! Play the damned voice mail. On speaker!"

Since deleting it altogether wasn't an option, I played it. We leaned closer to hear Rick's message. I toyed with the stem of the glass on the bar. Spun it around again and again.

"Reilly, I hope you don't mind. I got your number from the station directory." Billie's manicured eyebrows arched at Rick's voice. "Like I was saying before I was so rudely interrupted today by your compadre," he said, a distinct smile in his voice, "I'd wanted to ask you something."

Billie threw her hands up, itching to know—"So ask already, buddy boy."

He finally continued, "Would you be free Friday? I'm on the board of Mentors to Youth, and it's their annual event at the Park Hyatt. These dos are dreadful on your own, and, honestly, I'd very much appreciate your company."

Of course he's on the board. I rolled my eyes.

Billie grinned, mouthing "appreciate" the way Rick said it, an *s* not a *sh* in the middle of the word. He added, "Ring me back. Talk soon."

I moaned and dropped my head on the bar.

Billie shook me playfully. "Talk to me. Where did you meet Prince Charles?"

"Prince Charles ran into me," I muttered into my arm, still resting on the damp bar.

"Yup, you said. You did coffee," she said impatiently. *"And … ?"*

"No, I mean he literally rear-ended me. In the parking lot. At work. Idiot."

She went full smirk mode. "You're full of it! And his prize for being a dumb driver is to meet my hot friend over here and go for coffee." Grumbling, she added, "Jeez, you're lucky. Dude would be a legit troll if it happened to me."

I lifted my head and shook it ruefully. "Not happening. First off, arrogant AF. Second, he's kinda-sorta my new boss." That tingle, though. I admitted, "But he *is* pretty hot. No lie."

"And he *is* kinda-sorta asking you out. Let's call him back. C'mon!"

I was dismayed by the new dilemma. "Noooo, I'll call him later." Hardly about to risk an odd conversation with a sideshow of Billie heckling, I wiped my sticky arm with a bar napkin.

"He's … cocky. Been there. Alex thought he was God's gift. And Clark? Remember him, I wasn't *good enough* for his family. I can't—not with all the controlling, judgy stuff. They say women bring drama? Please. I can't do dude drama right now."

"If not now, *when?*" she echoed incredulously. "You got nothin' but time soon. You finally met a guy you vibe with. Forget those other guys. Can't keep livin' in the past." I shrugged but she persisted, her hands firmly on my thighs.

"Girl. The only thing you have to kinda-sorta figure out is what to wear Friday, you sexy thing," she said with an exaggerated wiggle. I shushed her affectionately.

The inquisition began. "So. What did we find out? Besides he's hot and a crappy driver."

"Not much. Turns out he's the CEO of Butler. Who, if you recall, just bought our station. *Issue.* Plus, seriously. What could that man possibly want with me?" I asked skeptically.

"I'm gonna smack you. I really am. You're a catch, and dude spotted that a mile off. Hey, you want my dad to have someone check him out? He's still got cop friends at the police force."

"No, I do *not*," I replied. "It's not like he's a psycho or a felon; he's just arrogant. Not a crime, last I checked." And actually—he was very *not* Alex in big ways—that poignant moment at coffee where I may have seen the real Rick for a moment, the one behind the curtain. Oz. The great and powerful. It felt as though there was a longing there, as though maybe for all his success, his world had become insular. Or lonely. Uniquely introspective. *Un*-Alex.

"How is Walter? The last time I saw your dad was when his barbershop group performed in that hellacious weather in Sheepshead Bay."

"The freakin' rain was horizontal. He still performs with 'em. Loves it. Talks about a move to Florida, the warmth—yada, yada, yada—but he'll never leave New York. Gotta get up and see dear old Dad soon. He always says hi to you two—we need to do a road trip again."

When we hugged good night, she punched me in the shoulder lightly. "Hey, you. It's been four years. You've done everything right. You can stop with the Sloan guilt. She's great. You can stop with the 'boys suck' thing. They don't all suck. Time to get your flirt on! It's harmless."

Sitting in my silent car, eyeing Rick's number in my phone, I knew I'd lived through enough to appreciate it that it could be the opposite of harmless. I'd been beyond disappointed before. Now back and steady; on my own was better than being with someone who turned out to be Mr. Wrong. That was my answer. No *no*.

I looked in the rearview mirror. Reached into the console for my M·A·C powder kiss lip gloss and slicked it on. Watched couples passing, people in pairs meandering to the Metro, headed to their homes, navigating their relationships. Harmless. Hardly.

No no.

CHAPTER 4

INFLUENCER

Late again! Damn merlot evenings. I quickly scanned the show sheet on my makeup vanity and looked for the "Life of Reilly" segment. Celebrity mixologist and chef José Maran was back, and he and I were creating dolled-up, alcohol-free mocktails. Warm, affable, always a dream guest. I exhaled; no worries now, this was shaping up to be a good day and a solid on-air piece.

Bonus points that I could dress home-casual since the concept revolved around the kitchen set. No need to change out of the snug, dark AG jeans that hugged in the right places. Or my favorite caramel Stuart Weitzman ankle boots. But just twelve minutes from being needed on set, the oversize men's oxford shirt I wore for makeup needed to go.

Debating the items on the wardrobe rack, I settled on a fitted ivory cashmere sweater. Just body conscious enough that it didn't look sloppy on camera. A deep V-neck revealed the teeniest hint of cleavage; honestly, I hoped the peek of skin might distract from the fact that I was no longer a dewy twentysomething like half of our on-air talent.

Once I was fully dressed, I opened the door—the universal sign that I was available when needed on set. The vanity lights flipped on; they were unforgiving at this hour, to say the least. The ivory washed me out badly, too monochromatic with blonde hair and fair no-fun-in-the-sun-lately skin. Quick fix: a swipe of sheer rose blush, and a more defined lip would help.

Sensing movement in the doorway, I assumed it was the producer summoning me to set. I didn't look up from rummaging through the cosmetics case for my go-to gloss.

"Need me?"

"*Need* may be a tad on the strong side." He laughed warmly.

Startled, I knew instantly. I still hadn't responded to Monday's voice mail. I'd decided ultimately that post-merlot wasn't the way to go. My liquid courage moments had been known to backfire.

Why hadn't I just called back? Why? Now I had to do it in person. And I didn't want to.

"Oh, morning," I said weakly, ducking my head until I found the tube. I was flustered that he'd shown up at my door unexpectedly, but I finally looked up. Rick stood grinning in my doorway. With his McDreamy tousled hair and a gorgeous blue-gray suit. *Dear God. Forgiven.*

Even better, he extended an espresso to me. I reached out to accept it. The cup was warm, the rich aroma drifting up. "Oooh, you have no idea how badly I need this," I said, gratefully taking a sip.

"Educated guess. May I?" He cocked his head toward the door, apparently intending to close it.

I nodded and caught my reflection in the mirror. *Shit!* My hair was still up in a messy bun from doing makeup; I yanked out the scrunchie and aimed for a beachy look. My only viable option. I swept an armful of cosmetics into the drawer and shoved hair products into a box.

He left the door partially ajar and took a few steps in. Leaned against my vanity. "Surely you're aware it's poor form not to return calls," he chided me with a twinkle.

Oooh. Very early to twinkle. I had less than nine minutes to José and his pear-muddled mock mojito. Rick pulled a metal stool close. It was far too small for a guy his size, but, undeterred, he dropped down so we were nearly at the same eye level. I swiveled to face him.

"This just isn't a good idea. At all. You're technically my boss now. Last I checked, mixing business with pleasure doesn't always end well."

A flash of disappointment dimmed his twinkle. Fleetingly.

"We're putting the cart before the horse, no? Worrying about the ending before the beginning?" His eyebrows arched. Even his eyebrows were eloquent. I'd been right; this was a man to whom few people said no. Why *was* I worrying about the ending, before the beginning? *Oh, that's right,* because things always ended. And I'd just recovered from the last ending.

He held my gaze earnestly. "Here's the thing. I don't own Butler Industries. I don't even run it. Franklin's chief executive. The company I work for acquired the company you work for. It's an investment for us—just like every other company we buy."

I wasn't sold.

He elaborated, "You and I won't have business dealings; we're not colleagues. Technically."

"Oh, he has me on a technicality!" I pushed back, slyly. "Just one question then: If you have so little to do with this place, if we're not colleagues, explain how it is that you're here in my dressing room right now."

That captivating laugh filled the room. I guessed my irreverence amused him. "I consider it my personal calling to hand deliver espresso to those in need. And I suppose I was hoping for an answer to my question."

I turned back to the mirror to swipe on the gloss and let him wait.

"Maybe, just this once, you could have a great time and worry about it later."

In spite of myself, I had to giggle. I'd heard exactly that somewhere recently. Seemed to be a universal quest to make sure I welcomed something akin to fun into my life.

"I know, I know, I should get my flirt on. So I've heard."

All doe-eyed innocence, he asked, "Doesn't anything about an evening with me sound enticing—or does it sound like utter torture to you?"

Zing—that thing between us again, the intangible one that defied description, the tingling at the nape of my neck. Using the mirror as middle man felt safer than turning to him directly. It blurred things. It took the edge off the magnetic attraction.

"It's not … torture," I said softly, shyly. Even studying him in the mirror, I was vulnerable and acutely unaccustomed to a man having this kind of effect on me.

"Well, that only leaves enticing," he teased. "It's all rather simpler than we're making it. At the risk of sounding foolish, you make me smile. That's it."

That dimple appeared, and the freckle. Very endearing. Perched on that rickety stool, he graciously awaited my response.

A light tap on my door. *Saved by the bell*; time to go to set. "Can I let you know? I …"

"Of course. Totally understand. Duty calls." With that, he was gone. He was heading in the wrong direction down the hallway toward the set.

He certainly had a unique way of appearing and disappearing in an instant—once he'd gotten what he wanted. This time, though, that was me—and he hadn't gotten it just yet. So I was willing to bet he wasn't really disappearing.

I called out as he loped down the hall. "Other way. You want the lobby and the parking area. You're about to walk into the air studio."

He glanced back. "Fancy that!" Pushing open the heavy metal studio door bearing the aggressive red sign with the warning No Admittance, he held it for me.

"Sorry, but to be on set, you have to have a special clearance." I added a little more sway to my walk as I sashayed past him. *Boom. Stick to your own playground.*

Stepping into the studio, he responded dryly, "Trust me, I have every clearance possible."

Of course you do. The studio was in full bustle mode. I moved into position on set amid a synchronized flurry of activity. "Morning, guys. José here?"

"In the green room ready to roll," replied my assistant, Bridget, consulting her cluttered clipboard.

Threading a lavalier microphone under my sweater, a male sound tech nudged it up over my midriff and clipped it on my collar. It had ceased to be awkward, a man sliding his hands under my clothing, I didn't feel it. It was just business. Union rules. Couldn't touch your own equipment due to liability issues. Rick cringed a little, watching the interaction. I imagined that kind of thing wasn't standard procedure during his days at the office of a private equity firm.

"José Maran? Is that your guest?" He stepped toward me.

"The restaurateur. It is," I confirmed. "Why?" I could feel the eyes of the on-air staff trained on us—wondering how it was that I was getting face time with the new boss.

"We worked together in getting restaurant food to shelters before it's wasted. Mention the money he's sending to Haiti from his new venture. He'll love you for it."

I knew about the mixers but not the charity angle.

Within two minutes of returning from commercial break, I glanced at bullet points printed on a large card and handed them back to Bridget. Googled the Haiti connection before tucking my phone away. Now in frame, I was unusually antsy and distracted. God, why did this feel like I was back in the auditioning days—Rick standing there and seeming to assess me.

Ambient studio noise ceased, the quiet happening quickly. The floor director made eye contact. She verbalized the counts of four, three, with the silent point at me for the two and one. We were live. On-air Reilly, large and in charge, kicked in. I smiled brightly. "Good morning. I have something special for you."

Introducing the concept of a fresh-fruit-infused mocktail, I ushered José up to the kitchen set. Oversize and outgoing, he was a hugger. He walked me through the paces of a well-muddled mojito while I zested a lime and prepped glasses to sugar the rim. Fellow on-air anchors wandered over from the other set to taste test the beverages, which always indicated a piece had gone well—no one willingly attached themselves to someone else's mediocre segment. Ever.

"Reilly, you have a future in mixology if you decide on a career change," José quipped with a wink before touching his glass to mine.

"Well, you never know in the unpredictable world of broadcasting. Good to have a fallback plan," I said impishly, well aware my bosses were watching. With ninety seconds left, I highlighted José's charitable efforts. I plugged his organic mixers benefitting hurricane victims in Haiti and noted the immense difference he'd made. His lopsided smile was appreciative. Over his shoulder, I caught Rick's eye—he was nodding; his twinkle was back.

José gave me a two-cheek kiss goodbye, both hands lightly holding my face. I'd swear, although I couldn't turn to confirm it, that the Englishman's eyes were glued to the exchange. And maybe to my derriere in the AG jeans. *Thank God it wasn't one of my boxy, conservative blazer days!* Lights dimmed on the kitchen set and brightened on the news anchors. Floor staff moved to the site of the next segment. "Clear," the director called from the booth.

While floor crew migrated, I could see Rick never moved, nor stopped watching. José made a beeline for him, hugged him and congratulated him on the acquisition. Sunny paused and chatted with the men, her hand tapping Rick's forearm for emphasis. Gus was in stage-one cling mode. I'd never seen him try to impress someone. Swaying from side to side, he was dowdy and colorless, but he was giving it his all.

As I stepped down off the set to return to my dressing room, my stomach flickered persistently with a peculiar sensation. *Butter-flies?* Knowing he was still watching, I stopped. I welcomed a new production assistant. I set up a lunch date. Ready now, my decision was made, and I knew what I was going to do. I turned back to Rick. He was gone. He'd disappeared.

Quickly, my eyes scoured the studio—he had just … vanished.

CHAPTER 5

FEATURE

Pushing open the hefty door into the hallway, no sign of Gus. Or Rick. I lingered in my dressing room. I took my time packing up and tidying the makeup area. Deciding he must not have desired my answer much or, worse, was unimpressed with my segment, I threw my gym duffel over my shoulder. Flipping off my vanity lights, I headed for my car and nearly ran into Rick as I turned the corner. He threw his hands up in pretend defense.

"Whoa, girl—where are you off to in such a mad rush."

"Sunny to set, Sunny to set," the sound system echoed down the maze of halls.

"Oh, I thought you'd gone." I couldn't help smiling. His eyes were inquisitive.

"Gone? Without the answer I came for? You don't know me very well." He laughed, leaning against the wall and toying with me. Sunny dashed to the studio, heels clicking and pulling on a snug blazer. When she'd passed Rick, she'd thrown me an envious "What gives?" look.

Finally, I threw up my hands in feigned resignation. "Since you're so persistent. Fine. I'll go with you." I smiled brightly, too brightly, probably. I couldn't help it. "I … I'm looking forward to it."

He threw back his head dramatically. "Are you now? Dear *God*, woman, must you make me work so hard for it! I've closed mega-deals with far less effort," he needled me.

Gus's voice rang out, "I need one more thing, Rick."

Rick spun around and headed back. "I'll be in touch about details. I'm looking forward to it too," he said over his shoulder as he headed back toward Gus.

I called after him, "Oh, hey—and thanks for the …" I trailed off. He was already through the door. "Tip," I concluded in his absence. There one minute, gone the next.

By the time I got home from the gym, Rick's assistant, Emma, had forwarded me the gala invitation. Her subject line was a chirpy "Have a great time!" *What have I gotten myself into?*

Scrolling through the list of prominent attendees, the ornate font screamed full-length-gown affair. Thankfully, I had a dress I'd worn to the Correspondents' Dinner two years before. A beautiful, strapless black Carolina Herrera gown that I felt special in. A delicately boned bodice topped with a sheer ruffle held away from the collarbone with a wired ribbon and a fitted silhouette that kicked out at the back to reveal just a touch of lavender tulle underneath.

Rick texted me on Thursday, again on Friday. He offered kind words on my segments and casually requested my home address so he could "come collect me."

Eyeing my great room critically, I shoved Sloan's boxes into the office. Fluffed the couch cushions and angled the hammered metal tray the way I liked it on the ottoman. It was still missing something. I clipped full blue hydrangeas from out back for the square crystal vase.

My gown hung from the hook on the dressing room door. With the steamer starting to hiss next to the sink, I shimmied the dry cleaner bag up the dress and over the hanger. I nudged the steamer through the layers of tulle at the back of the dress so it would fall just right.

Dropping my white terry bathrobe on the ottoman, I stepped into the gown and gently slid it up my body. It was so beautifully constructed it didn't even call for a strapless bra. The wired ruffle at the top was sheer and delicate. I adjusted it in the mirror, reshaping the ribbon. My hands behind my lower back, I slowly nudged the zipper up, fastening the tiny hook and eye at the top. The dainty teardrop amethyst earrings sparkled.

Uncharacteristically nervous, I took longer than usual retouching the makeup I'd done earlier. With a linen napkin draped across the bodice, I smoked up my eyes—dipping the small angled brush into deep-gray gel and nudging it underneath my upper lashes. The black satin clutch would hold only a travel-size gloss and mattifying compact. It would have to do.

A quick double rap on the brass knocker startled me. He was right on time. I slipped into my silver, strappy sandals and headed for the door. My heart skipped a beat or three when I reached the foyer and saw him. Illuminated by the exterior light, he beamed through the window in the front door. Dazzling. *My God*. Born to wear black tie, that man.

Was it the bustier-style top or the butterflies I couldn't quell that kept me from breathing? Rick mouthed, "Wow!" and put a hand to his heart.

"Thank you," I said, opening the door to him. My other hand unconsciously smoothed my dress over my rib cage.

Just steps into the foyer, he stopped without warning, nearly causing me to lose my balance. He turned, his eyes gleaming. "I've a brilliant idea. What say we get this over with?"

He moved in and tilted my face up with his finger under my chin. Lowering his mouth to mine, he gave me an intoxicating kiss. The other hand caressed the small of my back and pulled me closer. The real world fell away. Languidly enjoying my mouth as if it were melted chocolate, his tongue trailed over my bottom lip. He stepped back. Weakly, I half opened my eyes.

"And so it begins." His voice was husky as he headed into the house. *So it begins*.

I followed him, gesturing toward the bar, where I'd put out a cock-tail shaker, ripe pear chunks in a ramekin, and an unopened bottle of Havana Club rum. A near whisper was all I could manage. "Thought perhaps one of José's pear mojitos would be in order this evening."

Rick settled himself on a high-backed barstool and tracked my every move; I planned to exude grace re-creating José's mojito, the *non*mocktail version. I was doing well. Until the silver shaker I'd filled with ice cubes clattered to the tile, scattering ice everywhere. Startled by the commotion, he flinched. His eyes squeezed shut.

For a moment I thought it was exasperation. Maybe he was annoyed I wasn't the enchanting creature he'd conjured. *Stop. He's not Alex.* He laughed and began to gather stray cubes that bounced around, eluding him. I bent down to help. "Not to worry. I've got this, love."

No! The tiny word made me shiver. So silly: I understood *love* was just an English expression, but it felt like a very personal term of endearment. I watched the tuxedoed man who'd dropped down onto my floor handily cleaning up my mess. Tossing the cubes into the bar sink, he dropped a fleeting kiss on my hair in passing. "No harm done."

While he refilled the shaker at the dispenser, Rick glanced over at the landing to the side. The stairs that led up to the bedrooms. "Is Sloan here? Do I get to meet your daughter tonight?"

"Sleepover with the tennis team. Not that they sleep. I had to force myself not to text her to remind her about sunblock. I *really* need to let go." I laughed.

He moved his hand to my bare shoulder and squeezed lightly. "I like that: she's never far from your mind. Pity she isn't seeing her mum like this. How about we get her a picture."

With both hands, he turned me so the fireplace was in the background. He moved in next to me, draped his arm around me, and raised his phone for a selfie. "Ah. So pretty."

Surprisingly at ease, he reached for the bamboo muddler, pressed on the pear repeatedly with half turns. I searched for a particular glass. Leading me to the couch, he moved aside a few decorative pillows and sat close. His hand rested very near my thigh. I folded my feet under me.

As we sipped our drinks, he looked at me quizzically. Then asked if I got seasick. An out-of-left-field question. I shook my head.

"Here's why I ask," he said, and talked about chartering a boat for the day to tour Old Town Alexandria and Georgetown. "Sound fun?"

It did. And soon. I'd tried to tell him that I'd never experienced this; our attraction was undeniable, exciting, but I was not a jump-in girl. I was more cautious.

"It does sound fun. I … am I silly that this is a little over-whelming to me?" His eyes clouded over. "I mean, come on, even that kiss …"

"Not satisfactory?" he asked with a playful mock-frown. I couldn't stop the flush—or the giggle.

"More than satisfactory. You're an overachiever, clearly," I teased. "I'm just …"

"You're just … ?" he asked, nudging me lightly.

"I … have a limited …" I exhaled, paused; I was unaccustomed to sharing intimate details. "I met Sloan's dad when we were in college, so I'm not that …"

"You take your time with someone new," he concluded. I nod-ded, grateful for the save.

The reality, though: four lovers total. The high school first (Matt, great starter boyfriend, athlete, too young), most-of-college beau (Clark, a business major from one of the premier Newport families), one random model (Henrik, gorgeous but dull) in my few months of single life, and the end-of-college keeper (Alex, driven, devoted to me; we married at twenty-four—he couldn't risk "letting me go." Had to have a baby right away so he'd "never lose me."). That was it. Oh, and the one short-lived recycle, Clark. He'd circled back to give it another try when I was single. Ultimately, he couldn't "disappoint" his parents—by being with me, a newly divorced mother of a young teen. And my job: "Must she be so public?" A harsh lesson: the upper-crust, wealthy families didn't want to dilute that—I was smart, well bred—just not elite.

"To say the least. My friends say I don't even notice men. But this … will sound odd … I feel like my head is spinning with you sometimes," I admitted, heat rising to my face again.

"Ah, the head spinning. Thank heavens. Now I don't feel so crazy." He smiled, placing his cool hands on my cheeks to bring the flush down. *Sweet.*

"The good news is there's no need to rush things. I'm not going anywhere, are you?"

Relief washed over me. He hadn't gotten offended or taken it personally.

"Very cheesy but I confess: I hope this is our last first date ever. Time will tell." He rose from the sofa and consulted the white-washed mirror over the fireplace as he adjusted his bow tie. "In the meantime, best be going while we still feel like peopling."

I'd never heard that expression, but I knew what he meant right away. More than intrigued, I wondered, what would *peopling* with this man be like? Dreamy so far.

———

Descending the grand staircase to the ballroom, Rick tucked my hand in his arm. We moved down the wide marble steps, passing beneath elegant crystal chandeliers and an ornately painted ceiling. Regal calla lilies adorned the tables in vintage silver bowls.

My breathing got shallow as people turned to watch the newest couple arriving at the event. The large crowd began to close in on me; a familiar anxiety grew. I clutched Rick's arm. Smiling down, he loosened my clawlike grasp on his arm but left his hand over mine entering the room. "I got you," he said protectively. "I wouldn't let anything happen."

Any trepidation I had subsided. By virtue of a simple "I got you."

Placed at a table with other investment notables and board members, Rick was gracious and charming. With effortless manners, he waited until I was engrossed in conversation before melting away, and he always returned at the right time. Gliding from couple to couple, he introduced me with unmistakable pride as his hand rested lightly on the small of my back.

At one point, I was catching up with a fellow broadcaster I'd run into, Amin, and I could feel Rick's eyes on me—every gesture, placement of my hand when I giggled—for him. I looked back. He was holding court for a virtual receiving line as the sole representative of Butler, he had an admirable way of speaking to each person as though they were the only one in the room.

He tilted his head to the side when he spotted me with Amin—tall, caramel skin, blazing blue eyes—there was a reason Amin had made it big. Vaguely proprietary, Rick later inquired about him—I teased him for a moment, but relented quickly. I explained I wasn't his type. I said softly, "The blond man at three o'clock—that's his husband." But I saw it—jealousy. And it made me feel good. Desired. It had been a long time.

Once seated, there was a tap, tap. Rick tapped his finger next to the folded napkin on my charger plate. I turned inquisitively. A flicker crossed his face; he was trying to express something without words. Finally he scooped up my linen and draped it across my lap just as my entrée was placed on the charger. Clearly I should have done that sooner, but I half suspected it was simply an excuse to run his hand over my thigh.

His hand stopped between my legs. It lingered. Sucking in my breath sharply, I saw that sly smile that turned his eyes a deeper hazel. *Very naughty.* The hotel ballroom was whirling in fuzzy slow motion.

Rick whispered, his breath tickling my ear, "I'm going to excuse myself. You do the same in a moment. Find me by the coat check."

My pulse quickened. "What about ... ?"—the nearly full dinner plates were in front of us, but he was already gone. I wrapped up the chitchat I was engaged in and murmured my excuses.

He motioned me toward him as he stood at the coat check. In a quick gesture, he swept me into an adjacent room, empty but for extra tables and chairs piled high. Wrapping his arms around me, he kissed my hair. He inhaled deeply.

"Just needed a fix. This small talk will be the death of me." Reaching my arms around his neck, I put my lips to his. We melted together. We breathed in sync. His mouth was warm and responsive, the fleeting touch of his tongue was Cristal cool. People passing in the hall emitted trills of laughter; it came back to me slowly where we were. Dinner was waiting, and we were missing in action. At an ultraconservative affair. With a string quartet playing, for God's sake.

"You're so bad. We can't do this." I giggled. "Come on, you."

He bowed his head. "Fine."

"Well, after *one* more." Rising to my toes, I moved my mouth to his. He shifted.

I pulled him back to me, my hands sliding up his broad shoulders. "Just one more."

He slid out his crisp pocket square and leaned in to wipe away my smeared lip gloss.

"Absolutely not. No more. You're right. Not the time, nor the place," he said formally. "If you're very lucky, you might get more later," he teased, taking me back to the table. There was a unique sensation of floating, reentering the ballroom, my hand tucked in his arm.

I whispered, "If I forget to tell you later, I had a really good time tonight," unable to resist my very own *Pretty Woman* moment, unaware they existed in real life for real people.

CHAPTER 6

HOOK

I lolled beneath the sheets Saturday morning, contentedly one with my pillow. The high points of the evening scrolled through my mind. The tuxedoed man mouthing "Wow" in my door, that first magical kiss, a glass of port on my patio, sweet lovemaking that began outside and moved upstairs. In the night, we'd curled together, stretched apart, found each other again—lazily, I scooched my hand to the other side of the bed. I slid it up the cool sheet, back down—nothing. Opening my eyes, I glanced over and saw nothing but a tangle of bed linens. Just a sea of white sheets, king-size pillows, a fluffy goose-down duvet—and me.

I propped myself against a few pillows. The bathroom door was open, he wasn't in there. I listened intently—no sounds from anywhere in the house. Finally kicking off the covers, I pulled on faded boyfriend jeans and my soft old Capitals sweatshirt. I headed to the kitchen, stepped over the sandals that I'd kicked off at the bottom of the stairs. Slid open the patio door and looked out back. Nothing, no one.

No man, no remnants of a man. Well, that wasn't technically true. An unfurled bow tie lay across the lounge where I'd draped it after slipping it from his shirt. The only sign I hadn't dreamed last night. That and the distinct recollections of being touched, kissed, caressed. Running my fingers along the tie, the realization that I wasn't worth according more time to stung.

How had he slipped out—and when? I wouldn't even bother with the why. Nothing about the why was going to lighten my mood. Trudging to the Keurig, I dropped the tie on the kitchen counter and glanced at the digital clock on the oven. Nine o'clock.

He had run out early even when I'd said my daughter wasn't due back until afternoon. Moaning to myself, I thought, *Was the sex not good? Was I not good? No.* I'd just decided a split second ago I wouldn't dwell on the why—and I was already doing it.

There was a satisfying hiss, and the espresso began to drip deliberately into the cup. I'd gone about this wrong. I'd blown it. After waiting all this time. I'd made a critical error in failing to have *The Talk*. Guess that made love 'em and leave 'em acceptable.

I walked glumly to the front to get the paper, no doubt haphazardly across the front walk. With a start, I saw a man through my window, looming just outside the door. I shifted to the side and obscured myself behind the doorframe. I peeked out. He was big. And he wasn't moving on.

What the hell? A stranger was loitering at my door. This was why I didn't like being alone. I peered out again; he was on my steps. I grabbed my phone and pulled up 911.

The man glanced up. Rick. Flustered, I opened the door. He jumped off a stepladder, wearing a guilty-boy expression. As though he had been caught at something naughty. Saturday-morning scruff lent him a devil-may-care look. My anxiety subsided. *Mmmm.*

"I woke early, and I … wanted to do something special. You'd said how plain the front of your flat looks. Come see." Bronze hooks were now affixed to the sides of my door. Cascading baskets of vibrant flowers dangled from them. Drops of water escaped the just-fed baskets.

He hung his head. "Don't be cross. It seemed a good idea… . but I guess …" He had listened to what I'd said, and he had done something nice. For me.

"I guess ... it's just incredibly thoughtful. And unbelievably sweet." Trailing the back of my hand down his cheek scruff, my pulse picked up with a twinge of excitement. He hadn't left.

"Whew. That could've gone so wrong," he said with relief, adjusting the baskets and finding the optimal position. "Thought I'd have finished this before you woke."

I'd doubted him. I'd assumed he'd just taken off in the night. And I'd found out who he really was. He wasn't that kind of man; he was *this* kind of man. "I ... they're gorgeous. You're amazing to do that for me. Thank you. Can I offer my handyman coffee?"

His sleepy eyes shone. Holding my face with both hands, he moved his mouth to mine. "Good morning, beautiful. I would love to have a coffee with you."

Were my neighbors seeing this, this new man?

I looked down the street. Envy hit me—a sea of soccer moms and dads on the move. Hoisting smelly duffels, popping trunks already jammed with helmets and cleats. They headed to baseball, soccer, flag football. They were the very reason I'd traded in my SUV and gotten the small BMW this year. About to be unnecessary, my soccer-mom car had tugged at my heart every day; an inanimate object, and yet it had made me sad.

I closed the door on the morning exodus. Rick ambled over to the shelves of stacked books and photos. I cranked up the Keurig again and started his latte. That delicious man running his hands through his messy morning hair in my kitchen was a welcome sight. Just when I'd thought life had been about to get a little lonesome.

Was I really doing this? Throwing caution to the wind wasn't like me at all.

Sneaking sideways glances at him, I made espresso, steamed froth, plated biscotti. Rick was adorable and sexy in distressed jeans and a faded Henley top, but it hit me. He'd had the forethought to stash a bag in his car. A "just in case" bag? Or an "it always ends this way" bag? God, I was so out of practice; not that I'd ever been *in* practice.

He giggled at some of the baby photos and stopped at a square crosshatch frame. He bent down with a sweet look. "How old was Sloan here?" He pointed at a shot of her with my parents at Goat Island Lighthouse in Rhode Island. Moving next to him, I looked. Funny, it sat there every day, but it was still hard for me to see. I leaned in with a pang.

"Twelve. That's my favorite spot. I love a lighthouse, but *that* one is so special."

His eyes lit up in agreement. "I fancy lighthouses too. There's something so majestic about them. Huh. Your mum and Sloan have the same eyes! Moss green."

"They did. That was just before my parents died. She adored Nanny; two peas in a pod."

"I'm so sorry, I didn't …"

"No, you couldn't … Mom and Dad had a car accident. They were together." I studied the photo. Sloan and Nanny giggling (Dad in his ever-present bucket hat, Mom in her straw gardening hat with one cheery sunflower adorning it). I ran my finger along the textured frame.

"I kept those hats. I have them in a box. Under my bed." Blinking back unexpected tears, I turned away and pulled out high-octane ristretto pods. Rick's voice was almost hushed.

"You've had a tough go of it. It had to be hard."

The lump in my throat throbbed. "It was a lot at once. The divorce was just after that. Losing my parents made me realize I didn't have the marriage I wanted, the one they had," I said morosely. If he hadn't known before, he knew now—I was one inch from basket case much of the time.

"A lot of loss. Your parents. Your husband." The stream of espresso stopped with a final hiss. With tiny tongs, I dropped in sugar cubes, plopping them lightly into the cups.

"I ... I was glad my parents didn't see my divorce. God, they would've been disappointed in me. They believed in sticking together for life. I'm torn, though. At least they would have been here for Sloan—there would've been family around. It's like I deprived her of everything."

From behind, he ran his hands down the back of my arms. "And you, my girl, blame yourself."

"Always. It's what moms do." Picking up the porcelain cups and saucers, he said, "Not mine so much. She's a little different, but another story for another day."

He'd indicated there was some strain with his mother, and I didn't push him. I only replied with my truth. "No mother ever feels like she got it entirely right, but we do our best."

"Speak for yourself; mine skewed slightly less toward unconditional love and slightly more toward ... well ... completely conditional," he said ruefully. "Your daughter is lucky."

Moving out back to the patio, we arranged the cushions on the lounges. Unlike the front, the backyard was Saturday-morning quiet, a bright-red robin perched at the neighbors' feeder. Sprinklers clicked on, the spray swishing in wide arcs. The morning air was still crisp in mid-June. That would give way to warm, humid starts soon enough. Rick angled his body toward me, his soft shirt dangled over the frame of the lounge. His feet were bare. And prettier than mine.

"Change of topic. You're aware you were the belle of the ball last night." He smiled.

I flushed faintly. "I doubt that, but thank you. Could be an eye of the beholder thing."

"Pardon? You're doubting me? Not allowed," he retorted, kicking my lounge playfully. Reaching a long arm out, he yanked my lounge right next to his and turned his face to me. "Not to intrude, but I sensed you were a touch overwhelmed by the event at one point, maybe a bit anxious. I hope you know that I would never leave you to fend for yourself."

"When you said, 'I got you,' that fixed everything. I'm not always like that; just in larger crowds or where I don't know anyone."

He reached for my hand and ran his thumb slowly up and down the inside of my wrist. There it was, that tingle.

"I got you," he repeated, and sipped his coffee with a hint of a satisfied slurp.

My text pinged. I ignored it. My morning was plenty eventful as it was. I stretched my arms up and over the back of the lounge. I was savoring my man-on-the-patio morning.

Rick glanced at my phone. "Not to worry. Check it. Could be Sloan."

I leaned in. It was one of our producers. I'd tossed my hat in the ring when we heard Michelle Obama would be in studio Monday—just a quickie, she was on a mini junket in support of her book. There was protocol, hence the text; the Secret Service were thorough. Conducting a preshow studio sweep, they'd maintain an on-site presence all morning.

I told Rick the piece had gone to the anchor. "I didn't think I'd get it. It's been hard pushing the barriers from movie critic to encompass more lifestyle, female-forward material. She would've been a coup, such a super role model and advocate for young women, but …" Sitting up, I gathered our cups and the biscotti plate. Tried to shake it off. "Cynthia will do a great job. She's talented." I meant it. I added, "Anyway. Sloan's not due home till later. Stay for a bite?"

His face fell. "I'm afraid I need to pack. I'm heading to London for a few days. I'll see the family for a couple of days and then do some work in the city. Quick trip, though. Back on Wednesday."

Wednesday. Four days. He was leaving. Crestfallen, I replied, "Got it. London. Well, safe travels" (my standard send-off when anyone went away). Life felt like a series of leavings.

"Hmm, well, *safe travels* implies we'll speak when I return. As I understand it, and correct me if I'm wrong, London *actually* has cell service now, so perhaps we could stay in touch," he teased, lying on one elbow, square jaw resting on his hand. "If that suits."

"It suits. It definitely suits." He pulled me to my feet and held my hand against his chest before consulting his watch regretfully.

"Must away. Sorry." At the door, I tucked the folded bow tie in his pocket. He slipped both hands into the front pocket of my hoodie and tugged me closer, his incredibly soft scruff grazing my cheek. He murmured into my lips, "Wish I could just pack you in my luggage, whisk you away. I don't particularly care to find out what it's like sleeping without you, now that I know what it's like sleeping *with* you."

Sunday night, I pulled two seared tenderloins off the grill (thank goodness, Sloan's short-lived vegan chapter had ended). They were still sizzling when I placed them on a platter with char-edged porcini mushrooms. Nothing like a charcoal grill, its pungent scent filling the toasty evening air.

A text pinged. Change of plans. I can get her book to you tonight. Wanna handle the Obama interview in the a.m.? It was the producer. Goose bumps tickled my scalp.

I texted back with no delay: "Already read it. Loved it. And absolutely!"

The next morning, I hurried past the cadre of sunglassed Secret Service in our parking lot, in our lobby. They looked straight out of central casting. Dark suits, perfect posture. Already dressed and in makeup, I headed back to the green room. Certain people created a buzz in the studio; Michelle Obama was one of the buzziest. She exuded authentic warmth and grace as she rose from the sofa.

With five minutes to set, we chatted. *Becoming* would sell itself. She knew that, but it provided another opportunity to advocate for young women, the value of education, and overcoming gender inequality.

The in-studio vibe was super *on*—it wasn't every day we had a beloved former First Lady in. I knew it would be a winner when she kicked it off with, "I know you have a daughter a few years younger than my two. What's surprised you about being a mom?" My favorite interviews were ones where the subject was as engaged as I was. She was vibrant, prepared, and ready to go.

Seven minutes flew by—we laughed about the challenges of raising young ladies. She talked about enjoying her time off the radar. She plugged her Let's Move initiative, citing the importance of nutrition and fitness for our youth and beyond. Strong bodies, strong minds.

In the final moments, she leaned in. "I always say, and I'll bet you agree—gosh, our girls are probably so tired of hearing it—we can't let our failures define us." She was captivating, radiating determination and devotion to her crusade.

"Be determined. Be empowered. Be brave."

I agreed. "Arguably the most powerful thing we can instill in them. Facing challenges isn't optional; overcoming them is," I concluded, borrowing Rick's line.

She was quickly ushered off to her next interview, and I sat in the bright, bustling studio for just a second. Watching from the anchor chair, Cynthia turned to me during the break. Vietnamese and Persian, she was exotically attractive, if a little reserved most of the time. "You handled that well."

Not exactly the gold star, I smiled to myself, but I knew I'd done well. *I* knew it.

Elated, I returned to my changing room and hung my navy linen blazer back on the padded hanger. My phone buzzed: *I streamed it,* it read. *So you got the interview! I think I was more nervous than you.*

Rick. What is he, psychic?

I hadn't even told him about the change—it was so late in Europe when the producer had informed me. Did he watch every segment? Tapping on my vanity with a long, sable makeup brush, I realized, *No. He wouldn't.* In part delighted, in part distressed, I texted, *You were behind that. You pulled some strings, didn't you?*

His response: Isn't that what strings are for? ●.

I texted back quickly. OMG you can't do things like that, you'll make me a pariah here.

The moment I'd savored felt slightly sour; I hadn't legitimately gotten the piece. He'd had it taken from Cynthia. That explained why Gus hadn't popped his head in, or the director. I'd expected kudos of some sort, a job-well-done chat. But there were just crickets.

Him: One man's pariah is another man's princess. And, btw, you're welcome!

I was starting to get it; Rick went rogue when Rick wanted to go rogue.

CHAPTER 7

EMBARGO

On my way to the station Wednesday, the digital clock glowed brightly in the car. Three fifty-five. My stomach flipped, contemplating Rick's return. He was back tonight. Would I see him tomorrow? Probably depended on when he landed, what work had accumulated in his absence.

True to his word, he'd texted a few times a day from England. Called twice. Talked about the Obama piece, a new Japanese restaurant in the foodie-centric, gentrified Shaw area that I wanted to try (they didn't take reservations, but although he "abhorred" waiting in lines, he'd do it for me there, since I was dying to go). I asked about his visit at home; he'd offered little. He'd left earlier than expected, and that hadn't been well received. Particularly by his mother.

A text startled me out of my reverie. Back to the real world; my coworkers never texted preshow unless it was urgent. I pulled over. *Canceled guest, production snafu?* I'd just wanted an easy day at the studio. No drama. I fumbled for my phone. Another text lit up. *Not good.*

What? ... It was *him.* But ... it wasn't even four o'clock. Oh, the time difference, though—it was late morning in Europe. Placing my thumb on the control button, I read, *Happy Wednesday. How about a bite tomorrow? Early bird for you before you turn into a pumpkin?* And the second: *Actually, how about my place? I'm no master chef, LOL, but there's a lovely deck and it's meant to be a beautiful evening.*

Ummm, yes please! That man cooking for me, did it get more alluring? Aiming for a clever yet sweet response, I searched for the right carefree tone, but the headlights shining in my rearview mirror were too damn bright to think. I squinted in annoyance.

Wait, is that car flashing me? Am I pulled over illegally? Having gotten out of the car now, the driver approached me. Oh no, an unmarked police car—but what had I done to be pulled over? Worried, I fished in my glove compartment and pulled out my registration. Grabbed my wallet. Reached under my seat for the ever-present mace. On edge, I put the window down.

Holy hotness. It was Rick loping toward me. My hand pressed to my chest, my breath caught in my throat. I stared at him in his well-worn jeans and pale-pink polo. He chuckled.

"Didn't mean to put the heart across you," he said, quickly adding, "Didn't mean to startle you, I should say." My face lit up. "I grabbed a flight back late last night. I wanted to see you. And starting the day with a hug seemed …"

I was out of the car, my arms around his neck, before he stopped speaking.

"Sweet boy," I blurted into his cheek happily. "You're nuts."

His smile widened. "Boy," he repeated softly as we embraced incongruously on the side of the road across from Homeland Security, official vehicles slipping in and out through the gates in the early-morning hours.

"Care to come sit for a quick moment?" He gestured toward his car. "I took a mental note when you made coffee. You like it strong but sweet." He opened my door. Climbing into his immaculate car, I found two travel mugs in the cup holders.

"Strong but sweet," I agreed, flattered he'd noticed. "The best." In men, too, I mused.

Looking at me under the golden light streaming down from the lamppost, he tilted his head. He swallowed. "I'm just going to say this—and, yes, it's nuts. I … missed you."

"Full disclosure," I admitted. "I'm glad you're back."

"Fuller disclosure. I caught an earlier flight just to see *you*!" He laughed, one-upping me.

"Seriously? You only came back early for me?"

He groaned in embarrassment. "Good Lord, I'm not playing it very cool with you, am I?" I giggled. And sneaked a not-so-subtle look at the clock. *Damn*, I was going to be late again.

"Right then. Off you go. I can't be the reason you're tardy, although I'd sure as hell like to be," he said wickedly. Walking me back to my car, he draped his arm over my shoulders.

He produced a chocolate bar from his pocket with a flourish. "Breakfast of champions. I smuggled a Crunchie back for you. You must try it. It's honeycomb!"

"Honeycomb—then of course I'll have to try it. Thank you."

"So then. You're making me ask again. It would seem to be the way you like it. Dinner tomorrow? My place at five?"

I couldn't help the girly shrug. "Wouldn't miss it for anything."

He murmured, "It's a date." He kissed me lightly under the streetlight and opened my car door, tucking the Crunchie in the console.

Enchanted, I wondered what else there was to discover about this man, obvious attributes to the side. *Was he too good to be true?* I wondered, climbing into my car. What did that really mean anyway, more than I thought I deserved?

Rick fastened my seat belt and shut the door with his signature double tap on the roof.

Startled, I thought, *That man had very nearly gotten himself maced.* How had he known how to find me? Had he followed me? Whatever his method, he really *had* been dying to see me, a realization that made my heart flutter.

Approaching Rick's apartment the next evening in Foxhall Village, I clutched a bottle of red zinfandel, breathing shallowly with anticipation. I tapped lightly on the knocker.

The door flew open abruptly. The sight of Rick's back as he retreated greeted me. An unmistakable new tension in his body when he strode off down the entry hall stopped me. Massaging his neck with one hand, the other held his phone away from his ear. He spoke tersely.

"My time was very limited. You'll have to take my word for it. If I don't have a suitable amount of time when I return, I just won't come to the house, I suppose."

His mother. Had to be. They were still quarreling about his visit? Squeezing his eyes closed, he listened to her response and twisted his fist firmly into the granite counter. "Well, I didn't mean to disappoint, Mum. I never do. Truly. Talk soon." He looked for a moment at the phone, then took his head in his hands, twisting it aggressively to crack his neck. The crunch broke the silence.

"Sorry about that," he said hollowly. "I just wish ..."

Absently picking up the rabbit corkscrew, he swiveled it into the bottle. Approaching him from behind, I traced my fingers lightly down his back. "Do you want to talk about it?"

He shuddered. "Talking about it sounds dreadful, actually. Anything sounds preferable." Moving about the kitchen, he pulled glasses from the rack, lips clenched in a narrow line.

He opened the patio doors. His place was like a model home: sparely decorated but very handsome. Gleaming leather furniture, floor-to-ceiling windows just west of the sprawling campus of Georgetown University. Views down to the sparkling lights at the waterfront, the cafés that dotted the Washington Harbour boardwalk. Towering ceramic urns overflowing with flowers provided a privacy shield for the patio.

"Well. So it turns out you were right. The Crunchie was yummy."

He nodded and picked through the tidy drawers of the china hutch. That conversation still weighing him down, I wanted to distract him. I leaned on the cool granite of the island.

"You were sweet to do the drive-by. How did you possibly know where to find me?"

He straightened up stiffly. "What are you asking? I did that to make you happy. I thought you'd be chuffed. Now you think I was stalking you or something?" Downcast, he just stared.

"No! I was … it was just … I was thrilled you came back early. Happy to get a hug."

He rubbed his forehead and grumbled, "Great. Mum's peeved I didn't make enough time for her. Because I came back for *you*. And you're not at all pleased with me now either. Perfect."

"That's not …"

He removed the corkscrew, let it clatter to the counter as I spoke.

"Forget it." His voice was strained. He dropped his head back in frustration. "You know what? You should run. While you can. It would seem I'm a tough one."

Stunned, I echoed, "Run? Run from what?" I stood uneasily, a sense of foreboding starting to burrow inside.

"Women who fall for me end up hurt," he said, lost in thought.

Involuntarily, I backed up. What the hell had changed? I couldn't force myself to look at him.

I knew it then. *This is the moment*—I was about to have a special someone waltz right out of my life. Gorgeous, charming, successful; why had he made me feel so seen, so heard, only to hurt me? Doomed to repeat the cycle, I'd put myself out there. I'd thought he was different.

He said gruffly, "I just let women down. It's the truth."

I was shaken, angered even. *Must've missed this part of the Prince Charming fairy tale.* I trembled. I could only glare. He opened his mouth to speak, but I whirled around. Headed down the hallway runner for his door, one hand in the air to stop him from saying more.

"I can't … whatever was going on with your mother—I'm not your mother," I managed.

He stopped dead. "My *mother* has nothing to do with this. I'm trying to be real with you, help you out. You're so … skittish about …"

An agitated flush spread across my face. Was he using things I'd told him against me? I'd taken a chance on the wrong person. And I was surprised-not-surprised.

I snapped back, "Skittish. When men mess with me." I'd seen a glint of something in his eyes that I didn't like, that I didn't trust. It made me want to run. He reached out for me, but I was quicker. Already in the elevator, I heard him fumbling for keys.

I jabbed at the lobby button repeatedly. At long last, the door opened. I rushed out, nearly ran into Rick; he'd just exited the stairwell. The metal door clanged shut. I was mute. Fighting back tears of humiliation and devastation. The uniformed concierge politely averted his gaze, answering a phone that hadn't rung, his back to us as he stepped into the office.

Morosely, Rick beckoned me into a library off the lobby, a claustrophobic wood-paneled room laden with heavy antiques. I said curtly, "There's nothing else to say. No need to keep following me. I'm fine."

Sitting on the edge of a formal, satin sofa, in his pale chinos and creamy oxford, he patted the space next to him.

I walked to a chair instead and sat. *I can't do hurt again; I won't.*

He was deflated, his broad shoulders slumped. "I don't know how to do this. I'm not good at personal. I'm good at business. I … don't know how to let people in."

"Not like this. That much I can tell you. No wonder you're not good at personal." I'd thought he was so special, that together we were exponentially more special. I couldn't trust my own instincts.

He was grim and pensive. "But … don't pull away from me. I … just panicked." Dropping his head heavily into his hands, he moaned, "I can't get you out of my head. I literally hopped an early flight because I wanted to see you so badly, and then I go do this."

Staring hopelessly at the frayed carpet, he looked lost. Not at all his usual demeanor.

Though I fought it, my heart went out to him. This wasn't a man who seemed he'd be inept at anything whatsoever. Quite the opposite. People were in awe of him. I'd seen it. The gala, Gus, José, everyone I'd ever seen him with, come to think of it. He was in complete control of everything. Except me, perhaps. In this moment. *This is exactly what I don't need.*

I pulled my knees under my chin, my go-to when I felt alone. He watched me curl up, his eyes sad. No. If I didn't give more of myself, I couldn't be hurt more than I hurt now. Why had I trusted him of all people? A man who could have anyone. I shivered; he noticed, and he flinched.

"I guess I thought I was saving you from me. I didn't want to bollocks this up. I didn't."

My arms tightly around myself, I wanted to be even smaller. I wanted to disappear.

He floundered: "I can't blame you for leaving. And I can't stop you. Can I?"

I stood slowly. "No, not tonight. I … thought we were at a different place—I need to think. Just give me some time." Kissing his cheek—I had no idea why—I headed into the night.

Disoriented, I looked in each direction. Where the hell had I parked? I'd circled the block in frustration an hour ago; parking in his neighborhood was tight. Now I couldn't recall. That block, maybe; the well-tended elms looked familiar. Dropping onto a gold-scrolled bench outside the building, I contemplated not where I'd parked but what had just happened. If I left now, would I ever know what could have been … did I really want to run at the first sign of trouble?

There was no crystal ball, no playbook, for life. People had bad days; it happened.

I heard a tap. I looked up. No one. The streets were quiet, sidewalks empty. The summer air still fresh, not yet that DC-was-built-on-a-swamp swelter. Then a tap, tap, tap. With a start, I sensed movement behind me.

CHAPTER 8

EXCLUSIVE

Tap, tap, tap. Rick. Standing forlornly inside the foyer of his gracious prewar building, he had knocked on the glass door, gazing out at me in pain. My heart clenched into a fist. He motioned me over, both arms outstretched. I hesitated. I was still smarting.

Sitting there, my feelings had softened considerably; I cared about him, damn it. I already cared for him. He sounded drained. "It's not you. It's me. I don't have a good track record with women. I push them away. I don't want to do that with us."

Remnants of my agitation fluttered away. Replaced by—not quite nervousness, not exactly anxiety. Something unique to this moment, something more like hope. Fragile, but hope.

"Come," he asked, tugging on my hand, his fingers circling mine like a little boy. "We can start this evening over. I'd like to talk to you. I ... can do better. I want to..."

It would forever gnaw at me. What could we have had together? If only I hadn't squashed it, triggered by things I'd struggled so hard to overcome: mistrust and loss.

I let him lead me back inside. Waiting for the elevator, he gently rubbed my neck. A step behind us, an older couple entered and pushed the button for the ninth floor. The tiny man looked up with an elfin grin and bright eyes. I managed a wan smile in return.

"You're on channel seven, huh? In the mornings. I have coffee with you most days." He chuckled, elbowing his wife. She did the tilted-head, sorry-to-bother-you thing.

"You weren't kidding," Rick whispered when we exited the elevator. "They find you when you're not necessarily at your best."

I sighed. "Like I said, nature of the business. At least they're not the overzealous types—the ones who follow you around the market or take pictures of you surreptitiously—don't love that."

"Nor do I. That's a tad scary. I'm glad they've security at the station. You coming and going on your own, at all hours. That concerns me, quite honestly." Security was tight—and it got beefed up every time there was an incident anywhere.

He lit candles while we settled on the couch. Shimmering, sparkling bowls, scented lightly with fig. We drank wine. We talked. Really, *he* talked. Glazing over, he talked about his mother's tendency toward mood swings with him; his biggest fan one minute, his harshest critic the next. Hard to comprehend when he was young. She hadn't been that way with his sister, Claire, just with him. He alluded to undiagnosed mental health issues. He gripped my hand.

"We both lost our mothers. We have that in common. Mine withdrew her love. All a kid wants is Mum's love. I tried …" he stammered. "I mean, I'm over it now. It was ages ago."

That he wasn't over it was clear, but we'd all suffered through times that were tough to put in the past. "It must've been hurtful. I can absolutely see why you felt abandoned. A child needs to know the one person you can always count on to be in your corner is your mom."

He spoke of Maura; she'd broken his heart in his twenties, cheating on him with his then-friend Neal. He'd found them in flagrante in the flat they shared. As he told it, her parents hadn't liked him, even though they'd known him for years and all lived in the same village. Perturbed that Maura hadn't sided with him over her parents and made an impassioned plea on his behalf, he'd gotten cold with her. Distant. Or so she said. He held his hand up, "Her parents were extremely judgmental, made me never want to 'meet the folks' again. And she didn't have my back in the end. I went *seriously* off women then. Better off on my own than with someone who doesn't have my back. Lesson learned."

No serious relationship since; he preferred passing, superficial fun without commitment. Women tried to nail him down; he held out—for a great love, legendary. The stuff of movies.

He looked remorseful. "I … you were honest with me. I need to do the same. There were quite a few women—I know now that wasn't the answer." On a lighthearted note, he added, "At least the sowing-the-wild-oats thing is done. I just want to be a one-woman man."

True enough, that was the upside; I didn't have to deal with ghosts of girlfriends past. His vulnerability moved me. "I must sound a right mess," he moaned. "There's a reason I've never told anyone else these things before. I sound a fool."

"No one escapes this life unscathed. Everyone's got a story. It's all about the bounce-back, as my mother always said."

I commiserated, leaning against him, stroking his tousled hair.

Softly, he said, "The bounce-back. Your mother. Must be where you learned to be a great mom; you *had* a great mom." He traced his finger down my nose and touched the dimple in my chin. "What happened with Alex? From what you've said, it didn't sound like it ended well."

I nodded. His departure had been abrupt. Alex had shut me out immediately when I'd ended it; he'd vanished, up and moving his business. His life.

"In his mind, everything he'd done was for us, and I just 'kicked him to the curb.' He was angry; he'd done it all for me, to make me happy." In what was undoubtedly a middle finger to me, he'd relocated his agency to Los Angeles, seeing Sloan when travel brought him back east.

"My entire support system was gone. Sloan was thirteen. I had to make it happen. I had to get out of bed, make breakfast, get her to tennis, playdates." Though the memories weren't as painful now, they were still vivid. Candidly, I said, "It took time. There were days that simply existing hurt. But eventually I had to get back—to life, to my career. I had to get strong. Sloan deserved a mother that was present, loving her, every day." My feet were tucked under his legs on the couch, his hand rested on my ankle. I wanted to know more, everything about him, but not all in one night. We'd done enough for one night.

"Maybe we're both due for amazing times going forward!" I said optimistically.

"You *made* yourself do it, get through it. Because you had to be there for your child. You've gone through so much more than I have, and yet you're so … functional." His expression was one of total admiration.

Laughing, I crinkled up my face. Time to lighten the mood. "Oooh, really? I'm *functional*? That's so *hot*, exactly what I hoped you thought of me." I pushed him with my foot. Smiling finally, the dimple appeared—he moved his hand down my thigh, squeezing it sweetly.

I ran a finger over his lips and leaned in for a kiss. Those tempting lips. I started to sit up. "Not so fast. Get back down here." His hands were in my hair, holding my face to his, his mouth against mine. A surge of desire stirred deep within me. And within him; gliding his hands up and down my sides, he moaned. I looked in his eyes—what was this?

"I … this is crazy. What's wrong with us?" My cheeks glowed brightly.

"Wrong? This feels nothing but right to me." Scooping me up, he moved me to his bedroom. "You are an irresistible woman."

Hours later, we were still all wrapped up with each other. We'd kissed until my lips were numb; now we rested, entwined in his

California king bed. My body still quivered in the aftermath, and delicious aftershocks continued to roll over me.

He was startled. "Can I get you another blanket? You're shivering."

"Quivering, totally different. Quivering is good." He pressed his face to mine, deeply flattered.

"I love that I make you quiver. Now if you could only tell me it's never, ever been like this before," he said, pulling me into him, my backside curled against his warm front. His arms were slung around my middle, and the rhythmic sensation of his heart beat against my back.

"It actually *hasn't* ever been like this before. You're ... incredible," I said a bit bashfully, kissing his chest; here, there, everywhere. Never had sex been so exhilarating; even the evening of the gala, it was starter getting-to-know-you sex. This man *knew* me now, as no one ever had.

Lightly caressing my arms, my thighs, my tummy, running his hands up and down me, he murmured happily, "I'm so glad it's different with us."

"*I'm* glad. I ... I've missed a lot. Damn. Why do couples even get out of bed?"

An unexpected burst of laughter in the quiet bedroom. "Why indeed." Scratching my back with both hands, lightly up and down with his nails, I could almost hear him thinking.

He propped himself on an elbow. "I shared a lot with you tonight. Not a thing I typically do. As is evidenced by my discomfort with it." A pause.

"You still prepared to deal with me?" He tickled my rib cage, and I squirmed.

"I'll stick it out for a sec. But only for the quivering." Moaning at the thought, he lay back. Flipped me over so that I was half lying on top of him. Crooked his arm under his head.

"For a sec, she says. Rather hoped it would be longer."

"Could be. After all, I'm officially what they call ride-or-die. You know the expression?"

"I'm familiar with it. I'm a lucky man…"

With a start, he reached over to the night table and grabbed his phone. "It's ten fifteen! Won't you just stay here tonight? By the time you get home …" With Sloan over at Amy's, would I rather have headed back to my empty home or stayed exactly where I was? No question whatsoever. I whispered, "Wanna know a secret? I've never done a walk of shame. First time for everything." Snuggling together, we giggled.

Still entwined, he mumbled, half-asleep, "'Fraid I can't say the same. But they were just practice: you, my love, you're the real thing. You may think your boyfriend is daft, but he's all yours."

I nodded into his chest. *My boyfriend.* Twisting, he repositioned facedown on the bed, pulling a quilted pillow under him.

My mind and heart raced. He dozed off with an unconscious body twitch. "Sleep, get some sleep." My face nuzzled against his back. I breathed him in, not the soapy scent, but his essence. After an evening of passionate sex. Mildly musky, vaguely molasses-like, his own organic smell was hypnotic.

No doubt, he was a complicated man with many layers, but a man who perhaps just desired unconditional love like all of us. I hoped I'd always be his soft place to land.

Maybe, just maybe, I'm the Rick whisperer.

CHAPTER 9

AD HOC

With Sloan in Boston at her pre-orientation for four days, we took full advantage of the next few days and nights together. I was at Rick's place so often that Jim, the doorman, was a new friend.

"Reilly," he'd sing out, swinging open the sparkling door. "How was the show today?"

It was romantic freefall, I wouldn't have stopped it if I could. The day after our first evening together, I returned from the set to find a small square envelope protruding from the makeup mirror in my changing room. Scrawled on the front: *Reilly*. Someone had been in my room during the show and never mentioned it. Show policy, we didn't do that. Strange.

Slipping the envelope from the frame, I shook its contents onto my vanity. A shiny new key bounced out, nothing more. It was him. It was always him. As I turned the key over in my fingers, I picked up my phone.

"Richard Lynch here," he answered formally, for my amusement.

"Thank you for the key, Mr. Lynch," I said softly, eyeing myself in the mirror. I knew I hadn't smiled that brightly about a man in years. *You smitten kitten, you.*

"Rather a big assumption. What makes you think it's from me?"

Using his phrase, I shot back, "Educated guess. Since there's no one else."

"Oh, that's right! You have a boyfriend, so there's no one else. Must be from me then."

I closed my door against the bustle of coworkers headed to set and leaned against it.

"So it was a solid deduction. Hard to get anything past me. When will I see you?"

"As it happens, I can scoot out of here claiming client meetings at half-past one the next few days and take afternoons off. No one has a clue what I do or where I am." He laughed. "Meet me. Supper on the deck and an early bedtime, since you were deprived last night."

"Ooooh," I cooed. "You are mistaken. I did *not* feel deprived at bedtime last night. May I remind you about the quivering?"

"Fair, you were the opposite of deprived," he said with a dirty laugh. "Let me reframe. An early *sleep time*, that's where the deprivation part came in. We'll get it right tonight."

And we did; we got it so right. I'd been without a partner for so long I'd nearly forgotten the sheer joy of just being together. Over the next few days, he adopted the schedule of heading into his office early in order to dip out early afternoon—and spend the rest of the days and evenings with me. Precious times at Casa Rick, rarely venturing from the bed, addicted to being close and in each other's company.

The first afternoon I'd borrowed one of his dress shirts; it hung just to the top of my thighs. Ideal to welcome him home, beverage in hand. By the last afternoon, it had evolved.

Each day I'd smile, noting the rotating Post-its on his counter. One of his quirks: to-do lists, written longhand. Things got crossed off; eventually notes were torn up and thrown away. To be replaced by the next Post-it.

The last day of our mini staycation, I pulled a note off the pad and placed it prominently on the island. Just where he put his briefcase. At the top, I wrote, *To Do*. Underneath, I wrote, *Me*.

The door closed. His footsteps crossed the hall. A pause. Then he called out for me with a smile.

"Out here," I answered. "On the patio."

His eyes gleamed as he appeared in the doorway. Naked on one of his oversize bath sheets, planters shielding me from the street below. The sultry afternoon sun bathed my body. "Now this is what I call happy hour. May I offer you a cocktail?" He leaned down to kiss me. His tie dangled.

Half opening my eyes, I pulled him in by the silk tie, inch by inch, and said, "Something like that."

Tossing his suit pants and dress shirt on the chaise, he joined me on the towel, propping a couch pillow behind my head so I could see. Transfixed by his body and the ways he touched me, I watched; this was a brand-new me, the watching me.

Easy to spend time with, difficult to leave; with immense restraint, we pulled ourselves away every morning so I could head to the studio—once he'd made me a to-go coffee, he'd relax back against his wrought-iron bed frame and ogle me contentedly while I dressed. "Borrowing" one of his oxfords, I was using it as my new makeup shirt. It smelled like him, vaguely woodsy.

I protested weakly while he watched. "You can't gawk. It's three thirty a.m."

"I can't not look, forgive the double negative," he said, eyes shining. "Remind me to tell you every day what a beautiful woman you are. The word besotted doesn't begin to describe it."

My heart beat faster. "Your vision needs checking," I chided him. He pulled on the softest jeans (over nothing) and a sweatshirt (over nothing) and walked me to the elevator. Definitely difficult to leave.

"It would be so much better if we weren't slaves to this schedule forever. What was the project you wanted to do? I might know people who could help," he offered.

I'd told him about the lifestyle video blog I wanted to create, with my own YouTube channel, that it would certainly preclude me from keeping a demanding morning schedule. If I wanted to do it right.

"Mmm," I said, snuggling under his arm, tucking my hand in the pocket of his jeans. "I'd need a sponsor, professionals to set it up, online exposure. I'd love to, but it's overwhelming. I'll get it done, but it'll take years."

"'Dream big, make it happen.' You just need a little help, some connections." His finger pointed comically at himself as the elevator arrived. Goodbyes were the worst, and we moaned simultaneously as the elevator pinged open. Why did I always feel slightly tipsy with him? Maybe it was the constant overwhelming rush of endorphins that made me high.

"I'm not with you for your connections." I laughed. Tapping my cheek, I said, "Kiss, please." He obliged, and the door began to roll over. Thrusting his hand out, he blocked it; it reopened. His morning face with its faint shadow of scruff was guileless, adorable.

"If I had my life to do over again, I would only wish I'd met you sooner." *Swoon.*

With Sloan back in town, there was a new routine in place. I wasn't comfortable with Rick staying over with my seventeen-year-old present; she'd never seen me with a man other than Alex. In mere weeks, she'd be at school. My time would be my own. Too much my own.

Our visits weren't as frequent as when she was away—but what we lacked in frequency, we made up for in intensity. Amy hosted her for a sleepover every Friday; Billie facilitated while we looked for ways to spend time together, although she was not necessarily on board with the pace at which we were moving. Once or twice a week, he'd leave the office to spend the afternoon with me while Sloan spent time with friends on their never-ending farewell tour.

After a few weeks, I introduced Sloan to Rick, deciding on Comet Ping Pong in Chevy Chase. It had a cool neighborhood vibe in an industrial-style loft—and, of course, ping-pong. Maybe having an activity would take the pressure off. Plus they had the best pizza around—win-win. Still, though, I was nervous, concerned about how she would react to a new man in my life.

When we arrived, Rick had already snagged us a corner booth. A telltale pink box sat in the center of the wheel-style table; Sloan's hand flew to my arm, and she squealed, "Oh no, you did *not*. Georgetown Cupcakes are everything!" Cutting them each up, she made him try a bite of every flavor: he decided the carrot cake with the tart cream cheese icing was his favorite.

She laughed and mimed a gag. "Ewww, you mix your vegetables with your desserts. I don't know about you."

They must've played four rounds of ping-pong in the back. They were serious, the back-and-forth shots echoing through the place. He was good, but she bested him a few times. Not surprising since she'd played tennis for years. Her hand-eye coordination was on point. When she went to the ladies room, he whispered, "I let her win. Don't tell. Helps their confidence."

I wasn't at all sure that it wasn't his own self-esteem he was protecting, but who cared? It was ping-pong.

The next day, we took rental bikes down to the C&O Canal and grilled burgers out back when we returned. He seemed to get her right away, and she opened up to him easily. He even taught her how to drive his stick shift, my preferred method of driving growing up in New England. I'd always loved it, but teaching your child—it was something I'd never accomplished. I'd never even come close; he managed it in three outings. She glided to a stop in front of the house, dramatically pulling the hand brake up and dropping her head back against his seat.

"I get why you love it, Mom! I drive *manual*. Rick's the best driving instructor ever!"

I saw it. She was falling for him. I wasn't the only one smitten.

Before all Sloan's friends split off in separate directions, Rick had an idea, one that excited him immensely. A celebration for the families before the girls scattered. Having always wanted to rent a boat in Georgetown, he chartered a thirty-foot Bayliner, complete with captain, to tour the Potomac. It boarded at Gaylord National Resort & Convention Center at National Harbor, and it passed all the classic DC monuments. The only way to see them, he declared. From the water. He and Sloan started a list.

The list of girls looked awfully long. Eight or nine. How did that math work – the girls, their parents? "Doesn't the Bayliner only accommodate twenty?" I asked, putting a colorful fruit salad on the table, tongs hanging from the bowl. Sloan grinned, snagging a ripe strawberry with her fingers.

"Only? That's huge! This is gonna be awesome." Taking a break to go find her laptop, she wanted to create the perfect nautical, DC-style e-vite. God, I loved that girl right to my bones. Grateful that Rick was devoted to her, I leaned down and kissed his hair.

"She's right. Awesome. It'll be the first time I've seen the monuments from the water."

He tapped the silver pen on the notepad of names. "I thought I told you. Remember how you said Sloan had been sad about missing the daddy-daughter dance in May because of ..." He motioned at an invisible Alex. "I see this as a sort of make-good."

Puzzled, I put fruit into the stemmed bowls, dropping dessert forks next to each one.

"You know, just Sloan's friends and their dads. It would be lovely for her."

I absorbed that, a bit put out that the mothers weren't included in the festivities. That *I* wasn't. And she was my daughter. An exceptionally thoughtful plan, like he always was, but ...

"Well, hmm, if she only invited five girls, with both parents, the boat could fit everyone. And that way moms aren't excluded." Self-serving, sure, but it did make solid sense.

"We considered it, but she really has eight or nine 'besties,' as she calls them"—he laughed—"and it just seems she shouldn't be denied some kind of father figure–daughter figure celebration just because you and Alex couldn't work it out."

Was I really going to be petty about this? Begrudge Rick something special he'd conceived of solely with my daughter's happiness in mind. Something *I* couldn't provide her. I had to admit, the idea was unique. I just felt edged out of my own life.

Wanting to play along, to be a good sport, I said, "You're right. There were things she missed. Tell me what I can do for it. Food or ..."

His happy grin was laced with relief. "All taken care of; it's a one-stop shop. Fun food stations, a DJ playing their favorite music, the works." He stopped and squinted. "I really thought I'd told you. Wait. Here's a thought. There may be a chance I could upsize the boat, if you like. They may have something larger—that way we could have everybody, including moms. I could start from scratch on it." He fumbled for his phone.

"Absolutely not. It's such a thoughtful thing to do, and Sloan will be thrilled."

I meant that. I suppose I still felt left out, but it wasn't by design. He was trying to fill a void for Sloan, a void I'd left by divorcing Alex. I shook my head, and he put his phone down.

With plans in high gear, the day was on us in no time. Rick picked Sloan up at the house in his crisp white linen shirt and madras plaid shorts, she in her Rolling Stones tee (a nod to him, since he'd introduced her to their music). And off they went. Throughout the day, Brian and Rick sent photos of Sloan smiling in front of the Washington Monument, Rick at the helm grinning in a captain's hat, the girls posed melodramatically passing the Kennedy Center for the Performing Arts.

A group-hug shot. Amy singing karaoke; Rick and Brian playing backup, silly air-guitar stuff. That one stung a little; Billie and I should have been there. She came by at four; Rick was bringing the girls back to the town house and she was picking up Amy at my place.

A little past "curfew," awaiting their return, Billie and I sprawled on the bench in the courtyard, the smell of mulch thick in the air, birds humming their afternoon songs. She was quieter than usual. I asked if something was on her mind. Of course there was.

She looked at me sideways. "Not sayin' it's not a thoughtful thing to do. But doesn't it feel like dude is co-opting your daughter. A daddy-daughter day? Come on."

"I guess it could *look* like that, but if you saw how it came about, it really wasn't."

Hanging out the window of Rick's Range Rover, Sloan was all smiles. "How do you say no to that face?" Billie groaned and leaned against me, her feet propped on the bench.

Rick pulled to a stop and jumped out exuberantly. Sunburned across his nose, he grinned from ear to ear. "Hi, you two. We're all back safe and sound. Billie, Amy's bag is in the back of the car. I'll fetch it for you in one second." He jogged over to scoop me up in a hug. "I missed you every moment," he purred in my ear.

Billie slid off in the other direction. She sauntered to Rick's car and grabbed Amy's vintage-inspired tote. Tossed it in her trunk. Began the deep dive for her keys. "Ames, late for practice. That horrible Hannah girl will get your solo if you're not careful." Tossing her high pony, she turned sharply and pulled herself up to her full height—she had a few inches on him in her sky-high rope wedges. She saluted Captain Rick. Although, in true Billie style, it looked just a little like she'd flipped him off.

CHAPTER 10

MISCUE

Surfing waves of emotion from grief to pride in the young woman she'd become, I prepped Sloan's favorite meal for her last Sunday. Lobster pot pies were in the oven. The table was set. Whisking up a lemon vinaigrette for the mesclun, I swirled in olive oil from the pour can. I thought about texting Rick, who was late. Unusual for him, he was very regimented.

Selfishly, I was enjoying girl time, though, and he'd get there when he got there. Sloan was in and out, still packing—new tennis racket, her yearbook with the girls' notes. Billie sprawled on the club chair and twisted her long black hair into a thick, glossy braid. A thin suede headband tied across her forehead without a tinge of irony, the effect was very Cher, seventies chic. I'd missed her the past few weeks. What free time I'd had, I'd spent with Rick (courtesy of Billie's sleepovers).

Billie was consumed with renovations of her cottage in a funky part of hilly Glen Echo, where modern builds coexisted with vintage bungalows. So Billie. Her ex, Brian, was handy; he refinished her floors, installed wainscoting. A good ex, as exes went, he even helped her with her veterans' program. To be fair, she helped him too: he staged homes for sale, often calling on her for her eye. It was a unique trick making a home warm and inviting. So inviting that you envisioned your life there. They were still striking together:

he was blondish, solidly built, always in a Red Sox or Bruins cap. Nothing had changed—they were still the Bickersons, those two.

I'd so looked forward to Rick and Billie getting close. Having met a few times, she was … well … Billie. Teflon. She deflected his efforts easily. Watching the Fourth of July fireworks on the Mall from Rick's roof deck—its spectacularly bright two-minute finale, a gigantic glittering American flag illuminating the crowds beneath—she'd grudgingly admitted she could see why I was charmed.

"He … made that sangria from scratch? Because *I* like sangria?" she'd whispered.

"Tried three different recipes. Finally decided on the apricot."

Her eyes had widened, and she'd looked back over her shoulder at him, refilling everyone's drinks from the fruit-filled pitchers he'd brought up. Billie liked a different kind of guy—blue-collar, straight talking, more like Brian. She'd take to Rick eventually. How could she not?

Secretly, I'd planned tonight hoping she'd stay. If Billie saw how Rick had grown to care for Sloan, she'd see the human side of him, not just her gut instinct that it was too fast.

He'd been there for us in so many ways this summer, imprinting himself in our lives. Nepotism notwithstanding, he'd wrangled Sloan a month-long internship at Butler. Nothing fancy (manning phones, shadowing employees), just exposure to something she wouldn't have otherwise had. Undecided, like so many kids as she started college, she even toyed with a business major now after seeing the big-deal transactions at a private equity firm.

"We need to circle back," Billie said. She was agitating to revisit the story I'd finally shared about dinner at Rick's last month. "He actually said he sucks at personal, but he's awesome at business?" Setting her ice tea down, her mouth puckered. She mimicked him. "Babe, I told you. I'm Mr. Wonderful at *work*. I just can't be Mr. Wonderful at home."

"This is why I never told you that story!" I protested, irritated by the impression of him. "What about all the other things he's done and said? He's a guy who will be there, who will take care of things, take care of *me*." I sparkled when I talked about him. I couldn't help it.

"Not that you need taking care of. You've made it all happen on your own—the career, the kid. Even without Alex, without your folks, may they rest in peace."

I stared at my feet. "I know. I'm just tired of making it happen for myself. Rick believes in me *more* than I believe in myself. He thinks I'm an amazing woman, mother, broadcaster. If a guy you were seeing created a wonderful event for Amy, to host all her ..."

"Brian would flatten him," she snorted. She flipped her braid over her shoulder. "Oh, girl. Okay, okay, you're over the moon with each other. It's a freakin' fairy tale. Could be I'm a *little* protective." She added with a smirk, "But he's right; he shouldn't hurt you. 'Cuz I'll kick his ass."

"Settle down, Katniss." I laughed. "There'll be no ass-kicking. I got myself a good one."

Her forehead creased. "And you don't worry about Rick's relationship with Sloan?"

Aghast, I said, "Jesus, B, don't make it sound like he's a predator ..."

"C'mon, not saying that. But he's working awfully hard at developing something close with her, and somehow, miraculously, it excludes you."

Considering that, I shook my head. "I hear you, but no. He wants the best for her. He's as protective of her as he is of me. He's tried to be in her life in a way that she missed out on—with Alex leaving. For me and for her."

Coaxing her, I motioned to the pot pies, the smell of fresh pastry tantalizing—if she left, it was pickup or takeout for Billie and Amy. Billie had zero interest in learning her way around a kitchen—"Why, when perfectly good restaurants exist?" She hadn't even peeled the protective blue plastic layer off her oven yet. Good chance she never would.

"You should stay for dinner, B. I cooked for an army, as usual."

"Can't be away from the house that long. Amy's doing 'SAT prep,'"—the air quotes—"with a hormonal kid from school. Looks to me like he wants to hit more than the books."

I laughed. "Not getting in the way of that. It'll take two seconds for me to wrap a couple of these up for you." I reached into the oven with a mitt and put two pot pies in a box.

At the door, I saw what had kept Rick. He and Sloan were lounging on the bench in the courtyard. She was very animated, and he shoved her playfully. She tumbled to the grass. Laughing, he extended a hand to pull her up. Hell, he was practically her hero at this point.

Billie hugged me and took her to-go box. Dropped a kiss on Sloan in passing. "Kid. Work hard, be safe, and," she whispered wickedly, "have some fun! It's college, after all!"

Rising from the bench, Rick hugged Billie quickly, kissing her on each cheek. "Off so soon? Are you sure you wouldn't like to join us for supper, Billie?"

"Sorry, Lord of the Manor, gotta get back to my offspring. You crazy kids enjoy," she said tartly, hopping in her car. She leaned on her horn a few times in passing. Rick flinched. She smiled back innocently. One last, long toot as she made the right turn for home.

"She doesn't go quietly, that one. She's gonna be tough," he said, his eyes sorrowful. "I've tried, but I just … she's never going to like me. I don't know how to change that. I don't think she wants to share you—and I can't say I blame her."

"Stop. She's a softie. Lobster pot pies are about ready, you two. Come on in!"

"Lobster. You shouldn't have," Rick said. Leaning over to Sloan, he said something that made her laugh and look at me in mock alarm. "What's so funny?" I asked as she approached.

"Nice, Mom. Trying to kill the poor man after everything he's done?"

Confused, I looked to him. A few steps behind her, he was shrugging out of a linen jacket. He squeezed my arm and waved off her remark.

"Sorry to be such a pill. The fact is I've a deathly allergy to lobster."

"Oh God. I never thought to check. Oh, honey, I'm sooooo sorry. Let me dig up …"

He grabbed me around the waist and planted a kiss on me. "Stop. *You're* my lobster," he said. Usually I was the silly one; Rick had more gravitas.

"What does that even mean? 'You're my lobster'? You goon."

He was startled. "Sweetheart. It has *big* meaning. You're a New Englander—you know this! Lobsters are together for life. And *you're* my lobster." He grinned boyishly.

"Fine, I'm your lobster." I giggled back, a faint flush deepening. "And I never meant to kill you. I'll get you some of the leftover beef stew. No beef allergy you'd like to reveal at this point?"

He poked me comically, and held his three middle fingers up to me. Having done that once before, I was aware it was a gesture of some kind. One I'd never seen, one I didn't get. Like when Billie had first texted *TTFN*, and I'd eventually had to 'fess up, no idea at all that "ta-ta for now" was in such heavy rotation that it needed an acronym to speed things up.

I shook my head quizzically—he turned his back to Sloan. First finger, tick. "I." Second finger, tick. "Love," he mouthed. I beamed back.

Touching his third finger, I said, "You."

"By George, I think she's got it."

I leaned against his chest, our fingers intertwined.

"People," Sloan groaned, watching our little PDA. "Someone's hungry, and I'm gonna give you one guess." Rick good-naturedly gathered up the final things and got them to the table; Sloan filled the water glasses at the refrigerator. We settled in our usual seats.

"So it's all set for Friday then? That's the official move day?"

Sloan nodded, her mouth full. Too full. Trying to figure out how to swallow the too-large amount she'd jammed in.

"Well, I had a thought. How would you ladies like my assistance?"

Sloan jumped in for both of us: "*Yes, we could totally use you!*"

I pushed back a little, not wanting to be a bother. Rick had more than enough on his plate.

"You are not taking a day off work to move my daughter up to college," I said firmly.

"Just so happens, I've already made the decision! I wouldn't miss it," he said, patting my knee. "And as Sloan said, you two could use a little muscle on Friday. I'll get the truck when they open, and with three of us, we'll be packed and ready to roll by nine. Sound good?"

Sloan nodded. I couldn't decide if she was happier to have a semi–father figure or that she knew she was leaving me in good hands. Even at her age, she knew that post-Alex I had been in a bad way. She wouldn't have that concern leaving me alone now. Not with Rick around.

"So Sloan," Rick said. "I was thinking. What exactly might my favorite co-ed going off to university like? I thought to myself, perhaps a special reminder of home."

Mystified, her eyes looked back and forth between us quizzically.

"Something like this perhaps?" He pulled a box from under the table.

How does he do these things? I didn't even see him bring that into the house.

Sloan reached in around sheets of colored tissue paper and pulled out a whitewashed shadow box. Small photos hung from fuchsia velvet ribbons. Sloan and buddies—all dressed alike as Elle Woods for a movie night, me and Sloan under an umbrella in torrential rain, Rick and Sloan during the father-daughter boat trip—hammering away at hard-shell crabs, Sloan and Alex with a soccer ball from a few years back. She looked up with wonder.

"I have access to Facebook photos, too, you know." He laughed.

Overwhelmed, she checked out each photo. Then she shot him a look. "Oh my God! You got Lexy to help you, didn't you?"

He stared back vacantly: "Who? I have no idea what …"

"Um, Lexy, your social media person at Butler? 'Cuz I know *you* don't have a clue …"

Busted. "In my defense, once she got me onto your page, I picked the shots …"

"Wow. You really cave too easily. I have stuff to teach you." Giggling, she added, "Well, the idea was all you. With an assist from Lexy. This is the nicest thing ever."

"I'm glad you like it. It would be difficult to return it—seeing as it's all photos of you."

She grinned. "Mom—I'm gonna go Facetime Amy and show her!" And she was gone.

He'd mentioned the gift to me, but I had no idea the extent to which he'd gone above and beyond. *He even remembered the colors she wanted for her dorm room.*

He added slyly, "One more surprise up my sleeve. Care to show me around Newport after the move? You haven't been back since your folks passed. Maybe this is a good time. We can just chill out."

"Sounds amazing." I reached up to hug him. His strong arms circled me. His hands on my waist, he pushed aside the lazy Susan and lifted me onto the granite counter, moving his body between my legs. He bent down to kiss me. His hands drifted from my face, down my neck, toward my breasts. Batting them away playfully, I tried to hop down. His hands on my thighs pinned me, and he continued where he'd left off. *Sloan.* Firmly, I removed his hands.

Frustrated, he groaned. "Stop, love. She's occupied. We can hear her talking to Amy."

"I really can't. Sorry."

"You can. I just did the nicest thing ever for your girl. And now I plan to do the nicest thing ever for her yummy mummy." He pressed against me, lowered his mouth to mine …

"You did. And that girl is upstairs within earshot." I slid off the island, led him to the patio, and lit the citrusy, citronella torches. Settled on the lounge with a glass of port.

Distracted, quiet, he finally said it was time to go. After kissing me chastely at the door, he slipped out. I followed.

"Flower baskets seem to be dying," he said dryly. "You remembering to water them?"

"I … I am … you seem upset or something."

He just shook his head.

"Is it about before, in the kitchen? I just hope Sloan is finally seeing a really healthy …"

I was still trying to express my point, but I looked up and he was gone. His brake lights glowed in the night.

CHAPTER 11

OUTCUE

Rick arrived with the truck bright and early on a humid and sweltering moving day. He dragged dusty boxes. Hauled overstuffed trunks. Doggedly arranged and rearranged Sloan's things. Brow puckered, a slight scowl, he kicked the side of the truck, his frustration apparent. "Ow," he griped with a self-deprecating grimace. "Who said all men are great at packing?"

Determined, Rick stepped back. Eyeballed it again. Another adjustment, another box without a home. Still he studied the puzzle in front of him, a faint sheen of perspiration across his creased brow. Sloan tugged on her hair, sure precious belongings would be left behind.

"Honey, worst case, I'll send a few boxes up next week," I assured her. A last magical move, creating a spot out of nowhere, the last box was wedged in. A loud *whoo-hoo*, accompanied by a victory pose. Swaggering toward us, Rick had a hand on each hip.

"Ummm, 'scuuuuse me, I felt someone over here doubting my mad skillz," he said, pronouncing *mad skills* with an exaggerated Midwestern accent.

Sloan and I giggled; she high-fived him. Winking back, he headed to my office.

"If you can do without the moving man for a moment, I need to make one quick work call, and we can be on our way."

Sloan FaceTimed Amy, who was still in her girly nightie, her china-doll face sleepy. I packed water and rations for the road. Billie popped into the frame to blow Sloan a goodbye kiss. I leaned over Sloan's shoulder and waved at my friend.

"Morning, sunshine," I said. "Wish us luck."

"Who needs luck when you've got *him*? Am I right or am I right?" Such a wiseass.

I sassed her back. "With the vast array of options you've given me, I'll go with 'you're right.'" Sloan and Amy both giggled. Billie faux-moped.

"Fine," she said, pointing a deep-blue nail at me. "Just don't forget who drove the cheap-ass truck when we took the girls to camp at that godforsaken Lake Have-a-Lousy-Summer."

"Mother," Amy said for the fiftieth time. "Lake *Havamore*."

Billie smirked.

"Don't you worry, B. He could *never* replace you. You'll always be my number one," I said when Sloan was ending the call. Tucking her phone away, she tossed the bag in the back seat and dragged Rick from the house.

"Come on! Let's hit the road, people! Massachusetts, here I come," she sang off-key. Covering our ears, and laughing, we took our spots in the van. Many car games and life stories later, we off-loaded Sloan and her stuff. Excitedly, she began creating her Pinterest dorm room. The first possession to be placed in a spot of honor on the shelf in the entryway was, of course, the shadow box Rick had created.

We left Sloan and her new roommate, a gregarious southern girl, selecting their beds and closets and drawers. We promised to return in the morning. One last trip to get things the girls needed before heading to Newport.

Lingering in her doorway, I watched. My daughter was blissfully embracing the adventure ahead of her. Oblivious to my gaze, she hummed to herself. Made up the bed with the quilted gray-and-pink comforter set, enviably unafraid of the unknown.

Rick grasped my hand, pulling me away. "Let's give her some space." Space.

My girl was starting a new chapter of her life. *Makes two of us.*

As the reality of leaving Sloan here, in Boston, washed over me again, I craved a medicinal martini. Or five. The dimly lit little pub in our hotel looked inviting enough, caricatures strewn on the walls. Rick shepherded me in for a few cocktails.

After ordering my martini, Rick said to the waitress with the purple-tipped hair and rose gold nose ring, "Shake up another in ten minutes flat. This woman right here is going to need it." She grinned broadly. Gave him a thumbs-up.

Trying his best to distract me, Rick did an uncanny impression of Sloan's roommate, Rue, from Chattanooga, Tennessee. He mused about all college students suddenly looking like preteens. How meal plans now included Domino's and fast food. My mind elsewhere, I hardly heard. I forced a smile at his twang, nodded at the other observations. Unable to focus. My heart was heavy, the tangle of emotions barely below the surface. Rick laced his fingers with mine.

Choking back tears, I dropped my head to his shoulder. "Sorry. I'm a mess. But ..." I willed myself to not sob. "If I ugly-cry right now, you'll be humiliated to be seen with me."

The rubbing stopped. "Ugly-cry? I'm unfamiliar, but it's a bad thing, I can only guess."

"In my case, the absolute worst. My ugly-cry is legendary. And you know why? I'm allergic to my own tears. Who knew that was possible? My face blows up like a ..."

Chewing on his cocktail straw, he gazed at me. "I'm a bit lost ... is this still about Sloan? Rather thought you'd be happy to get your man full-time now, but you've got the blues."

With a start, it hit me—he was hurt. He'd gone overboard to try to make it all easier, to do everything he could possibly do—in anticipation of my excitement that it was just the two of us now. "Oh my God, no. It's just …" His expression had gotten darker. He put his hand up.

Distracted by the couple at the next table, he'd stopped listening, surreptitiously surveying them over my shoulder. "Jesus. Those two are going at it."

I heard raised voices, but I couldn't make out the words.

Rick said quietly, "Well, you're in good company anyway. She seems to be crying as well."

"Maybe she's just left her child at school too," I suggested morosely.

The man was surly with her. "Why are you so crazy?"

Rick and I eyed each other. It was always uncomfortable to be privy to people's private quarrels, and it was really hard to ignore in adjoining banquettes. A glass slammed onto the table.

"Men can be nasty pieces of work, can't they?" he said under his breath.

I was distracted. And drained. "Sure. Who really knows what's going on, though?"

The male voice at the next table erupted. "No, *you* stop. *You.* And right now."

Rick set down his glass aggressively and started to slide around the booth. Concerned he intended to insert himself, I tried to pull him back, my hand on his twitching biceps. "Sweetie. Don't. It's their business."

He waved his hand irritably.

"It can't always be your way. I'm sick of it," she complained.

"Zip it. I'm telling you!" the man said loudly to his date, his wife, whoever she was.

That was it. Rick slid the rest of the way. He leaned over and said emphatically, "Don't speak to her like that. That's inappropriate, especially in public."

"Sorry, Mr. Manners. Didn't realize you were on duty tonight."

Rick shot him a withering look. "You're making everyone uncomfortable. Most of all your companion."

Snarling, the man started to slide awkwardly out of the booth. "None of your fuckin' business, buddy."

Rick glared, his jaw clenched. I had rarely seen him angry; at himself sometimes, little flareups. This was different.

"Please," I said again. "Let it go."

The man, five foot eight, at most, had managed to stand.

Rick warned, somewhat pompously, "I don't think you want to do this."

"You got a lot of opinions," the guy snorted, a little drop of spit escaping. "And I could give a shit about any of them." He stood unsteadily, spoiling for a fight.

With that, Rick was up. Startled, I wondered what had possessed him. I hardly recognized him. His whole demeanor had changed: he was imposing, towering over the guy by a good three or four inches, broad shouldered, fists clenched. Our commotion had quieted the dim pub.

In an attempt to defuse it, I implored, "Guys. Sit. Everything's fine."

The guy jerked his finger toward the revolving door, wanting to take it to the next level. Rick was coiled tightly, ready for anything. Anything, it seemed, but backing down.

In a swift move, the man had swiped his companion's red wine and tossed it in Rick's face. Gasping, wine splashed all over him, Rick was humiliated. And angry. Getting right in the man's face, he hissed, "You bloody cretin …"

The manager appeared at our table, his ferrety features twitching uneasily. "I'll … I'll have your check taken care of. I'll need to ask you to leave at this time."

In shock, Rick turned to the rookie manager on duty, whose job it was to eject him.

"I'm sorry about the disturbance," I muttered to the manager, who moved on to deal with the other man. I nudged Rick from the bar. "Stop, just stop."

Outside the pub door, I wiped wine from his face with the linen napkin I'd snatched from the table. "Stop? Sue me for caring," he grumbled, gathering steam. "I will *never* ignore a misogynistic man demeaning a woman. Men should be men; that's the way Mum raised me. And to hell with consequences. That part's Dad. I hope someone would intervene for you. Or Sloan."

Stomping to the elevator and heading to our room, he stopped suddenly. "You had my back there. You supported me there, didn't you?" he asked.

I paused only briefly. "You meant well. They were wrong to ask you to leave. It wasn't you," I said.

Relieved, he nodded a few times. Loosened up a little. Smoothed my hair with his hand.

He headed to the bathroom. Sinking down onto the tufted chair, my head hurt. It had certainly been a scene, but he wasn't wrong. The man was no doubt at fault, berating his companion. Something Rick had no tolerance for. He believed women should be protected. Not to mention, it had inevitably been tough on him as well, the life-changing Sloan transition.

The shower spray started. Rick was rinsing off the wine, the day, the events downstairs. How long would it take him to shake that off? He was never made a fool of. He was accustomed to being the golden boy. And he hadn't been in the wrong.

Unsure of what the rest of the evening would bring, I pulled off my clothes. Threw on the hotel's heavy monogrammed bathrobe.

Then Rick's voice, "Sweetheart, you need to see this."

Tightening the tie around my waist, I went in to find Rick encased in thick glass, as content as could be. Several luxurious showerheads, all flowing at once, from the side, from the top. Dense clouds of steam rose and caressed him. I lingered in the doorway, transfixed.

"This is lovely, isn't it?" he asked. Dropping onto the settee, I watched as he sudsed up from head to toe, languidly, moving under the cascading water to rinse off, arching his back. I nodded appreciatively. I couldn't get enough. It was intoxicating.

"Now, see, *I* was talking about the fabulous shower—and you, you little minx, you're talking about me." He teased me. "So, are you enjoying this then?"

The lack of inhibition was alluring, nearly exhibitionism. I was enjoying it, though. He swirled the gel to a frothy lather. Looked through the steam to see if I were still watching.

"Well, I only see two choices for you, love. Either you come in or I come out."

I moaned. "Nooo. The shower show can't be over already. I'm just getting comfy here."

Reaching a long arm out to me, he echoed with a devilish grin: "The *shower show*. Well, get comfy in here. I'm lonely." He pulled at the terry tie on my robe. Nudged it to the floor. I stepped into the lush, steamy shower. He moved close, slathering rich shower gel over every inch of me, slowly massaging it to creamy bubbles. Sliding his hands around to my ass, he pulled me to him firmly. Wrapped one long leg around me. Trapped me in an embrace.

His eyes gleamed. Drying me with an enormous velour towel, he looked himself again. He tossed the towels to one side. He swept me up into his arms and deposited me on the pillow-topped bed in the bedroom.

He whispered hoarsely as his tongue caressed my ear, "Who said chivalry is dead?"

CHAPTER 12

CONVERGENCE

The next morning, with Sloan and her roommate in tow, we restocked the van in record time. Completely emptied the shelves at Bed, Bath & Beyond of anything with a gray-and-white palette plus a "pop of color," as the girls put it. With the combined efforts of Rick and a few freshman boys from their floor, the bags and boxes were upstairs in the girls' room in no time.

Fluffy towels were laid out. I hung a ruffled white cotton shower curtain and liner. I outfitted their bath so it would be ready to go. A must with the rest of the place in disarray. Dorms never seemed to get renovated, and it was standard issue: blond, manufactured-wood furnishings, gray speckled wall-to-wall, a dated bathroom. But it was home now, *her* home.

Sloan called to Rick, "Need you! I have an idea for stacking these beds to make more space." Hustling back, he assessed, and they pulled the sturdy bureaus to the head and foot of the bed on the floor, stacking the other bed to make a DIY bunk bed. They'd doubled the space in the room. He took her out into the hallway and she squealed, "Ooooh, so beautiful! That's …"

Peering out, I asked, "That's … what?"

Sloan smiled guiltily, and Rick stretched his legs, looking innocently at the ceiling. He cleared his throat.

"That's … a beautiful … room. Yes, it is. Well, we've done what we can do here."

"Okay, you two. Whatever." I grinned. Sidebar conversations weren't new for them.

"Well, then. Guess I've got it from here, Mom." All but shooing me away, Sloan dispatched me sweetly.

Shades of kindergarten all over again. I wanted to stay. The look on Rick's face said it was time; we should leave her to it. He nudged me to the car, and Sloan walked out with us.

She and I wept, hugging goodbye. Scanning the parking deck over her shoulder, the other parents leaving, we weren't the only ones. Not by a long shot. Leaning against the truck, Rick watched us fondly; finally, he swooped in. Draped his long arms around us for a group hug.

"It's time, I'm afraid. This isn't forever goodbye, just au revoir until Thanksgiving."

"Look after this one for me, okay?" She cocked her head toward me. He gave her an exaggerated wink and a thumbs-up before opening my door.

"Well. Call me sometime," I said to Sloan nonchalantly. "See? I'm the cool mom, the one who doesn't get emo when her girl leaves." We laughed, knowing that was far from the truth.

"Yah. I'll check in once in a blue. If I remember." She kissed me.

Rick squeezed her forearm. "Don't even think about moving from this spot until your mum can't see you anymore." He closed my door, and we were off. Sloan waved and blew kisses until we were out of sight. What had I done, just leaving her there? I ached to turn back, but Rick was right. It was time.

We picked up a vintage Corvette convertible after dropping off the unwieldy van. I was grateful that he'd suggested Newport, a welcome distraction from these last emotionally charged days. Standing behind me as we waited for the car, he clutched me to his chest.

"Not to worry, Mum. You've raised a wonderful girl."

Top down, headed toward Rhode Island, he periodically squeezed my thigh. We chatted over the wind whistling through the car about our own college experiences. And what was in store for Sloan.

"How I would have loved to meet your parents," he said. "I'd give anything to be able to thank the woman who gave birth to you. She was clearly a wonderful mother."

He wanted to thank my mother. The simple sentiment melted my heart. My mother would have been taken with that—"Thank you for this woman here."

"In lieu of that, I look forward to you meeting mine." He laughed. "Though Mum groused to my sister, Claire, 'He had to go to the States to find a woman willing to take him on.'"

Oooooh, so he's told his parents about me. He never mentioned that before. I still knew little about his parents other than his mother's issues with him. His father expected only the best from him; that was clear. Family dynamics can be so fraught. It was unfortunate the Lynches were so far off, though. I'd yet to meet them and knew how illuminating that would be. You could tell so much about someone by the way they interacted with their family.

Two hours later, I'd pointed out my high school and the now-purple clapboard home I grew up in. A bright purple—my parents would absolutely … never mind. My heart coiled, just briefly.

In Bristol, I showed Rick the casual dockside restaurant my parents owned, the place where I always worked during the summers, and he laughed at the image of me manning the Fryolator baskets.

"I'd give anything to see young Reilly frying clams."

I rolled my eyes. "Please. Clams, quahogs, cherrystones … my mollusk knowledge runs deep."

Finally, we pulled into the sprawling Gurney's resort and checked into a quaint cottage. After changing clothes and taming my convertible hair, we took welcome drinks to the Adirondack chairs overlooking Narragansett Bay and the sprawling bridge that crossed it. Having not been back since Mom and Dad passed, I'd mentally prepared to feel melancholy. But sitting there with my man, sharing the view I'd always loved, I felt peace, enjoying memories of them without being overshadowed by the tremendous weight of their absence. I'd begun to see my parents and my past in context.

"You want to know something crazy?" He stared off, lost in thought. "I'd always thought that one day I'd eventually do the picket-fence thing. Have a child. But when you meet the right woman, you don't want to share her. Good Lord. Does that sound selfish?"

"The children decision is such a personal thing. I can't imagine life without Sloan, but I also can't imagine starting over at this point. Are you *sure* you wouldn't want one—down the road?" Not only could I not imagine starting over, it was a tall order after forty.

He shook his head decisively. "I'm not cut out to be a parent, really. When I see the good ones do it—like you—I've always believed in doing what you do best. Maybe I'd bollocks it up. Maybe everyone in the world isn't meant to procreate."

"You're great with Sloan," I murmured, rubbing his thigh.

He put his hand over mine. "Because she's quite like you. And you're my favorite person in the world."

Ah.

The sun began to drop. The water morphed into a deeper blue. Whitecaps danced in the distance. Hypnotized by the bay, we watched the boats glide back in, their red and green side lights illuminating. I'd always loved the distinct smell of a marina, the salty air tinged with gasoline. He pulled me up.

"Show me. Show me the lighthouse you've told me about."

"Yes!" I squealed, half dragging him toward the footbridge. He finally got to see it. The spot I loved. I'd passed many hours there during my life, the only place to be when dramatic storms raged. In later years, coping with adult issues, my version of a chapel, my sanctuary. "She's small, but you can see her from most of Newport! Right through here ..." The front lights had just clicked on; the backdrop was deep orange with pink, horizontal streaks of sun and purplish clouds. "See what I mean. Magical, right?"

"Enchanting," he agreed, looking at me, not the lighthouse. He draped his arm around my shoulders. With the sun setting, we circled the lighthouse. He led me to a bench carved into the rock formation and sat me down. His breathing was strangely shallow. I dropped my head to his shoulder and placed a hand on his chest.

"Breathe. Honey, you okay?"

His eyes were glossed over, his voice thick with emotion. "My world is an entirely different place with you in it." Turning to me, he took my hands. "Do you remember saying to me that you didn't know how it could be, you didn't know what you'd been missing?"

I nodded, running my thumbs down the back of his hands.

"That's how I feel about you. When it comes to love, I had no idea what it could be like, how two people could fit together so effortlessly. I'd thought it silly—the notion of *you complete me*," he said slowly, slipping off the bench, on one knee before I knew it.

"I was certain from the time I met you. I love you—truly, madly, deeply—and I would be honored if you'll be my wife."

All sense of time and place stopped—there were shadowy figures, walking by hand in hand. They lingered to watch. I wasn't able to make them out; they were the fuzzy background of a movie shot. He was the main character, the only one I could see.

Your wife? Smiling so hard my cheeks ached, I searched his eyes. My heart swelled with love for this man. If I could just bottle this feeling …

"I love you too … and I …" No words. There weren't any good enough.

He let me flail around for just a moment; then that one naughty dimple appeared. Grinning, he rose from his knee. Reached into his pocket. In a daze, I wondered if there would be a box, but he produced only his key ring and held it out in his open palm.

Perplexed, I stared at it. He pushed a couple of keys aside: there it was, a platinum ring he'd slipped onto the key holder. Sliding it off, he held it up. Kissed it. Extended it to me to do the same. I did, holding his gaze. Not wanting the moment to end.

"Sloan helped," he beamed. "That's what we were looking at earlier. She's got good taste. It's Bulgari." A single tear escaped down my cheek. With one finger, as if it were a mirage, I touched the stone. Bulgari. It must've been $30,000. The number didn't compute. Like every other thought falling all over each other. He dangled the ring near my finger.

"So that was a yes, was it?"

Hell, I never actually said it! I managed a soft yes. Sliding the square diamond on my hand, the emotions of the day overwhelmed me. Laughing and sobbing simultaneously, I kissed him. He pulled me into his lap. Melting into him, the sun did its final descent. I cuddled in for warmth.

With day-trippers departing, he asked slyly, "Ever get randy in your special lighthouse?"

I pulled away at the horror of having adult sex at my childhood happy place.

"What? God no! Anyway, I'm sure it's locked."

Disappointed, he placed his hands firmly on my shoulders. He nudged me to the garden just beside the lighthouse. The area was in almost total darkness now, save for the twinkling lighthouse lights. He laid his jacket down on the grass. Put me down on top of it. Straddled me.

"This is to seal the deal. You're mine. Forever and ever."

I tingled in anticipation, my forever and ever love. Straining to be sure no one could see, I tried to resist, but he tightened his thighs. Held both my hands over my head with one of his. He wanted me here, now. I surrendered to the moment. To my fiancé. *My fiancé!*

Sheepishly rumpled, we returned to Gurney's half an hour later. Headed in for our dinner reservation. Rick and the manager caught eyes, an almost imperceptible nod between them. Showing us to our booth, the manager said, "Congratulations to both of you!" He pulled back the velvety drape and secured it with a twisted rope. Our table had been set with a gleaming silver champagne bucket in the center. I looked more closely. Touched the unique raised emblem: two lobsters with an embossed phrase. FOR LIFE. Lobsters, together forever.

"For life," I reiterated, my eyes misty, raising my flute for a toast, feeling my past, my present, and my future merging together in a magical way. *Luckiest. Girl. Ever.*

His glass raised high, Rick looked at me before sipping the bubbly. "For life. There's one thing first; I'd like to talk to you about something I need you to do for me."

The firepit lighting the way, we followed the pebbled, meandering trail in silence, the only sound our footsteps crunching on the path. Two chairs nestled together on one side of the pit beckoned, an oversize houndstooth throw draped over each. Rick threw mine over his arm until I sat, then draped it around me before seating himself in the other chair. The bronze fire crackled.

"I need you to do something, love. It's your schedule. It's too much for you, for our new life together."

The wind shifted off the water; suddenly chilly, I pulled my throw closer. "You ... don't want me to work?" I asked, shocked that he'd never shared that before.

"No! No, I know you enjoy what you do—and you're brilliant at it. I've given this ample thought, I've weighed the pros and cons. The only way I see this life working is for you to make a change," he said decisively.

Fingers on my temples, I opened my mouth: this wasn't just ...

"But actually—hear me out—it's a good *change*. It's time." His eyes were shining. "Start your video blog—your own hours, your own boss. I did the research. *You* are more popular than the station you're on. *You're* one of the highest-rated segments."

I nodded. I'd heard this every time I got a ratings-related bonus. So why would I want to leave when they still wanted me? "I can't even consider it for another thirteen months. That's when my contract ends."

"Not an issue. Leave that to me. Imagine it: *Life of Reilly*, the vlog. Exactly as you wanted. This is just fast-tracking the dream, *your* dream."

"Unfortunately, that's impossible. I actually passed that by Gus at one point, and 'Life of Reilly' is the station's intellectual property, so while that would help a ton, it's not an option."

"I may have buried the lead. I had a little tête-à-tête with Gus. He'll bequeath you the title. What good would the name be if you left? He won't find another Reilly to anchor."

He'd spoken to my manager. Made sure the project would be green-lit. My head spun. I'd wanted another two-year contract. I was due for a salary bump. I liked my colleagues (they'd become a family of sorts, one I'd appreciate with Sloan gone). I liked having somewhere to be.

"Realistically, it will take me time to find a sponsor, and that's an integral—"

He waved his hand. "Exactly the moment my connections come in handy. The truth is life is only getting more hectic. I'm being given more responsibility, presumably in anticipation of Franklin retiring. He doesn't want to work forever. He and Dory want to travel, enjoy their golden years, and I'm the obvious heir to the throne, if Franklin has his way. So maybe we get this vlog up and going while I still have time to help you. We wouldn't have security issues either. I worry about you at the station. Things happen," he added with a look of concern.

Dropping my head back, I stared into the starless night and tried to process the amount of change. Leaving the station, making a go of it on my own, nothing familiar remaining in my life. None of it was bad; no divorce, no death, no unexpected loss. Didn't change the fact that change was hard.

"Thoughts?" he pressed. "Do you see another way?"

Staring into the firepit, I pondered. "I don't know. I'll think it through …"

He smiled. "Do that." He nudged my thigh. "*Life of Reilly* can be up and launched in a flash. Sponsored. It's everything you've wanted, *and* it leaves us with a life, not a three a.m. wake-up call. I want a real life with you."

And I wanted one with him. Still. "I wasn't quite ready for it yet, but …"

Rick's face was illuminated by the rosy glow of the fire. "Come. I'll run you a bath, get you some bubbly. Let's enjoy our engagement tonight." Pulling me up, he playfully twirled the diamond ring on my finger. "No rush. You can decide tomorrow."

"Tomorrow? I thought maybe I'd take some time …"

Stopping on the trail, he said in mock dismay, "Yes, tomorrow. Arrangements need to be made for the wedding. Columbus Day weekend is the natural choice because it'll be easier for everyone, but that makes your answer an important and timely piece here," and he tucked my hand in his arm. "Make sense?"

Lounging in the spacious, jetted bathtub, a bottle of champagne in the lobster bucket to my side, I debated the idea while Rick worked on his laptop. What had he said? Pros and cons; let the head rule, not the heart; it's business.

Pros: my own project, content approval, civilized hours, the rights to retain *Life of Reilly*, and an unexpected partner who could make things happen that I never could.

Cons: I'd miss that grimy old station I loved. My motley crew of crazy colleagues that had become a family of sorts. That was really about it.

Not entirely true. There was one more dynamic to consider. I'd always believed there was what I called an "expiration date" for on-air talent—a few years more, a few years less, but an expiration date nonetheless. There would be a certain satisfaction in leaving the industry before it inevitably left me. Popping my toes up from the bubbles and back down, up and back down, I weighed the dilemma.

Wrapped in a pristine towel, I perched on the quilted stool for a while. It reinvigorated me, thinking about a new adventure, a new chapter. I was game. And ready for a challenge.

I wandered back into the main room. Tapping away furiously on the laptop, Rick looked up. "You're a vision." Seeing a new look in my eyes, he leaned on his elbows expectantly.

Decision time: the vlog was a gift I was being given on many levels. Crossing to him, I put my hand out and smiled. "Deal."

He rose from the chair and grasped my hand, his other hand closing over the top. "Deal," he responded, truly pleased. He looked me up and down wickedly. "I so rarely get to close deals with a woman clad in only a towel. Speaking of which, why is she even wearing a towel?"

He grabbed it and flung it aside as he picked me up. Hoisting me in the air, he laughed.

"Oh my God, we're getting married," he shouted, tossing me over one shoulder and carrying me onto the patio. Waving me like a trophy, he announced into the brisk dark night, "For life! I get my girl for life."

CHAPTER 13

SWEEPS

"October is the most exquisite month here, and you love the Inn at Little Washington. It's iconic. My mum and dad will be chuffed; my sister won't want to leave," he coaxed me.

Traveling back, I saw Rick's personal and business acumen in all its glory. Gracious with everyone, they bent over backward to create an event to please him, offering him options that didn't exist for a normal person. By the time we reached Reagan Airport, he'd nailed down a venue and a date. Inn at Little Washington. October 11. Only several weeks away, but he said the long Columbus Day weekend was ideal. Made a quick trip easier for Sloan.

A man who knew what he wanted. So, the Inn it was; lush, sprawling grounds tucked in the stunning foothills of the Blue Ridge Mountains. He reserved a block of rooms—for his parents, his sister, my brother, Sloan—and diagrammed a custom roof deck for the ceremony.

"You don't have music taken care of yet? What about the menu and flowers?"

"Must I do everything? Really?"

We sat, hands entwined, and made plans.

"I can't believe what you've accomplished. But can we talk about who's coming to this gorgeous event? I've got some close friends that … I mean, I'd like Billie and …"

Rick chose his words carefully. "I'm not so keen on that, actually, I'm afraid."

"Do you not like Billie? I mean, she can be lots of bark, but there's no bite at all."

"Of course not! That's not it at all. That girl loves you, and I appreciate that."

I looked at him helplessly, running my thumb up and down his. Slowly, he elaborated, "Hear me out. It's not personal at all. I just want this to be *us* and so, so special. And ..."

Rick stalled before sharing the real reason. "Here's the thing. Billie was your maid of honor at your first wedding. All of your friends were there. And that's *fine*! But this is *our* wedding. To me, if feels like *only* close family ... mine and yours ..."

Not the way I would have envisioned it, but I got his intention. Keep that circle tight, the tightest. Blood. I put my hand on his. "I understand. That's sweet, really. Just family. I love it."

If we kept the wedding intimate, it gave us more time to get to know each other in the short period of time we'd share, I reasoned. In any event, having booked a date several weeks away, there wasn't exactly sufficient time to plan something bigger. So *intimate* it was.

Rick booked flights for everyone. I chose the eclectic menu, a mix of upscale takes on British comfort foods, including shepherd's pie, and the Inn's specialty, duck a l'orange; the chamber music; the live wall of blooming flowers.

The dress! Calling in a favor, a stylist I'd worked with brought me some options appropriate for the venue, the season. With the fact that it was a second wedding, right away I was drawn to an off-the-shoulder vintage ivory gown—the simple bias cut was easy to wear and flattering on me. The creamy aged satin gleamed like candlelight. Juggling work and planning, the day seemed to be on us in an instant.

Gathering with us at the Inn, Rick's family was certainly more reserved than my own parents had been, but welcoming. The first evening we'd reserved a charming reception room with vintage tables and linens; catering trays were passed with heavy hors d'oeuvres, and a silver buffet cart held a full bar. Music and conversation from the other areas wafted in faintly.

Rick's mother, Diana, wasn't the warmest of women, particularly with him. On the austere side, she greeted him with an exchange of the briefest of double-cheeked kisses, in contrast to his father, who hugged him heartily and repeatedly. Rick tried to engage his mother with anecdotes, but she had a peculiar way of shaking him off and slipping away. Although cordial, I couldn't say she was much more forthcoming with me. His sister, Claire, told me she can be difficult to get to know—"She's not as demonstrative as the rest of us." Claire belly-laughed about the similarity between me and Diana. Five foot seven, long limbed and slim, sleek blonde hair past her shoulders, a deep dive of dimples, and green eyes— Diana was so like me you'd have taken *us* as mother and daughter. Rick said he'd never seen it, professed to still not agree even after everyone talked about it and marveled at it. We all had a good laugh about it.

After a few martinis the first night, Diana suppressed a sigh, pondering the huge olive on her toothpick. Her formality faded with gin consumption. "Rick says you're a 'remarkable woman' and a perfect mum, supportive to the nth degree. I don't recall him using superlatives like that before."

I assured her I was far from perfect, but that I did love her son. That I felt blessed to have met him. Unfortunately, she'd developed a nagging migraine shortly after arriving and remained in her room much of the weekend. The night before the wedding, though, she emerged.

Diana pulled a chair next to me in the study and reached into her small, structured purse. She pulled out a teeny velvet bag. "Now, you needn't wear this—but I thought perhaps. I had no idea what the perfect woman could use." She smiled, her eyes crinkling like Rick's.

Inside the bag: a bracelet—two bands twisted together, one platinum, one gold, dotted with small garnets, little ruby-colored crystals. "Arthur gave this to me when we were first married, and it seemed …"

Welling up, I kissed her on both cheeks. "You're so kind, and I'll … treasure this," I said. Suddenly at my side, Rick's father, Arthur, drew me away from Diana so we could have some alone time. He was a man's man, far more content outside with a cigar and the fellows, but he sat with me at the piano bar for hours. Bobbed his head along with the classics. Arthur humble-bragged about Richard—the fine man he was. How hard he'd worked to get where he was. His family held him in very high regard.

Will, my brother, was on-site now, better late than never. He'd come from Hawaii after all. Not one to be landlocked, he'd moved to Hawaii when I was still in junior high, in search of the endless summer, a surfer's true love. Still sporting longish sun-bleached hair, he glowed. I adored my brother, in spite of infrequent visits. My heart soared, and yet hurt, spending time with him. Selfishly, I wanted him in DC. I wanted family nearby. Now more than ever, since I was finally creating my own brand-new family.

Embracing Rick warmly, Will talked business with him over cocktails. Shared war stories. Will owned a business, a water-craft rental operation, and they commiserated about the challenges of budgets and staff. Pulling me over to join them, Will was all lit up. "Couldn't have written this one better. This one's brilliant, and funny, and he loves my sister." Looking down at me, he added, "Mom and Dad would adore him, how he is with you and Sloan. You know that, right?"

Nodding back, I smiled. I hoped they would've muddled through the Alex divorce with me and been pleased I'd rebounded. With a man who loved their daughter, and their granddaughter.

Will and Rick's sister, Claire, got on well. Will had played golf many times over the years in England and Wales; Claire had played for her college. It was a foreign language to me as they compared and contrasted flat links courses with mountain courses and their stunning cliff-top holes. Never without a pint of Guinness in hand. Made sense Claire played, because she had that same athletic look Rick had—tall; broad shouldered; Rick with lighter auburn, almost tortoiseshell, hair and a healthy dose of reddish freckles.

Tired but ecstatic, I felt sleep beckon. Closing my door, there was a gold box tied with a pink bow on my bed. *Something old*, the card read. Signed, *Yours, B.* Billie. She'd found a vintage hairpin, adorned with tiny crystals and gems; it would tuck nicely into the retro half-updo hair she'd helped me decide on. Flopping onto the brass bed, I called her.

"Runaway bride hotline," she answered. "Where do I pick you up?"

I giggled.

"I wish you were here," I said softly, guilty that my best friend, who'd been by my side forever, wasn't here. Knowing she felt left out, I also knew she'd never burden me with that.

"Me too," she replied. "So. My BFOTB duty."

In confusion, I echoed, "BFOTB?"

"C'mon, seriously. Best friend of the bride."

"Ah, got it now. You are definitely that."

"BFOTB duty is one question: You're sure this is what you really want? Like, really, really? It's my obligation to give you the 'never too late to call it off' speech."

"I really, really want this. I didn't realize what was missing until he came crashing into my life." I laughed. "We have an amazing thing together—and I want this for you, too, Billie."

She sighed. "Perish the thought. But as long as you're happy, and he treats you well, I'm all in favor. If that ever changes, I'll open up a can of whoop-ass."

"It won't change. Promise. Need to find Sloan, okay? Hey. I love you."

"Hey, love you back," she replied before ending the call.

Sloan and I got ready together in the over-the-top bridal suite, with its separate curtained-off, professionally lit changing room. Glamorous makeup area. Sloan pulled back the velvet curtain and stepped out. Her long blonde hair curled for the occasion hung in beautiful waves.

I caught my breath. She was so grown up in her vintage marine-blue strapless silk gown. "You're getting married, Mom! C'mere, sit." Taking Billie's gift, the glittery hairpin, she tucked it into my hair and smiled approvingly. I slipped on the bracelet that Rick's mum had given me. Sloan took my hand, the first time she'd done that in many years, as we walked to the rooftop.

"It's time," said the party planner, leading us to the top of the aisle at the makeshift altar. A lush wall of ivory and pink peonies of varying sizes and vibrant shades. Twinkling lights everywhere, hundreds of candles from tea lights to floating candles to tall pillars lining the entry. My exquisite bouquet contained deeper-hued peonies with tiny embedded crystals.

Sloan kissed me and headed down the aisle. A cellist played. Waving my hands in front of my eyes, I tried not to cry off the pretty makeup. The party planner shook my small train into place and said softly, "Your groom awaits."

Rounding the corner, I saw Rick, and the world stopped. He looked dashing, and, more importantly, his smile was dazzling and genuine. Walking to join him, I passed two chairs at the front of the aisle, empty but for one item on each: Dad's bucket hat and Mom's straw hat. *He thinks of everything.*

Toward the end of the evening, we dipped into the luscious chocolate fountain while family delivered sweet, funny toasts. Claire obviously adored her big brother. She held her champagne flute up with a boozy, toothy grin, her updo half-down, tousled hair falling.

"You've always been the bestest big brother a girl could want. You slayed dragons for me, and you'll do the same for Reilly. Cheers, kids!" She swayed slightly in high sandals, her turquoise silk dress sliding off one shoulder.

Claire confided that her mum had wanted to speak, but she got nervous in those situations. I related to that, I commiserated. She raised her shoulders, saying it wasn't so much social anxiety, more like *Rick anxiety*.

"Medical term?" I'd asked, laughing.

Claire acknowledged there had always been tension there. Mum could never do right by him—she hadn't doted on him enough, hadn't adored him enough to ignore his "mischief." She didn't refer to any mental health issues with Diana, and I didn't think it my place to ask.

On not her first glass of champagne, the secrets bubbled out, no stopping them. She gossiped: Rick had been a wild child. Money went missing from the chip shop he worked at, and he'd lifted a bike from a store (planning to return it), Claire said. He'd been a suspect in a home invasion, but nothing was proved. Rumors dogged him through the years, the way these things go. And years later, the family home of a woman, Maura who had spurned him had burned to the ground—so naturally there was a new round of speculation. None of it sounded like the Rick I knew.

"Claire," I said, "that's awful. It has to be so unsettling, for all of you, that rumors persist when he knows he's innocent and had nothing to do with it." I'd felt that poignancy in him, like someone on an island. *Had he always felt on his own, from early on?* I wondered.

She eyed me over one shoulder. "Guys don't give a rat's ass about rumors. But my mum—she has a hard time. She tries to ignore it, but it bothers her." Diana was no-nonsense: she had Rick make restitution to the chip shop, return the bike, apologize face-to-face. He'd argued even then that she was unfair to hold him accountable when other boys did it too. He'd been distraught she didn't support him, cover for him, the way other boys' mothers had. Explained the odd dynamic.

Claire giggled, her hand on my forearm (partially for support after another refill). "Hell, if he doesn't have a way—Maura's dad ran him down for a little chat and, by the end of it, was totally convinced Rick had nothing to do with it. My mum, though, she's still on about it. He can charm the birds out of their nest, but Mum's a tough one, not as susceptible."

Arthur hadn't wanted Diana to draw attention to his youthful foibles, lest it get in the way of his bright future. It had caused friction between the couple; Diana and Arthur had never spoken of it between themselves again. Rick and Diana had never bridged the chasm in their own relationship. Strange to me, since Rick seemed to desire her love and approval so badly—but who could ever really dissect other people's dynamics? Today wasn't a day for that anyway.

My brother, Will, was emotional. "You got it right this time, sis. Rick, if I could have conjured you up for her, I would have. You are a great addition to our family, and I have never seen my sister happier. So thank you, brother."

And Rick's dad, full head of silver hair, peered over his half glasses: "You've always gotten what you've gone after, son. Commit to this lovely lady, and you'll be just as successful in this marriage as you've been in the rest of your life!"

Sloan was darling and funny: "Pretty sure the term 'helicopter mom' was coined for my mother." (That elicited laughter.) "And now, thankfully, you have someone new to smother, Mom. Good luck, Rick!" (More laughter.) "But seriously, you two are hashtag couplesgoals, and I'm thrilled for you!"

Rick held his flute up and turned to my daughter. "Sloan." Her eyes sparkled. "Sloan. You are the light of your mother's life, and that makes you a very special person indeed." Claire wiped away a tear and grabbed her mother's arm.

"If we are hashtag couplesgoals—you are hashtag humangoals. Thank you for being such a pure, wonderful spirit—it is my pleasure to be part of your life. Your mom and I have something teeny-tiny for you."

I ... I knew nothing about this.

With that, he pulled the signature aquamarine Tiffany box from his pocket. The one girls swoon over.

Slipping off the white silk ribbon, she unfolded the tissue. She pulled out diamond studs. Her first. Nothing ostentatious; delicate, twinkling, teardrop-shaped diamonds. *Perfect.* Clutching the blue box, she beamed.

Rick faced me. My heart fluttered. Was this even real? Was this my life?

"They say that some people enter your life for a reason, some for a season, and some for a lifetime. I believe that's true, and I believe our lives have just begun. Together. If you'll raise your glasses one last time, I'd like to toast Reilly Lynch, my lifetime person!"

At our final breakfast the following morning, Claire cornered me, her index finger to her lips. "Got a little in my cups last night. Don't repeat anything I told you, eh?"

"Never, Claire. Don't give it another thought. Everyone's got a story, after all."

She squeezed my arm. Sloan ambled over, and Claire put her other arm around her.

"So back to Bah-ston, huh?" she said with the familiar Boston accent, a knack for dialects like her brother.

Sloan nodded. "This has been great, though. I'm so glad everyone could make it."

Will and Arthur pulled up chairs, plates of scones and lemon curd in their hands. Arthur said, "Chuffed you had so many Brit foods. Very nice nod to the English side of the clan."

Diana joined us in the final half hour, dressed to travel like her generation did. Hair glossy and straight, tidy cream slacks, walking shoes. She kissed Sloan nearly warmly and reached for my arm. Pulling me toward their waiting car, she tucked her arm in my elbow. "This was most lovely. And you seem a genuine and wonderful woman." Arthur opened her car door. Kissing me on each cheek, smelling of powder, she seated herself, and said, "Best to you, Mrs. Lynch." She closed the door.

Mrs. Lynch. There was another one now. Arthur clapped Rick on the back and squeezed us both, and we all said our goodbyes.

"Keep it up, fella. You two—keep living the American dream. Yee-haw." We laughed. Waving as they pulled off, Rick kissed me lingeringly—when he knew they were watching. Giggling, I pulled away and waved. The brake lights were nearly gone.

Rick turned, sharply. "On with it then. And let's not believe a thing Champagne Claire had to say, now shall we. She was a bit well sauced, bless her heart." He laughed fondly.

The long weekend concluded way too quickly, just when we'd started to bond. Heartfelt farewells all around, we scattered. The Lynches headed back across the pond, my brother back to Hawaii, and Sloan back to Massachusetts. Rick was taking me away for several days, but all I was told was to pack for New England weather. A casual getaway. Accustomed to Rick-size gestures, I must say I was surprised by the choice. I'd assumed there might be a glittery trip to an exotic locale. Still, though, when Sloan hugged me goodbye, she'd said, "You're going to have an *incredible* honeymoon. I want a guy just like Rick." She seemed to know something I didn't.

What exactly was in store for me now? Once we'd landed in Nova Scotia, I was puzzled. We drove and drove, and an hour passed. Turning onto a dirt road, we were in a tunnel of darkness, our headlights shining on nothing. Rick pulled over in front of a rustic, adorable lighthouse.

"Oh my God, is this one you can stay at? Sweetie, is this where we're staying?" Such a touching thought, it made me love my husband even more. Rick shouldered our two bags. Approaching the door, there it was: a beautiful copper plaque.

REILLY'S LIGHT, it read.

"How did you find this place?" I was awed by the incredible coincidence.

Immensely pleased, Rick pushed hard: the heavy metal door creaked open. He flipped each interior lantern on individually, illuminating the living quarters. The weathered welcome table held a document that he perused. Mesmerized, I took in the panoramic view overlooking the quaint seaside town. Reaching his arms around me, Rick held out the paper. It was a legal document, a deed; it declared Reilly Lynch the owner of this Nova Scotia lighthouse.

"For you." He held my face, kissed me. For a moment, I failed to comprehend. Wordlessly, I looked at the deed again. My name imprinted on it.

"It's ... mine? This is mine? You bought me a lighthouse?"

Do real people do things like this?

"Reilly's Light. And she's all yours. You always light up when you talk about your lighthouse in Rhode Island. Your safe place, your sanctuary, the place you went to put life into perspective. The place where my girl-geek 'watched weather,'" he teased me.

"Now, I couldn't afford one stateside, but I hope this makes you happy. If I can put that smile on your face every day ..."

Flinging my arms around him, I squealed with pleasure. And all I got him was a TAG Heuer watch! *Epic fail.* Who could have imagined: a honeymoon in a lighthouse? *My* lighthouse. He never ceased to amaze me.

The days and nights we spent there flew by. A haze of lovemaking, here, there, and everywhere, and the most magical sunrises and sunsets I'd ever seen. Cool mornings gave way to hot afternoons. You could see the energy in the atmosphere ramp up. Dramatic thunder and lightning-fueled storms raged some evenings. We viewed them through a vintage telescope.

Each night when the beacon illuminated, it stirred something deep inside me. Would I rather have been clubbing in glittery Ibiza or on an upscale safari in Africa? *No no.* I was exactly where I belonged. At Reilly's Light. So hard to say goodbye, but real life beckoned. Sloanless and jobless. But with a challenging new undertaking and a new husband.

What exactly was in store for me now?

CHAPTER 14

JUMP CUT

There were massive changes in the months after we married. After selling my town house, we moved into our dream home on a cul-de-sac in Potomac, beautiful horse country, just a few miles north of Billie in quirky Glen Echo. An environmental-green, center-hall colonial with random-width mahogany floors that Brian painstakingly refinished (with Billie as his day laborer when she could), extensive moldings, arched windows.

I oversaw minor renovations, and Rick took the financial reins; I was fine relinquishing them. I'd dealt with it on my own and barely kept my head above water, not because there was no money coming in, but I was very right-brain creative, and left-brain finances were alien to me.

"You're not much for investing, are you?" Rick noted when he looked over my accounts. "You realize you've over a million dollars between your divorce and your folks just sitting in savings? Doing nothing." I'd never considered the options. Fortunately, he'd hooked up with a super financial whiz that everyone wanted to be with, and he moved all my money to him.

Rick jumped in. He enthusiastically helped make the vlog a reality, each night hoisting himself up on the kitchen counter, his long legs hanging. Forever sticking Post-it notes to the counter that addressed every point necessary to make it work.

I designed a commercial kitchen a chef would envy and created a home I loved deeply; it was an ideal backdrop for *Life of Reilly*, the spot where I'd welcome subscribers into my world and we'd share—about life and love, work and play. Rick was a force of nature: organizing a production crew to set my lights and camera and create my YouTube channel with all the necessary vlog elements in place. Being a one-man operation, I had to be up to speed on how it all worked. Varun, Rick's tech guy, stuck with me until I was comfortable in my ability to handle it all myself. Truly indispensable. With the project nearly at debut now, I phoned Gus one afternoon, well past due in thanking him for the gracious use of the name. More taciturn than ever, Gus finally said, "Okay. I'm just going to … this is one hundred percent none of my business, Reilly, but tell me, are you doing this for *Lynch*? Because I have some real …"

I bristled.

"Gus, I'm doing this because it's a once-in-a-lifetime opportunity for me."

Was he really calling my husband, his boss, by his last name? And is there a hint of attitude there?

"Look. I'm talking to you like I'd talk to my kid. You know, Rick's job is doing due diligence on companies they're looking to buy—and probably dismantle," he snorted. "But have you done your due diligence on him? I just hope you know what you're—"

"Gus," I said stiffly. "If there's something specific you're trying to tell me, can you please be direct."

He mumbled. "Nothing specific. I just see a different side of him. He's tough. Maybe he has to be, what do I know? Look. You got a home here if you ever wanna come back," he said, ending the call.

Strange how Gus's attitude toward Rick had changed. The early days of fawning over him seemed to be well behind us now. Maybe Gus hadn't been happy about losing me—he'd never reached out to me. Nor had he thrown me any going-away party, standard when a personality departed. I'd just been swooped away from the station, never to be seen again.

That evening, I relayed the peculiar exchange to Rick (minus Gus referring to Rick as "Lynch"). His eyes narrowed. "He said I'm 'tough'? Maybe so. Because I have a real goddamned job. A lot of people depend on me. Christ, I have less respect for that wanker all the time. A man who trots other women around when he's got a lovely wife at home."

I raised my eyebrows, never having been privy to executive gossip. Gus? Frumpled, hapless Gus? He could hardly handle a one-on-one conversation with any of the women at the station without breaking into hives. The thought of other women was mind-boggling.

"Oh, Gus may not seem a womanizer. *That's* how he gets away with it." He thrust his chin out. "Not to worry, angel. We got what we wanted for you, and that's all that matters to me."

And so my baby vlog was born. When the time was right, Rick assured me, when I was confident in the execution and the content choice, we'd present early segments to his connections for sponsorship. Butterflies of anticipation were ever present. It was go-time.

The next evening, I did a trial run of an episode I hadn't planned to broadcast to get the kinks out. I logged onto my YouTube channel, and it was daunting to see the subscribership number at nine. The single-digit nine, only those of us that collaborated to get it together were aware of its existence. But I was undeterred, it was early. I dropped the lights using the remote. I smiled into the camera and automatically spoke to my best friend (the one we're taught to see when looking in the camera); that technique is the same whether at the news station or on a vlog.

I offered a fun twist on Super Bowl food. "With one super-simple meal, you'll satisfy everyone from finnicky kids to carnivores to food-sensitive friends. Create a grilled-cheese bar on your kitchen island or table. It's tasty *and* a fun activity, because it's a make-your-own. Put out anything. This one's a brisket and Jarlsberg. Here I made cheddar and apple-cranberry chutney—brush on the butter like this and grill your own signature creation." I pulled a perfectly crisped peanut-butter-and-bacon confection from one of the panini makers. "Voilà."

Then Rick's key in the front door. "I'm home! Something smells heavenly!"

I laughed. "Unplanned"—I smiled—"but I guess you get to meet the husband. C'mere, you ..." I urged him into the shot.

He was initially bashful, but then he gave a little wave to the camera. "Evening, Lifers," he said, my pet term for subscribers. "Mmm, this looks delish, don't mind if I do!" He leaned in to take a bite from the sandwich I held. "So this one right here is something, isn't she?"

"He might be just a little biased," I responded, tickling him lightly. Bending to kiss me sweetly on the cheek, he slyly tiptoed his hand to the platter. Snatched a grilled cheese to go. "Hey, you, I saw that!"

"Just one advantage of living with you. All right then, off to freshen up." His eyes twinkled; he loosened his tie. No question about it. I was going to have to broadcast this one after all.

Powering down the lights and moving aside the camera, I called up, "I'm meeting the girls at Brindle's. Obviously there's food here if you're hungry before I get back!"

He materialized, wearing only a crisp white towel around his hips after a quick shower, his dark hair still damp. He was disappointed. "Well, all right. I'd wanted to speak with you. Had lunch today with an old colleague whose company just acquired the Gillsen Group, and it seems ..." He stopped after dangling that tidbit.

"The Gillsen Group! It seems what?" I squealed.

"No, no, you're late. Go meet the girls. I'll tell you ..."

Squeezing his hands hard, I said, "Tell me! You're so bad. Just tell me already!"

Pretending to search his mind for the details, he finally said with an oh-so-casual shrug, "Between you, me, and the gatepost, as a lifestyle company, they embrace influencers. And they think you have rather a lot going for you. That you're getting into the vlogosphere at the right time. And Gillsen is on board to sponsor my wife."

"Oh my God, oh my God, oh my God," I cried. "I can't even. Gillsen. That's *big*."

"Naturally. Go big or go home. And you, my love, are going big."

"It's really happening," I said, throwing my arms around his naked torso, kissing him, again and again. "Thank you so much. I can't believe it!"

I couldn't stop smiling. He nudged the towel lower. "Sure I can't entice you to stay?"

"Stop!" I shrieked. "You'll make me later! I won't be long. Gillsen. You're amazing."

"I *am* amazing, you know that," he said with a wicked raise of the eyebrow.

Trailing me through the foyer, he playfully flashed me.

"Hold the thought!" I called back.

———

Brindle's was packed. The bar area was standing room only. Weaving through the crowd, I spied the girls. They'd secured a table down in the restaurant. Small bars dotted each corner, and standing lamps provided the light. It was a neighborhood place where the longtime owners table-hopped. There was a communal pitcher of fruit-flecked sangria already on the table.

After a couple of rounds of drinks, the stories got more personal. Barbara was going on, again, about how nonexistent her sex life was. How she couldn't manage to rev it up. A pint-size, perky woman, she'd kept her figure. It was enviable. And yet she hid it under mommy clothes. On my third merlot, I made a suggestion to inject a little fun, get *cheeky* with it.

"You've got the perfect opportunity. Eddie travels so much. Send him a video!"

"A video? Of what?"

Billie and I giggled at her confusion.

"Of *you*, Barbara!" Billie wiggled her shoulders. "A DIY. In lingerie, at most."

Delicately, I said, "It just says 'I miss you, I want you.'"

Barbara looked dubious.

"Okay, so last week when Rick was in California," I said in a near whisper, "I pretended it was a scene in a ... well, Barbara, I'll just say it's fun once you get into it. And even more fun when *they* see it." Flushing, I realized the sangria was speaking and tried to deflect. Unable to stop them, images of the tape I'd made rolled through my mind. Had I really done that? *Me?*

Emboldened by champagne, my inhibitions had faded. The body mousse I'd put on had a beautiful sheen and allowed my hands to slide easily. Kneeling on the bed, I turned to the side and looked back at the camera. Nice angle. In the monitor, the booty looked tight, the full breasts worth every penny. I coyly placed a hand over the one closest to the camera, not covering much. What fun would that have been? The other drifted down my toned, tanned midriff, slid down my thighs, wandered between my legs and lingered. I let myself enjoy it. "I can't stop thinking about you, and your ..." I'd said hoarsely. And what he'd sent back—a *Rick pic*.

"Reilly!" Billie screeched as though it was the tenth time she'd tried to get my attention. "So? You pretended it was ... a porno?"

The memories made my face flame self-consciously. "Jesus, Billie," I protested. "Very ... soft core. But yes, what you said!"

We all giggled, and I checked the time. "Oh, Robert," I called for our waiter with the universal hand gesture for "Check, please." Billie smirked.

"Freakin' party pooper. Maybe your keeper will give you a later curfew someday." The ladies laughed at her snarkiness. Robert returned with empty hands.

"Ma'am, your check has been taken care of. A dark-haired British gentleman came in and picked up the tab for the table. Lovely fella."

Annie swooned. "Oh my God. You guys are one of *those* couples. Sit on the same side of the booth, have pet nicknames. Bet you baby-talk each other."

Billie's face was pinched. "Prince Charming drove all the way over here? Why?"

"Oh, stop. So she'll keep sending him those videos, that's why," Barbara pointed out.

"Why not come in, say hi. Things that make you go hmm." Acerbic. Even for Billie.

Present Day

CHAPTER 15

TRENDING

The next few years flew. We were swept along by the fast-racing current of our lives. Rick and I worked hard and played hard. The vlog had been a huge undertaking, with shows twice a week and the preparation they entailed. My days were filled, exciting, albeit somewhat insular.

Missing my TV colleagues, I joined them a few times. Lives were evolving. Sunny, now married to a news anchor at a competing station, was expecting twins. Bridget, my driven young assistant, had gone with a prime opportunity to produce a fledgling show at PBS.

Most of my compatriots had been demoted or let go. There was an odd friction around it. The consensus was that Rick was behind the layoffs and that he'd had Gus do the dirty work. His directive: hire new, cheap talent. The bottom line was his only concern after assertions that "nothing would change." He'd told me, though. It wasn't him; it was Butler's assessment of the station's financials.

"Unfortunately," he said with a half shrug, "everyone is expendable."

I met Sunny and Bridget at a new bar by the studio, Circa. We rehashed some of the good times, avoiding the elephant at the table of the layoffs. Sipping her cosmo, Bridget whispered, "I swear, Reilly, you squeaked out in the nick of time."

Sunny's nose crinkled. "Bridg, it wasn't exactly dumb luck. It's not like Rick wanted *this one* around to see him backtrack on all his big promises."

Was that true? Had he wanted to protect me from being part of that? He certainly hadn't shared much. I'd had to hear it from the girls.

Rick's job was more demanding. Of those who have proved themselves, much was expected. Work days extended. Business travel mounted up. But he was held in high esteem. He had been widely considered to be the next Franklin when Franklin took a step back.

Franklin included us in the owners' annual getaway. Butler was thriving. Machu Picchu. Tuscan tours. The *Orient Express*. Trip-of-a-lifetime trips.

Franklin had been widowed last year. No kids, and now Dory was gone. After forty-four years: without Dory, her infectious laugh, he was rudderless. He lived for the firm now, adding to Rick's gnawing concern that he might not step down in time for Rick to attain that job.

Rick kidded, without much humor, that Franklin might be Queen Elizabeth to his Prince Charles. Maybe he'd never be executive chairman. He could remain the workhorse, dealing with all the draining day-to-day in a private equity firm. In Rick's favor, though, he'd settled down. With me. Franklin approved. He teased that I "spoke Franklin" even better than he did.

When Sloan graduated and was accepted right into her master's program (an MS in sports business), Franklin called me, wanting to do something special for her. I assured him that was unnecessary but thoughtful nonetheless. Days later, Rick came in beaming.

"You won't believe it. Look what I pulled off," he said, dropping tickets in front of me. For the Alaskan getaway in July. Not the expected two, but three, sets of tickets. Franklin had booked Sloan her own cabin in celebration of her big milestone. How touching.

"I'd *told* him that was entirely unnecessary, but it'll be awfully exciting for her."

His eyebrows furrowed. "Franklin called you? You never mentioned that."

"It's just been so busy and, really, I thought I'd dissuaded him. I guess not."

The memories of that trip were etched in my mind; the flight-seeing exploration of the remote Denali preserve, a jetboat excursion to magical Sitka (where Sloan's favorite movie, *The Proposal*, was shot). We had many photos of that trip scattered around; one of the few things that made it real that four years had passed. Now Sloan was in Philadelphia in graduate school. Closer, but never close enough for a mother. Life was hurtling by at lightning speed.

Life of Reilly was established. We'd seen steady growth. Subscribership hovered near the respectable five hundred thousand mark, thanks to network viewers migrating over and Gillsen's sponsorship. Naturally, Rick teased me that I owed it all to him. He loved that line. "No Rick, no Gillsen," he'd say. No doubt.

I made it a priority to find time together whenever we could carve it out. Not just your standing date night. Play time. Every so often, I'd pop by his office. The man was critically overworked. He left home at six and rarely returned before seven. His favorite banana–cashew butter smoothie in hand, I waved at his assistant and headed for his office with the cup.

"I'm so sorry. He's not here actually. I haven't seen him all afternoon," Emma said.

"Really? All right. I thought he was snowed under with budgets …"

She was frazzled. "I know, I need to get documents submitted, but he's been MIA for hours. It's that kind of day around here." She rubbed her temples. The little framed quote sat off to one side, there since I'd known her. *That which is behind you can no longer hurt you.* Emma didn't discuss her past, but she'd rebounded. She was positive and loyal to Rick, so I was pro Emma.

"Gotta keep that blood sugar up!" Handing her the smoothie, I said, "You're the one who needs the boost right now!"

She tugged at the straw wrapper gratefully. "Oh, thank you! If you insist."

"You know, Emma, Rick is lucky to have you. He's told me he'd be lost without you."

"You're nice to say so. I feel pretty lucky myself." She slid over to answer the phone.

Rick rounded the corner at that moment. "Look who's here. Nice surprise. I just have a few minutes. Today's been chockablock, but come in to the office!" Today, his desk had multiple lined Post-its, precisely placed side by side, a sure sign he was swamped.

The lobster items he'd collected over the years dotted his otherwise barren shelves. They were our little secret. Rick frowned on family photos in offices. They implied you were simply passing time there. The job wasn't your priority. When Franklin was in, he wanted him to see Rick wasn't distracted by anything non-Butler. But the lobsters were his reminder of me. Sweet.

Maybe this would be one of the days he closed the office door, and we'd be naughty. He loved a little respite from the grind in the form of some office "nookie," as he called it. Over the years, we'd close the door and he'd pull me into his lap. Gradually, he'd gone further, on occasion closing the door, showing me who was boss in that office. The memories were vivid. He was about to shut the door when Emma called out. *No!*

"Have you seen Alex? Or Caroline? She hasn't been around since morning either."

Absently, he ran two fingers across his brow. "Caroline was gone too? No clue there. Alan. Check the rooftop." A semi-joke.

Alan was one of the last of the dying breed of smokers. He'd be spotted on the roof several times a day.

"I didn't come empty handed, you know, sweetie." Explaining I'd brought him a smoothie, I told him I'd bestowed it on Emma when it seemed he was gone for the day.

"No worries. I'm in deathly need of caffeine at the moment." Once again, he moved to close the door. Another voice rang out. *Nooo!*

"Hey, hey, look here!" A tanned arm slid into the office and playfully wiggled a Starbucks cup. The woman holding it slid right in behind it. "Your fave." Caroline, the human resources lady, flounced in wearing dark jeans, sky-high heels and a fitted sweater. When had casual Friday become an everyday thing? Rick moved to his desk and skimmed an email. He tapped one back. Opportunity lost.

Without looking up, he said to Caroline, "I heard you'd been out of the office."

Her self-assurance dimmed. She balanced the coffee and a file. "Yeah, well, I'm back now. And … you're back, too, it seems." Her eyes drifted to me. "Hey. Long time no see."

I told Caroline being married suited her. She'd always been mousy, but she looked less matronly now. The sensible shoes were gone, replaced by towering heels to maximize all five foot three inches of her. The makeup was more subtle. Her hair was blown straight and highlighted blonde. She'd lost weight, as most brides did.

"Pretty!" I said, pointing at her new bling, an eternity band. Moving to Rick's desk, she pulled a coaster from his drawer, put the coffee on it. Tapped the cup with a long, tangerine nail.

"Triple shot. Took a wild guess you'd need a pick-me-up." She took the file clutched to her chest and dropped it in front of him victoriously. "You are gonna like this …"

Without a smoothie, and with Rick engaged in work, it was a good time to head out. I held my three middle fingers up as I left. Caroline dropped into my chair. She rolled it closer.

I waved a quick goodbye to Emma. Summoning me to her desk outside Rick's office, she said, "You remember Marchand's next Thursday, right? Not that I've got the details down." She ran her hand through her newly cropped, spiky hair with good humor. I laughed in solidarity.

"Oh, Emma. You're a rock star. I'm sure it's going to be great."

"Well, one important detail is in place! On a *Life of Reilly*, you'd created signature cocktails for callers, using their names and making a custom beverage. So this event is featuring the, wait for it, 'Butler Bellini'—champagne and pomegranate, Mr. Butler's favorite."

"Nice! Everyone likes a Bellini." I smiled, recalling the segment. I'd heard little about the event, just that Butler was celebrating a big year at the charming Marchand's.

Emma walked me to the elevator. "You heard Mr. Butler is coming? He's presenting an award to Rick. For 'stellar contributions.' He doesn't get to DC much anymore, so it's a big deal." She tapped the door as it closed. "See you Thursday."

Not long behind me, Rick returned and immediately jumped in the shower to revive before dinner. I settled in for the shower show and enjoyed the suds glistening on his broad shoulders and toned abs. It amused me that he soaped up every inch of himself, having just taken a total shower that morning. I handed him a large Turkish bath sheet when he stepped out.

"Seemed like a busy day today. Caroline's looking good, isn't she?"

He hadn't noticed the change. "Is she? I find her annoying. The HR figures were due two days ago. That Emma, though, a keeper. She's my eyes and ears, doesn't miss a thing."

"So. What else happened today? Any movement on either of the mergers?"

I loved hearing about his time at the office; he regaled me with each day's stories. Tonight, though, he was blank. He came up empty; for such a busy day, nothing had gone on.

"Just meetings. I don't know. I don't recall."

"Well, I guess the excessive meetings are all worth it—hence the celebration thingy." Figured that might lighten things. The event at Marchand's had to make him feel indispensable.

"I suppose. I'd just like the company to make that next move, and I don't think they will with ol' Frank at the helm. He needs to step down already."

I nodded. I'd heard that before. "Tricky stuff. Marchand's is Thursday, right? Have they given us details yet?"

Puzzled, Rick leaned his hip against the sink and looked at me in the mirror. He brushed his teeth, wiped the hand towel across his mouth. "It's not a couples thing. It's a business thing."

"I don't ..." I said uncertainly. "Emma told me all about it when I was at your office. It seemed like they expected me to be there."

"I don't know what she's thinking. It's not like that. I find these things awkward, really. You can't single out one person. It's all about the team."

"And if I know you, that's exactly what you'll say." His smile had an extra twinkle.

"Ah, you know me well. I'd be chuffed to have you with me Thursday. Everything's always better together. It's just that if the others don't have their partners, I don't feel it's appropriate that I should. It puts me at a different level. Sends the wrong message."

I'd looked forward to seeing him honored, disappointed I'd only get to hear about it. It seemed so strange to me that, even if other spouses weren't included, I wouldn't be welcome with my husband being honored. I couldn't conjure any reason why he wouldn't want me there, but it made me uneasy how unequivocally he'd stated that I wouldn't be accompanying him.

So I checked with Emma. Turned out the poor man was so busy he wasn't even up to speed. Emma said it was definitely a couples event. Electing to surprise him, I got the details from Emma. When the night came, I was pleased with the taupe cashmere dress I'd paired with dark Ferragamo boots and a cross-body bag. A look he'd always said showed off the "assets."

I still had butterflies. Special events were magical when you shared them; he was right. That first gala. So proud of me that he must have introduced me to everyone in attendance. So tuned in that he knew how to put me at ease with just "I got you." The memories of it lingered.

The man would be ecstatic when he spied me. Surprise.

CHAPTER 16

BREAKING

As I crossed the glass atrium, people weaved this way and that, holding pretty cocktails, wearing pretty clothes. Leaving my camel coat with the checker, I saw him, lounging against the mahogany bar. Manhattan in hand. Deep in conversation with Caroline and a new, young hire. Eyes playing across the room, he spotted me. I beamed. His head tilted to one side. Evidently, he was happy I showed, and he freed himself instantly. Pretending to be stern, he chastised me, "And here I thought I'd been so clear when I said *no*, love."

Adjusting his tie, I was saucy. "A wise man once told me there are no *no*s." I put my arms around his neck, grazed his cheek with my lips. A smile curled at the corner of his mouth.

"You are incorrigible. I'm afraid there are people I've yet to greet. Make yourself comfortable, and I'll bring you a Butler Bellini shortly. Franklin will be pleased you made it."

Up front, a tinkle of silver on crystal signaled a toast. Mr. Butler made brief but glowing remarks about Rick's achievements. Humbly accepting the praise, he bowed his head slightly.

"Richard," he started, using the formal version. He always did that. "You've accomplished great things, changing the landscape in Washington, DC, a major market for us. I'm proud to have you represent us—a gentleman and a scholar, as they say—but also as a valuable asset, and friend," he added, a choke in his voice. Not a man to show emotion—many weren't sure it was there at all—he held Rick in high esteem. I tried to catch his eye. I wanted to share the moment, but he had eyes only for Franklin. And the formidable brass plaque changing hands.

With a few people between us, Caroline was bursting with pride. She clapped her hands together vigorously when Franklin handed Rick the hefty plaque. And whistled when he warmly shook Rick's hand. Caroline seemed unaware that everyone else simply smiled their approval.

"Proud of my work spouse!" she called out, her hands around her mouth to be heard.

Something in the proprietary tone of that struck me. I leaned around Emma, who rolled her eyes at me subtly. I waved at Caroline. She'd had no idea I was there.

"Oh, hi! I mean, *work spouse* is just a phrase."

Right, I know the phrase. Maybe not one you use when the real *spouse is there.* Rough around the edges, Rick called her, but I was sure she meant well. Rick had a knack for surrounding himself with devoted women.

"Where's Dan? Is he here?" I asked, scanning for her husband.

"Didn't know partners were included. My bad. He's way happier watching the Nats play anyway, so win-win." She shrugged, smoothing her tight black slacks over her thighs, the red ruffled blouse dropping off her shoulder. She slid off toward the bar. "Want something?"

"No, thanks. Just waiting on the man of the hour." I laughed.

I turned my attention back as speeches wrapped. People began to disperse. Standing alone, waiting on Rick, I felt vaguely ill at ease. These functions were a little stiff. I'd said hello to most of the people I knew by name and now just stood to the side, nibbling on a bruschetta.

"Reilly!" One of Rick's managers strolled over to say hi. Dean was his number two guy. I secretly enjoyed his snarky attitude. Authentic in a sea of sycophants. He was more fired up than usual, positively edgy, rocking from one foot to the other, rubbing his newly buzz-cut hair.

"Gotta hand it to your guy. He makes shit happen, and I guess that's what counts. That and Butler thinking you're God," he said, sucking on an ice cube.

Proudly, I agreed.

"It's something. He's man of the hour," Dean went on, crunching and swallowing the ice. "I mean, if anybody really ..."

Rick materialized next to him, draping the arm holding the plaque around him. Dean shut down, intimidated in Rick's presence.

"Dean-o. Jack's looking for you at the bar." Rick whisked me away to greet Mr. Butler. He whispered, "Dean-o is overserved. Will wonders never cease."

I wished Dean had finished his thought, though. There was definitely something on the poor guy's mind. Maybe just that it was hard to be number two. Nobody's dream was to be number two.

"Reilly, my dear, I've looked everywhere for you. I was afraid you wouldn't make it," a booming voice called. Mr. Butler hustled over to me with an effusive hug and a pinch to my cheek. More rotund than robust now—he had no one keeping an eye on his diet with Dory gone.

"Mr. Butler! Miss this? Never. Congratulations on a banner year."

He shook my arm. "*Franklin*. Let's not forget. Richard had said you're a tad averse to crowds," he all but whispered, "and I understand that one. Dory was too. So. Looks like Bora Bora this year for the trip. I'm a little past some of the big-adventure things, getting to a different stage now. I wanted to pass it by you. You'll tell me the truth. Will folks enjoy it, even though it's not high octane?" He turned his stocky frame to me and rested a chunky hand on my shoulder.

"People can find all the adventure they like in Bora Bora, if that's their thing, but most of us would probably just love being in one of the most gorgeous spots on earth."

His eyes flickered with reassurance. "Now, miss. Your video blog. Quite the undertaking. I always meant to tell you Dory was wild about it. She got me watching. Throwback Thursday is a hoot—retro music and food. Fantastic!"

Franklin watched *Life*. The thought tickled me. "Can't beat a green goddess salad dressing and a Frank Sinatra sing-along. That would have been my parents' version of the perfect *Life of Reilly* segment."

He chuckled. "Your parents sound like my kind of people. Proud of you. The two of you." He eyed us approvingly. Rick beamed and tucked my hand in his arm. He was always heartened when Franklin expressed pride in either of us. He felt very inner circle and revered.

"Well, well, well. Kind of a power couple the two of you, now aren't you?"

"I'm not sure I'd go that far, but thanks." I laughed. He squeezed my arm affectionately.

"Flight to catch, I'm afraid. Nice to see you. Give your lovely daughter my best." Rick accompanied Mr. Butler to his taxi, opening his door, making sure his bag was stowed properly.

The crowd thinned. Odd I wasn't being escorted person to person tonight. Did he not want me by his side? Watching from the bar, Rick worked the room expediently. Solo. Faster that way, I guessed, took twice as long making rounds as a couple. I did miss being on his arm, though. He always said I was a good foil for him. That we complemented each other so well.

Caroline and Dean headed out together. Rick watched them, his expression almost amused as Caroline flashed a smile in our general direction. With most people gone, Rick finally relaxed. Sliding around the side of a big pillar, he crooked his finger playfully to me. He pulled me around where no one could see us and put his hands to my face. Kissed me. Then he backed away.

"And before you blast me. I only told you 'no spouses' for *your* sake. I know these events cause you anxiety, and I've always said I won't leave you on your own. This was an exception. Butler was here so briefly." Leaning in, he whispered, "I was with the prettiest girl here."

Running his finger down my collarbone, he moaned. He dropped his hands to grasp my ass firmly. He pulled me out into the night. He was in another world entirely, like the accolades were a drug.

In spite of strong assertions that praise embarrassed him, he was over the moon. He sang along with the wrong lyrics to oldies all the way home. Drummed loudly on the steering wheel.

It stayed with me. Dean's dark edge. "Did you notice something's off with Dean? He was wound up, or ticked off, or … I don't …"

"I know. Trust me. He played it all wrong, gunning for my job, spreading lies about me to Franklin."

Not surprised Dean aspired to the next job, but his methods were foolish. How disloyal. Rick had championed for Dean all along, only to have him bite the hand that fed him.

Rick was pensive. "As of tomorrow, he's not a problem. A nonfactor."

A *nonfactor*? "He wasn't a team player. How can you ever be sure after someone betrays you … ?"

"You *can't*. And he was drunk again. Butler folks know people. I'm just willing to bet he was picked up on a DUI. Bye-bye, Dean."

Something about his self-satisfied expression … I knew. I knew him.

Dean had tried to undermine my husband. Rick didn't deserve that—and he'd never tolerate it. I nodded slowly, exhaling at the realization, but I had a feeling, a gut feeling: "It wasn't 'Butler folks'; it was *you*. You set him up to get a DUI, didn't you?"

His "cat who'd just eaten the canary" expression said it all. He shrugged. "It had to be done. I'm not proud of it. No one made him have that fourth Jack and diet."

"So you had someone lying in wait after the event, knowing he'd have been drinking at it? How does one manage that?"

"Just as you said. If you know law enforcement, you ask a favor and you offer them a good reason to do it." He rubbed his thumb against his other fingers, the sign for cash. "Come, let's forget about that. Tonight, it's all about the event. And my hot wife." He grabbed me and swept me inside. Within moments, we'd left a trail of clothing through the first-floor rooms to the sauna. Rick's pants clung to the low-slung recliner in the corner, my sweater haphazardly across the area rug. A shoe here, a shoe there, kicked off in the heat of the moment.

Once inside, the heat only intensified. Rick was assertive, possessive. Pushed me up against the walnut-planked sauna wall. "Naughty girl. I was sure I'd told you not to be at tonight's event." He turned me around, tapped my ass with a firm spank. I was sassy in return.

"You don't tell me what to do. You're not the boss of me. You may have the corner office at work, but I'm the CEO at home, and don't you forget it."

"Oh, *really?*" he retorted. "You don't listen, love. Naughty, naughty, naughty."

With every next adjective, the spanks became hard, not just firm. Hard. Eventually, he sank down to his knees in the shower. Took my cheek in his mouth and clamped on, sucking vigorously. I squealed in pain. Pulled back with my hand defensively over my ass. His eyes cleared. He held me up against the steamy tile wall and continued, a little less aggressively now.

Maybe I hadn't felt exactly how harsh it all was due to the heat of the sauna. Once the sexcapades were over and we were in bed, my backside stung. Badly. Every time I tried to sleep, I'd turn over and the painful sensation would sear my behind again.

Creeping quietly down to the freezer, I unearthed ice packs to tuck under my derriere. Sometimes he slid from ravishing me in one moment to devouring me the next. As though he wanted to consume me. As though he was literally lost in the moment. On occasion, I wished it were less frenzied, but still, it was flattering, his deep desire.

———

When the shower started at six, I threw on a silky black robe to join Rick for the shower show. With sleepy, lidded eyes, he motioned at the love seat. My usual viewing spot.

This time, half teasing and half making a point, I backed up to the glass door. I slyly dropped the robe to my waist. First exposing only my naked shoulders and back.

Softly, he said, "Oooh, look who's coming back for more."

Letting the robe fall to the floor, I stood nude, leaving the developing bruises in full view.

"What do you think? Time for a safe word?" I smiled wryly over my shoulder.

I'd assumed he'd either laugh or apologize. I hadn't anticipated a snort. Rinsing off, only the pulsating water breaking the silence, he reached an arm out for me to hand him a bath towel.

"Safe word. Brilliant. Maybe 'I used to be fun.' Or 'wet blanket.' Too wordy?"

Whoa, what the … "Jesus, what? I didn't say …"

"No worries. I'll wear kid gloves, my delicate flower," he said, holding his three fingers up.

In shock, I tossed him a towel and pulled my robe back on. Tied it snugly. *OMG, I have black and blues. We're pretty far from kid gloves.*

Stunned by his reaction, I melted away to get coffee. *Damn, I didn't handle that well.* There he was, enjoying the afterglow in the shower, and I'd dropped my robe. He had every right to think I wanted to be ravaged again, we were perpetually at it, and what did I do? I called him out for sexual roughhousing. Something he's not even aware of when he's in hypererotic mode.

As I steamed the milk, it swirled and hissed. It weighed on me that he'd felt slapped down. It had begun to feel like walking on eggshells sometimes with him. The front door clicked shut.

Running through the foyer, I scooped up the remnants of last night's romp. His pants. My sweater. My midnight-blue lace bra hanging over the creamy floral lampshade.

Reaching the front door just as his car slid by, I raised my hand, waving as I always did. He never looked back.

CHAPTER 17

ANONYMOUS SOURCE

It had been years since I'd seen Miriam, my longtime psychiatrist. Maybe a tune-up was in order. I'd been a regular while I'd navigated my parents' deaths and the divorce in the same time frame—it had been Miriam who'd guided me back from that abyss.

In the sterile waiting area fifteen minutes early, I FaceTimed with Rick, who was attending a conference in Las Vegas. He thought it wise I was seeing Miriam. Said I'd seemed tense and reactionary lately. *I'm tense? Me?* That stung, but I held my tongue since it was a lose-lose; responding would be perceived as reactionary.

Frowning when I asked about Dean, he said evenly, "He's gone. I need a new number two. Someone who won't trash me to Franklin. Don't feel bad—I arranged a great exit package."

Miriam peeked in. I wrapped up our call. "All right. Miriam's here. Maybe we'll catch up later."

Her round face lit up, and she squeezed me around the middle, all she could reach at her limited height. "I was so pleased to hear from you again." Miriam was still all wiry gray hair and brown Birkenstocks. She'd never lost that ageless bohemian quality.

Not much had changed in her office over the years. The worn olive green couch, my favorite, remained. The requisite boxes of tissue on each table, the bowls of individually wrapped Life Savers. The soft, ivory bamboo rug was the same type my parents had in their den.

She was a nurturer. She always put me at ease straightaway. As I updated her on my recent life, she jotted notes before addressing the reason for the appointment. I'd left her a message telling her about the sensation of walking on eggshells.

"Rick gets so much admiration from everyone. And I adore him. I'm blessed to have him. It can be challenging, though, that I always have to see him as perfect. And be perfect myself."

"That could be stressful, certainly. What do you think would happen if you didn't show appreciation at every moment."

"I ... I think ... I'd be replaced with a newer model." I laughed, not believing that tired cliché for a second. Such a sad adage, I thought idly. People weren't dispensable.

"Well. And the anxiety? How would you quantify it? Are you apprehensive some of the time, much of the time, or all the time?"

I flicked a speck of dust from the thigh of my jeans. No doubt, my anxiety was more prevalent than in recent years but not as crippling as it had been post-Alex, post–Mom and Dad. "I always have this ... feeling my life could implode."

"So you're anticipating something will upset your world, because there's precedent set: that's what's happened before," she noted as she wrote longhand. "And what are you doing to de-stress?"

"I've gone back to kickboxing. I train at least twice a week, three times if I can."

Without looking up, she nodded. "Good. You'll want to keep that up. That's helpful."

The bucket chair nearly swallowed her as she sat back. She tucked her feet underneath her and asked about my sleep, always a topic of conversation in our sessions. I pulled a face.

"Well, it's never been great. You know that. It happens when you work all these different shifts, but I find myself awake in the night, just worrying ... about Sloan ... about Rick ..."

"Rick. What about your dynamic has changed? Is it the walking on eggshells ... ?"

"He's, I don't know, more temperamental. He's a little ragey or edgy about things that wouldn't have agitated him a couple of years ago. I feel like I was always the antidote to all that, but now I don't know how to help him."

Miriam's brow furrowed. "It's difficult to help other people. It may be more beneficial to figure out how you can process it, react to it, because it sounds like you think it's about you."

"Not really, he loves me. He's very protective of me. He can just be distant sometimes."

"Distant. In what circumstance? Always a similar situation?" Her copper eyes were thoughtful, engaged. The wind chimes outside her window played lightly, and I watched them sway.

"About work, I guess." I tried to articulate what had changed. "He used to look forward to sharing the events of his day. Talking them through with me. He solicited my opinions, found them so helpful." I leaned my head back on the worn couch. "He works more than ever. And he just lost his number two guy. More pressure on him, of course. And, therefore, on me." I didn't elaborate; it was a lie of omission. To my therapist.

I didn't mention Dean's DUI, or the circumstances. I knew it would derail the session. Dean was toxic, had lobbied for Rick's job, spread lies. All good reasons he should be ejected. I just wasn't sure Miriam would see it that way. No one made him get behind the wheel, as Rick had said, and he'd wanted to discredit Rick in Franklin's eyes.

"Anyway. He's more … impatient … he doesn't have time, or tolerance. He's used to calling the shots everywhere, I guess." I rubbed the back of my neck in the quiet room. She left a pause. She did that a lot.

"That seems to be something you gravitate toward. Defined by the job, craves control and appreciation, empathy challenged, some of the issues in your marriage to Sloan's dad too."

I hadn't thought about that. I'd stopped evaluating the Alex dynamic years back, once I was ensconced in a new, functional relationship. The comparison troubled me.

"And your sex life? Are you still active?" Miriam jotted in her leather-bound book.

"Oh, the sex part is great," I said, glad I could be authentic, not like the Dean omission. "Sometimes we're ... a little adventurous, I guess. He gets rougher than he means to, but it just comes out of complete lust. It's actually kind of flattering at this point." I giggled mildly.

Miriam pondered that. "Lust is good, but boundaries are necessary too. When you compromise your boundaries, you start to lose yourself." She made a note. "Certainly, ebbs and flows in relationships are natural, but they can be difficult. For the moment, let's get you to a less-anxious state."

Scribbling prescriptions for Valium and Ambien on her little white pad, she cautioned me not to drink with them. To take them as the bottle indicated. "This week, I'd like you to take note of specifics, not 'feelings.' Write them down. Moments where you perceive a shift, because when we're overtired and anxious, we can magnify things that in a better frame of mind wouldn't ..."

My text notification pinged loudly, reverberating in her quiet office.

Oh, damn, how rude! "I'm *so* sorry, Miriam. I would've muted it but I was just catching up with Rick in your waiting room ..." Fumbling for the phone to silence it, the text notification illuminated again. The entire message fit in the one visible line, unusual for Rick or Sloan, my two most-frequent texters. I took a second to look at it. To be sure it wasn't urgent.

You deserve to know. There's someone else.

That was all. The words didn't compute; they seemed to float together. And apart. *Someone else.*

I stared at the message absently. *I don't get it.* Whatever it was, it wasn't good. There was no way to take those words and twist and turn them into anything ... I looked again.

A panicky feeling rose in my throat. I couldn't swallow around it. *You deserve to know. There's someone else.*

CHAPTER 18

DEAD AIR

You deserve to know. There's someone else.

I'd read it right the first time. The sender wasn't in my contacts. The text came from an oddly formatted number—just 657-40. Anonymous. The room felt still. I couldn't get a breath. My windpipe clenched shut. I struggled to make sense of it, what it meant, who'd sent it.

Miriam shifted in her chair, uncrossed her legs. I'd forgotten I wasn't alone. Mutely, I turned the phone to her. She blinked myopically a few times and offered a thought: "I'm just wondering. Could it be it's not meant for you?"

Exhaling in relief, I looked up at her gratefully. *Of course!* The text wasn't for me at all.

"Pardon me, I'm just going to reply and say I think they have the wrong person." I placed my thumb on the control button to access the message. The instant I tapped on the text, it … just … disappeared. It slid up at an angle. And vanished.

Damn! Did I delete it by mistake? Where is it? Anxiety welling up, I scrolled and scrolled, but it was gone. Just gone. Miriam was disconcerted; she asked how that was possible. Reaching for my knee, she grasped it reassuringly. "Let's not get anxious. Let's check something."

She googled "disappearing text messages." Suddenly chilled and shaky, I couldn't ignore the only meaning the text could have.

It pierced my consciousness. A blinding pain behind my eyes came and went. Was this it? The sixth sense I'd had that something bad was …

In disbelief, hesitant to verbalize it, eyes on the worn bamboo carpet, I said hollowly, "Miriam. Someone's trying to give me a heads-up that Rick has another woman."

Saying it aloud, hearing it, was jarring. Miriam turned her phone to me; she'd found many methods to send a text that disappears once the recipient had read it. There were apps apparently, several ways to do it. So someone had sent it intending for it to disappear after I'd seen it. To protect the identity of the sender.

Why was someone doing this to us? People were so cruel. Was it someone with an ax to grind, someone Rick had let go? He was forever the henchman when someone had to be fired.

Jumping up abruptly, I let my bag tumble to the floor. "I have to go. I have to call Rick." I grabbed my jacket. Reached for my bag.

Miriam weighed in decisively, "Reilly. I think you should see his face when you talk. It's best you wait until he's back."

That was a body blow, hearing that. I needed to gauge his authentic reaction, see his expressions, his body language. To determine if he had someone else. A wave of nausea engulfed me. I tried to squelch it. I didn't want to assess his response. We're on the same team. We're co-captains. Only Rick could allay all my concerns, and he would. Once we were face-to-face. I knew he would.

After a sleepless night that Ambien didn't touch, I paced restlessly. Waited for Rick to come home. I didn't vlog. I didn't eat. Sitting numbly at Sloan's window, I watched. Waited for his Range Rover. And I drank wine. I tried dwelling on all the positives, but the negatives pecked away at them persistently, like birds at roadkill.

The sun started to drop, the baseboard heat kicked on. Finally his car rolled up. He'd fix this. He'd know who sent the text, and he'd know why. And it would be behind us. We'd laugh about it together someday.

Cracking the window for cool outside air, I sucked it in and watched him get out of the car in his typical travel attire. Well-worn jeans and an indigo sport jacket.

"Rick, hey buddy. Where you been?" called Barbara's husband Eddie from his yard as he tended to his new evergreens.

Rick sauntered over. "Leyland cypress? Love those, so lush." He ran his hand down one of the springy branches. "How's work? Get that raise, did you?"

Eddie brightened up. "Great advice. I pulled ads of similar jobs, and the going rate was for sure lots higher—and I used your stepping-stone idea, so the raise is gradual."

Rick high-fived him. "Good news, mate. Glad to hear it." I watched from the window, high strung and on edge. I wanted this conversation behind us.

Marilyn pulled her white Volvo to a stop in front of her house. Her husband had passed last year, and her own health was flagging. She popped her trunk, and Rick was retrieving the bags brimming with groceries before she'd even freed herself from the driver's seat.

"Marilyn, I'm walking in your bags, my dear." He disappeared with her groceries. Back outside, she squeezed his hands gratefully. "Thank you for mowing my lawn the other day. I'd been meaning to get to it."

He called back, "Don't give it a thought. Happy to do it."

Finally. Biting the inside of my lip, I watched him cross to his car. Hold out his fob. The trunk lifted. He pulled out his gray leather garment bag and tossed it over his shoulder. Loped toward our porch. *He looks normal. He looks like him.*

This was it; the door opened.

"Home at last," he called. "Sweetheart?"

See, it can't be anything. It can't. "In Sloan's room." Dropping the bag at the door, he put his head in the doorway.

"Why in here? Missing your girl?"

My face crumpled immediately. Hot tears gathered at the corners of my eyes. Sitting on the arm of the love seat with me, he massaged my shoulders.

"Ah, no, what's wrong? Has something happened?"

Jesus, get it together. Don't make a bigger deal of this than it is. I looked up. Those eyes of his—warm, inquisitive. I got lost in them, trying to speak. "I ... I got a text when I was at Miriam's. It was from a number I didn't know. It said ..."

My voice was strangled. His hands were still holding my shoulders. I blurted it out. "'You deserve to know. There's someone else.' That's all it said."

I waited. For the shocked denial, the hug, something, but his expression was impassive. A little knot formed in my stomach. It was diamond hard and throbbing.

"I ... it's just so weird. I mean, I know better than to ..." I trailed off, watching him. He shook his head from side to side. He was mystified. His eyes were vacant. As though my person had been changed out with this incredibly authentic-looking, blank Rick replica.

"Please just say something. Tell me it's not true," I pleaded in a hushed voice.

A bone-deep fear started to take hold. My guts rattled. He had to respond, didn't he?

Slowly, he smoothed a piece of lint off his black trousers.

"I'm not certain I even understand what it is you're implying."

"*I'm* not implying anything. The person who sent the text is."

Without looking up, he extended his arm for my phone, his face depleted.

"It's not there," I said. "Whoever it was sent a disappearing text. When I clicked on it, it just ... *disappeared.*"

He yanked his hand back. "So I'm meant to defend myself against a text that I don't even know ever existed?"

"It existed! Miriam saw it. It *existed!*" I sounded strident in the quiet bedroom.

"Good Lord. Let's say you did get that text. You're not an insecure woman. I was under the impression we trusted each other. Implicitly. At least I do."

"I do trust you. You know I do … but if you …" God, I'm letting him down. Why am I giving 'anonymous' the benefit of the doubt.

"If I what? If I got that text? I would never jump to that conclusion about *you*. Ever. You've always told me you have a hard time trusting. I suppose we're back to that."

"That's not fair," I said softly, straining not to cry. "This isn't about me. Someone …"

His hand over mine, his thumb caressing my knuckles sweetly, he said, "Exactly. Someone anonymous. You're in the business, or were. You know what anonymous is. It's someone hiding. Trying to stir something up. Where there's nothing. Otherwise they'd just come forward as a credible source of credible information."

I was forced to agree. "And there was nothing personal in the text. It could …"

"It could have been for anybody, about anybody. Bloody hell, you could send that to anyone in town and start wobbling marriages. It's insanity. Tell me if you get more 'anonymous' texts, you'll ignore them. If I believed the nonsense people chat, I'd go stark raving mad."

He rose wearily and stood in the doorway. "Honestly, I don't know when you think I'd have time for someone else, even if I wanted to. I do nothing but work. For all this." With a gesture around our home, he left the room.

I sat shell-shocked, unsure of what had just happened. He'd dismissed this information as petty gamesmanship, something to be ignored, given no credibility. When what I'd wanted were assurances of his love, his fidelity, his lack of desire for anyone else. A personal moment. Yet it had morphed into a cautionary tale; never believe "anonymous."

In the kitchen, ice cubes dropped into a glass. The bar door slid open. Rick was making a drink. Followed by heavy steps as he climbed the stairs to our room. I didn't know how long had passed, but the house was still. Still and dark. The early evening neighborhood hubbub ceased.

He couldn't have gone to sleep, could he? Did he really think he'd put this thing to bed? It was disconcerting to be left with more questions than answers. Was it a vengeful person he'd fired, the "malcontents" who inhabited his work space, as he called them. Was it a simple mistake? Or was there truth to it? A chill spiked down my spine.

Peeking into our bedroom, I expected to see him agitated. He was sleeping. Dread settled over me at the sight of Rick in repose, even as I was coming apart at the seams. I longed to climb in next to him. I wanted nothing more than to feel his long arms around me, to cuddle into our position, my back nestled in against his torso. I couldn't.

Backing away from our bedroom, I returned to Sloan's overstuffed couch. Finished off the bottle of wine. Took one Ambien, another two hours later. Sleep didn't come. Moving to her bed, I lay my head on her favorite childhood stuffed animal, the much-loved Holly the Hippo. Miserable and more alone than I'd ever felt, I willed myself to sleep.

Could it be true? It didn't make sense. I searched my mind for unaccounted-for time, instances when he'd been late getting home, unexplained absences—nothing. Nothing but work, work, work.

No. He hardly has time for me.

He had no time for someone else.

At least I hoped with every trembling cell in my body that was true.

CHAPTER 19

AMPLIFICATION

I never left Sloan's room that night. I didn't emerge in the morning, stalling until I heard the click of the front door, Rick's car roaring to life. He never came after me. Was it possible he didn't understand I was unnerved? From the bay window bench, I watched his car glide away.

Viciously ill, I suffered from a strange emotional vertigo—up was down; down was up. I staggered to the Keurig in the kitchen. Sat on the porch wrapped in a fleece throw. The third espresso didn't even break through the stupor. Up was down; down was up.

Maybe nothing helps after a bottle and a half of wine and a couple of Ambien. I texted Miriam about last-minute availability. She squeezed me in for a three thirty.

My phone pinged with a calendar reminder, a live vlog I'd scheduled for noon. *Shit.* With the coveted Gillsen Group sponsorship and a substantial subscribership, the vlog was no longer casual. Or optional. *Oh, nooo. This'll be something.* I showered in a fog. Pulled on a fitted black sweater. Tried to conceal the purplish crescents beneath my eyes.

Rick sent the most benign text: Clients chose Morton's for lunch. No surprise as it's expensed● So I'll just want something light for dinner. See you at 7-ish.

On autopilot, I replied: OK. Vlogging in an hour, Miriam at 3:30. See you later.

I knew I shouldn't attempt vlogging in that condition, but thank God, I had always been able to slap on my poise persona at will. Taking a breath, I dropped the ring lights into position and adjusted the color temperature. Placed a few photography umbrellas on the floor, hoping to diffuse the dark circles. Logged on to the *Life of Reilly* channel and tapped "Go Live Now."

The premise was that having it all was a myth. An affirmation of sorts, it revolved around absolving yourself of guilt when trying to balance working, mommy-ing, wife-ing ... but it resonated deeply with me as the opening graphics package rolled.

A montage of shots of Happy Reilly—laughing, clipping sunflowers, nibbling vibrantly colored macarons. The last fleeting image: Rick kissing me when he'd joined me on the debut vlog, his easy grin as he loosened his tie, looking so proud of me. I choked up. *I can't ...*

"No one has a perfect life, I certainly don't ..." I gestured to the all-glass walk-in refrigerator, a virtual farmers market inside. "Looks idyllic maybe. *Looks* being the operative word. It may look to many of us like other women have it easy." My lip trembled uncontrollably. "You know what? I can only speak for myself. This is one of those days where I'm barely hanging in there. I'm trying to remind myself it's just one day, one really sucky day, but it's just one day ..." This was live, and I was perilously close to oversharing. Certainly wearing my raw emotions on my sleeve. *Close it out.*

My eyes welled up. "It's all a juggling act, and sometimes you drop a ball. We just can't beat ourselves up about it. Life will beat us up enough as it is." A big fat tear dripped down.

This wasn't going well. I didn't have control. *Close it the fuck out. Say your goodbyes.* "Please know you're not alone. We all need to support each other. Till next time, live your best life!"—my usual sign-off minus the cheery tone. The incoming messages on the channel lit up. Trudging to the cluttered medicine shelf, I took aspirin, swallowing them down with water.

Damn it. The channel lit up with incoming messages, but they were about me. They were concerned. Had I crossed that fine line between being vulnerable and being a basket case? Continuing like this, there wouldn't be a *Life of Reilly* to obsess about. It would cease to exist.

Billie's number popped up as I loitered, waiting for a spot in Miriam's parking lot. It was going to take more time than the five minutes I had to fill her in. Part of me feared her reaction. She wasn't going to buy his explanation. No matter what.

Miriam blinked. She was silent when I relayed the conversation I'd had with Rick.

"Did he ever actually deny that he's having an affair?"

The word made me flinch. "Not really. He was perturbed. I mean, he was exhausted, so I get it. But I didn't exactly ask him that directly either. We don't even fight. I don't think we've ever raised …"

"You didn't ask him directly," she repeated, her brown eyes clouded.

"I mean, he implied he wasn't. Isn't. Where would he find the time?"

Her head tilted. "His words, I'm guessing?"

I nodded. It sounded sadly denial-non-denial in her office.

"Well. Reilly, he's certainly had his share of stress lately, and you've mentioned he can shut down in those times. Perhaps …"

A jarring rap on her door. "I'm with a client at the moment." Another insistent knock.

"Miriam, I know you're with my wife. It's Rick. I … I need to see her."

We exchanged a look. *Why is he here?*

She touched my knee and asked quietly, "Do you want to do this?"

I was at the door in an instant. Wary but hopeful.

With an armful of vibrant pink peonies and a tender hug, it was the Rick I knew, fully present. The concerned expression. The soft gaze. He looked like himself again, not the incarnation I'd talked to yesterday. Taking a Life Saver from the bowl, he removed the plastic and popped it in his mouth.

"I just couldn't wait until tonight. I bungled this so badly. Miriam, apologies for hijacking your appointment, but I was in a state." Devastated, he sat next to me. Miriam smiled welcomingly. She nodded encouragement.

"This is no excuse," he said, "but I was blindsided. To think you could possibly believe that of me. But when I turned it around, from your perspective, I understood. I didn't say anything to dispel your concerns. I was reeling that you'd doubt me, but I should have assured you there's no one else. You're my person—my only person. You are the last woman I'm ever going to make love to. And if there's more I should be saying, I ..."

I buried my face in his neck and cried, my cheek wet against his smooth skin. I breathed in the woodsy scent, my homeopathic cure-all. "No, there's not more. I'm sorry too. I was ... catastrophizing. I just wanted you to say what you're saying now ..." A tissue was tucked into my fist on my knee. Pulling away, I dabbed at Rick's moist neck with it. Miriam shook her head.

"That was for you, actually. For your eyes. But it's very selfless that you always think about him before yourself." Smiling through tears, I dabbed my swollen eyes.

Rick continued earnestly, "I don't know what that text was ... you saw the text, did you, Miriam? The one that vanished." She nodded. "All I can say is you know I'm not that guy."

Miriam counseled, "I think this is a good place to stop. You two need time alone. Just listen to each other and be kind." She dispatched us with warm hugs.

Rick said he had an hour's more work as he walked me to my car; then he'd be home. Tipping my face up to his, he cautioned that I shouldn't vlog in that state—his colleagues noticed. Caroline, Emma. "What if Sloan had seen that?" he asked.

Had I inadvertently made him/us a topic of gossip? I berated myself all the way home, the guilt gnawing at me. Pulling into the driveway, there was Barbara, walking her mini-doodle, Daisy. In pleated khakis, for Heaven's sake, taking her mommy wear next level. *Oh, Barbara.*

Fresh air sounded restorative. I parked and joined her. I pulled on my suede jacket. She chatted: Daisy was tough to train; Eddie was overworked as usual. A pause. She stared down the street and said hesitantly, "You heard about Adam?"

"Adam? The couple with the twins? No. What's going on?"

"Adam ... well, he sits at the end of the street when he pulls in most nights. Sits in his car and chats and laughs on his phone forever—*before* he goes into his house." She looked at me sideways, her lips pressed into a thin line. Daisy jerked on the retractable training leash.

"So. He talks on his phone? In his car. And that means ... ?"

"Well! There's exactly *one* conversation a man can't continue inside his home. In front of his *wife*." She nailed me with a knowing nod.

I looked back blankly. It had been a long day.

"The Mistress Call," Barbara said, sadly. "Obviously."

"Barbara! He's got twins. If I were finishing a business call, I wouldn't head into the house with those rambunctious boys either." I laughed off the neighborhood rumor mill.

She was dogged. "Doubt it's work. He's smiling and laughing. He does it more nights than not. I watch him. I can see where he sits from my kitchen window."

Adam talks in his car on the phone. That passes for scandalous in our neighborhood.

"Barb, my friend. You know what?" I held my hand up to stop her. "I'm fully subscribed with my own issues right now." At that moment, my phone vibrated. *Sloan!*

"Let's catch up soon. I'm gonna take Sloan's call," I said and picked up.

"Mom! You've been hard to reach lately!"

I'd been avoiding her. She'd sense something was off. I wanted to get everything back on track. Get it all in the rearview mirror so I didn't have to put her through my drama again.

"Oh, sweetheart. I've been swamped. I'm sorry. Did you get my gift?" She thanked me for the set of framed prints I'd sent for her apartment. All the seaside prints were by a prominent Rhode Island artist, one was of the Goat Island Lighthouse that we visited so often.

"You always find the best presents. That was the beach Pop used to take me to crab. Where he'd carry me over the rocky parts, and Nanny would wear her weird gardening galoshes, remember?"

I laughed. I remembered the molded yellow rubber boots, trowels painted on them.

She updated me on her classes at Temple and her internship with their legendary basketball team. She talked a little, very little, about a boy she'd had a few dates with. He was sweet, but between classes and the internship, dating was back-burnered.

She was stalling. Leading up to something. I shrugged my jacket onto the chair and waited. Inevitably, since she never missed a segment, she broached the subject of the vlog: "You okay? You seemed a little not-you today. You know you can always talk to me, right?"

I responded with false cheeriness. "Of course. Oh, sweetheart. There's just so much going on, but I'll fill you in when I see you!"

"You've always been there for me. I can be there for you now, you know …" Her voice was small. Sad.

My heart broke for having concerned my daughter again. It shattered into a zillion pieces. A mother worries about her child, always and forever. It should never be the other way around.

CHAPTER 20

ACTIVE PROCEDURAL

Any naive notion I had that life would just—*poof*—be back to normal dissolved quickly. Life was ... normal-*ish*. We did the same things, had similar conversations, but it was strained. Maybe it was me: it troubled me he never spoke of the text again. Had it been the other way around, I'd have revisited it many times. To assure him there was no one else. To wonder together who might've been behind it. Rick never did. He handled it his own way, the Rick way.

Coming in on the later side the next night, I was drained emotionally and physically. I'd spent the day downtown at a decorator warehouse opening to the public, finalizing plans for a remote vlog. Billie called twice, and I'd hit "Reject." It was impossible to take calls during a tour like that. I'd get back to her when I figured out what, and how much, to share with her.

Rick's car sat out front, but the house was dark. No lights at all in the entry room, the kitchen, the living room—no lights, but there was a luminous flickering outside. Dropping my bag on the coffee table, I moved toward the open doors. Rick's voice floated inside. "Out here."

The back patio had been transformed. It was an oasis, twinkling tea lights and silver pails with sweet-smelling hydrangeas and peonies dotted the bricks. Two lounges angled together, separated by a cedar table with shrimp hanging from a bowl of cocktail sauce and a charcuterie plank. Rick was like a boy proud of himself for pulling off a Mother's Day breakfast tray.

Why was it always this way? A simple conversation would have put my mind at ease. *Awful person*, I moaned to myself. This was the Rick way. I smiled. If this was how he proved his devotion to me, I'd appreciate it. His love language was definitely "physical affection," while mine skewed toward "words of affirmation"—but, hey, lots of mixed marriages worked.

"On your vlog, how to make any evening into a special date night, you said there's nothing that tons of votive candles and fresh flowers can't pretty up," he said.

I complimented what he'd done. How well he'd done it. I admired everything about it, noting the new candles and the effort he'd put in.

"See," he said proudly, "I'm a Lifer." Sprawled on the recliner lounges, he fed me shrimp. We drank wine. Crickets chirped insistently all around the property.

The flickering of the candles glinting in his eyes, he extended a hand to me. "I adore you. Every inch of you." His hand quickly unhinged the hook holding the back of my lounge up. Lying flat now, I laughed. Wanting me, even outside. Even with the recent tension.

"You're incorrigible. You know that, don't you?"

He reached one hand behind his head, snaked it halfway down his back, and peeled his T-shirt over his torso. He dropped it to the grass.

"Incorrigible? No." Pushing his jeans down his legs, he was naked now. He stepped over the pile of denim. Moving his mouth close, closer, he pulled back just before our lips met.

"Maybe, but only because every time I see you or think about you, I get hard," he said in a husky voice before lowering himself onto me on the lounge.

He pushed my arms up over my head and ran his hands down the inside, the wildly sensitive underside of my arms. His face grazing mine, he lowered himself to kiss and suck my neck, my ear. He batted my hands away every time I moved them to his biceps, or his chest, or his hair. Looking in my eyes, he grabbed his T-shirt from the grass. He twisted it around my wrists, yanking it until it was tight.

"You're the taker tonight," he whispered seductively, extending my arms back over my head. "You don't get to touch. You don't get to do anything—but enjoy. You're never selfish. It's your night."

Take, could I just take? Initially, I struggled. I longed for reciprocity. He ran his firm tongue down my collarbone, between my breasts. I moaned; tonight, I was a taker.

Removing a tie from the lounge cover, he held it up to me. Secured my feet together. He slid his hands up my thighs, pushing my dress toward my breasts. Exquisitely slow. He licked my now-bare midriff. I closed my eyes, reveling in the touch, our sighs, our moans.

He grabbed my hair and wrapped it around his fist, turning my face to him forcefully. His face hovered inches from mine. His breath tickled my cheek. He drew his parted lips across my jaw. It was torture, the waiting, but finally his mouth found mine and hungrily latched on. His hand loosened on my hair to hold my neck lightly, to pull all of me to all of him, my body writhing under his in the candlelight.

With a swift move, one hand cupping each side of my torso, he flipped me over with the same ease I flipped a turkey. Straddling me on his knees, I felt him hard against me. "Doggie style. Trust me, you'll love it," he panted, sinking into me. Crying out, in the silence, he clasped a hand over my mouth. I breathed raggedly around his fingers.

Facedown on the lounge, I eyed his reflection in the glass door. He was breathless, aglow with satisfaction. Blinking back hot tears, I pulled my chin to my chest. He was wrong. I hadn't loved it. It had felt like punishment. Or ownership.

He gently untied the restraints, unaware that the encounter had ultimately left me feeling violated. Smiling contentedly into the night, his white teeth gleaming, he said, "Seriously. Now *that* has to be worth five stars on my Yelp review."

———————

In the morning I sleepily made Rick a to-go coffee in a Butler Industries travel mug, still on edge about the way the prior evening had gone, the text, so much. While he sat unfazed, munching on marbled capicola from last night's charcuterie plate.

"I still don't get it. What would be the point of someone sending a text like that?"

Confused, he replied, "You're still on about the text? I thought we'd taken care of that. It'll make you scatty if you get stuck on it."

"I'm not stuck. It's just one of those things you'd like to have the answer to."

One hand in the air, he dismissed the discussion. "One we'll likely *never* have the answer to. Honestly, I think we've given it too much credibility as it is. Personally, I refuse to give it another second."

It lingered in my mind, taking up bandwidth, while he had already filed it away. If only.

A text pinged. Billie. Rick leaned in and read her message over my shoulder.

Soosh tonight at 6. Be there or be very effin' square.

His brow furrowed, he tapped out a text of his own. "Oh. Well, if you're off to do your thing tonight, I'll take one of the final two candidates for the number two job to dinner, I expect. You might've mentioned it, though, your plan with Billie. I try to keep you in the loop."

Too tired to explain that a plan hadn't existed, I offered a half-hearted "I meant to tell you. I forgot."

Yup. CU@6, I texted Billie back.

That day's *Life of Reilly* vlog was about accessing and harnessing your personal power. Power vampires tried to rob you of your strength, and the show would focus on how to recognize them and how to hold them at bay. My guest, a life coach and the author of *Your Boundaries, Your Rules,* was a provocative personality, with strong messages and advice about advocating for yourself in your own life.

Samantha Jamison offered suggestions for "renovating your life." Overaccommodating and compromising became a bad habit, Sam warned. "By dishonoring your own needs and wants, you train the people in your life to do the same. Have you ever found yourself not recognizing who you've become? Have you become a victim in your own story?"

I forced a response. "We all have at times. It's hard to see it when it's happening."

"Here's the truth: the *only* person who resists you defining your boundaries is the one who benefits so thoroughly from you having none."

That statement staggered me because Miriam talked about that, too, the necessity of boundaries. The things that I was tolerating now, the old Reilly would have never put up with. And in tolerating things, a new normal was set.

Viewer numbers were good, but I was rattled nonetheless, startled by how relevant to my life the content was. I dishonored my needs and wants, my boundaries. An uneasy, involuntary thought. I recoiled the second it entered my mind. I tried to smother it. I tried to suffocate it with lack of emotional energy. There was only one answer: there was someone else.

I was running on fumes, but Billie was heading out of town, and I did want to see her before she left. Well, I did and I didn't—maybe I feared what she might have to say.

She texted: Change of plans. Let's do Tap Room, Soosh is slammed.

A few minutes past six, I walked into the Tap Room. Dim, pub-style, mostly men drinking golden pints and watching the

Wizards on the big screens, John Wall giving it everything on the court. Intermittent cheers from the guys around the bar.

Billie was already there. Wine waiting. She tapped the rim of the glass when I slid in across from her: "Sit. Drink." That first sip slipping coolly down my throat, I shuddered.

She took a sip and fixed me with a look. "So what's up?"

"Umm ... you know that decorator warehouse opening, it's pretty cool, I'm doing ..."

She waved her hand impatiently. "I know, I remember." A pause. "Listen. I've been watching *Life*. What's going on with you?"

"Nothing really. Things are a little strange right now ..."

Her expression was no BS. "You aren't yourself. I'm not hearing much from you. Why is that?"

Raw from living in my own personal, not-knowing hell, I stared into the glass. I wrapped my fist tightly around the stem. If there was one person I could be my authentic self with, even in my state of fear and trepidation, it was Billie. Looking up, I managed, "I ... need to tell you something. A lot of somethings."

CHAPTER 21

OP-ED

Everything I'd been emotionally hoarding came tumbling out. The text, Rick's roller coaster of responses, the unsettling aftermath, some of the sexual details. As she listened, her blue eyes were ablaze with worry. Billie pinched her lips together with her fingers, twisted them, and tried in vain to keep herself from saying what she wanted to say.

"Girl. I don't like it. In fact, I'm sorry to say this, but if you want the truth, the real truth … I've never liked him." Her forehead creased over.

What the actual fuck? *You've never liked my husband, the man I'm going to spend the rest of my life with?* And now this. Exactly what I needed when my life was on the precipice.

"You never liked my husband? *Really?*" My voice was harsh, even over the bar revelers.

She crossed her slim arms. "I tried to. I wanted to."

You *wanted* to.

I shook my head, two, three times. "It's … it's lost on me why you can't just get along with him. For me. You know I'd do it for you."

She snapped her eyes to mine. "You'd stand by while your best friend was in some weird Stockholm syndrome thing? *He*"—she jabbed her finger toward an imaginary Rick—"is the captor. You're his willing victim. It's creepy."

I narrowed my eyes at her. Captor complex. Jesus.

"C'mon. He's been that way from the jump. Tells you you don't want to work at the studio anymore—suddenly you say that's the case. Tells you it's a good thing you're left bruised and violated 'cuz it means he's hot for you, tells you anything anonymous could never be true so the text is obviously crap—and now you're trying to sell me on all that too. And anything that doesn't fly, he'll just fix it with flowers and a tall, cold cup of his premium bullshit."

I slapped my glass down. "And this is why I'm not in touch. We're going through something. We're working it out. People do it all the time." I welled up. She opened her mouth to respond, but I cut her off with my hand very close to her face. "I ... I'm dealing with so much. I thought you ..." I fought tears, motioning between us. "I can't handle this, too, right now." Yanking my black sling bag off the bar hook under the table, I left her in disbelief.

I sat in my car, shaking. Considered what she'd said. *Stockholm syndrome.* As if. So I was his hostage, his brainwashed lover?

She never liked him. And she thinks that I'm trapped in some ... my heart shattered again. Had I just broken up with a lifelong friend? Wasn't that how "taking a break" usually ended? My support system was falling away. No, that was a lie. I was pushing it away.

A sharp rap on my window made me jump. Billie motioned for me to put the window down. "Listen. You're not off-loading me when times get tough, sister. And you *are* my sister."

I shook my head, squeezed my eyes shut. Why was I taking my anger, my fear, out on the wrong person? *What is wrong with me?* She'd been a loyal friend. We hadn't always shared the same opinion, but we'd always worked it out.

Reaching through the window, her chilly hand massaged my neck. It was so tight, so knotted. "Get in, Billie. Just get in the car already. It's cold. Don't mind me—I ... I'm just so on edge. I don't understand where my life went."

We sat together in the dim garage. "I totally get why you *think* you don't like him, why you were upset about not being included in the wedding, but ..." She stopped me with a fierce hug, even by Billie standards.

"You think it's about the *wedding*? It's so not. I'm scared for you. I don't think you're seeing things clearly." Scrappy Billie wasn't backing down. "Look me in the eyes. Can you say you one hundred percent believe the text was BS?"

My nerves were exposed and raw. Could I really say that? "Probably not," I said, sadly. "He hasn't been the same. He's *like* Rick, but he's ... not."

"And you are not the same you. I've known you twenty years, and you're a shadow of yourself. And you are gonna hate what I'm gonna tell you."

My voice was anguished. "I know you want the best for me. Tell me. Please tell me."

"You. Need. To. Know. For sure. You can't live like this. You could hire a PI ..."

"God, no. I can't do that. Anyway, I don't even have my own credit card. He'd see."

Billie was appalled when she asked about our finances. I knew nothing. I'd trusted Rick and his financial acumen. The man's a CEO. He didn't keep me in the loop about money matters. She asked if I'd kept the inheritance from my parents and the money from the divorce in my name. A rush of humiliation swept over me. I'd been so blind. I told her I'd put it all into the house since his money was tied up in the UK. And the rest was with his investment whiz.

Groaning, she googled. "See this? It's a spy store. You need answers. *Real* answers. They have all sorts of shit there. I don't know the half of it. But you gotta see 'em. Promise."

I wanted to just keep my head in the sand. On the other hand, maybe I'd confirm there was nothing to worry about. That he was loyal. That I could stop obsessing about the what-ifs.

"Fine." I committed, promising Billie I'd go to the store. No backtracking now.

"Don't wuss out," she warned. "I'm in New York for a few days, a phone call away. One way or the other, this is gonna be a good thing."

She hugged me reassuringly and headed to her car. Tossing her head back in annoyance, she did a U-turn. "Shit. You go. I left my jacket in the Tap Room."

"I'll wait. I'd rather see you get in your car." Scurrying in and out, she ran through the glass door with her vintage leather bomber jacket. Waved it at me in passing.

"Night. All safe now. You can stop worrying." She slid into her top-down convertible.

"Hey," I called after her, still unsettled. "I'm sorry about before. Are we all right?"

"Always," she answered, and blew me a kiss. I watched Billie's brake lights fade away.

Marching orders in hand, I steeled myself for the following day. The worst day yet. How would it be walking into a spy shop? Starting the snooping process on my husband?

The stark squeal of a siren, the spiral of police lights behind me … *No.* My heart rate accelerated. I pulled aside to allow the police car to pass, but it angled in behind me. I caught my breath. Exiting his car, a tall, barrel-chested man walked purposefully toward my vehicle.

"Do you know why I stopped you?" he asked after I'd handed him my license and registration. "You drove erratically exiting the parking lot."

I must be more exhausted than I realized.

"Just tired. I wasn't aware that—"

He cut me off. "How much have you had to drink tonight?" He shone a flashlight in my eyes.

"Nothing … not even a half a glass of wine." I'd left it on the bar when I was upset with Billie. The beam moved away from my eyes, and I squinted to see him, my vision blurry.

He had me exit the car. Walk a line. Touch my nose every so often. Recite the alphabet backward. A neighbor passed in her minivan while I stood on the side of the road. She averted her eyes. I was obviously under suspicion of a DUI. Humiliated, I asked if I could just take a Breathalyzer to prove it. The man scowled and shoved his hands deep into his pockets.

"Ma'am, gonna let you go this time." Abruptly, he returned to his car, his footsteps echoing in the night. He swiftly pulled away from his position behind me. So random, so strange. I *hadn't* been driving erratically. I knew they had a quota, but …

Grabbing my phone, I pulled up Rick's number. After all, he needed to know the police were all over it tonight. He'd have cocktails while entertaining his potential new number two and … clutching my phone, I stopped breathing. *Dean.* Jesus.

I was dazed. I dropped my phone into the console. Eerie co-incidence. Dean's DUI. The little hairs on the back of my neck tingled. Rick's justification: it wasn't entrapment; no one made him drink and drive. *Holy hell.* My mind was fuzzy. I couldn't think. No, Rick thought we'd be at Soosh. That was what Billie's text had said. He didn't know about the change of plans. He didn't know we'd gone to the Tap Room.

I exhaled. I was really letting my imagination run wild. Any-way, he would never. I could lose my brand, my sponsorship, my credibility. Dean, sure. Dean was trying to make him look bad. But me? He wouldn't do that to me. I was truly losing it to even consider that. I dialed him.

The familiar trill of his ring. He answered—the bustling sounds of socializing in the background. The laughter, the clatter of glass-ware. "Well, good evening, Mrs. Lynch."

"Hi. I … just wanted to hear your voice."

"I'm glad you rang. You girls had fun at Soosh, I presume?"

Suddenly, I ... I couldn't tell him I'd been pulled over on suspicion of a DUI. I didn't have control. I had to get control. I was barely hanging on, doubting everything, everyone. Was this the tipping point, the inevitable slide into my life going off the rails, the point of no return?

"Billie all right?" he asked, breaking the silence. That was a loaded question.

"I ... yes. Amy's teaching music at the conservatory."

"She's ... what's that you said? It's rather loud here ..." He raised his voice over the din.

"Amy's ... never mind. I'm just headed home now. See you later."

"Drive safe," he said, before disconnecting.

Tomorrow. No one knew where I was going tomorrow. Or what I was going to do. Or how vile I felt about it.

Least of all my husband.

CHAPTER 22

STING

Doing my best to be inconspicuous, I was woefully out of place in this Southeast neighborhood: more bail bonds joints than bougie blow-dry bars. Lowering my head, I slipped into the spy store. They didn't even bother with down-low signage. Just THE SPY STORE.

What the hell am I doing?

A geeky young guy glanced over as the bell on the door dinged. He wore a skimpy *Legend of Zelda* T-shirt, the graphic of the game so faded it was virtually colorless. He straightened the company ID hanging from his lanyard and approached me with an awkward gait. The scent of Old Spice wafted over with him, only making me queasier.

"If you'll come over to my counter, I can help you with whatever you need."

Normalcy, that's what I need. My life back, that's what I need.

Trailing behind him, I passed dusty glass cases jammed with boxes of various sizes. Each with handwritten signs affixed to the door: *Audio, Video, Tracking, Detectors.*

Standing at his counter, I froze. What happened now? I finally stammered, "It's just ... I need to know, I need to know if my husband ... if there's someone ..."

He was efficient, matter-of-fact. He'd dealt with some version of me many times before. A woman insecure in her relationship. Wanting to know. Desperate not to know.

Pulling out a laminated sheet, he pointed at options with a chewed-up pencil.

"Lots of choices when it comes to infidelity issues. You can jailbreak his phone. Or there's voice-activated pens or Nest cameras you put in his office. You can install just about anything, just about anywhere." He rapidly delivered his practiced spiel.

Staring helplessly at the cases, I was lost. I wanted to be anywhere else, doing anything else. I reviewed the list. As though any of those options meant anything at all to me. He let me look over the page. He cleared the phlegm from his throat and drooled it into a tissue.

"If you wanna know what I think, I usually suggest to start with a simple recording device for his vehicle." He rested his pencil next to the precise model he was recommending. "You got a key for his car?"

I nodded numbly. "His car," I echoed. "In case he happens to be driving around with her? I ..."

"Nope. 'Cause his car is his safe place, he probably calls her in there." He shrugged his bony shoulders. "That's what people do when they're involved."

Involved. My stomach churned loudly. I scanned the grimy store for a bathroom, if it came to that. It couldn't come to that. Not here. *Breathe.*

Yanking a small box from the cluttered case behind him, he pulled out a black metal unit. It fit in his palm. The dimensions of a fun-size candy bar. He held it out.

"See? This is how easy it is. It's got this magnet, attaches under the seat. It's voice activated, so you leave it for a few days, a week, and plug it into your computer to hear the voice files. Easy. Around here, we call it Surveillance for Dummies."

He collapsed into a lopsided smile. *Spy Store humor. Funny shit.*

"Hardest part is input and extraction. Getting it placed, getting it back. Takes balls, but you get answers real quick, *and* it's kinda legal. 'Cuz cars are community property." His droopy eyes assessed me, my questionable cojones.

I nodded six, eight times, considering what it entailed. Slipping the device back in its plastic sheath, he slid it back into its box. He nudged the box to a spot in front of me with his mangy pencil. Tapped on it. My cue to decide. The not knowing would kill me.

I said boldly, "How much?" and pulled out my silver wallet.

He bobbed his head, new faith behind those lidded eyes. "Right on, you'll do good. Forty-nine dollars plus tax."

Fifty bucks got you answers.

It was surreal, out of body, really, as he rang up the transaction. That was my grand plan, my sophisticated attempt at investigation? My own kinda-legal little black box that, once retrieved, might hold answers? And if it didn't, there was always jailbreaking his phone. *Jesus.*

"Lemme know how that goes. There's tons of other stuff you can do, but this right here is a real good start," he said, lowering himself onto his elbows on the streaky glass counter.

Is it? It's a real good start?

Sliding away from his register, I surveyed the store to make sure I didn't know anyone. I'd heard the bell on the door chime. The next customer was familiar. She tentatively approached him. Letting my hair swing down to cover my face, I looked at her. Her hands were tightly wound. Looking more closely, no, I hadn't met her—yet I recognized her. Fortysomething, Lululemon workout gear, concern etched across her pretty features. I knew her all right. She stuck out badly in Southeast too. I wondered how many of us made the pilgrimage every day.

Driving up Rock Creek Parkway after leaving the store, I reflected on our life. The parking lot tap. The proposal in Newport, the lighthouse, our home. The vlog. The way he'd always made me feel the best and the brightest. Since our chance meeting, everything had been more vibrant, more exciting, with him. Solemnly, I swore: if I listened to those files and there was nothing, no reason to worry, I would toss the miserable device. I'd leave my suspicions behind.

The next morning, Rick slipped his arms around me in bed in the early hours. He inhaled and kissed my neck. Pretending to be asleep, I made a muffled noise and adjusted to a new sleep position, farther from him. He pushed the sheets aside. Made sure not to rouse me. Swinging his legs out, he dropped his feet to the floor. Headed for the bathroom.

Eyes open, alert now, I waited. The shower door opened, and the spray started. I hastily threw on the sweatshirt and leggings I'd hidden behind the dust ruffle under the bed. Rushing through the bathroom, I said I was getting us coffee. Rick called, "No shower show? I just noticed I need a new gel from that drawer, if you don't mind."

Fuck! I have no time. I do mind!

Wound more tightly than I'd ever been, I rifled through items in his top drawer. Located the all-important shower gel. In a mad rush, not making eye contact, I thrust the bottle at him.

"Did you remove that little foil thingy inside so the gel can come out? The one that keeps it from …"

I snatched it back before he could finish. Unscrewing the cap, I grabbed for the teeny tab on the foil cover. Ripped it off. Twisted the cap back on.

"Good to go." I put the bottle on the ledge and made my getaway. Frantically, I dashed to the laundry room, my heart pounding thunderously. I shoved my feet into the gray UGGs I'd put there last night, pulled the recording device from the clothes hamper. Fumbling with the power button, I flew down the stairs. Damn shower gel. My time had already been limited. The window at Rick's sink had a direct view of his car; he'd be at that sink in four minutes.

Rushing outside, the chill assaulted me. I hurried to his car. Squeezed the fob to unlock it. The sound was jarringly harsh in the early hours on our quiet cul-de-sac. I did a loop around his car. Scanned the street to see if anyone was watching. No. No activity. *Breathe.*

Dropping down, I crouched on the far side at the driver's door. Double- and triple-checked. Yes, I'd turned on voice activation. Having practiced on my own car, I was confident. I knew exactly how the recorder clicked onto the undercarriage of the seat.

My hands shaking almost beyond usefulness, I opened his door. Thrust my arm under his seat. Waited for the device to click into place. No click. *Shit!*

The underside of his seat was completely different from mine. I hadn't anticipated that. Leaning in farther, I ran both hands up and down the cold metal components. Where could I attach this thing that it couldn't dislodge? It all took longer than in my car. My nerves were shot.

There—that was a solid spot. I waved the recorder at it, and the strong magnetic force abruptly jerked the device from my hand. Clamped it tightly to the metal rod. I attempted to pull it away, to be sure it was secure, that it wouldn't come loose. It didn't budge. *That's the best I can do.* Closing the door, I scurried back to the porch. My whole body buzzed on high alert.

Damn. Did I lock it? Stretching my arm toward his car, I squeezed the fob. It beeped. Locked. I'd done it. Planted a recording device in my husband's car. Trying to tamp down the adrenaline surge, I reached for the front door I'd left barely ajar.

Rick was on the other side, staring at me. Only a towel around his waist. He combed his hair slowly. *No. No!* Panic overwhelmed me. I had no idea what he'd witnessed. I stopped. I couldn't move. Couldn't think of what to say. Did he know I was about to violate his privacy?

"Paper never gets here before eight anymore."

Was he really apprising me of the paper boy's new schedule—or was he about to ask me what the hell I was doing in his car?

My throat tightened and choked the voice out of me. I rasped, "Used to be six thirty like clockwork." I didn't look up. I was afraid the terror eating away at my inside was visible on the outside. Kicking my battered UGGs to the doormat, I asked, "Espresso?"

"Double, missus," he replied. The hissing and sputtering of the Keurig commenced.

Pulling his yogurt and berries from the fridge, I sneaked a few peeks at him. Nothing remotely unusual. When had I become so duplicitous? A sleuth slash barista. Slash spouse.

CHAPTER 23

TWO-SHOT

Surviving the next five days was agonizing. Time ticked away unbearably slowly.

Staying busy and sane was nearly impossible. Training hard every day, I reached the next level of kickboxing. Kicks, punches, footwork, power—it released pent-up tension. And it gave me something to think about other than what might be on the recordings.

I made some superficial, feel-good changes. Buttery highlights. A little Botox. Some filler to make my cheeks "juicier." Had to work all angles: for the vlog and for my life.

The morning came, the day I planned to retrieve the device. It was recycle day. Rick had parked in the garage. Made it easier for the county trucks to access the trash cans. *Thank God, more accessible for me.*

When the shower started up, I threw my pink shorty fleece robe on. Stopped for a moment at the shower show. Rick slathered shaving cream on his face with a short, fat brush, swirling it around in the tin of cream, then on his jaw. Reached into the mirror tray for his razor.

Nonchalantly, I stretched, getting up from the love seat. "I'll start the coffee, all right?"

"No breakfast for me, client meetings with godawful pastries to look forward to."

I darted down the stairs and ran into the garage barefoot. Flipped on the overhead light. It buzzed like a bug zapper. Maybe the bulb was about to go. Pulling his fob from my pocket, I unlocked his car. Dropped to my knees on the grimy floor. Reached in for the device. Exactly where I'd placed it. *What the …* It wasn't there. It was gone. A sharp intake of breath. *No.*

In a panic, I tried another spot. And another. Nothing. *Shit. How did he …* Groping furiously now, my hands became slick, sweaty. My mind swirled with possibilities. I reached farther, my face pushed against the grainy leather of the seat. I strained to reach in even farther, my hand darting to all corners. There, what was that?

Something stuck out. Something cold. I couldn't quite reach it. I jammed my arm in another inch, my biceps hard up against the frame of the seat. Working my fingers around it, I touched it. The edge of the recorder. I took a raspy breath, not aware I'd stopped. The device had slipped up the metal rod to the farthest side of the seat, but it was still there. Still attached. Gasping, I tried to tug it from the thick rod. It resisted. I jerked it again.

My hand slipped off, banging hard on the floor of the car. Distraught, I crawled out and furiously scanned the garage. There. A rag for the car hung on a hook. I wiped my slippery hands on it. Climbed back in. Shoving my arm all the way in, I gripped the recorder tightly. Slid my fingernails under the edge and yanked. With a click, it fell into my hand. *Yes.* Curling my fingers around it, gripping it tightly, I pulled it out. Dropped it in my pocket. I hurried back inside. Time was limited.

Swiftly closing the door and locking it, I stealthily moved back into the house and slipped down the lemon-chiffon-painted hall. Stepped quietly to the landing at the stairs. Listened. The shower was still running. Perfect. I tucked the little black box in the pantry. In the nested mixing bowls, laying a smaller bowl on top. Covered it all with crisp white linen napkins.

Preoccupied with what lay ahead, I could barely make conversation. Rick looked at me with warm, questioning eyes; I forced a strained smile. Sipped at the coffee.

He gathered his things and retrieved his handsome chocolate briefcase. "No vlog today, right? So you taking class?"

"I … they're starting a hybrid kickboxing and Muay Thai. I'm … I'll do that one."

"Keeping it in shape. That's my girl."

Really. My stomach churned audibly.

Reaching around, he patted my tummy and trailed his fingers across it lightly.

"*Eat*. Did you hear that? You need food, love."

I nodded. I did need to. I couldn't.

He touched my lips with a finger, then lightly touched his mouth to mine. "Promise me."

"I promise," I echoed, closing the door. Held up my three fingers. Faked another smile.

Forever. His car sat forever at the stop sign at the top of the road—*Go!*—but once it made the right turn and disappeared, I flew into action.

Retrieving the device from the pantry, I grabbed my laptop from the office. Gathered things I might need. My cell phone. Pad and pen. A bottle of water, as if hydration mattered.

I set myself up in Sloan's room. At her bay window. If Rick returned unexpectedly, I'd see immediately. It had never happened before, but I could take no chances. My nerves were raw, jangled. Becoming almost hysterical, I shrieked out loud in the silent room—unable to position the thumb drive at the input port. It didn't fit right, damn it! It was faulty. It didn't work.

Only breathing deeply allows your mind to fully focus, my instructor repeated daily.

Slow down. Breathe. In, out. Consulting the manual again, I read the instructions in their entirety. This time, the drive popped in with a satisfying click. Past the first technological hurdle.

Spy Store Guy knew his shit. The process was intuitive. My lap-top screen lit up brightly with easy, clear access to each recording. Mesmerized, horrified, I could only stare.

"You have twenty-four new voice files." Six stark words.

This was it. *Breathe.* I stared at the screen, unable to move. This was the last moment ever that I wouldn't know. I wasn't sure I was ready for the not knowing to end.

Thirty minutes passed. Nearly an hour. Quaking, staring at the screen, I couldn't pull the trigger to eavesdrop on my husband's life.

"You have twenty-four new voice files."

Swallowing around the lump lodged in my throat, I slowly pressed the green "Play" button.

File 1. 10:29 a.m. There was a fair amount of ambient noise. It sounded like he had the window down. I leaned in and listened intently as Rick confirmed a lunch reservation. A knot in my stom-ach tightened. The confirmation, though, was for six. Had to be business.

File 2. 12:26 p.m. Rick and a male colleague in the car heading to the lunch. It was innocuous and mundane. The guy complimented everything from Rick's car to his public speaking techniques. *Gag.* Exactly the minutiae I thought I'd hear. He thanked Rick profusely for accompanying him to an appointment; he'd only closed that deal because the client was so enamored of Rick's claims of what Butler could do for their tech start-up, Butler's sweet spot.

File 3. 2:08 p.m. Rick got in the car. Then the passenger door opened and closed. A female voice. My heart in my throat, I dread-ed what was coming. "It's been forever," she said. I tried to focus. Did I know that voice? Rick said, "My apologies. Busy. Traveling. You know the drill." The young lady responded, "I *do* know the drill. No time for little old me. I know I twisted your arm to see me, but let's do this—maybe you'll even enjoy it," she teased him.

Enjoy it? Jesus Christ, enjoy WHAT? My fists pressed my eyes shut. I tried to breathe.

An eternity before he spoke. "I always enjoy an outing with you, Sandra." My already-agitated stomach flipped. I waited tensely. Sandra.

He added, "I'll certainly see it. Butler's always looking to acquire more real estate, but there just may not be enough upside to this property. For us, it's all location, location, location."

Thank God. I dropped my chin to my chest, my body heavy with fatigue.

File 4. 3:39 p.m. I listened as Rick left a voice mail. For me. Loudly enunciating via Bluetooth, "Call Reilly." He proceeded to leave me a voice mail message. I remembered that message. In fact, I'd saved it. I still had it. It had been unusually sweet. Said he'd seen a married couple at lunch. With absolutely nothing to say to each other. A smile in his voice, he'd thanked me for being so interesting and smart and funny. I listened to it again. This time courtesy of a recording device I'd placed in his car.

I'm officially the world's worst person, I moaned to myself.

File 5. 4:12 p.m. Again, two people got in the car. *Does the man go nowhere alone?* "Oh, thank you, sir," the woman said. He'd clearly opened the door for her. Followed by his own door opening and closing. The car humming to life. He flipped the radio station to jazz. *Jazz? WTF?* She said, "Mmm, nice." Rick commented on her shoes. Struck me as odd. He's not really a shoe guy. "Now that *is* a crazy-high heel, but I suppose they're not really meant for walking."

It could still be nothing. It could be nothing. Not meant for walking. Numbly, I twirled my wedding ring.

With a throaty giggle, she replied, "The reason they call 'em 'fuck me, honey' pumps."

Whoa. She was really laying it on. She was using that phrase to my husband?

"My first pair of Louboutins." She butchered the name of the red-bottomed shoes. "I still owe you a real thank-you for the giftie, and your office bathroom doesn't count." He let out a low, approving wolf whistle.

His ... bathroom? A searing pain shot through my body. Lodged behind my eyes.

"You know what? I'm gonna make good on that IOU right now. Move your seat back." He complied: the seat buzzed and slid farther from the wheel. A click: his seat belt was undone. *No, please, no.* The distinct sound that only a zipper makes. I froze. Stopped turning the ring.

At that moment, Bluetooth announced an incoming call. "Reilly calling." I heard my husband as he callously punched away, rejecting my call.

"Not particularly good timing, as it turns out," he murmured to her. They both laughed.

They're laughing. At me. The two of them.

Garbled now, she mumbled, "You could've taken her call if you really ..." followed by a sucking sound and a ...

It took me a moment. It hit me as hard as I'd ever been hit in my life. My hands flew to my head, holding it in place. No, God, no—this wasn't how this was supposed to go. I'm supposed to be relieved now, with a new lease on life.

The zipper, the garbled sound, the sucking, that woman's mouth was full of ... my husband.

It was like taking a bullet. My husband and I moaned at the exact same moment.

"Take her call? Now? Not a chance." His voice thick, he spoke to her in his lap, "Doll, you comfortable down there?"

"Well, it's not like your place with her seventy-two stupid pillows, but I'll take you any way I can get you," she said, having freed herself to coo at him.

My seventy-two stupid ...

Then she went back to the job at hand. Slurping. Her mouth filled to capacity with my contented husband.

In shock, in despair, I continued to listen. Unable to pull myself away. The sloppy sounds intensified. Stinging tears rolled down my face. His groans and her purrs became louder. More rhythmic. Rocking in time with them, I wrapped my arms around myself.

"Faster. Jesus, Caroline ..." The final moment I knew so well—that guttural growl I thought was reserved for me. A wave of anguish rolled over me, a riptide I couldn't escape.

I clumsily hit "Pause." My mind raced. Caroline. *You must be fucking kidding.*

Stumbling to Sloan's bathroom, I vomited. So hard that my rib cage ached. Unable to move, I dropped to her tile floor. There was the screeching of a feral animal.

Sobbing, screaming, my face lay in a puddle of my tears. I banged my head on the tiles, wanting to feel pain that wasn't my heart breaking into jagged pieces. I was bleeding out on the tiles of my daughter's floor.

No one should ever have to hear the person they love with someone else. I hoped to die. God, please take me. I'm not strong enough.

It was the truth all along. There *was* somebody else. Colorless Caroline. And they'd just slipped this behavior into their work schedule, his office, our car.

Jesus, was this what Barbara had tried to tell me with the gossip about the "neighbor" letting a woman into his garage? She'd been at my *home*. She'd referenced my *pillows*.

Fool. I'd been stupidly secure of his love for me. I'd lie around in boyfriend jeans and a distressed tee, thinking, *My man knows what's under here, and it's all for him.* Boyfriend jeans. While she was slinking around in four-inch stilettos and thigh-high stockings. I could have zhooshed it up. I was laboring under the delusion he loved me the way I was.

Had he ever really loved me? Had he been lying all along? I questioned everything.

The screaming, the howling, I couldn't stop. Our marriage was a mirage. I'd done it again; I'd believed a man wanted to create a world with me. That he'd loved me as I was. That he always would. He was a fraud. A despicable, disgusting, duplicitous fake. And I was his foolish ride-or-die. I flailed. I broke things. I flipped furniture. Rage and despair took turns kicking my ass.

Grabbing the poker from the side of the fireplace, I swung with all my strength.

CHAPTER 24

ON THE RECORD

"Beauty for beauty," Rick had said when he gave me the pale, watercolor Lladró figurines last month. Now in pieces, large and small, scattered everywhere. I'd smashed them to bits.

I hit #1 on my speed dial: RICK WORK.

"Mrs. Lynch!" he answered, with a lilt.

My voice was dead. "Take me off speakerphone."

"Would if I could but ..."

I couldn't contain a wild howl. "Take. Me. Off."

Alarmed, he picked up. "What the hell is going on with—"

I cut him off with a vengeance.

"I know about her!"

No response. I repeated the words, every word thudding like a block of concrete. "I. Know. About. Her."

"You are so damn suspicious." He sighed, sounding beleaguered. "Why can't you let it go? Our problem is ..."

Raspy and ragged, I talked over him. I knew full well how much he hated that. "Our *problem* is that you're having sex with another woman. You're lying, you're cheating, you're everything you've always pretended to hate!"

I dissolved into wracking sobs. He was appalled. Stopped in his tracks. It was finally time. He would confess the truth. He would tell me about *her*.

"Are you really still stuck on that? That's what you truly think of me?" He sounded resentful that I was so suspicious.

"It's what I *know* of you. I *despise* you."

His door closed immediately. "You are unhinged! Stop shouting."

"How could you? How could you fuck Caroline, for Christ's sake? In our car, no less, like you're fucking invisible. How could you lie to me for so long? Why did you keep seeing her after I got that text? You're *sick*."

"I, I ... ," he stammered in shock. Knowing now, for the first time, that I had him. I knew. "I ... she's pursued me for so long, it's ... it's just not a big ..."

I killed the call. I couldn't listen to anything he would have said. He knew he was caught. He *knew* now. We both knew now. We both knew that thing we could never unknow.

Like a caged animal, I couldn't settle. I jerked this way and that, eyes only on my phone. His work number lit up time after time. Then it switched. He was calling from his mobile. *Of course he'll come home!* I couldn't see him. I couldn't drive. I couldn't function. *I'll call for...*

His car careened into the driveway, as though rather than driving, he'd teleported himself. He squealed to a stop and opened the door, flinging himself at the porch in one motion.

I. Can't. Do. This. Frantically looking for somewhere he wouldn't find me, I tucked myself in Sloan's closet. He thumped around the house, shouting for me in each room.

Emitting a guttural yell, he slammed his fist on the end table in the foyer. He righted the chair and collapsed into it. Feet from Sloan's door. Then his voice. He was on the phone.

Silently, I rose out of the closet. Crossed to her doorway. Peered through the crack.

"I don't have any clue how she found out. I've no idea how much she knows, but she's off the chain. And she's nowhere to be found. God almighty, what a mess," he said, running his hands through his hair in frustration. He kicked a piece of Lladró away with his shiny black work loafers. Quietly, I had moved right in behind him.

"Yup. *What a mess.*" He jumped in shock. Stared at me slack jawed. His hand limply held his phone. I could see he was talking to "Max," who, obviously, was Caroline. Keeping her in the loop. How infuriating. I lunged for the phone before he could react.

"Caroline, this is Mrs. Lynch," I said in my chilliest tone, condescending, waiting for her panicked response. The flurry of words, a stammering apology.

Silence. Stunned dead air.

"I know you're not big on manners, but let me try to explain common courtesy to you: if you're banging your 'work spouse,' as you would say, the very least you can do is entertain a conversation with his real spouse."

Reaching around me, Rick tried to yank his phone back. I raced into Sloan's room. Slid the slim, brass metal rod across. Locked the door behind me.

"I ... don't wanna be involved in your ... you should probably be speaking to your husband about this," she finally managed, almost primly.

"Thank you. What a brilliant suggestion. Because this is only about my husband. Nothing to do with you at all."

Oozing sarcasm, I positioned myself by Sloan's door so Rick would hear every word. He paced relentlessly on the other side.

Irate at my attitude, Caroline tried to end the conversation, tapping something on her desk while taking my call. Busy dealing with employee issues, apparently. It would seem *this* is a pretty huge employee problem right here. Of course, I was no human resources genius.

"It's not appropriate for you to call me and say these things. I'm at work right now."

"At work? Well, as opposed to where, Caroline? In *my* family vehicle, in *my* seat, fucking *my* husband?"

When she spoke again, it was vaguely patronizing. The tapping ceased.

"Look, we're real sorry if anything we've done has hurt you. I'm not saying it's right, but I can only say I've literally always known we should be together," she concluded with a coquettish giggle.

A giggle. Perhaps the most inappropriate sound I've ever heard. Second only to her blowing my husband. Wrong in so many ways.

"IF anything we've done."

"IF we've hurt you."

He and I are the only "we"!

As *she* spoke down to me as if *I* were the interloper, it hit me. Her recent upgrades. The slimmer body, softer makeup, smoothly blown-out and blonded hair. She'd even adopted the french tuck of the blouse, subtly drawing attention to a toned tummy. From brassy to classy. She had morphed into *me*. To help herself to my husband. To steal my life away.

She'd elevated their dime-a-dozen blowy-in-the-car to something prettier. Something preordained. A predestined great love that no one could quarrel with. The bitter taste of *bitch* filled my mouth. I swallowed it back down hard.

"The thing is—" she began.

"The thing is, Caroline," I said, cutting her off. "Whatever you were doing with my husband is over. I hope you understand what I'm saying. This could be extremely detrimental for you."

She wasn't interested in anything more I had to say. It wasn't her first time at this rodeo. She'd fielded way worse than this. In a silky, unconcerned voice, she talked over me, "It seems this isn't going to be productive. I'm sure you have far better things to do."

"Well, you are right about that. I *do* have far better things to do," I said smoothly. "Like *call your husband.*" Snap. I killed the call and opened the door.

Rick dropped back into the chair, rocking and groaning, never having anticipated this turn in his life. How could he have? He was always the smartest guy in the room. He'd told me so. On many occasions. The smartest guy, and because of his success, untouchable. He favored the term *bulletproof.*

Rick looked haggard and gaunt. He held his ashen face in his hands.

"Jesus. What can I say? Maybe you shouldn't have blindsided her like that."

I *shouldn't have … ? I shouldn't …* I hurled Rick's cell phone at the brick fireplace, where it shattered on impact. That was the final straw for him. Rising from the chair, his face mottled and flushed, raw anger seethed from his pores.

"Grow up, Reilly. First off, you're not calling her husband and bollocksing that up too. This whole thing is already a right mess."

"Why is *she* your concern? I … I thought you loved me!" I slid down the wall, wailing.

He muttered something. Something about a mistake. A *"mistake"?* Picking up the wrong kind of bread at the market is a mistake. I thought I heard him mutter, "People make mistakes. It's not who they are. It's just a mistake."

My head thrummed, my ears buzzed. I couldn't think.

"You need. To get. Out. Of my house. Now."

"You don't mean that," he responded in astonishment. "This was nothing. Just a stress reliever with how pressurized work has been. I liked the attention, that's all. The newness. It's like it used to be with us when you found your … what did you call her? … your inner bad girl."

So it was my fault. I wasn't as lusty, as consumed with him, as obsessed. It was me.

My choking sobs continued unabated. I couldn't look at him. Would he look the same? Or would he look like that other person, the one who was deceitful, the one who laughed at me with another woman. My face was still buried in the Persian carpet.

He tried to placate me. "Please come off the ground. I hate that you're hurting. You're not that naive. Touching someone is nothing. It's not intimacy. It's not a relationship. It's who you share your life with."

I was perilously close to laughing at the absurdity of that. It had all sounded intimate to me. They were sharing something. A secret. And what was more intimate than that?

Reaching his long arms under me, he scooped my deadweight off the floor. Deposited me on one of the foyer chairs. I remained curled like a snail with my face turned inward. Rick dropped down to the floor, his arms still protectively around me.

Sniffles. Soft choking sobs. His. He was crying into my lap. Oh, that was what he used to do with his mother when she rebuffed him. He wanted her love so badly but ... *the poor* ...

I snapped back. No! I was *not* going down Sympathy Lane with him. I didn't move. Didn't rub his back. Didn't acknowledge his embrace. I was almost tempted to lift his head, only to see if his eyes were dry.

He murmured into my lap, "Why did I do this? What's wrong with me? Maybe I need help."

You need help, all right. Slowly, I extricated myself from his grip. I stood up. Stared out the window. *Funny.* I recalled when he'd been giddy with excitement that he was living the world "in vivid color" now. Only because of our great love. Ironic, all I saw now was sepia. Beige, gray nothingness.

Fiercely, he squeezed his eyes shut. Rubbed them with his fists, like a little boy upset with himself for crying.

"Women are so aggressive. I'm sorry, but I told you, they come on to me a lot. This time when it was offered, I'd had a tough day. I was ... weak."

The last thing you are is weak. "You said you were over all that—you're a one-woman man."

This felt like death, not betrayal. Death undoubtedly felt better. At least it was finite. An actual ending would've been merciful.

"Sweetheart," he said. "I *am* a one-woman man; it's you I love. I don't care about her."

"That's not caring? You have sex. You buy her expensive presents. You bring her into my home. You dismiss my phone calls when you get your precious time together—and you *laugh* at me."

I had no idea why *that* was one of the most hurtful things, but I had a wave of sickness reliving those conspiratorial giggles.

"You laughed at me with *her*. I'm just a joke," I said bitterly.

He was stunned at how much I knew. So many details. I could see the wheels turning. How did I know that much? And what else did I know?

Acidic bile rose again. It overtook me in an instant. Rushing to Sloan's bathroom, I could only dry heave, again and again. When it passed, I struggled to catch my breath.

Bleakly, I staggered to her bed and lay down. My entire body was numb with grief. There was only one thought on my mind. I was desperate to be certain that the affair was over. How could I be assured of that? Rick had to know how dangerous that affair was. That if it were revealed, to Butler, or publicly, it would spell the end of his impressive career. That meant so much.

And he had to understand that I knew I had the power to do that. It might be out of fear only, for himself, maybe for her, but at least he'd have to stop seeing her. That was all I could manage at the moment, my only goal in that instant.

Rick trudged into Sloan's room. Gingerly, he sat next to me on the bed. I lay staring out the window at the sepia neighborhood. He scratched my back lightly, the spot that I couldn't reach. *Don't touch me.*

You are not doing this to us.

Not turning to him, I spoke, "The affair was a big enough 'mistake,' as you call it. But the *who* is a bigger mistake." I twisted on the bed and looked up.

"She is a subordinate. You are her boss. *You* have a very tight morals clause."

His eyes narrowed. He rose from the bed. "Are you threatening me, love?" The voice had a new edge. He retreated to the foyer.

"I'm not threatening you. I'm stating the obvious. Franklin would fire you both."

The implication hung there. Staring each other down, we stood in the entryway. He looked incredulous.

"You *are* threatening me. I'm not sure I'd do that if I were you."

"Well, you're not me, *love*," I said, adding his term of endearment derisively.

Stony silence.

"You'd lose everything," I went on. "Me, our life. Your career, your reputation, the possibility of Franklin's job. All of it."

His lip curled, his body motionless; he just nodded rhythmically, repetitively. A bizarre bobblehead version of a man I'd once known.

"I can't be with you right now," I said. He threw his hands up to rebut. I cut him off, leaving no room for response: "Now. I mean it."

I stood at the window. Listened to him gather his keys. Close the front door. Crossing in front of me, his footfalls were heavy on the porch. I didn't look up.

He was gone. As I'd ordered. *No. Please no.*

Sitting in Sloan's window, the neighborhood carried on. Unaware. Barbara passed with her son and dog, barely corralling either. Adam and his heavily pregnant wife held hands as they pushed the twins in a double stroller. They walked back from the deli carrying brown bags, sharing a coffee. The new couple, whose names I didn't know, were running together. They raced the last block, collapsing on their lawn.

How had everyone else maintained relationships, trusting each other implicitly? Or had they? Was it an illusion? Was life behind the closed doors on our street what it appeared?

Forty-five minutes passed, my knees pulled under my chin. My arms wrapped around my legs. Self-soothing, I supposed. I rocked. I'd just wanted someone to love me. To look after me.

At that moment, the Range Rover came hurtling to a stop in front of the house. I jumped up. I'd said no. I'd said get out of this house. Racing for the door, I opened it and glared.

Standing at the far side of the porch, ostensibly to give me space, he appealed to me with baleful eyes. There had been a shift. There was a new gentleness.

"No," was all I could manage. "You're not the man I thought you were."

"I *am*. I love you for all your perfections, *and* for your flaws. And I know you love me like you've never loved a man—you've told me. This needn't define us," he said softly. I started to close the door. He pulled it back. "These aren't just words."

"That's exactly what they are."

His eyes glistened. "No. We have a whole life ahead of us. Think about it." He ran a finger down my cheek.

"Think about it: our girl, Sloan, getting married, having her own kids. We're not subjecting her to this. She deserves a real family, and we *are*." Referencing my daughter resonated so quickly and deeply that I was almost ill again. I grasped my stomach.

Sloan. She'd suffered through me being in a tunnel of anguish, post-parents, post-Alex. She'd emerged too. For what. For me to plunge her right back in. I couldn't tell her I was ripping another father figure from her. I couldn't upend her world again. I wouldn't. He may have been unfaithful to me, but he was faithful to her. She deserved that.

I fell into the chair, imagining miserably what life looked like without him. For me, for Sloan. It looked exactly like it looked last time. Devastating. Soul destroying.

Digging my nails into my fists, there was an awful sensation I was breaking apart, the pain in my palms the only thing assuring me I was still in one piece. Unbroken. Technically.

"This dalliance is not keeping us from the next fifty years together," he said tenderly, sliding in to spoon me on the same chair. *Dalliance, such a harmless term.*

He whispered into my hair, "You're my person. We're better together."

An adult orphan and a single empty nester. Alone.

Would I be able to forgive myself if I *didn't* give him a second chance?

"There's one thing you *didn't* say in all that," I said quietly.

"I'm sure I missed a million things …"

With my eyes swollen shut, my nose red and running, and a tear-stained face, I turned and tried to see my person in there. Slowly, I held up my three middle fingers.

Looking at them, his expression lightened. The smile was wide, relieved.

"Of course, *I love you!*" Stroking my face with one hand, he held his three fingers up with the other. "I love you to the moon and back!"

Feels like a long way back.

CHAPTER 25

SENSATIONALISM

Rick's strong arms circling me as we slept had always been a source of comfort, but after the events of the day, they were anchors weighing me down. Trying to drown me. I lay trapped. He snored lightly into my neck. The birds started chirping. The neighborhood circulator bus took its first roll-through of the morning. Finally he woke.

Bounding out of bed, he was keen to fix our situation, expediently and effectively. He would problem-solve this peccadillo the way he did every other challenge. As he always told new hires: being challenged is inevitable; being defeated is optional.

He kept up constant conversation over coffee. I replayed file 5 against my will. File 5 was on a forever loop. I couldn't make it stop. The jazz. The laughter. His zipper. Rick rousted me out of my insular hell. He put his hand on mine, the woodsy scent unsettling my stomach.

"Miriam said she could fit us in at nine thirty. I'm not sure where else to start, but I want to come clean with everyone, and I want you to know I will make this right."

"You must need to go to the office," I said with no intonation, just a dead monotone. He must have needed to confer further with cunning Caroline. Get their stories straight.

"Miriam seemed to think it a good idea for us to come in. I'm more than willing."

Gee, thanks. You're one of the good guys. "Sure. Fine. I guess I'll get ready." At least it was an excuse to get away from him for a minute. It choked me. This trying-to-make-nice thing.

Waiting for the water to heat up, I gazed in the mirror. Pasty, shaky, who was that woman? Blessed with solitude in the shower, I lathered up numbly. I cranked the hot water up so hot it stung. But it felt good. Or at least it *felt.*

Sensing movement, I turned. Rick ambled in and settled on the rose love seat, arm outstretched across the back, ogling me. Believing I'd be grateful for the attention.

"Classes are paying off. You look incredible." He glowed with admiration.

I gazed at him in disbelief and turned away slightly so he couldn't see me like this. Naked. Vulnerable.

"Can you … this isn't a spectator thing today," I said faintly.

I couldn't bring myself to use the phrase *shower show.* The things I used to find endearing now seemed elements of an empty charade.

He hadn't moved. Hot water still cascaded over my body. My hands slid up to cover my breasts. His bottom lip protruding in a pout, he rose. Slipped away. Left me on my own. The silence now broken only by the sound of the shower spray.

And fucking file 5. *Please let it stop.* I was despondent; the emotional cutting wouldn't stop. Jamming the palms of my hands deeply into my ears, I prayed to stop hearing it. The pain didn't dull file 5. It didn't mute it. His seat slid back; the seat belt unsnapped.

I was incapable of managing the simplest task. I pulled the same clothes I'd worn yesterday from the pile. Disheveled, but I was upright and clothed. The most I could manage.

The ambience in the car was oppressive. It hit me with a sickening thud. I was occupying the same seat as my husband's mistress. Where she'd … *Could I smell her?*

I jammed my hands between my knees and pushed them deep into the leather of the seat to stop the tremors. He flipped on the radio. No jazz for me. Sports. *Is that it? I'm just the everyday-girl now, the one who looks after him, and he always needs new and exciting?*

In stoic silence, I entered Miriam's office. She exuded empathy, guiding me to sit. I numbly placed myself at the farthest point of the green couch. Rick stopped when he got to Miriam. "I ... wasn't honest last time I was here. I was running scared, trying to cover my tracks. I'm hoping that now ... we can come out of it stronger. It happens, right?" he asked mournfully.

Her eyes bright, she put her small hand on his toned forearm. "It happens every day." Motioning for him to sit as well, she observed us.

The enormity of the moment hit me. Those tears again. *Damn it!* Handing me a tissue from the ever-present box, she said, "Unless you'd rather start somewhere else, I'd like to go back for a moment. Rick, you've had time to reflect. Assuming you were discreet and there were few people who knew, who do you suppose could have sent that text?" She poised her pen over the leather notebook.

Flustered by the question, not wanting to have that conversation, he crossed his arms. "I've no idea, Miriam. After all, you two are the only ones who saw it, and you say it was sent anonymously."

She added, "In situations like this, we have to imagine it's most likely someone with something to gain."

Rick sat stiffly, straight up against the slat-backed chair, legs uncrossed. "Well, we'll never know. And I find it best not to dwell, really."

"Dwelling won't help, that's true. Does it seem as though the only one with something to gain is the woman in question. She wants you free of your marriage."

Oh my God. Miriam thought it was Caroline who'd texted me. She wanted to blow up my relationship. She must've been damn sure she could nail him down if I ended things. Of course she was. She believed they were meant to be together.

"We don't *know* that," Rick said tartly. "In fact, I seriously doubt it."

I choked back sobs. "Nice lady. She may just get her wish ..."

Rick opened his mouth to respond, but Miriam held her hand up for me to continue.

"If she sent that text, she's not exactly the kind of woman—"

He cut me off. "This isn't about the text. This is about what drove me to do what I did. If we're to be honest, it's not like our whole problem is that. That's why we're here. Clearly we had issues, and I made an irresponsible choice, but it can't all be on me, can it?" He delivered this guilelessly, as though it somehow absolved him.

It was a stinging slap. My face even reddened as if it were physical. Having seen him deflect and refuse responsibility, I'd never seen him baldly reassign blame to the victim.

"You ... you're here to tell me I need to own a part in this? I thought you were falling on the sword, 'fixing this' and 'making us stronger.'"

"Nothing's just one person. That's why it's called a couple. I can only say I never meant to hurt you."

The chill from the drafty windows made me shiver. So did the implication.

"You never *meant* to hurt me? What the hell did you think would happen? What I didn't know wouldn't hurt me? What you do isn't wrong as long as you don't get caught?" I peppered him with questions, brittle and bitchy. "So you don't actually think the cheating is wrong, just that you should have been better at it? Maybe that's true. If *she* didn't text me, that means you were so flagrant that somebody felt obliged to clue me in! Do you have any idea how humiliating that is?"

As I vented, Rick helplessly looked to Miriam.

"Rick, it's going to take time for you to get context on your choices, your actions, and the impact they've had on Reilly and on your marriage. I'm going to give you the name of a therapist you might want to see for individual therapy."

His lips pursed.

"That's not to say you can't join Reilly on occasion here, but you have a lot to sort through, and maybe when you've done that work, you'll be able to understand this situation the way that Reilly is experiencing it. Make sense?"

Rick scowled. That wasn't what he'd wanted. He'd made the choice to come to a few appointments and to have Miriam's magic wand pronounce us healed. Agreeing to see his own therapist, though, he accepted the card Miriam offered.

"How has all this made you feel?" Miriam peered at me over her half-rim glasses.

"Like he's lying. Creating issues that supposedly existed to justify what he did."

He was dejected. "This is why I can't talk to you sometimes. You go on the offensive, dead-set on making me look the bad guy. It's what you do."

"*It's what I do?* This is on *you*. *You* did this. If *I'd* been the one who'd …"

"We *know* I've done this. We know I'm the villain here. That's not a question. But … you lie too," he murmured, woefully examining his cuticles.

"Do I? What do I lie about?"

His expression was pained. "Well, I'm not trying to toss you under the bus, but the other night, for starters. You told me you went one place with Billie, but you were somewhere else. Makes a fella wonder. An employee of mine saw you at the Tap Room."

I floundered; it wasn't the same thing. I'd just been too upset about the DUI to …

I'd had enough. "How dare you try to make this about me. I'm *done*!" I whisked past the two of them. Ran for the stairs. Slammed the door behind me. With him only steps behind me, I picked up my pace. He caught me and grabbed my arm as I hit the sidewalk.

"Who are you?" Pounding his chest, I sobbed, oblivious to bustling rush hour traffic in Kalorama. I didn't give a damn at that moment what the diplomats thought of me.

"Who the fuck *are* you?"

He held me. Restrained me, really, as I thrashed wildly.

"Stop, please stop. Everything came out wrong. Can't you understand this is hard, that I know you'd never do the things I did. That it makes me bloody *ashamed?*"

Now you're ashamed? Two minutes ago you were calling me a liar.

Emotional whiplash. As painful as it was sudden, it left me weak. Barely able to stand, I was groggy and fuzzy. My legs gave way. Rick moved in intuitively. One hand cupping my elbow, the other around my waist, he scooped me into his chest. Exhausted, I let him lead me to the car and take me home. He sat me on the couch in the living room.

Wrapping me in a soft alpaca throw, he held me. My teeth chattered uncontrollably. "Please. *Please*," he said. "You're stronger than this now. You can't go back into that hole. You don't want to be back there. You don't want a life that isn't the two of us."

It's not so much I "don't want to"—I can't imagine my life without you. The real truth was I didn't know who I was any longer without him.

We were a *we*; he was my igniter switch. He'd reinvigorated my world. I feared stepping off the roller coaster it had become; I feared nothing would be left when the ride came to an abrupt stop.

Rick went to the office for a few hours when he was sure I was settled. Sinking further into the soft leather couch, I tried to push it away. With all my emotional might.

That dark cloud of betrayal and abandonment floated close by. And it felt so much like it had felt before, when my world had imploded. Heavy and oppressive as it tried to smother me. It was dark and airless under that umbrella of fear. I wasn't going back there. I couldn't. Whatever it took to keep the cloud at bay, I had to do it. My world was at stake.

———

Six hours later, he returned to find me unmoved. I hardly registered his footsteps quietly crossing the house, but there was rustling. Sitting close, he laid things on the coffee table.

"Dinner. From City 41. No reason for you to cook. Your merlot," he said, and produced a few bottles. "And this." Pulling out a yellow lined legal pad, he tore off a page full of his illegible scrawl. "I had my first appointment with Gerry, Miriam's guy, just now, and I know I have real work to do. It started with this. This is my promise going forward. This is what's in my heart."

Extending them to me, he had a hopeful air about him. My eyes filled for the thousandth time. I took the papers. I read his words, hazy through my tears. The first sentences were simple:

My life could never be complete without you. I'm more disappointed with myself than you'll ever know that I haven't spent every minute of every day proving that to you. If you'll allow me, I intend to spend the next fifty years of our life making that up to you.

My heart ached. It was the Rick I'd known for so long. Genuine. Touching. I continued to read as he brought our dinner plates in. I leaned toward him occasionally with words I couldn't decipher, and he'd translate. We laughed about his woeful penmanship, the cloud dissipating to some extent. I could not descend to that place again without giving him a chance.

The sentiments he expressed were deep. Looking in the eyes I'd looked into for so many years, the emotion was real. He meant the things he wrote. It wasn't that I doubted his love for me. I didn't. No one could or would fake that kind of love. But was he remotely capable of the things he promised me. Could he uphold even the most basic tenet of marriage, *and forsaking all others* ...

Tragic that only someone you loved the way I loved him was capable of wounding you as deeply and thoroughly as he had me; that kind of gutting could only be an inside job.

CHAPTER 26

REMOTE

Two weeks later, Rick took me to Bermuda for a few days for a surprise getaway at a resort I'd always had my eye on. He'd packed me a bag and whisked me away. Like old times. It felt like another empty gesture—a Rick-size effort, for better or for worse.

He tried hard, though, to win me back. To assure me I could count on him. He spoke openly about his appointments with Gerry; he addressed the progress they thought he was making. The significant breakthroughs working through the process. He seemed genuine.

Candid and vulnerable, he even revealed that he now saw he'd started to morph into a different person. Admitted that maybe the corner-office mentality and all the yes people had led him to feel beyond reproach. Wasn't that what Claire had said? That he refused to be held accountable? That he'd never forgiven his mother for making him own up to his mistakes? Was that changing?

It finally felt like just the two of us again as we whiled away the mornings, intertwined on the luxurious pillow-topped bed. We watched the resort crowd heading out to parasail or snorkel in the sparkling blue water. We picked at scones and sticky plum jam on the silver room-service tray between us. His hand unconsciously reached for me, tracing the curve of my hip with his fingers. Sharing the newspapers, he'd peel off the business section, hand me the arts section.

Just Rick and Reilly again. Not exactly carefree, but had we ever been? No, we'd always had cares. We were card-carrying adults by the time we'd met. It was one of my favorite things about us, that we'd met as grown-ups. Having lived already, accomplished things, we both knew how precious it was to allow someone into your heart. We embraced the gravitas, as well as the comfort, of the *us*. As opposed to the *I*.

We even vlogged *Life of Reilly* from Bermuda together. Rick partnered me gamely as we explored the island, Gibbs Hill Lighthouse, and a British pub for an upbeat travel vlog, via scooter, Jet Ski, and paddleboard. He kicked my butt at the life-size chess game on the beach but bailed on limbo after the bar dropped. I made it another four spots. In a playoff, we balanced on the rolling log in the family pool. After surviving several jostles and sudden reversals, I was dumped in the drink. He showed off for another moment before jumping in next to me with a dimpled grin on his tanned face, his copper-flecked hair shining.

He was trying. The man was *trying*. And given the current circumstances, now was not the time to get complacent about sex. I ventured out of my comfort zone to keep life spicy, the way he liked it. We'd always had a great sex life, amazing chemistry, and yet since he'd *still* added another woman to his roster, I … I obsessed, honestly, about trying to retain my man, this marriage, my job, if at all possible. I hated myself for it, but I couldn't just pull the plug on us. I had to try *everything*. Desperate times called for desperate measures.

One evening, I unpacked a toy from the Pleasure Palace, fur-lined handcuffs. Not surprisingly, Rick took it further than I'd imagined. He handcuffed me wherever he was—to the Jacuzzi. To the armoire. To the wrought-iron chair on our deck. Hours passed.

This time, I was smarter. I made certain I had control over the scenario. Arranging to "meet" at an upscale watering hole, we'd spy each other across a crowded bar in Hamilton. Our chemistry would be so hot, so intense, that we'd pick each other up right there and then.

He craves new; I'll be new. I went as the anti-Reilly. Provocative and ready for anything. Thigh-high leather boots with a stiletto heel, the kind "not meant for walking," as he'd said. Black stockings. A short, sheer plum dress that revealed the black-lace bra underneath, a hint of nipple. A deep, red lip with tousled, dark beach waves—courtesy of an ombré auburn wig. I inhabited her world.

Strutting into the crowded gastropub feeling sassy, I tossed my hair and peeked up through my new, thick bangs. Men checked me out. I'd made it hard to miss me. I headed straight to the bar. No seats available. Leaning in to order, some breast showing, a dapper man in a blue sport jacket and plaid Bermuda shorts got up and said, "Please." He gestured for me to take his seat.

"So kind, thank you." I perched my boots on the footrest and showed off my long legs to full advantage. The bartender placed the triangular glass in front of me. He poured from the shaker. Martini straight up, two olives. The man who offered his stool said, "Fine looking drink."

Swiveling slightly, I replied, "Fine looking works." Although I hadn't spotted him, I felt Rick across the bar, his eyes on me. Watching me engage with another man.

The bartender leaned his long, tanned arms on the marbled bar top. "That gentleman over there would like to buy you this martini."

Moving my eyes to where he'd motioned, I was appraising. Aloof. Rick held my gaze. A smile slowly spread across his face. Assessing him, I let my eyes flicker up and down before turning back to the jovial barman, his weathered eyes curious.

"Please tell the gentleman that is a very tired approach, and I'll pay for my own drink."

When the message was relayed, the bartender clapped him on the back with a laugh, and they exchanged a look. "Women," it said. Rick raised one eyebrow and watched me intently. As I checked my cell phone. Sipped my martini. Nibbled an olive. Ran my tongue over the rim of the glass.

From behind me, his voice, "I certainly meant no offense. I just couldn't help notice you when you arrived and thought it might be an idea to say hello."

Spinning around on the stool, I looked him up and down seductively. "Well, *hello*."

"See, not so hard, was it?"

"I don't know. *Was* it hard?" My eyes drifting south, I lounged against the bar and displayed my body to full effect. "Come here often?"

"And *you* judged my tired approach? That's rich." He laughed and put out his hand. "I'm Ronaldo." *I got this.*

Hiding a smile, I said, "Charlotte."

"Not much left to the imagination there, Charlotte," he murmured, his gaze settling on my exposed thighs.

I leaned up and whispered sensuously, "You don't have much of an imagination then, do you?" and slowly pushed my already-short dress farther up my thighs. Dangerously close now.

He whimpered quietly. "Unfair."

"Oh, Ronaldo, I never said I play fair. You want fair, find yourself another girl," I replied, turning my back to him. He ordered two more drinks. Leaning over me, he was hard against my back. The pressure made Charlotte hot. Reaching around so no one else could see, I slipped my hand inside his thigh. Ran it up and down. He spun me back around.

"Charlotte, it's a little crowded in here," he said wolfishly.

We made quick work of the cocktail. He stood assuredly in front of me. I twisted and wedged one of my thighs between his legs. His eyes nearly rolled back. He squeezed my thigh and pushed my dark hair from my face. His hand on the back of my head, he pulled me toward him. Lowered his mouth to mine.

My voice husky, my hand against his chest, I pushed. "I don't do things like this."

"Well, you do with me." He grabbed my hand and sucked one of my fingers, never breaking eye contact. He pulled me up. "Come."

I followed, assuming we'd leave. Instead, he dragged me toward the restrooms.

I pulled back in alarm. "No, can't we just … ?"

"You're about to have a great time, Charlotte," he guaranteed as he moved decisively toward the bathrooms. I yanked him hard. He stopped. It was my voice now, Reilly.

"Jesus, sweetie, I can't. In *there*. I really—"

He snapped back and dropped my hand. "Oh for Christ's sake, fine. Why did you bother with this, if you can't just have some fun?" He headed for the entrance, pushing his way through to the street in an instant. I fell in beside him, trying to salvage the evening without having to end it in a grimy, public bathroom.

"Slow down. I just have a thing about public restrooms." I brought Charlotte back, her huskier voice. She flirted shamelessly.

"But I want to be with you, baby. Now. This your car?" I asked when he paused at the rental. He turned and the lusty look returned. I pushed him up against the car. Grabbed his hair with both hands, put my open mouth on his. The direction we never kissed, my face the other way, angled to the left. The kissing, the writhing, a stray moan, I imagined we were being filmed. I cheated my face to the "camera," and amped up my desire. Unlocking the car, we scrambled in, wild and uninhibited. I pushed thoughts of him with *her* in a car out of my mind.

Afterward, panting and perspiring, half-clothed, he laughed. Held me tight under the streetlight. I loathed myself for wondering in that moment, *Was he with* me *or* her?

"You are hot stuff, Charlotte." He was with Charlotte. So now there was another woman on the roster. Charlotte from the bar.

CHAPTER 27

A-ROLL

I craved normalcy. Balance. Everything was so fraught. The highs were high; the lows were an abyss. I didn't want to relive the days of life on the brink. Live vlogging twice a week was the only time I felt like myself, Reilly, in control of the dynamics of my world, taking back the reins.

Logging on to the channel to check the stats, I was horrified. Had I peaked? Viewership had dwindled by 10 percent, a significant problem. Was I not as engaging as I'd once been? It had been hard to bring my A game.

Kickboxing and Muay Thai became an even more important outlet; my body was strong, conditioned. Even if my mind was cluttered. My daily workout was the one time I was clear.

Prepping for Tuesday's *Life of Reilly*, I scanned my posts to determine a hot-button topic that would provide sticky content, noting what had spurred the most comments. With a largely female demographic, a recurring thread revolved around the #MeToo and #TimesUp revelations. A college friend, Millie, had been lauded recently for her brave piece in the *Washington Post*, examining the existing culture, its impact on women in the workplace.

So many firings recently, so many others shaking in their shoes knowing they'd participated in the same culture and were guilty of the same sins. The most recent, a preeminent news anchor for two decades, had been unceremoniously fired for his sexual transgressions. The massive amount of money he'd made for the network no longer mattered. We were suddenly in a zero-tolerance era for powerful men preying on subordinates.

I booked her as a guest. Millie arrived early and sat at the breakfast bar in the kitchen, hungry for human contact. She sipped a sugar-free Red Bull. Seemed she rarely came up for air; funny how you could live in the same town but only manage to get together every year or two with children, husbands, and jobs vying for your attention. She wore a tidy, beige blazer and a crisp white blouse. She checked her notes on her iPad.

I made sure everything was good to go as I lowered the camera and adjusted the ring lights. An inch this way, a quarter inch that way. I determined the optimal frame to have the two of us in the shot. Knowing this was a timely segment, I sent vlog reminders to the entire subscriber list. I was going to shore up my viewership. Today.

My mind settled uneasily on something. Hadn't Rick and I been an imbalanced couple, power-wise, when we'd started our relationship? Had that been part of the allure for both of us, his role of authority, the respect everyone accorded him? And hadn't he enjoyed acquiring my little "brand" and shining it up? Granted, he'd been right. I wasn't working for him in a day-to-day capacity, but still. Wasn't that inequality the genesis of the MeToo movement?

Millie informed me just before we went live, her thin eyebrows arched over her hipster dark-framed glasses, that she was still amazed. "It's happening everywhere, and they're uncovering it everywhere. Maybe you don't see it, being autonomous, self-employed. But at a place like the newspaper?"

"I've seen the coverage. Some powerful men have gone down."

"Sure, it's what gets covered, media moguls, news anchors. The magnates. But that next tier, the one that doesn't sell papers or get you to tune in to *GMA*. Dropping like dominoes."

My next question wasn't just idle conversation. I had started to wonder if there were any teeth in this movement for those "next tier" men.

"So … is it finally time for the Boys' Club to come crashing down, or is this just a public tsk-tsk, boys, and we'll be back to business as usual when it's over?"

She pointed her long, bony finger at me. "Long term, who knows? In the short term, though, they've got a *big* problem. There are a lot of men that should be terrified, hoping their truth doesn't get exposed."

I'll say.

Ironically, the next words out of her mouth were, "You're so lucky Rick's not like that."

That quick hit, zap. It was like a beesting. Made you wince in pain.

When *Life* went live, we talked about the importance of removing the inequality and toxicity from our workplaces. Millie was well informed and concise on the air.

"It's a slippery slope," she said. "There's no way *some* men are entitled to get away with *some* behaviors, unless we choose to entitle *all* men to get away with *all* behaviors."

I replied, "Those scenarios have existed in workplaces for a long time, but we're certainly more aware now of the collateral damage they cause."

With her bony finger, she tapped on the copy of the *Post* she'd put on the island. Repeatedly. "I talked to twenty-seven women. Twenty-four of them were affected in some way by upper-level management and their interoffice liaisons. Some were victimized, some overlooked for promotions because they weren't the chosen one. Some *were* the chosen one, and they were targeted by their peers. It's lose-lose."

"For the women," I said. "Lose-lose for the women. But it's changing now …"

She replied tartly, "It's a *conversation* now. That doesn't equal change. They say don't hate the player, hate the game. Well, without all those players playing, there wouldn't be a game, Reilly. You were in a field rife with it for many years. You certainly saw it."

Shifting uneasily, I was taken aback. "I wasn't privy to much aside from rumors. It's nothing new, but abolishing the culture would go a long way toward parity for women in the workplace. We'd all like to see that." Feeling a little disingenuous after my earlier insights, I deflected to parity. And back to Millie.

The conversation was engaging, and all the phone lines were lit. When we wrapped, and I powered down the lights, I checked the stats. Best numbers I'd had in months. *Yes.* More than a little relieved that I was rebounding, I poured a glass of Malbec when Millie left.

I answered emails and scoured the web for good content. Hearing Rick's key in the door, I moved to the foyer. He was wound tightly and swept by me without a glance. He dropped his briefcase loudly in the kitchen.

What had changed? Things had been better since Bermuda. I mixed his cocktail, made conversation about the vlog: Millie had gained traction at the prestigious newspaper. *Life* viewership had been huge.

"Her passion is commendable, but she's certainly adding fuel to the fire, isn't she?" He peevishly thumbed through the newspaper Millie had left on the counter.

Fuming one night, he'd watched the coverage of whichever mogul had just been ousted. Tumbled by some unscrupulous underling of a woman, Rick had thought.

He gestured to the TV over the fireplace. "Disgraceful. Exactly how Tiger Woods took the hit for every athlete doing the same thing. Poor guy's career was killed, and it will be the permanent postscript now when anyone says his name! When we should be talking about his legacy, his accomplishments."

"You've…. seen a lot of it," I countered resolutely. "Even Gus, you said he's …"

"All *consensual*," he interrupted, slapping the rolled-up paper on the island. "Nobody was ever coerced. Men have always had office flings. It's a tale as old as time, now isn't it?"

Only you can turn this into a fucking Disney movie.

While the interchange was intensely personal, we cloaked it in obtuse generalizations.

"But it's the … power imbalance that makes it hard for the woman to say no. It's flattering, an honor to be with the boss. And that dynamic trickles down to everyone else …"

"So you and Millie said, in every way possible. You're aware that my employees, and Franklin, and the Butler family, tune into my wife's vlog?" His eyes narrowed.

"But I didn't—it's the topic *everyone's* talking about. It would be odd if we –"

He snapped back: "You needn't slyly point the finger at me and every other powerful guy for public scrutiny. It's not a topic you need to dive into. I could ask the Gillsen folks what they think. I'll bet they'd say stick to the light stuff. People *like* you: you're honest; you're cute. A topic like that can sound bitter. Insecure. And by the way, it's men who run Gillsen."

Rick loosened his sky-blue tie and headed upstairs with his drink. I trailed by a few steps, still smarting from the slight, insulted by his implication that I should stick to arranging sunflowers in a mason jar. *Insecure. Insignificant.* And why was he still the middleman with the Gillsen Group. It seemed he could pull the plug at any time.

Halfway up, he said absently, "Oh, listen, I don't know if you're aware these exist, but our social media person said there are filters now you can use when you're shooting video. They soften age lines on your face, take years off, that type of thing."

The verbal slapdown, part two. *Ouch.* The lighting I'd settled on was flattering, or so I'd thought.

Reaching the top of the stairs, he dropped his head. "Jesus. That came out all wrong." He whirled around to see I'd stopped at the base of the stairs.

"I was not implying you *need* a filter. It was just something I heard about." He groaned dramatically, noting my pained expression. "But I know how this goes. I'll *never* live that down. Never. How can I keep being held accountable for things I never intended … ?"

"Well, if I'd said the things to you that you said to me tonight … you're aging ungracefully, you're superficial …"

He banged his hand against the wall. "Precisely. I can't. I can't do this with you. *I love you!* I tell you all the time. I always tell you how great you look. I tell you how entertaining the vlog is. I can't win."

Seething, he did laps around his changing room. "Being here, in this house with you, feels like a pressure cooker to me right now. This isn't healthy for either of us. I think we need to get some distance on this, look at it with fresh eyes down the road."

That final declaration made calmly, evenly, as though it were a natural solution.

I frantically tried to keep up with the careening topics of conversation.

"I don't …" I trailed off. "When you say 'distance' …"

Distance. He just watched me with a sour look. I averted my eyes as he added, "We don't seem to be able to steady this thing. You're all over the place. It occurred to me today after your vlog. I think it's best if I stay at the corporate apartment for a time."

Not sure I'd heard him correctly, I was silent. He draped his clothes over the door. Got into the shower. The corporate apartment. I dropped onto the sofa. I tried to make sense of the suggestion. Actually, it didn't sound so much a suggestion as a fait accompli.

After rinsing off, he just stood and stared out the small shower window.

"We can *date*. A do-over of sorts. I want my girl back, but it's just too heavy here."

On autopilot, I handed him a fresh towel when he stepped onto the mat.

"You want to date me? Well, why can't you just do that living—"

"We need to learn to trust each other again. That vlog ..." He screwed up his face. "You didn't have my back. You facilitated that Millie. I think we'd both benefit from a little space."

I was unable to keep up with the Rick Coaster. This man had just penned a love letter pledging fifty years of making it up to me. Couldn't recall a mention of a corporate apartment anywhere in those heartfelt scribblings.

I stared helplessly through the glass. Based on the look he gave me back – unsmiling, pensive – his intent was clear. His intent was to sleep somewhere else for the first time since we started sharing a bed, a life together. I was adrift, lost.

"But I didn't say anything about ..."

"No. You didn't. You just left it hanging. You left *me* hanging."

Pulling on perfectly weathered jeans, the long-sleeve cinnamon T-shirt I'd given him, he was impatient to still be entertaining this conversation. He switched into action mode.

A prepacked black leather bag appeared on the love seat in the bathroom. Rick added toiletries, a couple of our rolled-up Turkish bath towels. Seemed he wanted to be comfortable, pampered even, as he worked on our marriage. From the corporate flat.

"This will be better. You'll see," he promised, kissing me. "I'm doing real work on myself. Gerry and I think that this could be really positive for our relationship." Why had that been a postscript to the suggestion, an afterthought that his therapist thought this best too?

"Do we have a plan? A time frame? A ..." I sounded pathetic. I wished I could talk to the real Rick, not this imposter Rick who kept setting off grenades in my life. Not this distant, dizzying stand-in. I wanted the real Rick: the real Rick would kick this Rick's ass.

"Good Lord, *Reilly*. I've just said it's a pressure cooker with you. Can you think about taking the pressure off?" He spit out my name like it was the worst of the curse words, the one you'd say under your breath so you couldn't be held accountable. He used to say my name like it was melodic and inspired lyrical passion. Now I was the worst of the curse words.

CHAPTER 28

GLITCH

Click. Standing at the door, I replayed the conversation many times, a new forever loop. So I should have run interference for him. Protected him. Other cars came and went in the neighborhood. The familiar sounds of families, the kids shouting and the dogs barking, made it seem like everyone else got to keep their life, their home, their spouse.

Finally I staggered to bed. Only when the sun peeked through the gap under the blackout curtains was I aware it was morning. Rolling over in grief, a steel vise constricted around me. It suffocated my soul, my heart. Yesterday, I was unaware there was a corporate apartment, and now my husband was staying there. The pressure cooker he'd escaped—it continued to simmer and steam. The difference was that I was the only one in it now. He'd freed himself. He'd escaped the disastrous situation he'd created. *Save thyself.*

My insides burned. I moaned. I clutched my stomach. I knew what was next. Waiting as long as I could, I finally dropped off the bed to the floor and lurched unevenly toward the bathroom. Hurled remnants of last night's Cobb salad. I slid down the wall and propped myself on the tiles, trying to breathe, but the vile taste was still in my mouth. I wondered what his bathroom was like at the corporate flat. Was it as pretty as the one he'd left behind?

A text pinged. Rick. Morning. Hope you slept some. Fancy dinner at Fiola's on Friday? I can swing by and collect you at 6.

I stared. It had already been agony to send him to his office, and now, in theory, he could dash to the corporate apartment whenever the urge struck. And his urge struck often. I knew that.

Suspending disbelief had just gotten exponentially harder.

I texted back: *K*. He hated "K." I couldn't have cared less.

Why couldn't I walk away from him? Was he right when he said I couldn't make it without him? I wasn't a viable commodity any longer? He was watching my vlog stats too?

My daughter would resent me for upending her world, yet again, with my personal crisis. The Gillsen Group would distance themselves were it not for my connection to Rick. What miserable reasons to maintain the status quo.

I stood at the sink and leaned over to rinse my mouth in the waterfall faucet, swishing away the foul taste. With no vlog today, I blew off kickboxing and proceeded to drown my self-loathing sorrows. Hair of the fucking dog.

Day drinking had never been my thing, but I had no sense of time. It had stalled. I didn't wash my face or run a brush through my hair. Didn't brush my teeth; of course not, the mint cream would battle the Bloody Marys. I didn't even doctor them as I normally would to make the commercial mix more palatable. Why? I wasn't even tasting them.

Glass in hand, I stood before my empty bed and pressed my fist hard against my mouth to ward off the fear. Propping myself up, I slurped my Bloody. Ripped open a box of Wheat Thins. Exhausted yet incapable of sleeping, I dropped onto the bed and willed the next drink to put me over the sleep threshold.

An unexpected sound in the otherwise silent house. A key turned in the front door. Was it Rick? I tried to sit up. What if he saw me like ... but it was Sloan's voice that rang out.

"Mom? Surprise!" *No.* Running through the lower level and not finding me, she flew into my bedroom. "I know you're home, I saw ..."

In my doorway, she slowly registered my condition. Her startled eyes dropped from my face to my disheveled hair—to the drink in my hand. Trying to process that I didn't look like Mom, her eyes veered to the clock on the bedside table. Mine followed. That couldn't be right. Maybe the electricity had gone off at some point. Not even noon: 11:57. Did the clock need a reset?

She hovered hesitantly in her white denim jacket and leggings. Twirled her hair on her finger. "I saw ... packages on the porch. Have you not been out ... at all?"

Heat rising in my face, I put my glass on the table, motioned her to come give me a hug on the bed. Thinner than before, she felt slight in my arms. Her usually full face was delicate.

It wasn't judgment, but worry, I saw in my daughter's eyes. With a forced laugh, I could only dredge up the tired adage: "It's five o'clock somewhere. I'm so off my normal schedule, I've been working crazy hours."

Nodding solemnly, she sat next to me on the bed, her eyes big and sad.

"I'm so glad you're here." I summoned a chirpy tone. "How about I make you some lunch? How long can you stay?" Distracting her with questions, I swung my legs over the bed and willed them to hold me up.

"How about I make *you* a little something, Mom?"

Ashamed, I followed her. She pointed to the padded kitchen stool. I sat, my hands gripping the seat beneath me. I watched her assemble a ham and swiss on rye with mustard. My stomach roiled, but if it would please Sloan, I would get through a few bites. I hoped I looked pleased, not queasy.

"I just wanted to see your face." She used the phrase I'd said to her so many times over the years. I made myself smile. Got us each a Diet Coke from the drinks drawer in the refrigerator. Sometimes carbonation helped the queasies.

"What's going on?" she asked apprehensively, throwing her jacket on a chair in the breakfast nook. "I watch *Life*. You don't look like yourself. I … I haven't seen you like this in a long time."

I flinched at the reference. "I'm fine!" I insisted. "This isn't what it looks like, believe me. Let's get you settled and go for a walk on the C&O towpath. Sound good?"

She agreed. "We can talk. Sounds good. Oh! This was very last minute. I brought next to nothing. Okay if I hit up your linen closet for one of the extra toothbrushes?"

"Of course, sweetheart. That's exactly what they're for." I followed her, climbing the stairs, babbling about the happenings in the neighborhood. Picked up shoes I'd left on the landing to go back to my closet. She stopped abruptly at the door. I came to a stop behind her.

She stared intently at Rick's sink; the counter around it usually held meticulously placed products: hand lotion, face wash, two or three toothbrushes in the holder, his sterling silver comb. My gaze followed hers.

The water glass was there, the steel toothbrush holder, too, with one lone toothbrush, the bristles misshapen from heavy use. Nothing else. In stark contrast to the other sink, mine; there were eight or ten face and hair products on the counter. Toothpaste, a few toothbrushes.

Catching my own reflection in the mirror over his sink, I was horrified. Swollen eyes, bedhead hair, the sweats I'd slept in. *Is that what I look like? Is this what she's seeing?*

"He puts all his things in the drawers now. He read something about bacteria," I mumbled. Sloan turned to the linen cupboard outside Rick's changing room. The door to his closet was half-open. I had yet to notice, not having been back up, but the closet was thin on clothing. Half of it was gone. The shoe racks were nearly empty.

Sputtering, massaging her temples, she lost all color except for the intense eyes. She perched on the side of the bathtub. "What's going on? Are you guys … on the outs?"

"Oh my God, no. This … is me, not getting to the dry cleaner to pick up his things. It's on my list for tomorrow. Otherwise he'll have to wear jeans to the office," I said with a nearly believable laugh. "Don't let your imagination run wild, you."

Reaching into the cupboard, she took out a spare toothbrush and darted one more glance into Rick's closet. She quickly disappeared down the stairs. I stared back into the barren changing room. What must she think? Running down the stairs in hopes of saving this disastrous moment, I called out—gaily, I hoped. "You never said how long you're here. We could …"

Sloan turned back. "Mom. Will Rick be here tonight? Honestly, is he still even … ?"

I plumbed the depths of my mind. I conjured up a conversation that had never happened but *could* have happened, had things been normal. "I think he had a work thing tonight. Overnight in New York. That must be what he was saying this morning; I was half-asleep."

I brightened up for her, recalling a real conversation. One I could use to deflect. "Oh, *that's* why he reminded me about date night at Fiola's on Friday—because he's away on business." Picking up her Under Armour bag, I dropped it on her bed. She seemed a little lighter now. He and I had a plan. That sounded more like us. She pulled her jersey nightie out of the bag—it must swim on her now, judging by the size of her.

"He's been craving their puttanesca," I added. Details and embellishment, it could only help. "And their crusty bread—the only time he bothers with bread."

"Date night is always good." She smiled. "Fiola's. You're living large, Mom."

Putting fresh towels in her bathroom, having barely recovered from the brink of today's disaster, I did not feel like I was living large. My husband was, in fact, living somewhere else.

After a brisk walk, we left our muddy shoes on the porch door-mat. Sloan puttered in her room. I kept her company, curled up on her sofa. A text pinged. Rick. *Fiola's was booked for Friday, but Matteo did me a favor. Molto grazie* ●. I turned my phone to her.

There was a time, just briefly, when I considered confiding in Sloan. Glancing over at her, she had the weight of the world on those now-scrawny shoulders. I asked, "Is there anything else? Anything you're not telling me? Neither of us really looks ourselves at the moment."

Her spirits seemed low, she pulled her feet under her. "Going through a rough patch. You know how it is. My best friend in the program, Jess, she quit. She moved to Maine with her boyfriend. They're opening a restaurant. Cathy moved back with her parents to save money. With her commute I don't see much of her. So I just don't have anyone right now."

I scooched in next to her on the bed. "I'm sorry. Have you thought about talking to someone? I could get some suggestions ..."

"I found someone in-network on my insurance," she said, pulling his card out of the sleeve on the back of her sky blue phone case. "He's good, I think. I go to group. It's mostly girls in their twenties, anxiety, some food issues. It's not an eating disorder. My stomach just isn't right when I'm anxious. Anyway. It helps to talk about it." So mature now, looking after her own insurance issues, mental health issues. And then there was me. Looking after noth-ing: neither myself nor her. Back in that place of unconsciousness.

So wrapped up in my own shit that I had been unaware. That she'd been emotionally floundering. That she might be headed to-ward an eating disorder. That anyone had snags in their life beside me. My heart ached for my girl.

"Mom! Don't look like that," she exclaimed. "It's just standard stuff. No biggie, okay?"

Heartened that she could speak about it so openly, that she felt none of the stigma that I had in the dark days, I was hopeful. She pulled on her old sweats and fuzzy slippers.

"C'mon," she said, and tugged me. "Let's watch some *Gossip Girl*. We could use something mindless." I pulled out the panini maker and grilled up her favorite indulgence: crispy peanut butter and banana sandwiches. She ate the whole thing. Even if it was only to please me, that was fine. After an hour of Blair and Serena's romantic mishaps, Sloan fell fast asleep on the couch. I pulled the sage throw over her, smoothed her hair off her face just like when she was little.

This had to stop: the lies of omission with Sloan had to end. She wasn't a child. She was *my* child, always, but she was an adult. Dealing with her own adult issues, and I hated the thought of adding to that. The truth was she knew something was wrong. She knew it.

I slept harder than I had in recent days, maybe because my daughter was back under my roof. A door slammed loudly, jarring me awake.

CHAPTER 29

FEATURE

With a start, I grabbed my phone from the night table. Nine for-ty-one. Throwing on my faded cutoff shorts and a white tee, I raced down the stairs, sport flip-flops in my hand. I tried to recall the time of Sloan's train. Was it ten fifty-five? A note was propped on the counter: *Mom, I'm glad you slept. I didn't want to wake you so I called for a car. Do not worry about me. I'm doing fine. Hugs and stuff, S*

The door slam was Sloan. She'd made her own way down to Union Station. I loved dropping her there in the big circular entry, flags flying. *Damn.* I dropped onto a chair in the breakfast nook. In the too-harsh light of day, my head pounded. I struggled to rebound from a stressful visit and the concerning news that Sloan was having a tough time.

Need. Coffee … sometimes only Starbucks could cure what ailed you.

I tapped on the counter impatiently while a fledgling barista consulted her tattered prep sheet. She slowly tapped away at the espresso holder and packed the ground beans in tightly. *Finally.* She handed me the cup in the recycled sleeve. I savored the strong, sugary drink, heading home. How had it happened? The chasm in my marriage seemed so vast now. My daughter was going through a crisis of her own, and seeing me as she had likely compounded any anxiety she had.

Navigating the familiar, windy lane, I swerved around a sharp bend toward the single-lane bridge that should've been done away with years ago, I thought idly. Without taking my eyes off the road, I reached for my double macchiato. A sudden, chilling sensation.

What the hell? The car vaulted into a skid. Reflexively, I gripped the wheel harder. In horror, trees blurred; what had previously been behind me was now in front of me. The car was in a spin. My stomach churned. The minivan on the other side of the bridge had started to cross.

To one side of the bridge, a swathe of mature evergreens, to the other side, a dirt pull-off followed by a ravine down to the river. In slow motion and fast motion simultaneously, my car spun again. *Oh my God.* I had to choose—trees or ravine.

Brake, for fuck's sake, brake! I tapped first. They didn't engage at all. I hit the brakes hard, then jammed them repeatedly. Nothing. I seemed to gather momentum.

I was numb. Helpless. I fleetingly considered flinging myself out of the car, eyeing the spinning pavement to see if I could scramble far enough to avoid the car hitting me.

Perilously near the low guard rail at the start of the bridge, I chose. The bumpy dirt lot might slow me. The car lurched down the lip from the pavement to the lot and vaulted across the narrow patch heading for the embankment. *No. God no.*

I shoved my hands against the frame of the car and pushed my feet against the floor. Heaving to one side, I looked down at the river lapping at the ravine and braced myself. I was airborne. My head cracked violently against the window with the first impact on the jagged outcropping. My lungs contracted with such force I was sure they'd cave in.

After the first slam, sickening sounds of metal crunching and glass shattering. Strangled screams. Coppery blood pooled in my mouth, dripped off my jaw onto my shirt. *This can't be how it ends.*

A montage of memories flashed as I careened and banged my way down the rocky outcropping. Sloan. Rick. Billie. My parents. Like one of those forever-loop slideshows at a wedding. Or a funeral. I didn't get to say goodbye or I love you. Or I'm sorry. *An epiphany.* If I survived, it was my second chance. A chance to get back on track. Could that be why this was happening?

Another slide down the sheer outcropping, immense weight on the passenger side. The frame of the car shuddered massively. The floor mats launched, belongings scattered, scalding macchiato splattered across my chest. One huge clump of underbrush stopped the momentum. For a moment. Then the car shifted with a lunge.

The driver's-side doors screeched down the final dirt path toward the water. My face pressed with such force against the glass I couldn't move it. Then it all stopped. The intense crunching, the jarring hits. Stopped. At the water's edge. With a final wrench, the car dislodged and splashed into the rushing river, trunk first. Stopped by a boulder protruding from the water with green markings to warn kayakers. It heaved a final time before slumping into the loose silt.

An intense buzzing filled my ears. I was awed by the abrupt silence—the calm after the crash. But I was alive. I seemed to be alive.

Help, please, help! I screamed hoarsely, helplessly.

What I could see of my car was mangled, doors caved in, windows in jagged shards.

How could I escape this steaming, acrid-smelling carcass of a car?

My vision got blurrier and faded away to darkness. The agony brought me back, faded away, back again. My ribs, my foot, my neck, it was all excruciating. Fading away was better.

Was this how it ended? Could I just fade away?

No one knows you're here. No one can help. It's up to you.

I rooted frantically for my phone. It was lost in the chaos. *Shit.* A fist of gray smoke rose in front of me, dense and angry over the choppy water. The front of my car clung to a slate ledge.

In fear and agony, I peered through the half-opened sunroof at the rusty underbelly of the rickety overpass. My escape hatch, provided I could lift myself up. I jerked my jammed foot out from under the brake.

Crouching on the seat, I shoved my head and shoulders out and willed the rest of my body through. Excruciating pain as I squeezed through the small sliver of opening. The frame scraped along my spine.

This isn't how it ends. I get my second chance.

One last yank and I tumbled onto the hood of the car in a heap. The metal bounced me off, kicking me into the shallow, frigid water. It was a first step. I was out. Hot tears of hope and renewal. Rick would feel so blessed that we got our happily-ever-after. If I could just keep going.

It was unforgiving terrain in one remaining flip-flop and cutoffs. I tried to stand, and sharp pain pierced my left foot. I persisted. I would die trying, not die not trying. The underbrush gouged my legs. I dropped to all fours. The pain felt once removed, as though it were someone else's.

As if in a dissociative fugue state, Rick's voice wafted in. "Sweetheart?" A figment of my imagination, a cruel mind game, but I couldn't help myself. I looked toward the dirt pull-off and … I squinted at the lanky figure half running, half falling down the rocks. *How?*

"Rick?" I called. My heart pounded. Was it a hallucination I willed, or was I unraveling?

Sliding down the dirt path between rocks, he reached me. He was real. He lifted me from the ground. "You scared me. You're going to be fine. I'm here now." His voice cracked.

I extended my arms to him and touched the familiar shoulders; he gingerly kissed the top of my head. Circling his arm around my waist, he helped me up over steep outcroppings. Dragged me through craggy brush.

A small gathering of stunned people had gathered at the top. As we neared them, they shouted words of encouragement. My emotions were raw. I wept as I pulled myself up and over the lip onto the dirt. Looked at that empathetic little group: one man, a few women, a concerned collie. They'd been on my side. They'd willed me along. Just beyond them, paramedics pulled in.

A tiny blonde EMT rushed over; she instructed me to sit. Was it a teen intern, I wondered, or just an incredibly slight, petite … ?

She took charge. "We need to check you out before we send you on to the hospital. I'm Katie. Your name?"

"Reilly."

The witnesses inched closer. "Oh my God, we thought she was a goner."

"That was insane. Her car just flipped off the road."

"I think that's Reilly, y'know? *Life of Reilly?*"

Rick hovered while Katie checked me out. She kept me talking the whole time, to be sure I was lucid, I supposed. I was moved that Rick was there for me. *We're back. Maybe we're back.*

He stroked my hair while she checked my reflexes and my spine. She bandaged abrasions and deeper wounds capably. "What hurts? Scale of one to ten."

"Everything. My foot. My head. Nine, I guess."

"Could be a fracture." She prodded my instep with increasing pressure, and I jerked back. "Yup. You're going to be real beat-up and sore, but you made it."

"So can I go?" I pushed.

Before Katie could look up from her notes, an officer who'd been observing said, "Not yet. I have some questions, if you're up to it." Well built, with a blockish, Flintstone head that was too big for his hat, he shooed the crowd away with a jab of his stubby finger. Rick stayed.

"I'm going to need you to step over there," he said to Rick, motioning toward the others.

Rick didn't budge; he kept murmuring to me as though he hadn't heard.

"Please, sir. Step away," the officer said, sharply now. He stepped in Rick's direction.

"No, he can stay. He's my husband." I put my hand in his; the pain dissipated as I looked at our hands together. *It was worth it, after all.*

"Ma'am, I need to speak with you alone."

"Oh. I ... okay ..." Sensing Rick was resistant and oddly annoyed, I looked up with imploring eyes that said, *Please don't make a fuss.*

Leaning in, he kissed my forehead. "I'll be right to the side there." He loped off in the opposite direction of the onlookers. He held his middle three fingers up, and I responded in kind.

The officer sat me down. He asked me to describe exactly what had happened. I tried. I had frighteningly few concrete recollections once the car launched.

"I don't need to tell you how incredibly lucky you are to have survived this. The last two cars that went down there—well, they didn't end as well." Somberly, he took notes.

I was horrified they hadn't made it. Guilt washed over me. Other people hadn't escaped that ravine. They hadn't gotten to continue their lives.

I get my second chance. It's for all of us.

"So we've determined speed wasn't a factor in this accident." His eyes focused on the image of my crumpled car on his iPad. He swiped through photos. Off to the side, Rick was getting antsy, eyeing the officer.

"Gotta say I find this a little strange, and I've documented a lot of these scenes." The officer held my gaze with an unwavering, inscrutable expression. His next question stunned me.

"You've been through a lot today, a whole lot, but I need you to think, ma'am. Anyone else have access to that vehicle?"

"No one. It's just mine. No one else drives it." What was the implication, that my daughter or my husband had something to do with it? I refused to consider how ludicrous that was. This wasn't a *Dateline* special. This was my life—and no one was tampering with anyone's car.

"So no one has access?"

"No," I said definitively. "I … I was momentarily distracted. Other people have gone off the roadway right there too. You just said that."

And the other people hadn't made it. Unsteady and fuzzy, I knew how the end had been for them. I knew the utter helplessness. The trees started to spin, a blur of … seeing me get faint, he guided me to the ambulance. Rick tucked his phone away and addressed the officer. He spoke over the piercing scream of the siren as he helped me into the emergency vehicle.

"I'll accompany my wife to the hospital. Thank you for all you've done." The heavy door slid closed. I was in the quiet tin can of a car with an oxygen mask over my face. Unconsciously I tried to bat it off, nudge it away, in that moment failing to understand it would give me life, not take it away. The paramedic held it firmly in place without looking. She spoke to Rick.

"She'll need a way home, if they let her out today." *If.* He complied, jumping in his car.

The flurry of activity at the hospital was unnerving. The lights were bright, and the trolleys and trays clanged loudly. Doctors and residents called back and forth down the stark halls. Rick arrived and immediately pulled a chair alongside the gurney.

Countless doctors floated in and out. Scans were conducted. I was hooked up to multiple constantly beeping monitors. Hushed conversations were held just outside the door. There was no doubt I'd been severely banged up, but serious injuries were few. Likely due to my physical conditioning. Fractured bones in my foot, possible concussion, but time would tell. Abrasions, contusions, strained muscles. Numerous aches and pains. More would develop in the coming days. I was deemed well enough to leave. A mental health professional was last. Tall and plump, with her frizzy hair in a bun at her neck, she rolled a metal stool close to me.

"The thing with something like this," she said, her elbows on her knees, "it lingers in your subconscious. You just can't process a life-threatening incident in the moment; it lives on for some time." She consulted the board in front of her and continued, "I'd be aware of that, in your case. Particularly in your case." Her squishy hand reached for mine.

"Given your family history, your parents, I wouldn't rule out post-traumatic issues for you following this." She eyed Rick, his arm still circling me silently. "Her prescriptions are ready. Watch for signs in the coming days. I've noted them on these dispatch papers. Signs of concussion, post-trauma—you need to be her eyes and ears."

Strangely elated when they finally sprang me, I longed to be home. I changed from the blue hospital gown into my cutoffs, distressed threads dangling from the hem. Rick's hand protectively across my thigh, we headed to the house, where he fed me leftover Mediterranean chicken, lifting pieces on the fork and guiding them to my mouth. He flipped the big-screen TV over the fireplace mantel on and left it on HGTV—he set the volume low. There were just flickering lights and muted voices.

I knew he was reeling from the thought of nearly losing me. Quietly, we sat side by side. He was lost in thought. No doubt berating himself for recent strife in our marriage. Were the roles reversed that was what I'd have been doing. *We have another chance; go easy on yourself.*

He brought me water. Room temperature, the way I liked it. Laid my favorite Pepto-Bismol-pink blanket from Sloan's room across my lap and smoothed it over my thighs. I dropped my head to his shoulder.

"Did you want me to stay tonight?" The words filled me with a nauseated wave of disbelief. I stared into the fireplace. Had he missed something? I'd nearly died.

"Well, I'm alive, so I guess that means I'm fine to be alone," I answered softly, assuming he'd see that he wanted to be at home—for me, for us, and for our new chapter. I slowly absorbed that we may have had two very different experiences tonight. "I mean, you don't *need* to stay ..."

Nodding brusquely, he rose. He jogged up the stairs and re-appeared with jeans and a black T-shirt from my closet, dropping them on the ottoman.

"In case you want to change," he offered. I looked down. I was still in cutoffs and the T-shirt from the accident, coffee stains merging with darkened, dried blood spatters. He swiftly dropped a couple of Ambien and a few pain pills on the coffee table. With a glass of wine.

"Give me a shout if you need anything," he called from the foyer. The door clicked shut behind him. My eyes drifted up to the TV, flickering lightly, a marathon of the eternally devoted Chip and Joanna. *If? If I need you ...*

In the darkness, my heart ached in an entirely new and excruciating way. Pressing my palm against my chest, I hoped it would mute the pain. This pain was far worse than any physical injury from the accident. What was it that doctor had said? It was too much to process.

This was not a man who cared for me. It had taken nearly losing my life to gain that clarity. He left me after that accident; he never came back that night.

The truth was unavoidable. But it was the truth. My husband would have done more for a stranger.

CHAPTER 30

KICKER

I'd finally drifted into an oversubstanced, fitful sleep (thanks to merlot 'n' meds) on the couch. Yet somehow I had no idea how I'd stumbled up. And there I was, unable to stop my sudden tumble down the steep stairs, even as I grabbed wildly for the handrail. *No.* That only propelled me down. I hurtled again. Over the rail, plummeting down the deep, damp, stone well beyond.

I clawed at the moss-covered sides of the well. So cold, so damp, so hard. And incessant banging … it …no, I'm not going to make it. I bounced off the jagged stone again. My head cracked against the rock. Tucking into a ball, I anticipated the next slam against the side …

Loud rapping roused me slowly; I was bleary, heavy. But I wasn't careening down a well at all. My pulse raced uncomfortably. I slowly emerged from what had been a nightmare. A terrifying odyssey. I tried to focus.

The inescapable light pained my eyes—underneath my lids felt gritty, scraping when I blinked. Every part of my body hurt. My head throbbed, and it didn't seem my neck would be able to support its enormous weight. The surface my head lay on was ice cold and unforgiving.

Ceramic tile. Disconcerted, I twisted my head. Tiles. I wiped my mouth. Drew my palm across the sleep drool that had formed between my face and the tile. The green glass tile, the guest bathroom. I was on the floor in the bathroom.

The bar for a new low had just dropped to the lowest rung with a deafening clatter. I searched the recesses of my brain. How did it happen that I was prone on the floor? I came up empty. I gagged.

Pulling myself to sitting, I could only guess I'd headed to the bathroom in my overly medicated condition. And never made it back out. I didn't remember heading to the bathroom. I must have listed to one side, fallen to the ground, and remained there for God knows how long. Until now. It had been a long time. Every part of me was cold and shivering.

I'd passed out. I was unconscious. By the toilet. Like an indigent. I'd lost control. I'd lost it. Ashamed, disgusted that I was spiraling—cloaked in haziness, a vague memory of Rick returning last night. Sitting near me for a moment, disappearing at some point. That didn't make sense, though. Why would he have left?

Was that a hallucination, a drug-and-drink-fueled mirage?

Aggressive rapping with the brass knocker now. *What the hell?* Rinsing my face, limping into the foyer, I spied a frazzled Billie through the door. She snatched her aviators off and threw her arms up. She mouthed something, no doubt filthy, and gave me her signature withering look.

"What gives? I've been calling you all afternoon, and I was freakin' worried!" Grabbing my phone from the island, I saw four voice mails, all from Billie. The most recent sent at three ten. What the hell time was it? Three twenty-one. Had I been on that floor all day?

The vague scent of Rick still clung to the phone, or was I imagining that too?

"Well, you look like shit. Glad you're alive …" She swooped in for a bear hug.

"No!" I yelped loudly, pain shooting through my ribs, my neck. Stepping back in horror, she took in the bruises and cuts on one side of my face, the bandaged calf, the limping …

"I was planning to call you. I had an accident yesterday. This sounds insane, but ... I ... I flipped my car somehow. A few times. I'm okay but ..." I listed to one side; this was the longest I'd stood upright since the accident.

Frightened, she guided me back to the couch and sat herself across from me, paging through the dispatch papers from the hospital on the coffee table. Eyes frantic, she breathed out, "Jesus H. Christ. Start talking."

Spinning, launching into the river, and climbing out of the ravine. I told her the harrowing tale. It all sounded unthinkably awful, recounting it out loud for the first time. She could hardly bear the gory details. I let her know that it was Rick who had come to my rescue, virtually pulling me to safety. That he'd stayed with me at the hospital.

All the time I spoke, she inspected my gouged foot, checked the bandage for fresh blood. She looked closely at the bruises and scratches on my face, my neck.

"The police that were there, the EMT, they said if Rick hadn't been there, it might have ended for me like the couple of people who didn't get as lucky," I informed her. Not exactly what they'd said, not even close, but he *had* been there, and he *had* helped me when I needed him—even though it had since become sadly clear to me that he was less than devoted.

Still rattled from the accident, from passing out in the bathroom, I wasn't sure I could give Billie the real deal just yet. She'd worry. She'd seen me in the abyss before, the black hole. Never one to miss anything, she scanned the room. She was ablaze with anger on my behalf.

"Stop. My ears are bleeding. Speaking of Prince Charming, where the fuck is he?"

Too depleted and heartbroken to continue to cover for him, I told Billie about what had gone on while she was away. Dean, the DUI. That he was spending time at the corporate place. That he hadn't stayed after the accident; he'd left me to go there once the hospital released me.

"Jackass. Just left you on your own. So you're separated?"

"*No.* God, no. It's … I'm sure it's temporary." I flushed.

The look she shot me was the jaded one of a cop's daughter. I loved my friend for pushing, for caring, but I was almost unable to tell her. Was it grief, or was I mortified I'd recovered from the Alex era only to find myself mired in what Billie would certainly deem a far-worse situation. With a far-worse guy.

My eyes filled, and a few tears plopped onto my upper cheek, one after the other. She slowly slid in next to me, her signature patchouli fragrance lightly enshrouding her. My flesh prickled with shame, an agitated heat rash of humiliation.

"He … ," I began miserably. "The implication of the text was true. He had a girlfriend. Or has, I don't know. At the office. And … I don't know if the apartment has to do with her, or if he ever meant this. I don't even know anymore."

I fumbled in the drawer and handed her the moving letter he'd written. Scanning it, there was no change in her expression until she dropped it back on the table and crossed her arms in front of her. Her lips trembled.

"It's not fair, damn it. You treat that man like gold. Does he not understand loyalty at all, developing a real trust with someone? What the hell does he expect you to do, just accept this?" she asked, motioning at the yellow paper. "It's words. Well, sorry, Charlie, actions matter too. And his actions *suck.*"

Billie grabbed my phone and hit his number, her mouth curled into an angry frown.

"Hey, love," Rick answered.

"Sorry, not your 'love,'" Billie snapped. "I'm confused. Why is your wife here alone at a time like this, after an accident like that?" She clicked on speakerphone.

"Ah, look who's back in town. I know it all *sounds* quite dramatic, and it was, but she's fine. Trust me, I was there. I should know."

"Yes, you *should* know. Here's the thing, Rick. We're supposed to be here for the people we love when they need us. How *could* you?"

"Well, *Billie*. Here's the thing: she asked me to leave last night, if you must know. And she was in quite a state, so I didn't think it wise to distress her further."

Billie looked at me inquisitively. I shrugged helplessly. I didn't think that was how it had gone down, but it had come out of the blue, it had happened so quickly.

She persisted. "Still. Doesn't matter; you could've called me, or stay just 'cuz it's the right thing to do." The silence reeked of disapproval. It just hung there.

Rick offered an icy, "Are you seriously implying my wife drove off a cliff and I just left her? Of my own volition. You may not think much of me, but even you know better than that—"

She cut him off. "I don't, though. I just find it hard—"

He returned the favor and spoke over her. "Maybe just sit this one out. It has nothing to do with you."

"Thanks for the suggestion, boss, but I don't remember asking for your opinion," she snarled back. I jumped up and grabbed for the phone, but he was gone.

Billie stood inches from me, nose to nose, trembling with fury. And fear.

"You're a real smart girl. You know something's not right here. And if you *cry* again, I'm gonna *kill* you!"

I stood unsteadily, her eyes boring into mine. I had no words. Helping me to the soft suede chair in my office, she seated me gently. Tucked a squishy pillow behind me.

"You asked him to leave? Why the hell would you do that, girl?"

Weary, overwhelmed, I tried to recall the exact words, but it was fuzzy. "No. I think he asked if he needed to stay, and I ... I was sure he would, I didn't ..."

She waved her hand, dismissing the semantics. "And it's for sure this was an *accident*?"

"I ... what else ... that's crazy. I was distracted. Tired." Another lie of omission. Stop.

She glowered as she dialed her dad, Walter, on my phone and put me on with him. It was quick. He was an ex-cop, after all—no nonsense, no fluff. Walter said he'd have a guy in DC check out my car at the lot it was towed to for any signs of foul play. Get back to me ASAP.

"There won't be any. That's not Rick. You guys don't know him."

"Look. He's gaslighting you. You're not thinking straight. None of this," she said, gesturing around. "None of this is right. Or normal. Capisce?"

I agreed. None of this was normal. It all looked the same as it always had; it just wasn't. What had happened to my life? "I used to wonder how I got so lucky."

"Yah, well, when you start askin' yourself how you got so lucky, you damn well didn't."

Making my way slowly to the kitchen, I got Billie a Dasani for the road. She dug for her keys and asked carefully, "You seein' him again? Will he stay here? How's that gonna go?"

"Rick's taking me to Fiola's tonight. We're ... dating. He wants to romance me," I said, aware of how pathetic that sounded. Crunching her face in disgust, she yanked on her keys.

"Well, at least you'll have to freakin' eat. Those jeans are hanging off you."

She wasn't wrong, I tugged at the loose waist. "I can only hope bony is the new thirty."

Her Converse high-tops squeaked on the wood floors when she spun back to me. She shook, like a bottle about to lose its cork.

"That garbage come from him? That you're-over-the-hill, you're-worthless-without-me shit? Gaslighting. Dude's manipulating you, but good."

CHAPTER 31

CLICKBAIT

Fiola's was adorned with twinkling white lights everywhere. Matteo was at the door when we arrived and welcomed us warmly. "Grazie mille, mio amico," Rick said with a double-cheeked kiss. Matteo chatted animatedly in Italian, using his hands as much as his words. He ushered us through the back to the main kitchen, which was the original cottage, whitewashed brick, with a walk-in fireplace—in contrast to the ultra-modern, stainless commercial ranges the chefs were working.

Rick whispered with pride, "Matteo arranged for the cranky chef to create a chef's table. Just for us." The chef's actions were like a choreographed ballet, every element synchronized beauty. The food was exquisite, plated art; the enticing aromas of fresh garlic, ripe tomatoes, and pungent cheeses were the only reason I could get any food down. As conflicted as I was about my life, the entire show was a much-needed distraction from the turbulence churning inside me.

Rick ordered me a martini and a Manhattan for himself. As our private soiree at the chef's table progressed through the amuse-bouche, the salad, entrée, and cheese course, Rick's mood lightened. He'd pulled off a special evening.

As we drove back, neither of us mentioned the apartment or his plan for the evening. We talked about anything but. "I spoke with the insurance people today. I didn't think that was anything you'd want to handle." True, I had no desire to relive that accident or deal with the details, yet it brought me back to our first encounter. Rick going rogue. Dealing with insurance, not dealing with insurance, whatever worked for him in the moment.

Now Rick taking control was just another trigger. I almost died. Did it even matter?

"They said they'd cover a rental car until we decide on a new vehicle, but I declined. I was certain you wouldn't want to drive."

My face reflected in the glass of the passenger door frightened me: my eyes were dark holes, and deeply shadowed cheekbones reflected the blackness of the night. The streetlights gleamed around the edges; I touched the odd negative of myself.

"I'll have to at some point—I can't be a complete shut-in. I'll get the rental, and I'll drive when I'm comfortable," I said flatly.

"Perhaps. But why put yourself through that? It's not like there's so much you have to leave the house for. And if you do, I can take you." That taxi service sounded like pure misery.

"*Driving Miss Daisy*. You'd get tired of that. I'll just get the car." I got the distinct sense he liked that I was housebound, dependent on him. Even during a night at Fiola's, we were remanded to a private room. My world kept getting smaller.

He recoiled. "*Driving Miss Daisy*. You did not say that. You sound like my mum. That's what *she* calls it. Christ." He barked a short, aggrieved laugh of contempt. At Diana. Or at me.

In the silence that followed, he wistfully grasped my hand. "I do wish you had let me stay with you after the accident; it was upsetting not to be with you, not to be able to check on you."

I turned away from the window. "That's not … you asked if I needed you to stay …"

"No. That was you … you *told* me to leave. You left me no choice," he said firmly, his face etched with concern and, quite possibly, irritation. At me.

Revisionist history. I wasn't even in my right mind. "To be fair, it was your decision. I was in pain. I was awake all night hoping …"

"Ah, no. You don't recall things the way …" Tightly, he ended it. "Not to worry, it's in the past. I sat in my car outside in the driveway all night, in the event you needed me."

I stared at him. I was stunned. He sat in his car overnight? If he'd wanted to leave, he would have left—not stayed at the house all night. Just when I'd thought he was a lost cause—that *we* were a lost cause. I'd been inside, praying he cared. He'd sat outside, proving he did.

No denying that heading into the house together felt familiar, like the good years, the great years. Flipping off lights, we walked through the warm, inviting kitchen and living room. Rick said tenderly, "I do wish I could sleep with you tonight, but I can see you're still in pain."

His arm circled my waist, and he helped me up the steps to our room. Gently removing my clothes, he grabbed one of his soft oversize jerseys, dropped it over my head, smoothed it down my thighs. He extended his hand, palm flat, fingers beckoning. Was I supposed to hold it?

"*No electronics.* You need to sleep tonight. Trust me, doctor knows best," he said, and gave me three pills (one for sleep, two for pain) with a glass of wine. Placing the fluffy, down-filled comforter over me, he retreated quietly with my phone tucked in his blazer pocket.

"I'll stay in the spare room tonight. I don't want you alone."

He's staying. He doesn't want me alone. And tonight, he's not outside. He's inside. Comforted by not being on my own, not technically, I fell into a heavy induced sleep.

Groggy, coming to gradually, my eyes fluttered. What had woken me from that near coma? Maybe it was as something illuminated on the bed. I tried to focus. What was that? The light was from my cell phone. Under my hand. Rick was kneeling next to the bed. He was holding it too. My phone. A look flickered across his face when he noticed me awake.

"You'd retrieved this in the night—bet you don't even recall. You really need to unplug," he said sternly, removing the phone from my hand. *Shit, he's right. I don't remember that at all.*

Reaching for the memory of getting up, grabbing my phone, it was nowhere. I had no recollection whatsoever. After what had happened the previous night, passing out cold in the bathroom, maybe he was right—I couldn't trust myself. Maybe I did need him policing my electronics, chauffeuring me around. I had become a very messy person.

"Plus I love just watching you sleep; you look angelic. Always have." Holding up those three middle fingers, he took my cell and left, gently closing the door behind him.

When I finally came to, late in the morning, Rick was gone. No note, no nothing. Not that going to work required a note.

When Rick relieved me of my phone, he usually left it charging by the Keurig, my inevitable first stop. He hadn't left the house long ago. Left me a still-warm cappuccino in a bowl-style ceramic mug, the ones we'd brought back from Provence, evoking bittersweet memories of evening strolls, croissants, vineyards. Lifting the lid, I took a long sip. I could almost feel it enter my veins directly. Vacations, vineyards, simpler times—it felt so long ago, the images nearly out of reach. It certainly seemed we were never getting back to that place.

I checked my messages. Billie's dad had texted when we were dining at Fiola's: *Gimme a jingle. News about your car.* Walter. Retired for years, he still answered the phone like he had a desk job. "Walter," he barked gruffly into the phone.

It was poignant hearing his gravelly baritone after all these years. Billie and I used to get the girls to Brooklyn to watch Walter perform with his barbershop quartet, but that had stopped when the girls' lives became consumed with sports, friends, school.

"Hello again. Thank you so much for—"

He jumped in. "Here's the thing. Had a guy head to the lot where your car is. He was a detective for years, also a helluva car guy. Owns Buddy's in Rockville, if you ever need anything. He gave it the once-over. Electronics looked fine, no brake line issue. Only thing was all the lug nuts on one wheel were real loose. Said it looked like you had new tires recently?"

"I did. Rick took it in a few weeks ago; a couple of the tires were getting bald."

"See, it could be a lazy tech. They get to that last tire and just drift. Could also be purposeful. Normally wouldn't have the kind of accident you did; you'd skid maybe. But you had the ravine working against you. Hard to believe somebody would do that, but you know him best."

Did I? Billie would think the worst, but I was pretty sure I knew him better than that. When you have an answer that makes sense, why dig for something deeper and darker?

"There was one thing, though. There was a GPS attached to the undercarriage. Seems your old man wants to know where his wife goes."

I was stunned … a GPS? As though I did anything exciting. Or questionable. What could he possibly want to know? I stared out the kitchen window. Watched two dark squirrels tumbling on the deck. *No.*

That would explain how he knew where to find me the day of the accident. And … oh my God … when I'd changed plans with Billie, Soosh was busy, so we'd gone to the Tap Room. Rick would've known that. He could have been behind the DUI. My mind couldn't quite light there, but there didn't seem to be another answer, try as I might to summon one.

Disturbed and distracted by Walter's revelation, I did what I always did. I logged on to my YouTube channel to respond to *Life of Reilly* messages, and I scrolled through comments. I'd incorporate suggestions subscribers made so that they truly felt part of the *Life* family, because without them, there was no family. The invaluable feedback kept me apprised of the hottest-trending topics and interests among my demographic.

One recent post had elicited a flurry of activity in just the last few moments. Certainly that would be a hot topic to create an episode around. I absently clicked on the post, noticing the initial post that incited the comments was actually a video. I hit the little square in the upper-right corner, and the small video enlarged and filled the screen.

The video played. A woman. Writhing on a bed naked, hands covering very little of her bare breasts, touching herself, using evocative language. Not *she*—me. I froze.

The posted video was *me*, completely nude and sexually provocative, and it had been linked to my own YouTube channel. The air was sucked out of the office. In the stark light of day, my creative I-miss-you looked more porn flick than Valentine's card.

It was *that* video—the one I'd shot and slyly sent when Rick had been traveling. The titillating reminder of what he had waiting back home. *Holy fucking shit,* I breathed. I'd never used his name while taping, nor made it clear that it was fun couples play. No, this looked like a full-on porn shoot, albeit low budget and arguably mild by most standards. But for a vlogger whose brand was wholesome All-American, this took on a whole new, tawdry look.

A lengthy string of comments followed, a dozen already, and it had only posted thirteen minutes ago. The first was quick to judge; she commented that she'd always thought Reilly was a sham. Presenting this dream life, this Martha Stewart existence, while actually doing porn and God knows what other deviant things on the side. I couldn't look at the rest.

I tried in vain to delete the offensive post. As administrator, that should have been my domain. But it hadn't been posted directly to my channel. It had been posted independently and linked to mine. Which prohibited me from deleting it. Time after time. *Oh fuck, oh fuck, oh fuck.*

CHAPTER 32

RAW FOOTAGE

My body tingling with apprehension. I was reeling, and I attempted another work-around to delete it. *How does something like that get out there?* I'd sent it only to Rick, of course. He compulsively deleted my saucy photos and videos immediately. Always concerned inappropriate content would be seen on company-owned devices. That Franklin could get wind of something sketchy.

How did I get rid of this? *Now!* This had to go away. Now.

I battled the urge to call Rick, my go-to. Instead, I pulled up the Butler directory. Varun, who'd helped me with the vlog, who'd given me the tutorial for *Life*—he'd be able to help.

I watched more comments crop up. Some labeled me trashy; some said a video was a hot thing to do for your person. And harmless. Not to me. It was *out there*. I needed it gone. Now.

Ice cold, I thought through the implications of leaked celebrity sex tapes. Paris Hilton, Kim Kardashian. Pam Anderson. The backlash they'd endured, the efforts to mitigate the situation. The effect on their reputations. *Oh, right. Insane comparison. Those ladies ultimately benefitted from their tapes in many ways.* In a conservative town like Washington, DC, this video wouldn't exactly be brand building. Stigma building, yes; brand building, no.

Varun picked up on the first ring. "Mrs. L. What can I do you for?"

My voice wavered. "Varun. I need your help. It's ... personal." He took me off speaker.

"Anything. What is it?" Rick had always said he was discreet. I'd have to count on that.

"Pull up my channel. You'll see a video that someone posted to my ..." I stammered.

One step ahead of me, he already had it on his screen. He groaned. "And you tried ..."

"Everything you showed me, but it was linked, so I ..."

He tapped on keys, clicked on links. He muttered under his breath as he worked, "M-kay, if you go in the back way. Let me try ... this ..." The tapping persisted. *Jesus.* If Gillsen saw this ... oh, nooo. My daughter could see this. Everyone could see this. My head throbbed as the magnitude resonated with me.

I couldn't stop; I watched as I sucked on one of my fingers, seductively slid my hand lower. I was aware Varun watched now too. How humiliating. New comments posted.

Varun's tapping stopped. The video suddenly stopped on a still frame. My back was arched. I looked "skanky," one poster noted. I stopped breathing. Within seconds, the box where the video had lived was empty. Just the frame, no embedded video. Was that it? Was it gone just like that? Another long moment later and the comments disappeared, all at once. In their place, an automated phrase: *This content is no longer available.*

"Holy shit, is that it? You were able to ..."

"I deleted it," he replied. "Permanently. Any associated data isn't cached; it's gone."

It had been up only fifteen minutes and twenty-nine seconds. An eternity to me but hardly viral at this point. I tried to calm my nervous palpitations. Tried to think.

Varun. So discreet, indispensable. Is that why there was so remarkably little about Rick online? I'd found it odd when I'd googled him. Had Varun whitewashed Rick's online presence?

The clicking resumed. He mumbled, "I'm verifying. I'm attempting to regain access through other means, and ummm … it's nowhere now. It can't be discovered."

My head on my desk, I moaned. My life was entirely out of control. I struggled to get air in my lungs. "Varun, do you have information on the poster? It was only on my phone."

"People hack phones all the time. Lots of people could poach it. As for the originating IP address, the poster used one of those services that routes through other countries, to maintain the privacy of the poster. Can't help you out there," he said. "Shitty what people can do with a little technological know-how."

I was shaken. "It's … not great. Can this be between us? I'm sorry to ask, but …"

He stopped me midsentence. "Don't you give that one more thought. I would *never.* That is your business, yours alone. Reilly, I'm … you don't deserve that."

"Thank you. Truly." I could finally exhale.

I'd been careless. I hadn't deleted it. The sad truth was I'd thought I looked hot, that my body wouldn't always be that tight. Renewed my confidence to see myself that way. That confidence now gave way to something more akin to self-loathing. *We could lose everything over my vanity.*

Light headed, I lay on the tapestry office couch and considered my options. Only two real possibilities. One: ignore it; maybe only a handful of people saw it in that fifteen-minute window. It was possible. Two: acknowledge it, own it, put it in context.

Ignoring the post was risky. Not a huge amount of people had seen it, but what if someone screen grabbed it? The other concern was that whoever had managed to poach it and post it could do it again. So it could still present an ongoing problem for me and for Rick. *Shit!*

Acknowledge it—how would that work? What could I possibly say about a video like that? Having never been involved in a scandal, I didn't exactly know. *Think.* The biggest issue was that subscribers, among those Rick's work family, would think that I do porn and I'd be seen as a disgrace. That would be a black mark for both of us, to say the least.

Would my subscribers understand the saucy video if I explained the genesis, if I put it in context? Something born of love, playfulness, a private moment between married adults. One way to find out. As my mother said, "You know the truth when you hear it." And that was what I was known for on *Life.* I shared myself; I lived my life out loud, in good times and not so good.

Decision made. I had a live vlog scheduled in two hours. I knew from being at a news station that you tackle a crisis quickly and head-on. I logged on to my YouTube channel. Dropping the camera down, I adjusted the angle higher. Looking slightly up into the lens lent a certain accessibility for a vlog like this. I tested the ring lights and added a warm, golden filter.

Sitting at the makeup vanity, I made mental bullet points. Shorter vlogs retained viewers. I was going to keep it tight. I sponged on a dewy bronze moisturizer and emphasized my lashes. I swept on clear fibers for bulk and length and followed with a swoop of inky mascara. I wanted a natural look, like the women who watched. I wasn't some floozy fake. I was one of them.

I set the timer for four minutes. Opening graphics aired. I forced myself to breathe.

"Hey, Lifers. It's been a day already, and it's only noon." I mustered a wan smile. "We've shared tips with each other about how to keep our relationships spicy, and, well, I practice what I preach. Sometimes, maybe like you, I need to think things through a little better. I don't want to make a bigger deal of this than it is, but I'd like to provide a little … context."

I elaborated on the most intimate of things as I looked up into the lens.

"I love my husband. I'm attracted to him. I miss him when he's gone." Tears threatened. Though the emotions were genuine, it certainly seemed all that was in the rearview mirror.

"Once in a while, I'd leave him an alluring message on his phone. Sometimes I'd snap a sexy picture to remember me by. And then I had the bright idea to ramp it up."

My dry throat ached. I swallowed hard around the throbbing lump.

"Lifers, I … played around with the video camera. I was sassy. I was totally feeling myself. And I wanted to make my man smile on a day when he sounded stressed. So I created a little vignette … it was harmless fun, or it was meant to be. To say: 'I miss you, can't wait to see you.' Did I exhibit the best judgment?" I laughed ruefully and flushed, my hand over my eyes.

"Probably not. Not the first time, not the last time, I'm afraid. All we can do is learn the lesson and keep it moving." Watching the timer count down, I concluded with a lighter aura.

"So until Thursday, when we get tips from closet guru Brandon B, live your best life!" Switching off the LED lights and the camera, I knew one thing. I had made a decision for myself, for my brand. As my vlog guest had said, it was time to take back my personal power.

A thud out front broke the pensive silence. On the porch, a delivery: a slender stick extended from a vase, and a powder-blue card tucked into the plastic prongs had my name on it.

I wasn't entirely surprised that Rick had reverted to his old ways, but the selection was not Rick. They weren't the kind of statement he usually made. These flowers were daintier, more subdued. A petite arrangement of roses, chrysanthemums, and calendula in shades of cream and peach. That struck me sideways, in a time where everything struck me sideways.

Was he making some kind of point? I detested the color peach. I'd always said it was just a glorified beige, an apricot that lacked attitude. Rick always sent colorful flowers—vibrant gerberas and peonies, bright cornflowers and foxglove, reminiscent of the wild English gardens he grew up with. Or exotics. He was allergic to ordinary.

I picked up the standard-issue frosted vase and deposited it on the kitchen counter. Automatically, I dug out a long glass bar stirrer and added water, stirring in the packet of plant food. I didn't remove the card from the envelope. It would be another meaningless peace offering, one I could drop in the drawer with the others. A slim drawer cluttered with cards.

Exhausted from the events of the day, I wanted to fling the thing into the trash, but I resisted. Since Rick had the habit of coming and going at will, I didn't want him to see that I'd junked his gesture. I pulled the envelope from the prongs and slid the small card out.

I've been thinking about you. I hope this finds you well. Take good care, Emma

Emma. It hadn't even crossed my mind that the flowers would be from anyone other than Rick. He'd told her about the car accident, I guessed. What a thoughtful way to reach out. I wondered if she knew, being the "eyes and ears" of the operation, that Rick was spending time at the corporate apartment. My mind hummed. I considered Emma, her position at Butler. Her daily exposure to Rick. And to Caroline. Her unwavering devotion to her job, her boss.

I scrolled through my phone for Emma's direct line. A recording announced the call had been forwarded. After the transfer, and two more rings, she answered, "Emma Davis."

"Emma, it's Reilly. I just wanted to thank you for the beautiful flowers. That was very kind."

A pause.

"Well, I wanted to do something. Hard to know what. Like I said, I hope you're well."

"The accident was traumatic, for sure, but I'm doing fine considering. Really."

She was puzzled. "Of course. Right. The accident. Well, glad you're good."

Odd. She didn't seem to know about the car accident. So what were the flowers about? Did she know Rick was spending time at the corporate flat? Was she concerned for us?

With nothing to lose, I said, "Emma. You've always been on the front lines with Rick, with Butler. I expect you have some idea what's going on with us."

"I really don't ... I mean, I quit last week, as I'm sure you've heard," she said nervously. "I'm at the branch in Chicago now." So that was the reason the call had forwarded; she was no longer in the DC office.

"Wait, what? You quit? I hadn't ... did something happen? Is everything okay?" I found myself walking in small circles, my arm pressed tightly to my rib cage, phone clutched to my ear. The buzzing in my ears almost drowned her out.

"I can't ... I'd been there too long. I'd seen ... too much. I ran interference for him, through every episode, but at some point ..." She took a deep breath.

"You *did* deserve to know." Emotion strained her voice. "You deserved to know long before that. I'm just so, so sorry about everything." With that, she was gone.

I did deserve to know. Emma. Emma had sent the text. She knew about everything. Of course she did. She watched all the comings and goings. Every episode? *How many were there?* She'd believed in him. She had been as devoted to Rick as I had, for longer than I had.

Something big must have transpired to change that. For her to leave him for good. Emma had no doubt been deeply disillusioned, possibly heartbroken. *She'd been Ricked.*

That which is behind you can no longer hurt you. Her desktop plaque. I could press Emma for more information. I was certain she knew more.

But I'd finally reached a personal saturation point. *About damn time.*

CHAPTER 33

FACT CHECK

Forward momentum, one step at a time, one kick, one jab.

I was determined to be in top condition, both for my state of mind and for my physical confidence. For several days after the accident, I'd had to abbreviate my workouts. Now I doubled down, even though I thought some days at that dank gym would be the end of me. Muay Thai was kickboxing on steroids. It was mostly men at Urban Boxing, but they made me welcome, with a grudging regard for the fact that I kept returning. Dragging my sorry ass out after most sessions.

Deep breathing allows for clarity of mind and emotion.

Gym air was noxious, heavy with perspiration, moldy shower rooms, old shoes. And determination. I'd come to like it. This wasn't like the rest of my world. It was gritty. It was real. Not a place for words, a place for action. A place to embrace your inner badass. Reading the stencils painted in red on the black accent wall one more time, I committed them to memory.

"My aim is accurate—I've trained it. My mind is sharp—I've honed it. My body is strong—I've made it so." Accurate. Sharp. Strong.

Having jumped rope and shadowboxed for twenty minutes, I'd broken a sweat. Breathing heavily, it was time for my private lesson. I was pleased with how I'd done in early sessions, but they'd revolved mostly around punches—kicks and jabs, that was more difficult for me. I booked the incredibly fit, disciplined Hoon to work with me individually on my form.

"Economy of motion. Don't signal a kick or a jab is coming. If it's a dropping jab, use your body weight to help you." He demonstrated on his assistant, Dale, and then had me drop a jab on him. I stepped in. I jabbed. I knew my technique wasn't right.

"Again," he kept saying patiently. It was about repetition. "It should feel as natural to you as brushing your teeth." Jab, jab, jab. "You will disable with a thumb jab, done properly."

The repetition was grueling, and my frustration grew. Yanking my ponytail tighter, I groaned. I let my aggravation work for me. *Jab.* Hoon's cracked front tooth appeared. He'd broken a smile.

"Look here," he said. We leaned in to check out the video he'd shot. "See? You kept your elbow in, not flailing. That gave you the power. You're coming along."

There was a heavy clap on my shoulder. Brian, in soccer shorts and a backward Sox cap. "Hey, lady. Heard you joined Urban and that you've been here a lot lately. Planning on kicking ass and taking names?"

"If need be. You just never know when you'll need to these days." He gave me that crooked grin, his face tanned and weathered.

"Billie says the same thing, only I'm afraid it's *my* ass she's planning on kicking."

"Nah, she loves you. She just has a funny way of showing it," I teased.

"Ha," he said. "Strong stuff today. Looks like you made the Hoonster smile."

"I noticed that. Hoon smiles? Who knew."

Brian laughed. "Good to see you here. Dreary when it was all guys. Listen – don't be a freakin' stranger, okay?"

I agreed. "We'll do dinner soon." Throwing a towel around my neck, I went to my car. Tossed my bag in. My phone vibrated in my pocket.

A text from Rick: Are you trying to ruin me? How did that video get out? Tell me you deleted it from your phone.

I narrowed my eyes. Damn, it was always about him. I resisted a snarky response.

I tapped back: I thought I had. I hadn't.

Seesawing. At moments, I'd hoped he hadn't seen or heard about the video, but there was definitely part of me that wondered if he'd posted it. Not that he would want his colleagues to see it, but there was a way. Varun had taught me.

He could have chosen *where* and *to whom* that got posted: after all, I'd created various lists I posted from. Not every subscriber got every notification every time.

Rick: I need space. I'm vexed. This foolishness could have been the end. What if Franklin had seen the video—or that bizarre effort just now to ameliorate it? The Gillsen Group can cut ties with Life any time, I did a handshake deal with them. You need to remember that.

I'd anticipated an expression of support, concern maybe. I hadn't done it on purpose. People make mistakes. Rick prided himself on being someone who doesn't make careless mistakes, as mere mortals do, recent evidence to the contrary. Somehow, incredibly, he still felt superior. And, it seemed, he was threatening to pull my sponsor. I'd have nothing.

Was I losing it? Could he have posted it? And why? To impress upon me again that he controlled the sponsorship of my vlog? Would he go that far to corner me into submission?

What was the word Billie used? *Gaslighting*. I had a vague idea, but was it a real term or a Billie-ism? On edge, I grabbed the laptop and typed in "gaslighting." Almost every result highlighted the word *narcissist* in the clinical description.

Reading the first, the second, and the third results, I was dumbstruck.

Reading the traits of a narcissist, I was strangely familiar with them. I read through them again. My husband had dead-on exhibited eleven of twelve from very early on. My breathing was labored.

Narcissists were charming, wooing you relentlessly with gestures large and small. *Check.* Three a.m. roadside hugs and lighthouses. Hanging flowers at my home. Shadow boxes. Hand-delivered espressos. Surprise getaways. Even now: Fiola's, sleeping in the driveway.

Narcissists were smart, successful in business. *Check.* He had climbed the ladder strategically, arguably ruthlessly. His words. I recalled Gus and Dean and their nearly palpable, growing disdain for my husband. Probably due to his tactics.

Narcissists despised those who dared to suspect that they were less than perfect, who saw they were acting the role of an empathetic person. *Check.* Billie saw cracks in that facade early. And Dean, look where his doubts had gotten him. And his mother, she'd stopped buying his act when he was a wily teen.

Narcissists got away with behavior mere mortals wouldn't, so they didn't fear reprisal. *Check.* Things that made you go hmm. Was Caroline really the first, or was he just convinced he was too smart to be found out? The DUI, the video—a normal person didn't think that way.

Narcissists trained you to accept their "illusory truth": if they told you anything enough, it became your truth. *Check.* If they implied you were undesirable, you were nothing without them. It was fact. If they told you wrong was right, it became the truth; they framed it so effectively as fact.

Narcissists "got" you immediately. Morphed into what you desired. Made you feel your prettiest, most desirable. *Check.* My history with Rick flashed in montages. He'd "learned" Reilly early. I longed for a man devoted to me, only me, to be my peer, a partner; what a coincidence he wanted just me so badly he wouldn't even share me with a child. It was paramount to win over my daughter; Rick had wooed Sloan as though she were his newest acquisition.

"Love bombing" described our early times perfectly. *Check*. It was a whirlwind. I recalled the dizzying pace. No time to breathe, think, question: the romance freefall couldn't be stopped.

The interim stages were so accurate it was chilling; the "devalue and discard" phase summed up recent history. The nagging feeling I'd developed that I wasn't good enough any longer. I made poor decisions. I embarrassed him. The discard phase that happened when they no longer saw you as one who was unconditionally taken in by the image they'd created. If you no longer saw them as perfect, you instantly became the enemy. And I had.

Alarmed, I had to talk to the one person who could provide insight. I called Gerry's office and made an appointment under an assumed name. Good chance Rick's therapist wouldn't see me otherwise. Explaining who I was when I arrived, I told him I had reason to think Rick was a sociopath, a narcissist. Gerry was tall, wiry, angular, wearing wide-whale corduroys and driving loafers. He closed his door.

"I'm sure you understand that legally I can't speak to you about a client." Exhausted and unnerved, I spilled so much, so quickly, that he had a hard time keeping up. He squinted over his narrow, frameless glasses; his light-gray eyes were clouded.

"Here's what I can do for you. I can speak in generalities. *If* this person's a narcissist … *this* is how it manifests, and *these* should be your concerns. If that's helpful."

In other words, I knew Gerry was about to tell me things I needed to know about Rick. He sat at the edge of his padded leather office chair. I nodded, desperate for help. Tucking my hands under my thighs on the chair, I tried to keep myself grounded.

"Narcissists aren't typically dangerous, except to your psyche. One exception. When a narcissist is unmasked, when they have a lot to lose *at your hands*, they stop at nothing."

My breath caught in my throat. That was Rick. *What am I dealing with?*

"Having no conscience, no empathy, serves them well. *You* are simply an opponent to be dispatched once you see the flaws. You're a pawn in their game now. They've already gone all in with the new model, and you are simply an old supply source that's outlived its usefulness. And lacking any impulse control, they just keep seeking fresh stimulation."

"If I'm an ex supply source, why would he still want to have sex with me?"

"Sex is a *critical* part of how they define themselves. Their sexual prowess equates to their success. Sex is how they get you under their spell, how they maintain control over you. Sex is their currency. Pure and simple. And currency is everything."

"But suggesting, or agreeing with him, that spending time in the corporate apartment ..."

Gerry was quizzical. "I don't know what you're referencing. Rick saw me once. That's it. Just the one time." I was shell-shocked. So many times he'd referenced Gerry's sage advice, but it was all fabricated. To prove that he was a good guy. That he was really trying.

"Typically, a narcissist would just evaporate out of your life because you mean less than nothing to them now. One exception. When they must continue to manage you to ensure you won't do anything to create repercussions for them. They *need* you to stay invested; they *need* to convince you they still love you. When they don't need to manage you any longer, they'll ghost exactly as they wanted to do from the very moment you discovered who they really are. Narcissists you're a danger to," he cautioned, "are malignant."

Malignant.

CHAPTER 34

HARD OUT

So I was doing battle with a malignant narcissist. Who may have just tried to destroy my career. And my reputation.

I grew angry watching myself in the mirror as I dried my hair. The man who had always been there for me, vowed to always take care of everything, he sure was MIA now. The love of my life was an illusion, created to please me. He no longer existed, if he ever had. I wasn't tolerating avoidance anymore. I wasn't going to text and call, hoping he'd pick up or respond. Done. Pulling the brush through one last time, I hung the chrome blow dryer on its hook and dropped the round, vented brush in the drawer with a crack.

Yanking on my jeans and a soft fleece top, I grabbed my car keys and headed to the garage. I was pulled up short by the eerie emptiness of it. Just a wall cluttered with leaf blowers, random cans of paint, metal snow shovels. Of course it was empty. I'd totaled my car. I was without a vehicle, and that had just slipped my mind.

My memory, or lack thereof, was scary. The gaps weren't surprising, though. There was so much going on. I called for a car. My agitation grew while I waited on the porch.

At the Butler garage, I entered the elevator and pushed the button for the eighth floor, Rick's office. I intended to have a real conversation today, a come-to-Jesus, as they say. What was he doing? What did he want from me?

When the doors opened, the reality hit me. Emma's area sat devoid of personal items, her affirmation plaque gone. Touching her empty desk, I found it hard to believe she had jumped ship after so many years of dedication. What had that woman seen and heard?

There was a tremendous whirring sound, migraine inducing. I turned to see the custodian, a stubby man overpowered by the backpack commercial vacuum. Doing the final deep clean before they vacated and settled in the new offices they'd leased. We passed, moving in different directions. He grunted loudly each time he stooped down. I pulled my hair around my face and pretended to check my phone. Seemed most of the Butler employees were already at the new location. Cubbies were empty. Random half-packed boxes sat here and there.

Rick was still there. His door was ajar. Light emanated from his office. My determination grew to get answers, and my pace picked up. An angry cauldron churned deep within me.

Getting closer, I heard his voice. "Do you understand how vital it is to act on this *now*? As you're aware it's not the first time."

And her voice. "I know. You can imagine how upsetting this all is."

Her voice. Sloan's. I stifled a gasp and edged my back against the doorframe. I looked in. All that was visible was the corner of the laptop screen: Sloan, in a red Temple Owl sweatshirt with her tiny chin trembling, looked like a scared teen. It was a Zoom call. A husky man in a flat tan suit occupied the chair next to the desk. He had thinning reddish hair with longer strands at the sides. I'd never seen him before.

What the hell was this? He was authoritative with my daughter: "Elaborate on that."

I peered in again; the office looked stark. *Oh,* all the lobster trinkets and items he'd collected over the years had disappeared. The shelves were barren. Our memories—gone. And likely not boxed for the new office. My eyes moved to the screen. Sloan's face was pale, thinner.

She stammered: "Look ... I ... know you're worried. I am too. Mom didn't seem right the other day at the house."

They were conferring about me. My legs quaked uncontrollably. The anger was stunted, held hostage by a newer, growing apprehension.

"And you've seen her like this before, out of control, on the edge," Rick said, sadly. "There's more, and I'm so sorry to show you this. *This* was her condition the other night, unconscious on the bathroom floor. Just passed out."

My husband held up a picture. I couldn't quite see it from my vantage point, I strained further over. It was a black-and-white photo. Of my face squished into the bathroom floor. I was drooling. Passed out by the toilet. My stomach seized. Sloan moaned.

So he *had* come home. I knew it. He had taken a picture of me at my most pathetic and compromised, the state he had induced. It went exactly as planned. He had let himself back into the house later and found me there, splayed across the ceramic tile. He'd snapped a picture rather than help me. He'd printed it out. A photograph he now shared with my daughter.

Who was already dealing with her own life, her own problems. Every inch of me was trembling: a melting pot of fury, guilt, disgust. At him, at myself. The humming in my ears intensified. I forced myself to listen to Rick's words. Concentrate. Stay in the moment.

"This isn't going to end well if we don't help her. She drove her car off the road. She slammed into the river, not surprising when she's in this kind of condition."

Sloan gasped.

It was the first she'd heard of the severity of the incident. I hadn't wanted to upset her.

Rick added pensively, "Honey, we have to consider whether it was intentional."

My insides heaved. My knees buckled. The framed paintings on the hallway walls dizzily rose and dropped … was I collapsing? *Intentional.* Clutching my mouth, I closed my hand hard over it—to keep from howling. Convincing my daughter that I had actually …

Sloan protested, "Mom would *never* …"

Rick interjected. "The way you saw her, at eleven thirty in the morning. You've seen her vlogs. She's struggling. She's told me that she feels like she's back there, in that place. Where she was after your dad …"

I'd never told him that. I wasn't back in that place. I wasn't. I clenched my teeth.

The suit in the chair spoke up. "This is often the best way. When your family loves you, they protect you from yourself. Legally, it's termed *parens patriae.* While you may be able to coerce an adult to enter a program, the majority of the time they leave before treatment is over. When you can prove a person is a danger to themselves, such as rendering yourself unconscious, or getting into a near-fatal car accident, family members agree to have the person seek treatment. This program addresses coexisting issues: addiction, but also depression, etcetera."

I gripped the doorframe with both hands, afraid I'd fall into the office. Trying to coax my daughter to join forces with him, *against* me, to have me put away. Convincing her I was a menace to myself. That these unthinkable incidents had all been at my own hand. That the accident was perhaps not an accident at all.

Sloan's voice was strained. "I don't know anything about the place. Would I get to visit?"

The suit spoke. "I'll send you a link to a virtual tour. You're encouraged to visit. It's in Delaware, so it's convenient. It's important for family to be involved in the process."

Rick nudged gently, his signature move. "Sweetheart, she won't fight this if you're on board. I know you could never live with yourself if something happened to your mum when you could've prevented it." He played the guilt card masterfully.

Sloan wept raggedly. She raised her hands to cover her face, her moss-green eyes bright with tears. Her chest heaving. That broke my heart; my tough-yet-tenderhearted girl. Not a girl to cry easily. *I will never forgive you for this. Ever.*

These evil men manipulating the mind, the loyalties, of a young woman. I fought an urge to throw the door open, to scream, *What about the DUI? What about leaking the video?* I couldn't technically prove either of those. I'd only sound more unhinged, providing proof an intervention was the only viable option.

"It's hard, I know," Rick comforted her. "But you see why I can't live there right now, don't you? She's not well. And sadly, she shouldn't be on her own at a time like this either."

Sloan wiped her eyes with the raw, unfinished trim of her sweatshirt sleeve. Tugged at the blue hood strings. "What if … what if I just come home from Philadelphia? I've been so worried since your calls and texts that I … my therapist spoke with the director of my program. They agreed I could take a little time. Do some distance learning from home while …"

Rick pulled his eyebrows together in concern. "Honestly, I think it best if—"

"But … just hear me out," she said, picking at her cuticles. "They'll give me a month. I can devote that to Mom, getting her well. And I can be back to finish coursework and graduate."

The suit spoke up. "Your mother needs professional help. Personal support, too, of course. She'll need you during this. But the program is custom designed to help her. She'll have her own team of doctors and therapists. Trained to help her get to a better place."

Her eyes drifted away from the screen. "I … I need to think about this. This is a lot …"

"It is," Rick agreed. "The plan is to do this in three days, so get back with me tomorrow. And I have to ask. Please don't share this with your mum; it will derail everything. It's one thing if you choose not to participate in her wellness plan, but *please*. When I married your mom, it was 'in sickness and in health'—I owe it to her to help in any way I can."

The suit backed him up. "That's critical. Do we understand each other, Sloan?"

It revulsed me to hear him use her name. As though he knew her. As though he knew us.

"I understand," she said sadly. "Rick … I … probably don't tell you enough how much I appreciate how you care for my mom. You've been nothing but supportive, and I will never forget that. Ever. The fact that you still want to help her, when it's all … kind of a mess."

He humbly accepted her compliment. "I only want the best for her. I always have."

"Look, I … have to go, but I'll call you in the next couple of days. I just need a minute," Sloan said, a sounder ending the zoom call. There was a pall in the office. Leaning back, Rick's leather recliner squeaked. The headrest smacked against the wall.

"Not easy, that one. Like her bloody mother. She going for it?"

"Damned if I know," the suit responded. "You might have yourself a problem there."

Rick rapped on the armrests in frustration. "Well. Challenges aren't optional. Overcoming them is. There is a solution," he said, raking one hand roughly through his hair.

"There's always the other way," the suit responded. *The other way.* His chair scraped loudly as he pushed away from the desk.

Frantic that the meeting was wrapping up, I was blinded by a surge of adrenaline. I fled. Shoved the steel exit door and stumbled down eight flights. Emerging at the parking level, I stood right at the over-the-top signage reserving Rick's spot. Saved for our hero. *Galling.*

Nearly catatonic, I slid into the booth at Carla's Café, empty but for a teen couple cuddling in a booth, half reclined on the tired red vinyl bench, canoodling away from Mom's watchful eyes. Only coming up for air to check out the mini-jukebox.

Billie was waiting, twisting her chunky braid. She shoved an old-school white cup across the dingy, checkered vinyl cloth. Coffee dribbled over the rim and pooled in the saucer. Dark, nearly viscous. I recoiled, certain my system couldn't tolerate drinking it. Or maybe even smelling it. Carla's reeked of bacon, days-old fry oil, and burned coffeepot. I sank onto the seat, nauseated, and dipped the napkin in the water glass. Pressed it against my clammy face and neck.

"What? Jesus." Her eyes were wild. "You sounded freaked the fuck out."

"I haven't told you everything. And it just got worse. So much worse."

At a loss for words, Billie flailed her hands, begging for answers.

"First," I said, stuffing the nausea down forcefully, "I have to text Sloan, let her know I'm okay. And tell her to lie low for a minute."

Billie slapped her hands on the booth with a sharp crack. "Stop. What the *hell* is happening?"

Trembling, I spilled everything. All the despicable things I'd never wanted Billie to know about Rick. That now he was co-opting Sloan to his side to put me away. The details of the affair, the drugging, the phone hacking. The narcissistic disorder.

"Back up. We're blaming this shit on a disorder? Like … he has an issue so he's not responsible for any of the …" Billie scoffed.

"Gerry says it qualifies as a disorder. His mind is disordered, but he also says narcissists can't usually be fixed. Especially the malignant ones. They win, no matter what they have to do."

Rummaging in her fringed bag, Billie located her phone. Nailed me with a look. Held up one finger. "So. Sloan needs to know you're all right." She held up another finger. "*And* she needs to be out of reach of Rick."

I nodded. She cracked her knuckles and shifted on her seat.

"Listen. I need to tell you something. Truth is I've shared some of this with Amy. Hard not to, since she's been living at home. Teaching money sucks. And I overheard her on the phone talking to Sloan. Saying she thinks you and Rick are having problems."

She tapped her phone. "Just say the word, Amy'll be on the next Amtrak to Philly. Take Sloan to a hotel. Put her concerns about you to rest and keep her off the radar till this is done."

Sloan was priority one. Amy knew enough of the real story to keep Sloan from abandoning her life, the progress she's making. Running back to me, afraid I'm spiraling. Sweet, dear Amy was just the person who could talk Sloan off the ledge.

"Do it," I said. "Send Amy. Neither of them should be alarmed. I just want to be one hundred percent sure they're out of harm's way." I shot Sloan a text to let her know Amy would be in touch, and *please* not to worry. I couldn't even call her, I was incapable of speaking suddenly. Dropping my head back against the padded booth, I squeezed my eyes shut.

Getting Amy on the phone, Billie went full-on drill sergeant. The next express train was in forty minutes. Amy needed to get to Union Station. Billie booked a suite at the Radnor Hotel. "Yah, Ames, it's bougie. But I want you girls to stay put, so live it up till you hear from me."

My stomach began to settle once there was a plan in place to keep Sloan away from all this, to allay her fears. Now I prioritized what I wanted out of this. What I needed. My home. My vlog. Anything I was rightfully entitled to. Couldn't prove the DUI, couldn't prove the accident, but with Walter finding the GPS, we knew. We just couldn't prove it. Now, though, he wanted to have me put away, even enlisting Sloan. He was devious, ruthless, used to winning.

One dynamic played into my hands: right here, right now, this was a seminal moment in time for men in positions of power. An impossible time for a guy like Rick to be outed. And he knew I had proof of an inappropriate relationship with a subordinate. Information he was clearly concerned would leak, if his reaction to Millie's *Life of Reilly* appearance was any indication.

I fumed and pushed Carla's glass salt (with-rice) and pepper shakers around the vinyl-topped table like chess pieces. Purposefully. Move one. Move the other. Move one.

"I am not going to be institutionalized, and I am not letting him woo Gillsen away and leave me without my vlog. Proof of the affair is one thing, but proof of financial malfeasance, felonies—*that* I could hold over his head. That's leverage."

He kept nothing at the house. It was always locked up tight at the office. But between offices during the move—there was only one place he'd keep anything. The corporate apartment.

All he cares about is his reputation, his big job. He'd do anything to protect them; without those, he felt he was nothing. That was what I needed to hammer him with. Hardball.

I said defiantly, "I'm going in. It's the only way."

Billie gagged on her coffee and dropped the mug back onto the saucer.

"Going … in … where?" she asked super slowly, as if English wasn't my first language.

"You know where. I'm breaking in. Tomorrow." I leaned in. "The key is on his ring."

"You are not serious. If you try to get it, go to a hardware … Jesus, do you … ?"

I googled "Copying keys app." Just three words. I exhaled sharply, turned the phone to Billie. She grabbed it. Apps existed. I didn't have to steal the key. I just had to have *access*. And I did. It was distinct, octagonal; he hadn't tried to hide it.

Scrolling through the reviews, I was stunned. And more than slightly skeptical. But 768 reviews—all with four-plus stars—saying, "It worked for me," couldn't be wrong. I searched the app store for that specific one. KeyMe. *I'll be damned.*

"Jesus H. Christ," Billie breathed.

There it was. The app copied a key exactly using only a photo of each side. That was all. Two pictures. *This can't be aboveboard.* The app automatically put itself into invisible mode on your phone after you used it. Was that even legal adjacent?

Didn't really matter, I was doing it. After I downloaded the app to my phone, all that was left was to create a foolproof way to get his key ring away from him. And there was only one possibility: get him to the house. And separate him from his keys.

Easier said than done. Obviously if he stayed overnight, I could grab it in the middle of the night. But I couldn't bear to share a bed with him now; those days were over. We were over. Make nice over dinner, yup; make fake love to him, nope.

"So. Nine times out of ten, he still heads for a shower immediately. Showering off the day or the mistress—*Who knows?*—but that was definitely my best shot. The keys will be in the changing room, but *he* is in the shower." I shrugged. As though I had it locked and loaded.

She flinched and blew out hard through her mouth. But we both knew it was my only chance. Risky, but my only chance. She bit the inside of her lip but finally nodded. She was with me whatever I decided. "*Okay.* But you make goddamn sure he leaves your house at some point so I can follow him. I'll find that apartment. Trust me. You do your part. I'll do mine."

Practicing on my own keys for half an hour, I had the technique mastered. Hovering the phone over the key on the grimy diner table exactly in the center of the frame earned you an "Accepted." You'd met the criteria, the signal you could flip the key. Repeat the process. The final step was the most daunting: take the photos to the hardware store to have the key cut. And see if it worked.

Provided I got photos tonight and the key tomorrow, provided I gained entry, I'd be out front of D-Day (the intervention) by one, maybe two days. Could I even get him to the house? I was willing to bet I could. He needed to keep me soft to him, Team Rick. For a few more days.

Hitting speed dial #1, I said in a wispy voice, "Hey, you. I have an idea."

CHAPTER 35

STAGGER THROUGH

"How about dinner at home tonight?" I said, disingenuously referring to it as home. I had no time left on the clock and only one way to get his key. Everything rested on this.

"My, my. Look who wants to spend time with her husband," Rick said petulantly.

"Don't be silly. I want to make it up to you about the video thing. I feel terrible."

His attitude improved in the face of an apology. Always had. "Not your fault. Careless to have saved the video, but understandable. You looked ... spectacular. I haven't got the feeling that anyone from my company saw it, as it was just an online post."

And it was all about *you.*

"I'm glad. I ... don't want to make trouble for you. You work too hard to have me mess anything up for you," I said in a most heartfelt way. "See you tonight then?"

"Sounds perfect. See you at home tonight."

I kept the meal simple. Pasta. Mushroom raviolini with brown butter sauce. Roasted asparagus. Like a cat on a hot tin roof, I swirled the butter unconsciously, wood spoon circling the brass pan again and again until the sauce reached a caramel shade. And had that smoky fragrance that made my stomach flip.

Adrenaline shot through my limbs. My fingers and my feet tingled painfully. I looked out the front door. His car was there.

He just sat in it. For ten, twelve minutes. Cell phone to his ear. He smiled, the light from it illuminating his square jaw.

Finally, he dropped out of his car. Striding across the porch, the motion lights flipped on. He looked like Rick. A cheery wave at Barbara's husband tending to his landscaping. Adopting my on-air persona, I aimed for calm, cool, and collected. I swung the door open.

It's all so fucking awkward now. Touching his hands to my face, he kissed me. I couldn't respond. I couldn't summon anything, but I nuzzled up against him. I pressed my cheek against his. My stomach flickered with revulsion at his light scent, the touch of his evening scruff.

He murmured into my ear, "It's nice to see you. It's nice to be home."

Our years-in-the-making routine carried us past the initial wooden greeting, the vibe between us quickly settled into a new stagnancy.

Sorting through the deep pile of mail on the counter, he tossed catalogs and neatly stacked bills. He drained a pint of ice water, refilled it, ice cubes loudly clinking from the dispenser. He pulled the recycle bins back into the garage. Aligned them meticulously.

I pulled out utensils, linen napkins, and terra-cotta pasta bowls painted with black kalamata olives. Checking the digital clock on the oven, I tilted my head and pretended to calculate cooking time. It was agony that he was here. He wandered toward me. "Anything I can do to help with supper?"

Showtime. Plastering a small smile on, I said, "I got this. You know, looks like you have time for a quick shower, if you like, sweetie." I averted my lying eyes, swiveling the corkscrew into the chilled pinot grigio bottle.

"Maybe not tonight …"

My heart sank; with those words, all hope was gone. Any chance I'd had evaporated. My chest was so like the corkscrew, coiled far too tightly. It was over.

Dully, I sat at the island. Half-heartedly feigned digging around in a drawer for something, moving aside spatulas, salad tongs, knowing all was lost. Game over. My eyes on the golden flecks in the granite, I willed myself not to cry. I couldn't string two thoughts together, not even one lucid one. My mind was the place thoughts went to die. A sharp crunch startled me. I looked up, having forgotten he was there.

He had his hands behind his head, elbows spread. With a swift crack of his neck, he said, "You know what, don't mind if I do take a shower. Ghastly day today."

Score! Guilelessly trailing behind him with renewed hope, I poured a glass of wine to take up to the bathroom. He saw I didn't have one. He raised an eyebrow. "No wine?"

"With dinner. I think I'll hold off until I've gotten the food under control."

Not a chance. I have one shot at this.

I perched on the pale-rose, damask settee, tucking my bare feet under me to watch. He'd like that. Time slowed; he turned the faucets on to warm the water. Swiveled each knob to precisely his liking. The soothing sound of the shower spray filled the bathroom.

He brushed his teeth, in and out, up and down, the electric toothbrush vibrated. A new application of swirled white-and-green toothpaste on the oscillating brush. He ran it over his tongue repeatedly. Placed a new tube of cream by his sink. Hung a new loofah stick inside the shower. All the while still wearing the navy jacket that held the keys.

I forced myself to stay put. Time stopped as he leaned against the sink and watched me while gargling blue liquid deep in his throat. He pooled it into the sink, the medicinal smell swirling up. Finally, he stepped into the changing room. Hung his jacket on a hook. I couldn't look away. Dropping the rest of his clothes across the hamper, he loped past me, naked as always. Fleetingly assessed himself in the reflection of the shower door before hopping in. Narcissist.

The instant the glass door shut, I melted into the changing room, maintaining a conversation the whole time. "So what's going on with that new merger? You think it's going through?" I called out, trying to extract the keys as quietly as possible from his jacket pocket, curling them into my palm to keep them from jangling. His voice was louder, since he was speaking over the shower; that gave me the chance to place the keys on his sleek black vanity with minimal noise.

"Does it seem like something you'll need to spearhead at this point?" I pressed on, separating the octagonal key from the pack and bunching the rest together. There was a slight metal clink. I froze. Listened intently.

Did he hear that? Is he getting out of the shower?

"Sorry I didn't hear that. What did you say?" I asked.

He was still talking. He detailed the merger. The members of that team. He added callously, "I've spent the past few hours doctoring the financials to make it all work. Gotta do what you gotta do, right?"

He'd stopped even worrying about repercussions; maybe he *was* bulletproof. Maybe if you thought you were, that was what you became. Narcissist.

"And more layoffs," he groused. "Always. The bloodshed continues."

I'll say.

Pulling out my phone, I touched the app. It folded open. Hands trembling, I held the camera at the corners, hovered over the key. *You must be still,* it informed me. Trying again, I steadied my forearms against the edge of the bureau. I took a shot.

"Accepted."

Yes!

But as "Accepted" popped up, the camera clicked audibly. In response, I coughed loudly, as if I'd swallowed the wrong way, hoping it would cover any noise. I hit mute. *Rookie mistake.*

"So did you know the O'Haras are moving in a few weeks?" I nearly shouted to mask the sound as I flipped the keys. "I can't remember if I told you."

"You did. Something about a job in California, was it? Or Las Vegas? I can't recall." His resonant voice covered the distinctive sound of keys as I gently turned the whole ring to get the other side. With the phone on silent now, I held the camera directly over the key.

First attempt, not "in frame." *Shit.* Tried again. Still not in frame. Agitated, I gripped the phone more tightly, my hand unsteady and slick. Moved it so ... slowly ...

Oh my God. I did it. *"Accepted."* The automated response guaranteed I'd successfully submitted; it offered a list of all local hardware stores where I could obtain a copy.

The moment felt tragic and triumphant, all at once. Jubilant and joyless.

"Right the first time, California. Coronado, actually, which is somewhere I've always wanted to go. Remember we talked about it? So close to downtown San Diego, that gorgeous old hotel ..." Quietly sliding the keys from the armoire, I pushed my clenched hand into his jacket pocket and unfurled my fingers to let them drop.

I tried to compose myself. My heart was beating almost visibly. He was still rinsing off, soapy froth rolling down his limbs. Blithely unaware of what had just transpired. My breathing was shallow; the steam was oppressive.

Lying casually across the love seat, I watched; he turned off the water, squeegeed the glass door, gave his signature full-body shake like a dog after a bath. *My God, I used to love that.* Our routine. I handed him a fluffy white bath sheet when he stepped onto the mat. *Normal.*

"I'll go finish off the pasta. See you in a minute." Palpitations subsiding, I slipped down the stairs to the kitchen. I poured a glass of ice water. No cocktails, not tonight. Nothing to slip a medication in, no slippery slope of an evening.

Moments later, he appeared in faded jeans with his now-empty glass of wine. Promptly refilled it.

Plating the pasta and the char-tipped asparagus, I sprinkled toasted pine nuts on his; he pulled out my chair at the table. Poured me a glass of wine. I touched my lips to it and rolled some onto my tongue, let it ooze back down the side of the glass when he looked away.

Can he tell something's amiss?

Dinner chatter passed for normal, albeit anemic. I forced a smile. I asked perfunctory questions. We ate. He finished off the bottle of wine. I cleared the bowls and utensils; he opened another bottle. Our usual dance. One foot in front of the other; you got the key, now get him out.

He poured from the new bottle, the golden liquid approaching the rim of the jumbo glass. Draining it like water, he loosened up and sighed. Rubbed his chest vigorously. He tipped his still-damp head in my direction, his hair curling around his ears.

That I-will-have-you leer appeared. He assessed me across the island, moved purposefully toward me.

Shit. No. I willed him to not want to "make me his" tonight, the phrase that had cropped up too often in recent years. I needed to keep it calm. I couldn't risk making him angry.

Sex is his currency; sex is how he controls you.

His mouth was on mine hungrily. He tasted of Listerine, wine, and pine nuts. His hands moved up my arms, slipped around the back of my head. Firmly, he pulled on my hair. Tugged my head back. Sucked on my neck. Hard. *Just respond, even a tepid response.* My despairing moan passed for passion; at least I hoped it had.

"Not now," I whispered, attempting to finesse my way out of anything intimate. "Let's just leave it at dinner tonight. It was nice, there's always ..."

Ignoring my request, he retained his grip on my hair. He moaned, hard against my hip bone. *Can't you feel I'm not into this? Into you?* I couldn't fake anything more. I tried to pull away. He yanked harder. "What the fuck do you think you're doing? Stay still." He pinned my arms behind me roughly, needing only one of his hands.

His aggression was unsettling. One hand held my wrists firmly, the other grasped my neck and squeezed. Not lightly, as in the past. That had been titillating at one point. This was different. I was trapped against the granite, his body weight leveraged against mine, his hand tightly around my neck.

"Tell me this is how you like it." He tightened his grip. Things started to get hazy.

"No! I ... I ..." My shriek echoed through the kitchen. *"Get off! You're hurting me!"* I gasped for air, and my fingernails scratched down his arm.

CHAPTER 36

NOT FOR ATTRIBUTION

My lack of cooperation threw cold water on his desire. He pulled back. His lids were heavy. He stared in disbelief at the pink scratch marks developing on his wrist. Wiping one finger across his lips, he gazed at that fingertip, and a small, dimpleless smile formed.

"I should think you'd be thrilled I still want you at this stage."

"I couldn't breathe," I said, holding my sore neck. About to ask him to leave, I sensed a new twist. An ominous one. The room dimmed. It darkened rapidly. A vicious rain started, pelting the slate roof and echoing through the kitchen.

"Bollocks. You're playing games. Stop."

That just hung in the air. Is he referring to sex? The role-play games?

"You just keep digging. For what? To fuck with me? That doesn't end well. I'm tired of this. Here's the bottom line," he slurred, proceeding to tick off points on his fingers. As though he were firing an errant employee and taking perverse pleasure in it.

"Short-term marriage. No shared kids. You are an 'earner,' or could be if you'd kept a real job." Tick, tick, tick.

What the fuck? I mean, we agreed ...

His diatribe continued: "You have no assets, none. No house"—again he ticked his fingers each time for emphasis—"no pension, no savings, no nothing." Tick, tick, tick. "Without me— no sponsor, no vlog, no career." Tick, tick, tick.

So he'd rob me of everything else to bribe me into playing nice on the vlog. I could keep my sponsor, provided I made him out to be a good guy.

"That's what you're worried about? You want to leave me penniless? Well, that's not happening. *I* put all the money in this house. That deed's in *my* name. Plus the money I put with your financial guy."

That knowing smirk disturbed me. The driving rain continued; it changed course, slapping against the picture windows, pinging off the glass.

What does he know that I don't know?

I persisted, "This house is *mine*, and I get half of everything else. That's 'marital assets.'"

Furious, I clung on to the island and shook. That was all that mattered. All he'd wanted to do was build me up—to tear me down and leave me with nothing. Destitute, no dignity, in a rubber room somewhere in Delaware.

I provoked him. I wanted him to know my information ran deeper than a contract-breaking affair. "This house is *mine*. Even if you torch it, even if you burn it to the ground, it's still mine."

His face froze, his glassy eyes slitted. "Even if I ... ?" He drew the words out slowly: "What was that you just said?"

"Even if you burned my house down. Arson," I repeated savagely, driving the point home. "Not exactly a new concept to you, now is it?"

He stalked upstairs. Hostile steps rang back. I ran after him and took the stairs two at a time. A thunderous crack outside. The storm was getting close.

His face distorted. "I wasn't involved. I didn't do it. Are you accusing me of setting fire to that bitch Maura's house—thirty-five years ago? There was no proof, just nasty bloody rumors." In a peculiar bark, he added, "And ... and they built a much better house after insurance paid out—a McMansion, for Christ's sake."

I looked at him in the mirror with disgust. Who was he? Who was the real Rick?

"You fucked with the wrong girl!"

He whirled around. Pushed me onto the love seat.

"You never really had my back." He moved his face within inches of mine. "Worse, you've vastly underestimated me."

"Have I?" I asked quietly. "I don't think so. You take what you want, no matter the cost to anyone else."

His eyes flashed. "How could you have flipped on me? I thought you loved me. Why in God's name would you contact law enforcement? Why would you involve Walter? That wasn't very wise, love."

The room was suddenly airless, a toxic vacuum. How had he known I'd talked to Billie's dad? My mind stalled. "He hadn't been well, so I just checked in."

His eyebrows arched into two severe inverted vees: "Is that so? Just 'checked in'—about your car?"

The pieces were clicking into place. When I'd woken in the night to find my phone between our hands. The times in the morning, after a night I couldn't remember, after the overserving and doubling up on meds. Those times I'd smell his scent on the phone. The reasons he continued to see me, only to gain access to my phone.

Walter had texted me. "News about your car." *Oh my God.* Why had I doubted myself?

Light headed, dizzy. My skin was crawling. The shock was consuming my flesh like locusts. Unconsciously, I scratched at my arms, my neck. Still, he wore that patronizing look, unaware of what he'd just revealed. I could barely manage the words, "*You* were in my phone. Exactly how are you getting into my phone?"

Stupefied, he busied himself throwing random things in his bag. He had blown it.

Is this the only reason he ever saw me, shared cocktail hours with me, made love to me—to get access to my phone? All to see what I was doing, how much I knew. And whatever else he was doing in my phone.

Moments, images; the slideshow flashed quickly. Finding him on his knees, putting my hand on the phone, smelling him on it. Blood rushed to my head.

He finally mustered a reply, "Well, it's not rocket science. You leave that phone unlocked all the time. Anyone would look. It's only natural." Flustered by his uncharacteristic misstep, beads of sweat had formed at the corners of his temples, and one shiny rivulet dripped down his jaw.

"That's impossible," I informed him. "My phone's on auto lock." Preemptively, I shut down other lies, ticking them on my fingers exactly as he had so dismissively.

"And you don't know the code, because there isn't one. And you can't bypass security. You may as well just tell me. How did you get in my phone?" Tick, tick, tick.

I stared him down. He was done with the cat-and-mouse game. Wiping the beads of sweat away with the back of his hand, he dropped his head like he'd been nothing more than a naughty boy. He dried the back of his hands on his jeans and looked at me dismissively.

"Fine. I retrieve your phone after you pass out at night, with or without my help," he said coolly. "And, yes, I slide the phone under your hand and put your thumb on the control button. Don't look so damned dramatic. You'd do it too." The confession. Followed immediately by the justification.

Is he saying he drugged me? I gasped for air, my fingers clawing at my throat. Would I? Would I do it too? If he only knew I had photos of his key as we spoke. The depths to which we had each gone frightened me.

"What else was I to do? I needed to know what you were up to. What you thought you had on me," he said, dropping his bag on the sofa nonchalantly. There was something like a smile curling his lips, but his eyes crackled with a cool antagonism.

Holy shit. Drugging me. Hacking into my phone. All because I could cost him his job, his reputation, some money?

It was chillingly clear now: Rick skulked around in the dark of the night, refilling my glass, slipping me medication, making sure I was out. He would slyly slide my phone under my hand and touch my thumb to it. Then he'd hide somewhere in our home, scroll through my texts, my emails, whatever he could find. I watched him in petrified stillness.

He moved to the window, his hands on the sill as he surveyed the storm. The storms we had loved watching together. His expression equal parts disdain and dominance. That wasn't Rick; he *looked* like him, very like him. A bolt of lightning crackled and shattered the quiet.

You fucked with the wrong girl.

"Oh my God, Rick. You've really complicated things for yourself now," I said with faux concern. I conjured an empathetic shake of the head. "You've got a very serious problem now. The affair was bad enough. But you just went straight from *philanderer* to *felon*."

I got this. I didn't relent.

"I'm sure Franklin Butler will be most impressed when I reach out. Now, if I remember it properly, and correct me if I'm wrong, but doesn't your morals clause cover both of these issues—sexual misconduct *and* felonies?"

His athletic body tensed like a copperhead ready to strike. He hissed, "Rubbish. It's not a *felony*! People do it all the time." He threw his hands up. "Which one of us do you think they'll believe? You, with your little YouTube thingy? Or me, the one who makes them boatloads of money."

He stated that with immense confidence; maybe it really was all about the Benjamins.

"My little YouTube thingy. You mean the one where I can talk about my life, my marriage, what *really* happened. That one? Yes, I think that could present a problem for you."

His lips curled mirthlessly. "A rather empty threat. You can't present a problem if you *don't* have a vlog." There it was again, the insinuation that he'd made me, that he could break me.

He picked up his weathered leather overnighter. "I'm finished with this lunacy. And *you* are stark raving mad if you think you are going to do anything to diminish me in the eyes of Franklin," he yelled back up the stairs. The gloves were off.

The front door slammed, the brass knocker reverberating. Moving to the window, I watched his car peel away in the downpour, windshield wipers flapping wildly in the night. *Madness is right.* As he rounded the corner, Billie's car swerved in behind him. Visibility was low and heavy rain persisted, but she doggedly tailed him, keeping a few car lengths between them. Her bright-red brake lights kept time with his. They were both heading to the apartment. Only one of them was aware of that.

CHAPTER 37

WRAP

"On my way to you," Billie crowed into the phone, fifteen minutes later. "We've got ourselves an address. And it ain't no corporate flat." Of course it wasn't.

But we had a key (sort of). And an address. The thunderous downpour moved east. It faded to a constant, quiet swishing of rain.

Shaking violently, I was ill, but I didn't cry. The well was bone-dry. He had gone too far, too often. *Enough.* Enlisting Sloan? *Enough.* I sat in total darkness on our—kill that—on *my* bed.

I was done. Disgusted that he planned, as a final affront, to take complete advantage of me by any means possible. His only goal to leave me with nothing. That was what mattered. Keeping his own nest feathered and keeping me silent. Terrified at the monster he morphed into when he felt threatened, I wondered about the many red flags I'd ignored. Why I'd not only accepted them but gathered them into some pitiful bouquet that passed for love and devotion.

I'd justified his unconscionable behavior at every turn, his rages, his backhanded insults, his infidelity. His entitled, I'm-be-yond-reproach approach to life and love. I'd willed him to possess the qualities I'd imbued him with. All because I needed to believe that he loved me, that he loved Sloan, that he fixed every prob-lem. Fixed, hell, he'd created the problems. Here was where it had changed: *I* would fix them. *I* would get my life back.

Slamming the door, Billie flew up the stairs. She grabbed a towel and dropped onto my duvet, dripping but victorious. She had his address. Flipping the bedside sconce on, she held her phone out. "Got somethin' for you."

Not only did she have his address, she'd received a simple text from Amy. Just a selfie. She held up the picture: "Not for nothin', but Amy says Sloan is doing real well. That this answered a lot of questions. That she'd started to wonder about Mr. Wonderful."

Stinging tears now, but not about him. Tears of relief, for her. The selfie: in the lobby of the Radnor, Amy and Sloan perched on an enormous cream sofa. Amy was taking the shot, and with her other hand she dangled a bag of Thunderbird's Philly cheesesteaks. Sloan blew a kiss. I pinched in on her; she had some color back in those cheeks.

"Thanks, B. Jesus Christ, thank you so much." I was finally able to breathe.

"You got it. Hey, what the hell is that on your neck?" I touched it self-consciously. "Is he hurting you?"

"He did tonight."

She snarled, "I swear to God. I could Betty Broderick that dude."

I nodded heavily, having had the thought myself. *It's a plan. A bad plan, but it's a plan.*

She ranted as she shoved the yellow towel through her wavy black hair: "If I ever told Brian *any* of this, holy shit, he'd ..."

"Well, you're not. We're on a serious timetable here, and I have to figure out tomorrow."

Coordinating our movements for the next day, she said, "All right. We'll hit the hardware store first thing, make sure we've got the key. Then we'll watch him leave his place. I'll go sit at his office garage—till you text me to come back."

I replied slowly, "No. It's Tuesday. He spearheads the Tuesday afternoon think tanks. We know without a shadow of a doubt he's there for those. They're mandatory for the whole company. We can do a drive-by at Butler's garage first to confirm the car is there."

Getting into that apartment as soon as possible was the only thing that mattered. Before I lost my nerve. Before sanity and common sense prevailed. Before the concept of breaking and entering resonated.

I couldn't move. Subdued beneath a sea of pillows. No longer fluffy and lovely, the pillows joined forces, conspiring to smother me. They melted onto my face, oozed around my chest, congealed into a suffocating glob. I strained to claw at them but had no arms, no hands. I jerked my chin to my chest. Tried to create a small pocket of air. I sucked in hard. The pillow blob drew in with my shallow breath. Gloppy gel filled my nose and mouth. Solidified in my throat. Choking it out, I heaved to the side—coughing and gagging—and lay across the moist, tangled mound of pillows, panting. Had I slept at all or was my subconscious simply not allowing rest?

Trying to shake off the dream, I got dressed to face the surreal day. I pulled on dark jeans, a long gray tee, and a cropped ivory sweater. I retrieved the wig from under the sink and positioned it just right. Smoothed the bangs down. The mirror didn't reflect that the malignancy was eating me alive; what looked back at me passed for normal.

What a fucked-up itinerary. A typical day would have gone something like gym, Whole Foods, *Life* prep. Today's itinerary: first stop, the hardware store to pick up my husband's key. Second stop, my husband's garage to check on his car. Third stop, my husband's apartment.

Billie and I got in her Prius in silence. It was beyond gloomy out. Last night's lashing rain hadn't quite cleared—it just hung there thickly. Rick called it "soft," meaning neither raining nor not raining. That inexorable in-between that could go either way. So heavy that you wore it like another layer.

Billie pulled past the grate draining water from the lot and dropped me just beyond the door of the store. I moved past the gas grills, folding chairs, and garden flags and headed to the back corner inside. No one was at the key kiosk. I looked around impatiently. Suddenly a bulky man popped up from behind the metal counter. I reeled back. The man wore a faded brown work smock that matched his eyes. "Need something?"

Thrusting my phone toward him, I showed him the app, fully expecting a blank stare in return. Eyeing the two photos, his eyes flitted back and forth. "I seen these. I gotta scan for the coded specs in there. Hang on." He disappeared into the minuscule, cluttered space behind him. I waited. And watched the enormous, round old-school clock over the door.

Three minutes ticked by, it felt like three hours. The moment was surreal. Was this my life? I was just a few lousy decisions away from being a *Dateline* special. Keith Morrison's velvet voice-over would make even hardware store key-cutting ominous. "Oh, my ... ," he'd start.

The key guy reappeared. Lumbered over to a small steel machine. He grumbled, "Always has to be unique key bitting, can't just go with generics." He revved up the machine and whittled away, cutting the key in less than a minute. The burning smell of metal dust hung in the air. Without even glancing up, he reached over the antiquated register and handed the key to me. That easy. After all the hurry-up-and-wait, I was holding his key. Comparing it to the photos, I couldn't see any variances. It sure looked like a match. *Unbelievable.*

Rick's compulsory company-wide meetings were on Tuesdays. Three o'clock. That gave me time. The man liked the sound of his own voice. Confirmation he was at the office was the final and essential piece. Billie flashed her lights at me from across the lot.

Nearing the office, I said, "I don't want to drive right into his garage. I'll jump out here and meet you over there." I pointed to the gas station on the corner. At the side exit to his lot, I jerked on her black oversize bomber jacket. She idled next to the station, looking as nondescript as she could in a baseball cap, her hair pulled through the back in a wavy ponytail.

Slipping into the dank garage, I made a sharp turn. *Please God, don't let him be standing there.* Looking past the Hondas and Volvos, veering around the electric car stalls (empty as always), I had no trouble finding his reserved spot. Poking my head around the corner, I saw, yup, the Range Rover was there. First hurdle. Turning back, two women headed to their cars; my head down, I pulled a U-turn and slid out through the monitored gates. On the other side of the building, gathering dark hair to my face, I crossed the bustling street against the light. Approached Billie's car from the far side. She was keenly focused on the door where she'd dropped me, her nose to the window.

I reached for her door, yanked it open. She jumped and rapped her forehead sharply against the window. "Damn it. Don't sneak up on me like that. Car there?"

Breathless, I dropped onto the fabric seat. "It was there. Sorry, I was avoiding Butlerites."

Heading toward the love nest, Billie kept up a rapid stream of conversation. As though she were dropping me any old place. "Just keep your wits about you. Make every second in there count."

You think? My grand plan was to freak out and snoop through useless shit.

I carefully shoved the octagonal key into the coin pocket of my jeans. Tried nudging it to see if it was secure. Every nerve on high alert, I buzzed with trepidation. And determination.

Billie kept talking. "Key can't slip out? Phone fully charged?"

I squashed a visceral urge to make a break for it. *Breathe.*

I looked down the quaint courtyard, an enclave of brownstones. Refined, far-from-prying-eyes row houses. "Third door on the left. It's red." A lone woman passed at the end of the courtyard, a dotted umbrella over her shoulder—the gloomy, dreary day was ideal for breaking and entering. Not a lot of people around. It rolled over me as I took in the unfamiliar surroundings that my husband spent time here; he had a life here. A life that didn't include me.

"Okay, Mama. Showtime. I'll keep watch at his garage till you text me to come back." She all but shoved me onto the sidewalk in her oversize jacket and my dark wig.

Some fucking disguise.

Conveniently near the outlet of the pedestrian courtyard, I spotted his steps. Beyond the enclave with its potted cherry blossoms was Georgetown's famed M Street. Chic cafés, bougie boutiques, water taxis. *Corporate apartment, my ass.*

Painted clay planters sat out front. A copper watering can next to them. Someone took great care of this little place. I waited impatiently for two rambunctious teenage boys to leave the courtyard for the park. They crossed the street, and I moved quickly to the red door.

I tried to pull the key from the coin pocket. The shaking was nearly uncontrollable. One finger fit in snugly. Trying to extract it carefully, it slipped away and clattered to the steps. I stooped to grab for it. The key bounced into water pooled at the base of the steps. I pulled it out through the murky puddle of last night's rain. Wiped it on my shirt. Slid it in the lock quickly.

Fuck. The key wouldn't turn. No movement at all. None. I tried both directions. I yanked it back out. Nothing. *It's stuck!* I tried to muscle it. Wouldn't turn, wouldn't come out. Frozen, I was momentarily paralyzed. By the what-ifs. The what-nows.

Damn it! I knew it was too good to be true—an app that makes a key. *I'm screwed.*

Not about to give up, I wiggled it. Gently at first—back and forth, back and forth. I scanned the courtyard, alert to any movement, any sound.

Do it. One chance. Think. Sometimes a newly cut key is … *holy shit!* I twisted harder, and this time it turned, stuck a bit, and then one final tinny click. I pushed my shoulder against the old door. It heaved open. I was inside. In the entryway of my husband's love nest.

CHAPTER 38

CALL TO ACTION

The darkness was stifling. Dark plantation shutters covered the courtyard-facing windows. The wide slats were drawn closed. Slim slivers of light slipped through, streaking the wood floors. I forced myself to take a breath. There was a cloying, musky scent mingling uncomfortably with the sharp smell of bleach. Shutting the heavy door instantly, I looked for a keypad indicating an alarm system. Ears alert for telltale beeps. Nothing. *Someone's watching over me.*

My eyes started to adjust. A distinctly feminine touch, furnished with things I'd never seen. Tiny occasional tables. A tufted, leather ottoman, decorative tray on top. Soft area rugs. A silver candle with several wicks—that was the musk. Always made me gag.

The only familiar items: two of our lush Turkish bath sheets piled spa style on a little table outside the bath. Several tasseled pillows from our guest suite were strewn at the top of a bed I'd never seen. One of our high-thread-count cashmere throws across the floral couch.

Guess I'm decorating your love nest, one luxurious linen at a time.

In a dim corner, a small pre-fab office. His distinct ruby-red laptop sat closed on the desk. A pleather stool beneath. I switched my phone into camera mode. Ready to screen grab.

The desk drawer resisted when I pulled it. It squealed loudly on loose tracks. On top of a tidy pile, a tiny beige envelope. It contained a lone thumb drive. Turning it over in my fingers, I plugged it into the laptop. Despite knowing exactly what it was.

A still screen popped up, a big play arrow in the center. Unmistakably me, even in a still. Mid writhe, mid moan. The sexy video I'd sent, the one made out of love, the one he'd said he'd deleted. It was Rick: Rick had posted it. Rick had deleted it. The hairs on the nape of my neck tingled.

He plans to ruin me. Obliterate my brand. Discredit me in every way. Sliding the drive out, I slipped it in my pocket. I dug in the back of the drawer and found a loose ChapStick, not very different in size to the drive. I tucked it in the envelope. Hoped fervently he had no reason to open it soon. What else would he do to me?

Under the envelope, a large lined Post-it. His handwriting. Still taking notes: his to-do lists or must-ponder lists. When he handled them, he tore them into pieces. Disordered mind, that was what Gerry had said. Employing a tactic like that fueled his sense of being in control.

I caught my breath; it was a simple list, childish really. Two columns: pros vs. cons. Me vs. Caroline. Mine topped with an *R*, hers with a *C*. As though we held equal places as he debated our attributes. Our shortcomings. Twisting the knife in the same way hearing them laugh when rejecting my call had. The *R* column read: "Sexy. Smart. Funny. Sweet."

And why the hell wasn't that enough—sexy, smart, funny, sweet? Enough was never enough for a narcissist. If you no longer idolized them, you were nothing. Two options: you were pedestaled or demonized. *I'm a demon.*

I couldn't look at the *C* list. Except to notice there were no cons. Just pros. Only pros for the one who does you in my house, our car, your bathroom. Sure, she hadn't been *Ricked* yet. I flipped the note over. My hand flew to my throat.

Incredible. And yet not.

The work spouse wouldn't have to wait as long as the real spouse had. On the backside of the note: two more lists. One marked Vegas, one just the letter *J*. Looked like Caroline had competition already. Who was *J*? Did he even know Vegas' name?

In disbelief, I screen grabbed it. Pressed on. Papers sat neatly on an open blue file folder. The deed to our home. As he'd implied, it was only in his name now.

Jesus. That was my money, and it's gone. And the pension form showing the funds had been protected and were solely his. There were documents where I'd waived rights to any marital assets. And I'd e-signed every paper in the pile with my curvy electronically formatted signature.

And there it is. The real reason he needed access to my phone. He was sending me documents. Hacking into my phone. Signing them *as me*. Another felony. He wasn't wrong, though. Nothing I had was admissible. Hard to prove he'd hacked my phone, signed papers. It may all still be inadmissible, but it was a preponderance of evidence I was compiling.

Taped to the laptop in the lower-right corner, the back of one of his business cards, his password neatly written on it: "CarpeDiem50." *Seize the day*, the Latin he prided himself on.

Placing the phone on the desk, I opened the computer. His screen saver photo was of a naked woman, her face coyly averted from the camera. *Who* ... leaning closer ... was that me, my breast? No, I had a beauty mark right ...

Shimmying on the desk startled me. It was a text from Billie. Get out. He left through the front door on foot. Couldn't catch him on the one-way street.

A sickening sense engulfed me. I had taken too big a risk: *You can't see him?*

Billie: He was walking. I couldn't get the car around. I'm looking.

Rigid with terror, I couldn't blow my only chance. There was no time left.

Keep going, keep going. I typed in the password. His home page came up.

"Expense Accounts" icon—I screen grabbed the front-page summary of each month. Spreadsheets detailed everything—the who, what, and why of everything the company paid for.

Billie: Get out. I mean it.

Her Louboutins, Porsche Cayenne lease, world-class travel, hotels, spas: he'd falsely assigned each "company" expenditure to someone the company found acceptable to woo for business purposes. *Finally.* Definitive documentation of fraud as well. Or was that embezzling?

Since Rick was the financial whiz, I made a mental note. Check with him to confirm which felony category that fell under. Fraud or embezzling.

In a minute. Found more stuff. I hit "Send."

"Reilly insurance." I opened the attachment. He'd upped my life insurance policy to two million dollars? Why? As a healthy fortysomething, it wouldn't seem much of a concern, or would it? Two million reasons.

Click, click, click.

Dizzy, unsteady, I stumbled to the kitchen for water. To the side of the sink was a small oval dish. In it: his wedding band, the one I'd slid on his finger at the Inn. Inscribed: FOR LIFE.

Next to the ring, silver cufflinks. One an x, the other an o. Dummy, you're supposed to wear the cufflinks she gave you to the office so she can enjoy your little secret.

Prominently placed on the kitchen windowsill, the solid brass plaque that Franklin had handed off to him at Marchand's, his voice swelling with pride for his "Richard."

Billie: I'm driving. Saw him. Maybe coming there. Get out.

Face-to-face with him. At his lair. The image crippled me. I had more than I needed; time to get out. Listening intently for any sound in the courtyard, I hurriedly put his desk the way it had been.

What the ...

I'd overlooked something: the large brown envelope under the laptop. Pulling out two sets of papers, my hands went ice cold.

The first sheet was topped with an official-looking silver seal. From the circuit court.

A legal separation document confirming that we, Richard W. and Reilly A. Lynch, had officially separated. We sought a dissolution of our marriage. Rick listed the corporate apartment, thereby establishing residency. *What the hell?* He'd requested the separation; I'd signed it. He'd filed it in our jurisdiction over three weeks ago.

Blindsided, I touched my finger to the raised seal. It was legitimate. Legally binding.

We're legally separated, nearly divorced. He figured out a way to mitigate that extramarital affair into a nonissue.

I looked at the closing lines; I'd agreed to an uncontested divorce. To be granted after thirty days. Two days from now. *I'm fucked once that divorce goes through. In two days.*

I moved my index finger to the seal again ... *Divorced.* Screen grab, keep it moving.

Billie: Are you out?!

I replied: *Almost.*

The other documents. A psychiatric advance directive, from the institution in Connecticut. "I, Reilly Lynch, do willingly grant legal decision-making authority to my 'agent,' Richard W. Lynch. Mr. Lynch will serve as my advocate during my time ..."

I'd abdicated everything—my marriage, my money, my career. My control over my life. So this was the "other way" the suit had mentioned; if he couldn't get Sloan on board, he would just e-sign my rights away. To him. My stomach roiled. *Breathe.*

I obsessively replaced each item. To the millimeter, I hoped.

My phone vibrated, the buzzing indistinguishable from the sounds filling my ears. Billie: *On foot. M and Willow. Urgent.*

M and Willow! Now it *was* urgent. Four blocks away. Shaking convulsively, I replaced the envelope, the stool. No time to comb through night tables, the closet. *To what end, anyway?* I knew all I needed to know, more than anyone should ever know about the one they love.

Loved, I reprimanded myself harshly. *Loved.* I moved to the front door and reached out.

A footstep creaked on the outside stairs. A man's voice. My heart in my throat, I backed away.

CHAPTER 39

ACCOUNTABILITY

A rising terror threatened to immobilize me. I scanned the unfamiliar apartment for a spot to hide. The minuscule coat closet in the corner, maybe. *Damn*, it wasn't for coats after all. It was shelved. I whirled around, looking for a back exit.

Keys jangled as they were pulled from a pocket. *His* pocket. *Shit*. I'd waited too long.

The voice again: Rick. Who was he talking to? Had someone joined him now?

I was nearly incapacitated. No back exit. Where could I go? Where could I hide? The bed: too low. The kitchen cabinets: too small. The skinny broom closet at the end of the hall.

I jerked on the door. It was empty but for a shaky wooden crate. Crouching on the rickety box, I curled my feet up under me. I barely fit. Another footstep on the stairs, and a key slid into the lock. I closed the door. Just as the front door opened.

Rick groaned in frustration. There was no other voice; he was alone. Only silence, he must be on the phone. Pushing my body hard up against the wall, I could see through the splinter of an opening where the door hinged. At the end of the hall, he stood impatiently. In the near dark. He banged his fist on the wall. Jumping at the thump, I nearly tumbled from the box.

His attempt to not lose his temper was testing him. "Already told you, mate. That plan has changed now. There's one way. She has to go. Not basic car nonsense this time; that was just meant to be a small thing, undermine her a bit."

I had to go? My heart hammered wildly. He couldn't have meant … he was behind the accident. He was truly evil. He'd only wanted to undermine me, scare me, and yet he'd almost succeeded in killing me.

He dropped his briefcase to the floor. Flipped on the light switch and turned toward the closet. I leaned away from the wall, terrified he could see my eyes. What would he do if …

Breathe. Silence again. Panic surged through me. Deep breaths were the only thing that allowed the mind to focus, especially during fight or flight. In, out.

I texted with trembling fingers: I'm safe. Out of sight. Wait in the courtyard.

Billie's response: Copy. Don't do anything stupid.

Define stupid. I eyed my surroundings. The old door to the closet I hunched in had a huge gap at the bottom. Opportunity. Pressing "Record" on my phone, I placed it quietly at the opening of the door, microphone facing the room.

He no longer hid his condescension, sharply rapping his phone against the wall before speaking. "Did you *hear* me? I was assured *yesterday* I'm getting Franklin's job. He's taking a step back. New plan. She's a liability now. I can't have a messy divorce."

"*Or* a wife with a public platform, God forbid," he ticked off.

"*Or* a wife who is institutionalized. Insane isn't an option," he ticked.

"The stakes are higher now. The highest. She can't just be silenced. She needs to be *dead*. Got it?"

The pain in the deep cavern of my soul was unbearable. He tossed the word out so cavalierly. *Dead.* I leaned my head against the wall, and images scrolled through my mind: being hunted by his hired gun. Never knowing, always waiting. Hiding.

None of my hard-fought efforts mattered now. None of the proof I'd just compiled. He wanted me eliminated. So he wouldn't lose his shot at Franklin's job. The job he'd coveted for so long; his deep-rooted fear the board wouldn't approve of him. This was everything to him.

Destitute didn't seem all that bad now; it had just been trumped. By *dead*.

A muted squeal, the thrump of a cork being wrenched from a bottle. "The *how* is your job. I don't care to know details. I simply want to know when it's done. It's awfully hard to bear such a tragic accident," he said sadly. A glass placed on granite. Liquid was poured generously.

"The gentleman is automatically accorded everyone's empathy—you see? The widower that soldiers on. And when he finds love again, whoever it's with, everyone will be on his side. He deserves it, after all."

The cracked plaster of the walls in the tiny closet squeezed in on me more tightly; my cell was airless and claustrophobic. He was so remarkably unconcerned with having his wife killed that he was toasting to it. So unconcerned with leaving Sloan motherless that he would enjoy a full-bodied cab while organizing it.

Anxiety was no longer inanimate. It clawed at me unrelentingly. From the inside out. An alien straining to escape the confines of my body.

It was ominous, his shoe tapping persistently. It was a countdown-to-dead metronome.

I'd been right; he'd stop at nothing. The best thing that ever happened to him—being offered the position of a lifetime—was the worst thing that had ever happened to me.

I could go to Franklin with everything I knew, everything I had, but I'd still have a target on my back. And still face the risk that Franklin would turn a blind eye: Rick, after all, was what he could deliver financially. Who he *was* didn't matter, as he'd said. If he was still able to bring in the big bucks, his transgressions would be forgiven. Ignored.

Footsteps as he moved close to my spot. Then none. I didn't breathe, didn't move. The anxiety was overwhelming, the space stifling. Beads of sweat gathered at the base of my wig and dropped onto my neck.

"I'm familiar with the concept of time," he said sarcastically. "And I'm aware it's not much. But it's what you have. Twenty-four hours. You've the home address. She takes classes at eleven at the shopping center. Day after tomorrow is one of her vlog things, and that *will not* happen. She's a goddamn loose cannon."

Looking down, the red "Record" button was still lit, his voice still strong in the apartment. The smartest guy. On audio, asking for his wife to be killed. In a tragic accident. I could be taken out by his person at kickboxing. When the very reason I was there was to protect myself. I couldn't think. My brain jammed. Clammy, cold, I tried ... tried to think.

Like Gerry had said: When you posed a true threat to them, they'd stop at nothing. Their lack of empathy and moral compass came in handy. I wasn't getting out of this alive; he was seeing to that. The fraud didn't matter, the divorce papers, the other women. Even his attempt to have me institutionalized didn't matter. The game had changed dramatically.

He sighed, as if concluding a tedious business transaction, and opened the door to his bedroom. I finally exhaled. He wasn't five feet from me any longer. My pulse steadied.

"Just make it happen. And the tall dark-haired one you saw her with—it would make me extra happy if she were to be part of the tragedy. That one is bloody relentless, dog with a bone."

For the first time in the suffocating closet, I fought back tears. Billie. He would have her killed, too, if, in a happy accident, we were together at the time his guy chose to execute the plan. The guilt: of not having believed Billie's gut, of not fully sharing with her because I wanted to be right about him. And now this.

A sob lurked in my throat. *No. No!* I was so selfish, and Billie would pay the ultimate price. For having shown me unconditional love. *How ironic.* Rick had so highly coveted that quality in any woman in his life. Except for in Billie, because she saw through him. Doubling over, images of a motherless Amy drifted into my mind. The collateral damage of my choices knew no boundaries.

And me, what was left for me? What about Sloan? Would he work his magic on her if I never escaped this madness? I had to. That wasn't an option. This wasn't happening like this. Sitting ram-rod straight, I pushed my back against the wall and took strength from its rigidity.

As Rick told his new hires, facing challenges wasn't optional; overcoming them was in your control. The challenges had just become more daunting, the stakes higher. Fixing things with my daughter, saving Billie, saving other women from Rick, getting out of this situation alive, those things were not optional. Everything else was. Fuck everything else.

He concluded, "Let's get on with it then. I'm leaving town tomorrow. I'll pay a visit to a few of our other offices. I mustn't be anywhere near here. Be in touch."

My mind started to clear as I looked down at my phone. It was on record. Oh my God. I could make sure he was held accountable for once in his life. I could make sure he couldn't harm anyone again. *Now* I had what I needed. Proof positive that would put him away for a long time. All I had to do was escape. I got in. I could get out ... somehow.

He pulled down a suitcase, dropped it to the floor with a thud. Rick was voice-to-texting: "Ciao bella period. Arriving McCarran Airport tomorrow at ten fifty period. At Bellagio by noon period. The Cypress Suite smiley."

Likely Vegas. No shame in that man's game.

The shower spray started, the bathroom door closed. I hadn't expected that. I trembled with relief. There it was. Opportunity.

My opportunity to get out. I waited. I wasn't rushing it. Once I was sure he was *in* the shower, that was my moment. He wouldn't be able to hear anything in the hallway. Opening the door a few inches, I listened intently. A creak, a click—the shower door opened and closed. The water sounded different now. It wasn't hitting the ceramic; it was rolling over a body. It was muffled. I exhaled.

Pulling my feet out from under me, I went to place them on the wooden floor. Leaning into the room, I rose from the closet and sneaked a look at the bathroom door. Still closed. Shower still running.

A jangle of keys at the door startled me. I stopped. I was just jumpy. Could be the town house one over. A key slid into the lock, this lock, this flat. In front of me. The silver door knob turned. Just a little. In slow motion.

The knob turned more, and the door was pushed partly open. An arm reached in, a woman's arm. All lavender nails and tinkling gold David Yurman bangles. The hand dropped a quilted overnight bag on the floor. I breathed shallowly. Backed away as the door continued to open into the foyer. Frantically, I slumped back into the tiny cage, pulling the door behind me.

Billie texted: WTF. Did I just see a woman go in?

Me: Yes. Don't move.

There was a creak. She pushed the heavy door closed behind her. Dropped keys onto the duffel. A quieter thud, a purse maybe. The clicking of heels down the entryway, rhythmically tapping on the wood floors. It was *her*. Or one of the hers, at any rate.

The steps stopped; a glass was put on the counter, and the cork popped lightly out of the bottle. Heels poured herself some wine. Pulling my knees closer to my chest, I held the door in place in front of me. As near to being closed as I could get it, praying it was near enough.

The clicking started again. With a light tap on the bathroom door, she called out to Rick. I knew that voice.

We-were-always-gonna-be-a-couple Caroline.

"Hey, boss." She opened the door to the bathroom. Breezy. Carefree.

"Hey, love. Grabbing a quick shower. Out in a sec." *Love.*

Back in my spot, my face was squished up against the peeling plaster. I watched her through the sliver of an opening. I narrowed my eyes to see more clearly. She really had done her best to turn into me, wearing my signature dark stretch jeans, a V-neck fitted sweater, hint of a tee peeking out from the bottom. The layered look I favored. That Rick favored on me.

"Your car was in the garage when I left; thought we crossed wires."

"I walked. Since I'm in Las Vegas and San Francisco for a bit, it's better left there than these narrow Georgetown streets. The dings will be the death of me."

"Gotcha. Traffic was a mess. Must've been stopped by the Watergate for ten minutes for the motorcade." She kicked off super-high-heeled taupe boots, one after the other. Clunk. Clunk.

My mind was racing; she was getting comfortable. Shoes came off. Likely they were staying in when shoes came off. I was *not* listening to them together again. I couldn't. File 5 started: the zipper, the garbled sounds, his climax. My stomach clenched viciously. I couldn't.

"Steamy," she said. "It's gettin' hot in here," she crooned to the Nelly song. To my husband. Slowly starting to peel the flimsy black sweater up her torso, she leaned back when it cleared her head, and she was rolling it down her arms—my opportunity. The second she leaned and disappeared from sight, I darted from the closet.

Dashing to the front door, I swiped the sweat from my neck and pulled open the door to the outside. Billie sat on the back of a rounded bench, nearly obscuring herself behind one of the cherry blossoms. Thrusting her hand up high, she frantically beckoned. I breathed, really breathed, for the first time, and reached back to pull the door closed.

Rick's voice, tantalizing and inviting, floated out from the bathroom. "Joining me for the shower show?"

I didn't feel the anger just yet, my hand on the knob. How had our life together culminated in this impossibly surreal, implausibly abhorrent vignette? He'd simply swapped us out—*my* shower show, *our* shower show, had just been handed over to her, the next iteration. A toxic combination of fury and disgust slapped me. I reeled from the impact. Along with the stark realization that I was, in this instant, capable of potent, untethered rage.

It wasn't the betrayal—it was the cruel, abusive way he treated women, all women. Not that I cared about this woman, but she had no idea what she was dealing with. She had no idea the extent to which we were all disposable. Looking back at her vibrantly patterned, optimistic Vera Bradley bag perched so confidently by the door, I had to do it. I had let his manipulations twist me up for so long, make me question myself for so long, control my relationships, my career—not a minute longer.

I held my finger up to Billie, it was a "give me a minute" finger. *Fuck it.* Give me a goddamn minute.

She threw her hands up and mouthed a terrified, "No."

No was right. This was not how this was going down. I was not skulking out into the night, slinking down the courtyard. Fleeing. As if I were the felon. Disgraced. Discredited. He was not getting his way this time; he was not winning. I would not explode. I would not rage.

Fuck it. Easing back into the foyer, I closed the door, Billie still flailing in concern. I would be grace under pressure. Calm. In control.

I reached over to his desk. Slid open the drawer. It scraped again. I slipped out the Post-it and crouched behind the chair. Held the paper against my chest. Had they heard the squeal?

"Not tonight, babe. Had my hair done. Their blowout is sooo much better than mine. I need it to last as long as humanly possible." She giggled.

They hadn't heard, still obliviously making random small talk, about blowouts no less. Just another woman, a different day, more mindless chitchat. Nothing new. Except the woman.

I knew precisely what would undermine a woman's love; I had *been* that woman, after all. For way too long. With him, every woman would eventually be that woman. Clutching the note, I made my move. *I got this.*

Sliding into the bathroom doorway, I leaned against the doorframe and feigned irritation. My eyes drifted back and forth between Rick and Caroline. "I was under the impression it was just the two of us tonight, love. Change of plans?"

Ensconced in the glass shower, Rick listed sharply to one side. One hand jerked heavily up to the wall. In the midst of rinsing out shampoo, head arched back into the water stream, his face flipped to me. His mouth gaped like a trout. The shower flush vanished, his skin so pasty that his five-o'clock shadow looked like burned sesame seeds strewn on raw dough.

And *her.* Her body rigid with shock. Her jaw dropped in astonishment. Sweater in her lap, she was clad only in a violet push-up bra and jeans. She almost failed to recognize me, her watery eyes spasming—twitch, twitch, twitch. That I was there, in his bathroom. Holding a key to his love nest. Wearing a sexy, dark tousled wig. Her head tipped involuntarily, and her highly glossed lips tried to form words.

"He likes an assortment of women; you know that. I wear this when I'm 'Charlotte,'" I purred, using air quotes. Smoothing my dark bangs in the mirror, I wiped a finger under one smudged eye and conjured a raven-haired vixen. "Right, sweetheart?"

Sputtering, Rick stood naked and dripping, his face slack. His eyes narrowed, they darted furiously between me and Caroline. Only the spray of water broke the eerie near silence. After opening and closing his mouth, he mustered, "What ... how ... did you get in here?"

I acted dismayed. "That's how you want to play this? You got your schedule of ladies mixed up and you want to act like … what … you're not still seeing me? Not very chivalrous."

Matching looks of shock. His and hers. Incongruously, my husband stood nude, generally his preferred state. In front of me, in front of her. And Caroline sat in front of him, dressed like me. Two women, virtually interchangeable from a distance.

Mistrustful of me, she shifted her back to me and addressed him. "You're not still seeing her, are you? You swore. You said there would be no other women. Your sowing-your-wild-oats days were done."

I smiled benignly, knowingly. "He used the same line on me. Did you get the 'I never understood *you complete me* until I met you' line?" I asked.

Shifting her flinty eyes back, she was less certain of him now.

He shoved his hands through his tangle of hair. "'Course I'm not seeing her. I've no idea what she's up to. This is madness." Slapping his head to the tiled wall in frustration, he let out a piercing groan; a vein popped out by his eye. It throbbed darkly against his wan skin.

The woodsy-scented steam was rising. He composed himself slightly, pulled himself up to his full height. Turned off each of the shower knobs. Slowly. Meticulously.

He murmured quietly to her, "You know it's only you. It's only us. Don't let that one play games with your head. Now call nine-one-one. We have an intruder."

She gripped her phone tightly, trembling.

Without turning to me, he said in a nasty tone, "Get. Out. This is trespassing."

Dangling the key from my fingers, I replied, "Hard to see how that works. Since I have this. Where exactly would I have gotten it?"

"I've no idea. But just like you clearly had some sort of device in my car to know what you knew, how do I know what else you might be willing to do?"

I nodded smugly. "Well, I did learn from the best. The one who put the GPS on *my* car."

The steam started to dissipate, the glass of the shower clearer. Rick stumbled as he shifted, steadied himself. His mind revved in overdrive.

Caroline eyed him with growing trepidation. Waiting for more of a denial. About seeing me, about the GPS. About anything. I'd been there. I knew what that was like. Desperate to know if he was really all yours, if he was who he presented, and at the same time desperate to stay in the dark. Simply wanting to believe your happily-ever-after.

Rick repeated, "Nine-one-one, Caroline."

She numbly bobbed her head. Her perfect blowout, tainted by the steam, had started to frizz badly at the temples. She turned her phone screen up and reached a finger out. I placed the Post-it between Caroline and her phone.

Her eyes drifted toward it. I pointed at the two columns: *R* and *C*. She scanned them and blinked. With a new wariness. The softer look she'd adopted vanished, and her natural coarseness returned.

"You said it was a non-relationship. But here ..." She jabbed her finger at the note. "Sexy. You told me it was a sexless marriage. That's why she couldn't give you the kid you wanted."

I flinched at the lie. Vilified again. He sneered: "For Heaven's sake ..."

"Funny, smart, sweet. And I'm ... 'laid-back,'" she read, caustically.

Rick slapped his open hand on the vintage black-and-white tiled wall and moaned. "*Yes.* As in not high maintenance, like her. I will not continue to justify this, Caroline. I won't."

Her voice was haunted. "Trusting, devoted. Doesn't this all just translate into ... I'm easy to manipulate? Starting to seem like that's what you do."

The anesthesia effect of the shock was evaporating; she was an open wound now. Raw. Nerves exposed.

"It's not what it looks like. I must've written that long ago. You know me better than that."

She muttered. Drained a long gulp from the wine goblet. Squinted at him and clutched her phone in its leopard glitter case, a remnant of the not-yet-classed-up-for-Rick era.

I flipped the note over. Trailed a finger up and down the other two lists. "So J and Vegas are ancient history too—and that's why he has the note right on top of his desk drawer."

Rick growled when I turned over the note. Caroline whimpered pitifully. She self-consciously slid her bunched-up sweater over her torso to cover her naked midriff, her garish purple bra, blotchy flesh spilling out. Pulling myself up next to her on the counter, I sat. I thrust my feet flat up against the heavy shower door and lodged my back against the wall, wedging the door closed. Impossible to open from the inside.

Rick thrust his formidable shoulders up against it several times. It shuddered, but the door didn't budge.

I turned to Caroline. She wouldn't look at me; she couldn't move her gaze from Rick. Her eyes were tormented. But bound to his. She was wavering.

"I'll get this all sorted. Stay with me here." He was wooing her. His accent became more pronounced, the lilt amped up for effect. Her lip trembled. She would trust him. She was under his spell. He was her drug of choice; she just needed more—and it would all be better.

"What've I told you? You're my soul mate. We were always meant to be together."

Transfixed, I watched. He'd started to get her back under his spell.

"Soul mate," she echoed. He almost had her back again, back where he liked his women.

"Possible." I tossed my dark, wavy hair over my shoulder. "But those things he bought you—the Louboutins, the Porsche—Butler paid for all of it. You could be an accessory."

Reaching out, I tapped on her Yurman bracelets. "Good bet those are Butler's. And that's not even part of what he's been up to—financially, legally. Did he tell you he drugs me, hacks into my phone, signs documents that waive my rights to my home, our money?"

Rick talked over me and directed himself to her. "She's delusional. She's unwell. I've told you that; you can't believe this nonsense."

"And he was on the verge of having me institutionalized," I informed her.

"For your drug and alcohol problems. I told her all about it. You pass out. You drive your car off the road. I was just trying to help her, Caroline. You know I only wanted the best for her, even though she …" He held his hands up helplessly, his face radiating decency. She nodded. She'd heard his stories about me.

I watched him channel his charm, get some swagger back. He was intuitively creating a new lane. Polishing the corrosive tarnish off his halo. Soon to be a paragon of virtue once more.

Holding up my phone, I waved it back and forth. They turned simultaneously. Four eyes fixed on it, aware it meant something, unaware of what that might be. Time stood still.

With conviction, I pressed "Play" on the file I'd recorded. Caroline watched me, guardedly. I watched him. He was unsure, for once, what to expect. The not knowing, the dread of what someone might do, what they were capable of. He had inflicted it often. The file started to play.

Rick's voice: "The *how* is your job. I don't care to know details. I simply want to know when it's done. It's awfully hard to bear such a tragic accident. And the gentleman has everyone's empathy—the widower that soldiers on. And when he finds love again, whoever it's with, everyone will be happy for him. He deserves it, after all."

Whirling around to her, his face mottled with anger, he approached the glass of the shower wall. "Care Bear, it's not what it sounds like. You mustn't start doubting me now."

All color had drained from her face. "*Whoever* you're with. Whoever? Even after you would have her killed, I still wouldn't get you?"

"Of course you would! Those others … they …"

Her breath caught in her throat as she tried to absorb that he was acknowledging … unexpectedly dropping her head back, she dissolved into yelping barks of laughter, mirthless and hollow. It echoed in the confined space. She pressed her fists to her mouth.

Her glassy eyes were rimmed with pink, anguished as she gazed at Rick. She tugged her sweater over her head. Jammed her hands through the sleeves and shook. She'd been *Ricked*.

"Fucker. You promised me a life. I left my husband for you. I have nothing now, nothing." Her whole body quaked. Slipping to her feet, she was unsteady; one hand gripped her stomach, the other the counter.

He coaxed her along. "You mustn't overreact here. We're a team." His eyes glinted, they bore into hers and willed her to comply.

She shifted her gaze to me. Drew her palm across her runny nose. Strangely simpatico, she and I. The enormity of his lies, his betrayal, his behaviors; it was sinking in. Her dream was dead. It had been snatched in an instant. She'd stopped breathing. She was strangely silent.

"Care Bear," he whispered.

Caroline twisted to look at her reflection in the mirror, and Rick behind her. She mumbled in a disembodied voice, "I deserved this. Just when I thought I'd finally gotten lucky. I should've known. I'll never get lucky."

Gagging on bile, her breath became labored. She was panting. Her pupils dilated. Her lavender nails pawed at the collar of her sweater. Caroline was hyperventilating.

"Breathe," I said. "In. Out. Come on. In…"

Inhaling through her nose, exhaling through her mouth, and again, her color improved. She moaned, clutching her stomach.

Rick watched the exchange scornfully. "Care," he implored her. "This is when you prove your love for me, right now. There's two of us, one of her." He jerked an elbow in my direction.

In a hoarse monotone, her lips hardly moved. "You tried to have her killed. Killed," she repeated, her gloss-smeared mouth curling with contempt.

"All because of Mr. Butler's job? It's worth that? You're a sick son of a bitch."

His eyes were angry slits; he was naked, still glistening with unrinsed froth trickling down his limbs. "Oh my God, you are failing to understand …"

She was contemptuous.

"No, *you* don't understand. I protected you; you'd have been fired, except for me. Now I get it—you *used* me, to keep your job, to get Butler's job. Keep me happy and I wouldn't get you fired. I just didn't know that when I wasn't useful anymore, you might have me killed."

She snatched her boots from the floor and stood with her back to me. "Grab your shit. Let's get outta here," she said and trudged out with her wine.

It was time. Time for it all to end. He was going to get what was coming to him. I looked back at Rick, encased behind glass, his hair matted, foam pooling at his feet—he was pathetic.

Unaware Caroline still hovered next to the door sliding into her leather boots, he appealed to the one left standing. Me. "Please, love. It's always been you. I will make this whole mess right. You know I will. I can make anything happen." His chin was high. He held three fingers up against the steamy glass.

"That's his gesture for 'I love you.'" I showed Caroline, ticking off the three fingers.

She flung her glass at the shower. The burgundy beverage dripped down the wall. The goblet shattered to the tiles. Stalking into the foyer, her heels tapped furiously.

"If you think I'm protecting you going forward, you got another think comin', *boss*."

My feet still propped against the door, I stared at him in his cage. "This is what it's come to. You had everything, but you're demented. You're vindictive. You've deceived people all your life. Except your mother—she knows you're a liar and a thief and an arsonist. What she doesn't know is that you're fine with being a murderer, too—but she will," I promised him.

He kicked the door. "Don't talk about my *mother*! Don't ever say anything about my *mother*!"

Sliding off the counter, I turned to leave. So tragic, in so many ways. Our accumulated history that had breathed new life into my existence, the abiding moments of deep love I'd hoarded in my heart, the bond I'd believed unbreakable. Movement glinted in the mirror.

I heard it first: a ferocious thud. Seconds later, I felt it: a screaming pain bolted through my head. Dazed, I looked up at Rick's reflection in the mirror. He'd viciously shoved the glass shower door at me, and it had caught me squarely on the back of the head. My vision was fuzzy; my dark wig lay across the sink. My gaze drifted to the living room. How could Caroline not have heard that disturbing crack and come to investigate?

Rick stepped out of the shower, an impenetrable look on his face. Before I could move, he lunged for my phone on the counter and grabbed it. My vision cleared some. I turned to him.

Smirking maliciously, he tipped my phone. This way, that way. "What'll it be? Care to let bygones be bygones? Without this, you have nothing."

My mind thrummed, I assessed options.

Never moving my eyes from his face, I was still. He was still. Both of us expressionless.

Never signaling the move, I cracked the side of my hand down on his extended wrist with force: my phone clattered to the tile. I snatched it before he could.

A smile played at the corner of his lips. "So that's the way she wants to do it." He walked out of the bathroom, calmly wrapping a towel around his hips.

His eyes scanned the living room. No sign of *her*. The front door was ajar. The quilted overnighter gone. She'd grabbed her stuff and slithered away. I was alone with him.

Thanks, Care Bear.

Turning to me with a victory sneer, he put his hand out. Beckoned for my phone. My phone was his biggest problem. He would deal with the rest.

His fingers sharply motioned. His body: stiff, tense. My body: taut, on high alert. I was in the zone now, the one where everything falls into place. You didn't miss anything. Your reasoning skills were tactical, strategic. *"Accurate. Sharp. Strong."*

Slowly, I extended the phone toward him. With a devilish wink, he said, "Who knows, sweetheart, you might even get to keep me if you play nice. It seems to make the most sense right now for both of us, don't you agree?"

I opened my hand and dropped the phone just before it reached him. It clattered to the floor at his feet. He instantly leaned down to get it. I let him. I wanted him to. I watched him bend down for my phone with one hand holding the towel in place and the other reaching out.

I got this.

Opportunity. Jerking back my dominant arm, I slammed the boniest part of my elbow down into the softest part of his exposed neck. *Jab.* The crunch was sickening. In an instant, his body splayed out, collapsing awkwardly onto one arm. His chin jammed jarringly on the floor. Scarlet ooze pooled from the corner of his mouth. No movement. Eyes half-opened, unfocused.

Placing my foot on the back of his neck, I applied pressure. From deep in his chest, a primal croak. I swiftly scooped up my phone, tapped out 911. About to press "Call," I was suddenly off-balance. Rick yanked my calves, and I plummeted to the floor.

He was up, hovering over me. Racking my brain for the next move, I scooched myself back along the wood planks, trying to create space between us. He was in control now. He had me where he wanted me.

With his bare foot on my chest, he pushed me the last inches to the wall, pinned me. He grabbed me by the arms. Tossed me across his couch like a rag doll.

"I can still be the grieving widower. Trust me, no one will ever find your body." He crouched next to me, his mouth twisted and dripping blood, his hands around my throat. "You never loved me. You never had my back like someone who loves you should."

I kicked my feet; I flailed in his grasp. In response, he clenched tighter. Everything felt so far away … my ears were ringing, buzzing … *stop fighting him. Stop.*

Options. The jab to the eyeballs. *I can do that.* Gathering my resources, I took a last, quaking gasp and went completely still. Limply, I dropped the one arm I'd had up against his chest. Ceased my breathing entirely and closed my eyes. Let my lips fall open slightly. His hands relaxed around my neck. He moved closer to me. I felt his breath on my face. Opportunity.

I angled my fingers for the jab. Then …

A hideous thud. With a staccato grunt, Rick toppled heavily onto me and listed to one side before sliding off the sofa. He lay in a heap on the floor. A gaping wound to the back of his head opened, and blood overflowed the indentation. A bright-red yolky ooze. I had to look away.

My gaze drifted up. There, looming over him, a hand hoisted the hefty brass plaque. The one that Franklin had personally handed off to Rick, the presumed heir to his throne.

It was Billie.

The police siren pierced the quiet courtyard as cars pulled onto the cobblestones and screeched to a halt. A rosy spiral of lights illuminated the room.

CHAPTER 40

END SLATE

Three months later, my dusty rental Wrangler hugged the curvy Nova Scotia roads. Fundy Coast Drive presented extraordinary sights as towering sandstone cliffs topped with club moss rose majestically from the whitecapped bay. The Flower Pot Rocks had a coppery sheen in the high afternoon sun. Driving no longer paralyzed me; in fact, the immediate responsiveness of the manual transmission inspired a sense of power and control.

Reaching into the pocket of my weathered windbreaker, I tugged out my phone and dropped it on the passenger seat. I swerved the Jeep into the dirt viewing lot and tugged on the hand brake. I pulled up my emails. Scrolled down to the one from Maria, the prosecutor. The one that had arrived earlier in the day. The one I hadn't yet read.

I'd spoken with her only once, several weeks before. I'd informed Maria that, after much consideration, I wasn't prepared to testify against Rick. I wasn't sure I could face him. Having just completed a six-week program working on techniques to deal with my post-traumatic symptoms, I avoided anything that might trigger me. I was in recovery. From Rick. And recovery was one day at a time.

Although they could compel me as a witness, they'd stated no intent, given the situation. Unfortunately, the criminal charges that carried the greatest sentences revolved around me: the commission of a murder, violating the Electronic Communication Privacy Act (hacking into my phone), identity theft (signing legal documents as me). Franklin had summarily dismissed Rick in the aftermath, but Butler Industries' reach was limited to financial malfeasance.

The subject of the email read: "Update." I opened it. Maria was informing me that the recording I'd made of Rick wouldn't be admitted into evidence. In the District of Columbia, a one-party-consent jurisdiction, one of the parties involved in a conversation had to be recording it for it to be legal evidence.

My heart twisted. I stared out at the older couple holding hands as they helped each other traverse the rocky walkway. Would Rick wriggle out of this? Would he evade justice again? Without evidence of the commissioning of a crime, that part of the case was impossible to prosecute, but there were other charges with less-serious penalties attached. Maria assured me they'd persevere, even though it was a daunting blow. *Onward,* she'd written.

Onward. My last contact with Rick played in my mind. We'd locked eyes over the police cruiser in the courtyard. He'd tried to shake off the officer who'd dared to shove his head down to clear the door as they'd put him in the back seat. He'd refused to speak a word without an attorney present and quickly assembled a dream team of lawyers who had gotten off high-profile defendants widely considered impossible to acquit. The look he'd shot me had sent a shiver through me. Blank. Vacant eyed. As though we were strangers passing in the courtyard and one of us just happened to be in steel handcuffs. The memory was still in the archive, although less vivid as the months passed.

The Jeep roared to life. Downshifting at the next switchback, I saw the lighthouse rising up behind the hill. I slid onto the parking pad and saw my front door ajar, framing an image that would forever stay with me. A new forever loop. The tableau at the kitchen island: my people, the ones who were always there, no matter how bleak life got. Billie, in her long, gauzy skirt and cherry-red ballet flats, pulling plates and glasses from the rough-hewn shelving. She playfully micromanaged Sloan and Amy while they cut lemons into wedges for the pitcher of ice tea.

"Who's waiting on lobster rolls?" I called, dangling the Rudder's bag toward them.

"'Bout time, Mama. Got some starvin' Marvins here." She dumped the paper-wrapped loaves onto the old, brightly tiled utility cart I was using as a kitchen table. There wasn't much talking as we dug into the rolls overflowing with sweet chunks of lobster.

Billie leaned in to me with a smirk. "Lobster? Is it just a coincidence that we're enjoying a meal that would actually kill your ex? Very meta."

"Coincidence." I smiled. "Let's clear all this away so I can get back to my job, people."

I got misty logging on to the YouTube channel for my scheduled first vlog back; for so long, I'd feared my passion project might fall victim to the dynamics of my marriage. Panning the camera around the perimeter of the rustic kitchen, I captured the views through the metal-framed, lightly rusted windows. The boats bobbed in the bay, the quaint town below dotted with vibrantly colored cottages. For today, at least, this replaced the former *Life of Reilly* opening montage. I was all about living in the present and anticipating a new future.

I positioned myself back in the shot and secured the phone to a tripod. "Afternoon, Lifers. Coming to you today from stunning Yarmouth, Nova Scotia. Excuse my hiatus; I was dealing with a personal situation, and I hadn't been able to be transparent about it—but that stops today. You're only as sick as your secrets, and I have nothing to hide."

I pulled out a painted stool and sat. My throat was unexpectedly tight, but I kept my chin up. "My marriage is over. It was hard to accept. I thought I knew what my future held. Who it held. And I … I don't know what's next. I don't have the answers. I'm not even sure I have the questions. But that's okay. What doesn't kill you makes you stronger, right?" I managed a smile; the soundtrack lightly playing was, of course, Kelly Clarkson.

"I'd like to ask one thing of you; it's important. When someone shows you who they are, believe them. The first time. It's easy to make excuses for people you love, to turn a blind eye, to accept the unacceptable." I paused to reflect. I considered how to explain what I'd been through. It had been unacceptable, yet I was the one who'd tolerated it. I'd nearly let it destroy me.

"I've learned this: we can't stay in toxic situations. It kills your spirit over time. Today, I want to empower you. Muay Thai expert Hoon is showing us easy self-defense basics. Share this video with every woman you love. I've posted it to the channel. *That's* the real start of taking back your personal power. Goal number one in the coming year. Let's promise each other."

And I talked about the future. "The Gillsen Group continues to partner with me as we rebrand going forward—we are now *Life in Progress*—something I think we can all embrace. The focus will be on enriching our lives, advocating for ourselves, knowing what we want. Thursday, I'm excited to welcome world-renowned relationship expert Anna Arlens, and she'll take your questions. Until then, live your best life."

I signed off and powered down the portable Lume Cube light panel.

Hopping up from the creaky couch, Billie shot me the finger pistols. "She's baaack."

Amy clapped her hands and hugged me sweetly, singing along in her buttery alto to the tune now playing: "Miss Independent," with sassy lyrics about the fearlessness of strong women. Billie and Amy were mesmerized by the sun starting to set. They sighed in unison.

"This is the life, huh, kid? We need a lighthouse, or a castle maybe. Yah. A castle."

"Mi casa es su casa; you guys have beds here anytime," I reminded her, looking over at my friend. Something glinted in the sunlight. A band of canary-yellow diamonds on Billie's right-hand ring finger. Tapping the ring, I said, "Anything to tell me, B?"

Two spots of bright color perched high on her cheeks. I'd never seen Billie blush.

"Same thing I told him. If he behaves himself, I'll move it to the left hand."

Brian.

Amy teased, "Please. Those two were never really *apart* apart. Dad was just waiting for Mom to get a little more chill."

I nearly choked on my iced tea, stifling a laugh.

"Chill. Well, thank God he's patient. I always thought you'd end up together. I'm thrilled for you two."

"He's a hard one to get over. He may be a big goofball, but he's *my* goofball," she said, rolling her eyes for effect. "Oooh—and you need to teach me to cook when we get back."

"*Mother.* She's not a miracle worker!"

Billie hip checked Amy and reached for the phone vibrating in her pocket. "Awww. It's Goofball." With a coy smile, she drifted away. "Hi, sweets."

Out of the blue, a jarring thud. The vintage floors groaned. Sloan was practicing a Muay Thai move Hoon had demonstrated. She deftly dropped to the ground with a ferocious jab. She looked up from her knee-jab position on the floor, her eyes clear. Her new swingy shoulder-length bob was sophisticated. It tugged at the mom in me, but Sloan no longer teetered at near adulthood.

"Is that the gist of it, Mom?"

I confirmed what she already knew. "Um, yes. That's *exactly* the gist. Who knew you'd turn out to be the badass in the gang."

Sloan pumped her fist and threw her toned arms around me. "I learn from the best. OTC."

"OTC?"

She poked me in exactly the spot that made me squirm. "One tough cookie, Mom."

"Got it. That makes two of us, sweetheart. I love you. And you know what? I think you are going to love being in New York."

She'd been offered an entry-level position in a Manhattan sports management firm when she finished her master's, and she started in three weeks.

"I'm psyched. I mean, the money is nothing, but it's New York! Hey," Sloan said, turning to Billie and Amy. "Are we still meeting in Manhattan next weekend—Brian said you all could make my modest fourth-floor walk-up look like *Architectural Digest.*"

Billie let out her husky laugh. "Full of promises, that one. Of course we're coming. We're staying at Walter's in Brooklyn, but we're all work during the days at Sloan's stupendous studio."

"All six hundred ten square feet." Sloan giggled. So did I; she and I had painstakingly measured her cozy space more than once so that we could replace her overstuffed everything with space-saving anything. Billie beamed, watching us, and sashayed over.

"Oh, hey, guess what time it is. Time to make amazing new memories. How 'bout you two say 'cheese' or something equally idiotic?" She angled to get the bay views in the picture and motioned us closer together.

I slipped my arm snugly around Sloan's waist. She pressed her cheek lightly against mine. I flashed Billie a smile. Click.

The ladies dispersed to grab jackets for a tour of my favorite spots. I retrieved my phone from the tripod and read Maria's email again. Did they have enough without me? Would he go on to do more of the same? Would that choice to back away from the process haunt me? That which is behind you can no longer hurt you. It no longer had power over me, unless I allowed it. I had come a long way. And I wasn't allowing it. *I got this.*

"There's always one right thing to do," my mother had been fond of advising whenever I'd faced a conflict. And I needed to do that one right thing. For myself and for every other potential victim. Rick may have gotten himself the dream team, but I had right on my side. I'd been strong-armed for long enough. I espoused empowerment; I needed to embody it. It would be empowering to hold my hand up and tell the truth, the whole truth, and nothing but the truth.

I hit "Reply" to Maria's email and deleted the subject line, replacing it with "Change of plans." I put a few more words in the body and paused—not to reconsider but to let the magnitude of the moment sit with me.

"You can count on me. I'll testify." The "Sent" notification echoed in the quiet. *Whoosh.*

If you enjoyed *Blindsided*, please take a moment to leave a short review. Thank you so much!

AUTHOR'S NOTE

Not a mental health professional but having long been fascinated by the human psyche and psychological domestic suspense as a fiction genre, I wanted to delve more deeply into the characteristics that make this type of coercive relationship dynamic possible. Many of us might automatically ask, "Why didn't she/he just remove themselves and leave the partner?" For the purposes of this story, I homed in on one particular disorder that lays fertile groundwork for a dysfunctional relationship with a codependent partner, though there are many.

A WORD ABOUT NARCISSISTS

Narcissists can be both extraordinarily easy and disturbingly difficult to love. Seemingly blessed with a charming, dominant personality, narcissists lack a core self. Their self-image and behaviors are other-oriented in an attempt to validate their self-worth.

The gods sentenced Narcissus to a life without human love. He fell in love with his own reflection in a pool of water. He died still hungering for its response. Like Narcissus, narcissists only "love" themselves as reflected through others' eyes. Commonly believed to love themselves, they typically loathe themselves. Their inflated self-flattery, perfectionism, and arrogance act as a shield. Emotionally dead inside, they hunger to be filled and validated by others. Sadly, they're unable to appreciate or reciprocate the love they do get and alienate those who give it.

To be psychologically diagnosed with narcissistic personality disorder (NPD), the person must exhibit grandiosity and a lack of empathy, exhibiting at least five of the following traits:

1. Has a grandiose sense of self-importance and exaggerates achievements or capabilities.
2. Dreams of escalating power, success, and a more ideal love.
3. Believes he or she is special and can only be understood by, or should associate with, other unique or high-status individuals or institutions.

4. Requires excessive admiration, particularly from their mate. Should that cease, they withdraw their love. Expecting unconditional love themselves, their own love is thoroughly conditional. It's based upon being idealized to a higher state.

5. Unreasonably expects special, favorable treatment or compliance with his or her wishes.

6. Exploits and takes advantage of others to achieve personal ends.

7. Lacks empathy or moral compass for the feelings and needs of others.

8. Envies others they deem to "have it easier" or believes them to be envious of him or her.

9. Has arrogant behaviors or attitudes, usually disguised behind a false humility.

Empathizing with narcissists is complex, but they didn't choose to be the way they are. Stunted development in childhood is often the cause: whether an unnaturally close bond with an overindulgent mother or an overcompensation to parental harshness or criticalness.

Narcissists are the epicenter of their relationships; they choose mates as extensions of themselves. What others do is not right, nor is it appreciated. Those in their lives must meet their endless needs—for admiration, service, love—and are dismissed if they don't. Those unwilling to cooperate are expendable.

ABOUT THE AUTHOR

 Veteran broadcaster Erica Hilary has been a consistent voice on the airwaves in the Washington, DC area for 20 years, having hosted shows on WASH 97.1, Z104 and MIX 107.3. In addition to being a seasoned on-air personality, Erica is an actress and public speaker. She is a cancer survivor and an advocate. Some passions include cooking (from indulgent comfort foods to spicy ethnic cuisines), travel off-the-beaten-path (and learning just enough of the language to muddle through without a translator app), photography, hiking, independent films (preferably tear-jerkers), and her two kids.

HTTPS://ERICAHILARY.MEDIA/

photo: courtesy of Asico Photo (Joy Asico)

Made in the USA
Columbia, SC
02 December 2020